Karin Baine lives in Northern Ireland with her husband, two sons and her out-of-control notebook collection. Her mother and her grandmother's vast collection of books inspired her love of reading and her dream of becoming a Mills & Boon author. Now she can tell people she has a *proper* job! You can follow Karin on Twitter, @karinbaine1, or visit her website for the latest news—karinbaine.com.

Susan Carlisle's love affair with books began in the sixth grade, when she made a bad grade in mathematics. Not allowed to watch TV until she'd brought the grade up, Susan filled her time with books. She turned her love of reading into a passion for writing, and now has over ten Medical Romances published through Mills & Boon. She writes about hot, sexy docs and the strong women who captivate them. Visit SusanCarlisle.com.

THE SINGLE DAD'S PROPOSAL

KARIN BAINE

NURSE TO FOREVER MUM

SUSAN CARLISLE

MILLS & BOON

First Published in Great Britain 2019
by Mills & Boon, an imprint of HarperCollins*Publishers*
1 London Bridge Street, London, SE1 9GF

The Single Dad's Proposal © 2019 by Karin Baine

Nurse to Forever Mum © 2019 by Susan Carlisle

ISBN: 978-0-263-26957-4

MIX
Paper from
responsible sources
FSC C007454

This book is produced from independently certified FSC™ paper
to ensure responsible forest management.
For more information visit www.harpercollins.co.uk/green.

Printed and bound in Spain
by CPI, Barcelona

THE SINGLE DAD'S PROPOSAL

KARIN BAINE

MILLS & BOON

For Karen and Andrea,
who brought Triathlon Dad to my attention!

Many thanks to Mary, Geordie, Diane and Michael,
who allow us to share the Spanish sunshine with
them, and Chellie, who always has my back. xx

CHAPTER ONE

'TRIATHLON DAD IS finally in the building,' Summer muttered under her breath as Dr Rafael Valdez made his way to the day-care centre.

He was still some distance away but she followed his progress along the walkway from the main building and the reactions of the patients and staff of the clinic as they stopped to stare at the handsome Spanish surgeon. It was hard not to, even for someone who'd quit her job at a prominent hospital and come to this island to escape the temptations of handsome men and the chaos they created.

Although only a couple of miles off the coast of Boston, Maple Island gave the impression she was far from the troubles she'd left on the mainland as it was only accessible by ferry or light aircraft. They were still susceptible to the same wintry weather here as the city she'd grown up in at this time of the year, but there was a distinct vacation vibe about this laid-back place that meant it never really bothered her. It wouldn't be long before the sun was shining again and the influx of tourists would double the size of the population. As long as she didn't dabble in any holiday romances, or any romances for that matter, she could live here happily.

Unfortunately, her job as a child-care assistant in the staff nursery meant it wasn't as easy to avoid Dr Valdez as she'd prefer when he was a reminder that, despite her vow, she wasn't immune to handsome men. He was fit in more ways than one with the perfect body to match those dark good looks, honed by all the swimming, running and cycling around the island that had also earned him his sporty nickname. He was a perfect treat for the eyes but that was all he was to Summer, or ever could be. Even if he wasn't a co-worker—she'd learned to avoid them at all costs in romantic notions, since she couldn't keep moving after every failed relationship—he only had eyes for one girl around here.

'It looks as though he has a fight on his hands this morning.' Kaylee, her colleague, had apparently noticed the object of her attention too.

The love of his life, his three-year-old daughter, Graciela, was one of Summer's charges and the reason she got to spend more time with him than was good for her. Regardless of the physical attraction she might harbour towards him, they were often locked in battle over the best way to care for his child's extra needs. There was a personality clash that cancelled out the allure of his outward appearance, even if his single-dad status hadn't already put him at the top of her off-limits list.

The last time she'd lost her heart to a father-and-child combo she'd mistaken her ex's relationship of convenience for love. Whilst she had been throwing herself into that nurturing role to look after his son Leo, thinking it was leading up to a permanent arrangement for them as a family, Marc had been using her as a stop-gap until his baby mama came back on the scene.

She wouldn't make the mistake again of giving her

trust, her future, to someone who didn't appreciate her worth beyond her child-minding skills. Since she was already paid to do that for Rafael Valdez, she knew the score. If she let herself get drawn into the middle of another parent-and-child set-up she only had herself to blame this time around.

She watched Gracie turning round and running off in the opposite direction for the umpteenth time, taking them twice as long to reach the nursery than usual. Instead of demonstrating more patience, her father simply swung her up into his arms and marched on despite her protests.

Summer had witnessed her fair share of toddler tantrums but a child on the autism spectrum needed extra-careful handling and would have no concept of making her father late for work at any age.

'Something must've happened this morning to make them late. He hasn't even had time to dry his hair.'

Even from this distance Summer could see his still-wet hair glistening in the sunlight. That wasn't a big deal in itself, but whatever had caused this disruption to their routine had the potential to become an issue for Gracie. Summer loved working with the little girl but she had communication issues and learning difficulties that often led to these bursts of temper.

She caught sight of Kaylee smirking at her. 'What?'

Okay, so she was imagining Rafael's dark hair curling at the nape of his neck and soaking his collar. It didn't mean anything other than she noticed the small details in other people's lives. People-reading was part of her skill as a child life specialist, even if her job here required more of her child-care services for now.

Alex Kirkland, the medical director and one of the

clinic's founders, had employed her with a view to eventually moving her into her preferred position. With the extension of the children's ward in the future she would be needed more in her role as a child life specialist to help the young patients cope with their illnesses and prepare them for whatever medical procedures they faced.

She was happy to wear either hat if she could stay here, leaving the mess of her personal life back in Boston. It wasn't as if she was missed when Marc and Leo were back living as a family with his ex and her own mother had her second husband to support her instead of Summer.

'Nothing,' Kaylee replied, obviously meaning everything as she did a double take between Summer and the two figures she hadn't been able to take her eyes off.

'Oh, shut up!' Summer hit her playfully over the head with a soft-bodied panda she'd been minding for one of the children.

Not for the first time she wondered where the child's mother was, or any other family for that matter. There was very little known about the spinal surgeon other than what a coup it was to have him on board here. Despite his sterling reputation as a surgeon, she'd found him difficult, stubborn and resistant to taking on any friendly advice. If he had that attitude to people other than her it could explain his single status, regardless of him being so smoulderingly attractive. Even she experienced that flutter in the pit of her stomach when he was near. She'd seen how loving he could be with his daughter so she knew there was a soft heart in there somewhere.

It might come across as judgemental but sometimes she thought parents often didn't try hard enough to salvage a relationship when children were involved. Broken families would always be a source of pain to her when they represented her own difficult background. The children suffered most when the parents decided they couldn't live together and, in her case, not only had she lost her father but he'd taken her stepbrother too, severing all contact between them and leaving her feeling incomplete.

Robbie may not have been her biological sibling but she'd grown up thinking of him as her big brother, someone she could turn to for advice or comfort, and losing him had been akin to having a limb cut off. Since then, she'd lived her life always feeling as though something was missing, and the loss of a mother had to be even more devastating to a child of Gracie's young years.

She never talked about her mom and she'd noticed Dr Valdez didn't wear a wedding ring so there didn't appear to be a significant other anywhere in the background. There was a chance he was nursing a broken heart, which would explain his defensive behaviour. It was the same reason Summer had come to Maple Island in much the same mood at first. Perhaps he was finding life as a single dad difficult. Given time, he might get back together with his ex again too, just as Marc had when he'd left Summer out in the cold over a year ago. Apparently, it was easier to share the parenting of a small child with their *actual* parent rather than someone who'd been learning on the job.

Men with motherless children were double heartbreak waiting to happen because when things ended you lost them both. Regardless of the love and time given to help raise their offspring, when the relationship was over an ex-girlfriend didn't have any right to remain in the child's life. Losing Marc had been difficult, but having five-year-old Leo taken away from her too had been devastating when she'd come to think of him as her own. Until Marc had decided to forgive his ex for cheating on him when she'd asked to come back and, just like that, Summer had been surplus to requirements.

That bitter taste of loss and betrayal tinged her objectivity. She knew nothing of the secrets the Valdezes might be hiding and she intended to keep it that way, having sworn not to get involved with another family outside the workplace again. If and when she decided to date again, her requirements for a suitor would include being single with no dependants or exes lurking in the background.

She doubted Rafael had any desire to jump into the dating quagmire either. There certainly hadn't been any talk of him seeing anyone since arriving on the island and his devotion to his patients, including the ten-year-old Walsh twins who'd suffered severe spinal injuries and were taking up a lot of his attention, didn't leave him with much down time.

She might not view him as relationship potential but she could see he was a good father, trying to give his daughter the best start in life and struggling with the demands of juggling his home and work life. It couldn't be easy for a busy single dad contending with the special needs of an autistic daughter and Summer would never dare criticise his parenting skills but it wouldn't hurt him to ask for or accept help once in a while.

Her own mother had been equally as pig-headed when they'd been left as half of a family when her father had taken off, refusing financial or emotional assistance from any quarter. As an adult she recognised how her mother must've been hurting badly to be so determined to do everything on her own and prove she didn't need a man around. Except Summer had been the one to suffer, forced to grow up too quickly and dragged into the conflict between her parents by having to choose which one to live with. She hoped Gracie would never be subjected to that kind of stress when it could have such a devastating impact on her development.

It hadn't been fair to Summer as an eight-year-old to put her under that much pressure to pick sides, but emotions had been running high and she'd been compelled to stay with her mother since her father had been the one having an affair. Once she'd made her position known, her father had demanded custody of her stepbrother and moved abroad to start a new life with the woman he'd left them for.

They'd all been devastated by the split but her parents had wanted a complete separation, things having been said and done that neither could apparently overlook in order to let the siblings maintain contact. Perhaps they'd imagined they had been young enough to forget and would get over it, but she hadn't and now she didn't even know where to start looking for Robbie.

With hindsight she could understand why her mother had chosen never to rely on anyone else after that epic betrayal, but when her health had suffered, Summer had been the only one there to pick up the pieces.

Unable to work full time, there had been no money

to fund things every other child took for granted and it hadn't been long before she'd been taking on after-school jobs to supplement their income at a time when her teenage peers had been going to parties or shopping for clothes. She'd never resented her mother for those sacrifices but when she had eventually married again Summer had gone a little wild, exploring her sudden freedom and leaving her responsibilities far behind. They hadn't really been close since. She'd even been replaced at home.

Summer had no wish to interfere in anyone else's life but Dr Valdez didn't have to be Gracie's whole world. There were no parent-of-the-year prizes for running yourself into the ground, only more problems for the child when there was no one else around to lend a helping hand.

She'd studied hard to enable her to work with vulnerable children and she knew how much time and patience it took to communicate effectively to make any progress in their development. If he would simply give her the chance, she was willing to share everything she'd learned to make their lives a little easier.

'Hold this for me,' she said, handing the plush toy to Kaylee, and left her vantage point to meet them in the corridor, persuading herself her actions were based purely on Graciela's needs.

When she reached Rafael, he'd changed tactics and was murmuring in soothing placatory Spanish to his daughter. Summer's school-level Spanish was rusty but she recognised *'Te amo, mija'*, because he told Gracie he loved her each time he had to leave her in child-care to go to work. It melted her heart that he could be so curt with people at times yet wasn't afraid to express his feelings for his daughter. She wouldn't have been human if she didn't wonder what it would be like to have him whisper sweet Spanish nothings into her ear too, or experience the delicious shivers up her neck when she imagined him there.

'I can take her from here if you'd like?' Graciela immediately stopped fidgeting once she took her hand.

It had taken weeks to get her to this stage when she'd screamed the place down every time her father was out of sight at first. There were still problems with those who worked with her on late shifts when Rafael was on nights at the clinic, but she was lucky Gracie responded to her so positively.

'We're fine, thank you,' he insisted, yet as she dropped Graciela's hand, the little one began stamping her feet. The low whimpering in her throat began to build until it would soon become that ear-piercing shriek to let everyone know she wasn't happy. It was difficult for children like Gracie to communicate their needs effectively and the tantrums were often born of frustration.

Summer stood her ground before Rafael's stubborn pride, or lack of faith in her ability to do her job effectively, distressed the child any further.

'If she's happy to come with me now, it means you can get to work quicker.' It was logical to anyone who wasn't a helicopter parent, who didn't trust another soul with the care of their precious offspring, that she was offering him the perfect solution.

'Graciela, would you like to come and have a teddy bears' picnic with us this morning? You can pick any toy you want and we'll spread out the tea set for the party.' Addressing her directly didn't always elicit a response but on this occasion Gracie made her preference known by clinging onto Summer's forearm with both hands. Her triumphant smile was a victory for common sense and a sharp contrast to Rafael's frown, but he didn't try to sway his daughter any further in his direction.

'Here are her things.' Her papa shrugged the sparkly pink backpack down his arms to give it to her. As well as proving how comfortable he was in his own masculinity, the girly, child-sized bag he carried for his daughter emphasised the broadness of his shoulders and gave Summer a temporary moment of fancy. She'd seen his muscles ripple at the swimming pool as they powered him through the water at breakneck speed and could easily imagine the upper-body strength he possessed. One flex and he could probably burst the straps as if they were made of tissue paper.

Simply thinking about that display of machismo awakened her girlish appreciation…and was it hot in here because she was in desperate need of a fan right now? Here was a man so strong in body yet he had no problem setting aside the discomfort many men would've shown with such a small act to make his child feel comfortable in her surroundings. He had a gentle way with his daughter she hadn't fully grasped because he did it in such a quiet way without making a fuss or expecting ebullient praise, like Marc often had.

Perhaps she'd merely convinced herself Rafael had an inflated opinion of himself because she'd pigeonholed him right along with the last single dad she'd known. There was also the possibility she was finding excuses not to like him because she knew she was developing quite a crush.

Summer graciously accepted the handover and did her best to ignore the zing that came from the simple brush of their fingers during the exchange. The increased heart rate and tingling sensation where he'd touched her was nothing more than a sign that she knew she was playing with fire here. She shouldn't be thinking of him as anything other than a parent at the day-care centre but forbidden fruit always seemed that much more tantalising.

'She'll be fine, Dr Valdez.' It was her turn to dismiss him so she could get on with her job without having him distracting her with his muscles and sexy accent. She might also have to start wearing mittens if she was to prevent herself from going into raptures every time they came into brief physical contact.

He bent down to kiss the top of his daughter's head before walking away.

'Thank you, Miss Ryan.' He tossed a measure of gratitude back over his shoulder. It should have riled her when she was blatantly an afterthought but she drank it in like an eager-to-please lapdog, thirsty for praise. The only consolation she took from being such a slave to her hormones was that this exchange would probably stay with him for the remainder of the day too. If only because he'd been forced to accept her help in some small way.

Just breathe. Rafael did his best to keep walking and ignore the urge to look back. He didn't think he'd be able to handle the sight of his daughter happier to co-operate with a member of staff than with him. The whole attraction of coming to Maple Island Clinic had been the idea of having Graciela close, and though he was relieved she'd stopped her theatrics this morning he hated the idea that someone could do a better job than him of looking after her.

His career was always going to keep him busy but he'd been sold on life here with the excellent child-care facilities Alex Kirkland and Cody Brennan had told him they provided on site when they'd lured him away from Boston Harbour Hospital. Although everything here on Maple Island had lived up to expectations, it hadn't made the separation anxiety any easier. After his wife Christina had walked out on them he'd been doing the job of both parents and he was under pressure not to fail his daughter the way her mother had.

So far, it didn't seem as though he was making a great job of it. Summer made him feel inadequate when it came to looking after his daughter for the simple reason she was doing a better job of it than he was. Regardless of his workload, he always made time for a leisurely breakfast together before he dropped her off at nursery. It was the one meal he was guaranteed to spend with his daughter. He appreciated that quality time together and he was sure that on some level Gracie did too.

Those rare family moments had been few and far between for him as a child. As Spanish nobility, his parents had always had more important business to attend to and had often dined elsewhere or at different times from their children. When they had been at home dinner had become an elaborate affair where he had been preened and polished before being allowed to dine with whatever dignitaries had been in residence. If at all.

It was a small rebellion against that regime by making breakfast a casual occasion, eaten whilst wearing pyjamas and before a hair or a tooth had been brushed, but it was his and Gracie's ritual. He'd slipped up this morning by oversleeping and thinking he could get away with a juice box and a cereal bar on the go. It was never going to be that easy when he'd ripped her from her usual morning routine.

His mistake in sleeping through the alarm had been compounded by having the battle to get Gracie through the nursery door in Summer's presence. It was bad enough leaving other people to do most of the caring for his daughter when he was working, without anyone witnessing his epic parenting fail. Summer in particular was always offering advice on how he could best manage Gracie's challenging behaviour, as though she knew her better than he did.

Okay, she was acting in the best interests of his little girl and on some level he was grateful for the one-on-one attention she was receiving in day-care with regard to her extra needs. However, times such as this succeeded in making him feel guiltier than ever about his workload and the possibility he was neglecting her in any capacity.

It was absurd, of course. Graciela was his life, his reason for being, but he found it difficult to trust again or rely on anyone other than himself to do right by her. Christina's sudden departure had impacted on every area of his life and he'd had to employ the help of his young neighbour, Mags, to babysit whilst he'd tried to make permanent day-care arrangements. They'd used her before without any problems on the rare occasion he and Christina had gone out as a couple for the evening. One emergency late-night call-out had changed everything.

Although it had been last minute, Mags had agreed to mind Gracie overnight while he went to the hospital to perform emergency surgery on a car-crash victim. He'd thought his daughter would be safe in her own home with someone he knew and trusted. Mags had never offered him a true account or explanation of what had happened that night but from what he'd gathered, the lure of a party in the neighbourhood had proved too great to resist. She'd left Gracie alone and his baby's cries had been heard and reported to the police by other concerned neighbours.

He'd been confronted at work by police and child protection services as though he'd been the one to abandon her. Even when a tearful Mags had confessed what she'd done, Rafael had been subjected to interrogation and suspicion by social workers to the point he'd taken leave from his job to prove his devotion to his daughter.

Eventually he'd had to return and put some level of faith in agency childminders since they had the relevant checks and qualifications. However, that overwhelming feeling of guilt for what had happened, or what could have happened, had never left him. Even then, he hadn't been able to shake the notion the efficient, professional women who'd enabled him to return hadn't cared for Gracie much beyond their pay checks. Not the way Summer did.

Graciela had flourished since coming to the island and it would take time to come to terms with not being her sole source of support. He was thankful that there was someone who could reach her where others had failed but he was wary of their developing bond. Simply because it was drawing him closer to Summer too and that wasn't somewhere he should be when he was supposed to be concentrating on his daughter.

He'd been hurt too much to risk another entanglement and though his head reminded him of that at every given opportunity, his senses and his body were more easily led astray. It was difficult to keep that security wall in place when Summer kept breaching it with a look or a touch and the sweet scent of her perfume that smelled like candy.

In any other circumstances he would have welcomed someone else's devotion to his daughter but he hadn't let anyone get close to them since his wife had broken their hearts. He'd always been attracted to strong, independent women and Summer wasn't afraid to challenge him when necessary but he would never be distracted again when it came to Gracie's welfare.

The way Summer was already so integrated into their lives was unnerving but Gracie had never responded so well to a female influence. Not even her own mother. Christina had been hurt by her refusal to interact with her at an early age, had taken it personally when it had merely been a symptom of her condition. She'd been embarrassed when their baby had failed to reach the milestones of others her age. In the end she'd simply told Rafael she wasn't cut out for motherhood or marriage and had gone back to the single, carefree life she'd apparently missed so much.

The irony was that he'd been able to get the help and advice needed to aid Gracie after she'd gone. Christina had been in denial that her baby could be anything other than perfect, when Rafael had known all along there had been something wrong. Once he'd been able to get a diagnosis so they knew what they were dealing with, it had been easier to cope. If Christina had hung around she would've watched her child reach all those milestones, if slightly later than her peers.

It hadn't made life as a single parent any easier to have a daughter with special needs and there certainly wasn't room for a Christina replacement. He couldn't trust anyone not to hurt Gracie again.

Miss Ryan had to remain a mere bystander when it came to his family. Otherwise he was doomed to repeat the past and the opportunity to come to Maple Island would have been wasted. He hadn't relocated here for anything other than the stability it offered Gracie. Bringing another woman into their home wasn't going to achieve that, only offer more possibilities of heartache when she decided Gracie was too much reality for a pretty young blonde to handle.

Rafael had had his time of putting his wants first when he'd left his family behind in Spain to come and study medicine in America. Unlike his parents, he wanted what was best for his child, not necessarily what was more acceptable for them. That selfishness and all the other negative family connotations he'd turned his back on could stay in the Mediterranean as far as he was concerned.

Rafael's mood hadn't improved at all by the afternoon. As usual he'd had a busy morning catching up on the day's schedule, meeting the team at the facility to discuss the status of their patients and prioritise his cases depending on the urgency of their conditions.

One of the reasons he'd relocated to the clinic had been the hope it would be less demanding on his time, making more room for Gracie, with fewer emergencies coming in at all hours of the night when they were primarily a rehabilitation facility.

However, his caseload was always full, dealing with back-related conditions that required surgical intervention. The clinic's reputation, combined with the privacy and beautiful surroundings provided by the location, made it the ideal hiding place for the rich and famous wishing to recuperate away from the glare of the spotlight and the paparazzi.

He understood that mind-set to some extent. Unknown to his fellow islanders, he was a bit of a celebrity in his own right. In Spain, at least. The eldest son of a duke attracted more attention than he'd ever been comfortable with, and though he'd been glad to leave that cosseted lifestyle behind to come to America and study anonymously, it had caused a huge fallout with his family, but he didn't regret the sacrifice he'd made when it meant he and Gracie retained their privacy.

The majority of Rafael's clients here tended to be sports stars keen to recover from injury as quickly and quietly as possible and the on-site rehab facilities provided everything they needed post-surgery.

He didn't follow American sports himself but even he'd heard of Tom Horner, the ex-football star turned commentator, who was here for a lumbar discectomy to relieve his sciatica pain. The procedure Rafael was carrying out today was to remove the herniated portion of the lumbar disc pressing against a nerve.

'*Buenos días*, Doc.' The All-American hero slapped his meaty hand into Rafael's and shook it vigorously. Even now, in his fifties, the man was a powerhouse, the strength of the handshake alone reverberating through Rafael's limbs so he dreaded to imagine how much damage a hit from him in his heyday would have caused.

'*Buenas tardes, Señor Horner.* Are you all set for your surgery today?' The surgery unit was still in its infancy at present but sufficient that they could carry out procedures on an outpatient basis. Any major operations were still carried out at their sister hospital, Boston Harbour, and patients were often transferred here for secondary surgeries as well as rehabilitation. Sometimes they had a team out from Boston to assist and other times Rafael's expertise was required back on the mainland and the sharing of skills was working successfully so far.

'I can't wait to have it done and get back to normal.' From his appearance alone no one would be able to tell this man had been in pain for some considerable time. A lot of people tended to look vulnerable sitting in a hospital bed in their gowns, waiting to put their lives literally in the hands of the doctors here. Not Tom Horner. His hulking frame dominated the space, the fabric of the flimsy gown stretched to accommodate him and he was as intimidating a presence as ever.

'You know you'll have to take it easy for a while after surgery? We'll discuss it at length post-op but we need to make sure you avoid any undue strain to keep your spine in proper alignment.' He knew Tom's kind, having started out in sports therapy. Sportsmen didn't make the easiest patients, wanting to shake off injury as soon as possible to get back on their feet and back in the game, often ignoring rehab advice to their detriment.

'Don't worry, Doc. I've hired a place on the west

side of the island where I'm doing nothing but resting up until I'm fighting fit again. As far as anyone
knows, I'm on extended vacation and I want to keep
it that way.'

'Of course.' Although wear and tear on the body
was all part of the ageing process, Rafael had treated
men and women who saw it as a sign of weakness, almost something to be ashamed about. Whilst it wasn't
his business who his patients did or didn't tell about
their health problems, it was his duty to ensure there
was some after-care in place at home. 'Do you have
any family or friends over with you who can help you
out during your recuperation?'

He hadn't seen any evidence of a support system
even at the initial consultation in Boston before Tom
had followed him out here, over the moon at the prospect of having his treatment in private.

The big man's cheeks turned pink before he answered. 'My daughter's here, fussing around. She insisted on coming with me but as far as the ex-wife is
concerned we're on a father-daughter getaway. Terri
can read me better than her mom ever could and knew
there was something going on.' He threw his hands up
in exasperation and the fact his daughter had got the
better of him made the corners of Rafael's mouth tilt
upwards for the first time that day.

Daughters had that knack of tying their fathers up
in knots around their little fingers. Thankfully that
bond didn't break even when the marriage did. At least,
not for him. Gracie's mother hadn't had any problem
abandoning her child but she'd never taken to being a
parent the way he had and now he was doing the job
for both of them.

The responsibility of motherhood had curbed her nights out when he'd been working and unable to mind their daughter. A baby with special needs had been a step too far for a woman who had still thought and acted like a single twenty-something. It had almost been a relief when she'd ended things because they'd been able to stop pretending she was a wife or a mother. It was entirely Christina's loss she'd never got to be part of her beautiful daughter's life, the daughter who'd exceeded all of those damning predictions regarding her development.

He'd made a success of his life without the assistance of his family and at least Gracie had a father who loved her and would do everything he could to ensure she thrived.

'I'm glad you have someone to make sure you do as you're told. It will help your recovery.' The clinic staff would operate, provide medication and follow-up treatment, including physiotherapy, but there were practical things Tom would require at home to smooth the transition from the clinic.

'Don't worry, Terri's at the beach house now, adapting it for the return of the invalid. She even insisted on buying me slip-on loafers for the duration of my stay so I don't have to bend down to tie my laces.' The absolute horror on his face that he should be subjected to such an atrocity was comical. Rafael silently wished Terri good luck, hoping she would prove equally as stubborn as her father. She'd probably have to tie him down to prevent him from rushing his recovery.

'Think yourself fortunate to have someone willing to take care of you. Not everyone does.' He had a momentary lapse into self-pity, considering his options should he ever find himself in the same situation. There were no loving family members around for him to rely on. It was a sobering and ironic thought that he'd probably have to pay someone to provide that assistance.

If he'd stayed in San Sebastian, as his parents had wanted, and had never left Spain, he would've had every medical or child expert available to the eldest son of a duke. Therein had lain the problem. He'd never wanted to remain tied to that lifestyle, living off ancient connections to the royal family and trying to stay relevant by portraying himself like his playboy brother to the paparazzi.

This life of anonymity had suited him better, even though his family had seen his move to the States as a betrayal of his heritage. He hadn't spoken to them since but as they hadn't accepted him for who he was, he knew they would never acknowledge Gracie for being different either. She wouldn't fit into the perfect family they preferred to parade for the cameras, neither would he subject her to those expectations.

He had played along for a while for appearances' sake but Gracie wouldn't understand that's what she was supposed to do and she shouldn't have to pretend to be someone she wasn't. It was better for her to be loved for who she was, even if he was the only one in her life able to give her that unconditional love.

Unfortunately, that left him with no next of kin here if anything should happen to him. Tom should appreciate someone caring enough not to back away when he needed them most.

'Not as fortunate as you, Doc, that's for sure. Oo-ee!' Tom's appreciative whistle was lost on Rafael.

'Excuse me?' He cocked his head to one side, waiting for an explanation when he could see no reason why a successful pundit would exhibit the slightest bit of jealousy towards him.

'Forgive me for speaking out of turn but if I had a wife who looked like yours, she wouldn't be an ex.' The bawdy laugh didn't help unravel the mystery for Rafael, only deepened it. He had no idea how anyone here would know about Christina, but if they were acquainted with her they'd also be aware nursing anyone wasn't in her DNA. Her job was strictly in medical research and she wasn't hands on in any way unless she was in a club with her girlfriends in the early hours of the morning and looking for some male attention.

'I think you must be mistaking me for someone else.' He decided not to go down that dark alley and dismissed it to concentrate on Tom's notes.

Unfortunately, Tom wasn't so easily deterred from whatever it was he thought was going on in Rafael's life.

'I saw you this morning with your family when I came in. Beautiful. You're a very lucky man. We weren't good together, me and Jess, but I miss having that closeness with someone, you know?'

He didn't know, staring at him blankly for some time before it dawned on him who his patient was referring to.

'Oh. Oh!' An image of him handing over the care of his daughter to Summer in the corridor popped into his head. He supposed to an outsider the mistake was understandable but it did knock the breath out of him that Tom had assumed her to be his wife and Gracie's mother. Did she really appear so comfortable in either role?

'Summer's not my wife, she's—' What exactly was she? An employee? A co-worker? None of those titles accurately depicted how significant she'd become in their daily lives yet he couldn't describe her as a friend either. Not when he was trying so hard to resist having her play a part in his personal life for his own sanity.

There was no discernible line between work and personal matters when Summer's efforts with his daughter broke through any perceived barriers. He reaped the benefits at home with Gracie's improved verbal and motor skills apparently honed by the time and energy Summer had put into working with Gracie.

However, with every achievement she accomplished, guilt took a bigger nibble at his conscience— that if he'd spent that time with her instead he could've been the one to further her progress. Except that would have prohibited them from moving to the island, having an income or helping countless people with his surgical skills.

He had to accept some things were out of his control. Including thoughts about Miss Summer Ryan, which seemed to be coming much more frequently and less about educational matters.

Contemplation about her current relationship status, how she was spending her evenings or if she liked him beyond her official capacity were not things he should be concerning himself with if he considered her only in her role at the day-care centre.

He wanted to get to know her but with that came a whole web of complications he couldn't afford to get caught up in again. Investing emotionally in someone other than his daughter left him vulnerable to another rejection or worse, more heartbreak he could do without when he would still have to get up every morning and carry on for Gracie's sake.

'Summer's my daughter's nursery teacher,' he filled in, unwilling to give his patient any further insight into his complicated personal matters. 'Now, are you clear about what's going to happen today in surgery?'

'Could you run it by me again, Doc?'

'I'm going to make a small incision in your lower back and insert a small tube that will act as a corridor for me to access the herniated disc with minimal tissue disruption to the surrounding area. We'll use local anaesthetic and some mild sedation so you won't feel anything.' Sometimes there could be irritation afterwards caused by the operation itself but once the bone spur or disc material causing the pain was removed, patients usually felt an improvement.

'That's all I need to hear.'

'I'm sure we'll have you back on the football field in no time at all.' He closed Tom's file with a smile and tucked it under his arm.

'I spend more time behind the sports desk these days but I appreciate the confidence.'

They parted on a friendly, firm handshake but the exchange had shaken Rafael. It wasn't the fact someone had assumed Summer was part of his family that bothered him. No, it was that the idea wasn't totally unappealing to him. Exactly why he should try extra-hard to push her out and prevent her from doing to him what every other person close to him had done and let him go without a fight.

CHAPTER TWO

'SEE YOU TOMORROW.' Summer waved off another of the little ones for the day as her parents finished work and came to collect their baby.

People came and went from the nursery at different times according to shift patterns or unforeseen overtime. The clinic even provided a live-in night service for those hard-working doctors and nurses who had to cover nights in the clinic and required extra child care. The set-up was all to keep disruption to a minimum for the families of the employees here, and attracted the best medics in their field for that reason.

The day-care aspect of her job could be seen as a step down on the career ladder when she was a highly qualified child life specialist. However, the position she'd held in Boston had proved difficult to transfer from when it was in such a competitive field and she'd needed something, anything, to get her away from her ex-boyfriend and the wife he'd reconciled with.

It had turned out her skills had become useful for the small children's wing they'd later opened at the clinic. Although there wasn't yet a need for a full-time child life specialist, she'd come to an arrangement with Alex and Cody to go wherever she was needed most.

Currently, she was content to help keep the children entertained at day-care but the arrival of the Walsh twins on the island had ensured her diary was full in both areas.

'Papa?' At the sign of activity around the door, Gracie came to stand beside her with her pink backpack clutched in her hands.

'Not yet, Gracie. Your papa was working very hard today so he might be a bit later than usual.' The erratic hours were something the staff accounted for but it could be difficult for the children to comprehend. Especially for the younger ones or those like Gracie with learning difficulties. It didn't matter how often she was told her father wouldn't be taking her home yet, when she saw other parents arriving for their sons and daughters she expected to leave with them. The best thing in these circumstances was to try and distract her until Rafael did get here.

'Home.'

'I know you want to go home, sweetheart. Why don't we make your papa a nice picture while we're waiting?' Summer eased the bag out of her hands and hung it back on her coat peg. With the aid of some glitter and glue she could try and keep her busy enough to forget his absence temporarily.

Summer wasn't privy to the family circumstances but from observation she could see life wasn't easy for father or daughter without the mother's presence. What Gracie needed more than anyone or anything was stability and currently the sea of ever-changing faces managing her care was doing nothing to aid that.

There was no one nominated care-giver at present, with different staff managing her needs according to the rotas and time sheets. The attention Summer provided whenever she could seemed to calm Gracie down, the meltdowns less frequent during her shifts. Perhaps it was because Gracie trusted her, or that she took more time trying to understand her than the staff who might not have as much as experience with special needs children, but she responded to Summer. Sometimes.

Without speaking or making eye contact, Gracie put a purple crayon into her hand and in her own way indicated she was supposed to contribute to the picture too. Summer pulled up one of the tiny chairs to join her at the colouring table.

'You want me to do something?'

'Draw,' Gracie demanded, tapping the page impatiently.

With confident strokes Summer drew the bold outline of a flower, which her co-artist set about obliterating with a succession of colourful scribbles. She didn't mind staying on even when her working day had supposedly ended. It wasn't as though she had anyone waiting for her at home, or anything of a social life that necessitated consideration.

The child's learning difficulties would probably require extra assistance when she reached school age but for now Summer was of the opinion she was the most qualified person in the nursery to look after her. There was no formal arrangement in place but if Rafael, the day-care manager and the medical directors agreed, she wanted to put herself forward to care exclusively for Gracie. Outside her clinic responsibilities, of course. That way there wouldn't be a stream of strangers coming into her life day and night when

Summer was willing to be there for her every minute she could, and offer that stability Gracie was lacking.

The biggest obstacle to overcome in that plan would be Dr Valdez himself and his insistence he could do everything single-handedly. If this morning was any indication, he was resistant to any offer of help. He'd been so defensive about the idea of her accompanying Gracie to nursery for him one would've thought she'd come from child protective services to take her from him permanently, not do him a favour.

'Your father's going to love this.'

Gracie smeared glue and glitter in between the now indistinguishable petals, turning the flower into a sparkly, purple blob she was sure the proud daddy would display along with her other works of art.

There was no verbal response from her protégé but once Gracie was interested in something it often became her sole focus. Although that could be problematic in public places, it did prove useful when Summer had to go elsewhere. Like now, as she saw Rafael through the window, striding towards the nursery unit.

She wanted to intercept him before Gracie spotted him and shut down any chance of a private talk about future arrangements for his daughter.

'Kaylee, could you watch Gracie for a minute while I talk to her father?' Summer quietly caught the attention of her colleague, trying not to disturb her art student or alert her to her father's appearance in the process.

'Sure.' Quickly and quietly, Kaylee slid into the seat she'd vacated and Summer hoped she could achieve her goal before the switch became apparent.

With ninja-like stealth she slipped out, closed the

door gently behind her and managed to accost her target in the hallway.

'Dr Valdez, could I have a word with you about Graciela?' She positioned herself directly in front of him, forcing him to come to a halt.

'I'm late. Sorry.' He rubbed his hands over his face, giving her some indication of the day he'd had. His dark brown eyes were hooded and heavy as though he hadn't slept well in days and it made her more determined to offer some assistance. She wasn't sure the man knew how to relax but she'd been around enough children with special medical needs to understand the toll it could take on the parents without them realising the importance of self-care.

There was also her experience of watching her own mom's health decline rather than accept outside help. All those years of hard manual work her mother had done to earn a living, taking on cleaning jobs where she could, had caused the early onset of arthritis and limited her mobility at a relatively early age. If they'd given in and let someone else into their circle of trust, that might've been prevented, or at least delayed.

Summer opened her mouth to assure him she wasn't here to scold him or delay him any longer than necessary, only for him to dodge around her. She backed up, praying there was nothing in her path she could fall over as she tottered backwards, trying to keep up with him. In the end she resorted to grabbing his arm to get him to stop, almost knocked completely off balance by the discovery of the taut muscles beneath his pale blue shirt.

It must be the swimming, she mused, before her mind

drifted towards his cycling and running regime and what effect that might have on other parts of his body.

She shouldn't be thinking of him in such a fashion but her imagination seemed to run wild where Rafael was concerned. Not only was it a conflict of interest when he was the parent of one of the children she worked alongside, but he represented everything she was afraid of in a potential partner. He had a young child she was already attached to, and they worked at the same clinic so any romantic daydreaming about him was a disaster waiting to happen.

By blurring that line she would put her job and her heart in jeopardy. She was afraid she mightn't have any choice in the matter when she was fixating on something as innocent as touching his arm and reacting as though he'd given her a lap dance.

Rafael stared at the hand on his arm, then at her, his eyebrows raised at her audacity. She had to fight through the foggy muddle of her brain now flicking through snapshots of him in cycle shorts and sweat-drenched running gear to search for words to string a sentence together. Perhaps she really should think about getting back into the dating scene—restricted to single men she didn't work with—if her body was so desperately craving some interaction with male company.

'Gracie. There should be a constant in her life.' It didn't quite articulate everything she'd intended but it was the gist of why she'd come out here to him and sufficient for that dark scowl to slide over his face as he began walking away again.

'I was in surgery. It couldn't be helped. I'll collect her now and we'll be on our way.'

No, no, no. This wasn't going the way she'd planned at all. She'd merely succeeded in ticking him off even more.

She spun around and was forced into a half-run to catch up with him this time.

'Can you stop so we can talk properly?' Okay, she was verging on the bossy side of insolence in a professional capacity but the man was infuriating at times.

He pulled on the brakes with a hiss of air through his teeth. 'What exactly is it you want, Miss Ryan?'

Miss Ryan. Not Summer, as every other person on the island referred to her. She was sure he did it to annoy her, keeping things formal so it was impossible for her to penetrate his defences.

'Sorry, I wasn't criticising you. What I meant to say was that I'd like to offer some assistance with Gracie's care. I thought I might take on sole responsibility for her nursery care where I can. I'd have to run it past my superiors but I think that continuity of care when you're working would help her flourish. You saw yourself how stressed she gets with change.'

'This is about us running late this morning?' He shook his head, any possibility of him agreeing to her plans evaporating before her eyes.

'No.' She refused to be embarrassed about standing up for what she believed in, although her temple was throbbing with the threat of a stress headache. This was so much harder than it ought to be and he was making it that way. Or it could be her recent inability to express herself adequately. Something she'd never had trouble with previously.

If it wasn't for their common goal of getting Gracie

as settled into island life as possible she'd have given up explaining herself and gone home for date night with a tub of mint choc chip. Unfortunately, that wasn't going to help anyone and would only make her feel even more nauseous than she was for having started this conversation in the first place.

She took a deep breath and cleared her mind of everything except the little dark-haired girl who lived predominantly in a world of her own and started over. 'As you're aware, I have experience of dealing with children who have specific needs and I was merely suggesting we could discuss an arrangement for Gracie. I would have no objection to taking over her care, day or night, if it suited you, rather than having a variety of new faces parading through her life.'

He studied her silently for a moment too long, those dark eyes scrutinising her every word and body language as though searching for her true intentions. Well, he had nothing to fear. As far as she was concerned, it was about time someone else stood up for Gracie along with her father.

Finally, he said, 'I don't think so,' and left so abruptly Summer gasped at his brusque dismissal. No discussion. No explanation. No gratitude. She was sorry she'd even approached him about the matter when she didn't appear to be anything more than a nuisance to the busy surgeon.

Rafael didn't stop to hear any more or break into a smile until he walked into the nursery unit where he was assaulted in the face with his daughter's painting. Summer reached them as they were preparing to leave, no further conversation apparently warranted as he took his daughter's hand.

'*Vámonos*, Graciela.'

Let's go. He may as well have added they needed to get away from this crazy lady by the way he was staring at her. As he swung the child up onto his shoulders and walked away, singing to her in that deep Spanish burr, Summer wondered if he had a split personality or simply a Summer Ryan aversion when he was so wonderful with his daughter and his patients.

Her sigh was full of regret for the tunnel vision he had when it came to Gracie's guardianship but also because, no matter how she tried, she couldn't get Rafael to like her. Although extremely rare, it was still soul-destroying when issues occurred between her and parents of the children she worked with. This was worse, when lusting after him wasn't something they could easily work through together. The best that she could hope for was that he'd learn to tolerate her for Gracie's sake and she'd get over this crush, soon, before it began to affect more than her concentration.

Supper. Bath. Bed. It was a routine Rafael had been able to implement with Gracie from an early age and had been working very effectively. Until now.

'Come on, Gracie. We're both tired. Why don't you put your pyjamas on and I'll read you a story in bed?' He'd given up on the other two stages now when the walls were coated in the supper he'd made and he was soaked from head to toe with bath water while Gracie remained bone dry.

'No.' She ran off again down the hall away from all thoughts of sleep when it was all he wanted to do.

He pulled the plug out of the bath and drained away what water there was left in the tub and used a towel to mop up the rest on the floor. She'd got into the bath initially but, rather than sit down and play with her toys as usual, she'd stood screaming and kicking the water until he'd had no option but to lift her out again. Rafael couldn't stand to see her distressed yet he didn't know what had set her off tonight.

'*Por favor*. Please, Gracie.' The toddler pulled off her bath robe and streaked away from him, screeching at the top of her lungs.

At the lowest point of his day now, he was tempted to reconsider Summer's proposal. If he withdrew the inference that he wasn't being a good enough parent to manage alone, he still didn't think it a good idea to turn over responsibility of Gracie's care to someone else merely on their say-so.

Once the red mist had dissipated he could see Summer had meant well and he should've been more appreciative of her interest, more gracious in his refusal of the offer. After all she had nothing to gain in making herself available for Gracie except, in his mind, the possibility of undermining his position in his daughter's life and taking the moral high ground. He knew it was a ridiculous notion but he was so unaccustomed to having people help it made him wary.

The last time he'd felt backed into a corner, forced to ask someone else to share the responsibility, he'd almost lost his daughter and had had his commitment to her questioned. It wasn't easy for him to swallow his pride and his fears and accept genuine support when it was being given freely.

If Summer could see the two of them now she'd be entitled to wag a finger and say, 'See? You need me,' before providing the calm voice of reason his daughter might be more inclined to listen to than her father. He'd worked alongside Summer enough in the clinic with the twins to have experienced that patience she had with the children and the rapport she was able to build with them individually. It was the same with Gracie.

If he was honest about why he didn't want her involved in his life beyond the clinic, it was that building panic at the thought of letting her get too close to his daughter, or him, on a personal level. She had a sweet smile to match her easygoing nature around the kids and it was impossible not to be impressed by her dedication as well as her beauty, but he hadn't moved to an island to find himself in exactly the same situation he'd left in Boston.

He couldn't afford to start relying on her being there for him in case the time came when she decided she'd had enough too. Then he'd end up back at square one, having to fight through his own grief to support Gracie on his own. It had taken this long to get where they were and now they were happy he had no desire to get knocked back down.

They'd been through too much to have to face that kind of devastation again. Unless he was guaranteed to have a partner willing to be by his side for the rest of his days it was pointless even forming an attachment. Eventually even this beautiful young woman would tire of their demands on her time and want to move on.

Too bad that self-preservation seemed to manifest in his grouchy alter ego intent on protecting him from Summer's charms. His attempt to keep her at arm's length simply seemed to spur her on to display a dogged determination and passion that did nothing to diminish his admiration for her, even though he couldn't show it. He had enough on his hands trying to wrangle a three-year-old to bed without debating the pros and cons of getting into another relationship. There simply wasn't room for another female whirl-wind to wreak havoc in his life.

'Graciela Valdez, will you please come here and put your pyjamas on now?' It was half command, half plea. He was willing to forget the last few hours of Gracie Armageddon if she would get into bed and finally go to sleep. Then he might get an hour or two to wind down before he had to do this all over again. Obviously, he needed to retire earlier than he had last night to avoid oversleeping again, when they were still experiencing the effects of that slip-up now.

He'd known Summer's assessment was correct about the disruption to Gracie's routine setting her off on the subsequent trail of mayhem and chaos. Some-times it was easy to forget this cute bundle couldn't be railroaded into things she didn't want to do for con-venience's sake. Logic didn't fit into her life the way it did for most.

He heard the handle turning on Gracie's bedroom door before she emerged, dressed, if not in the night-time attire he'd have chosen for her.

'That's what you're wearing to bed?' He was re-signed to letting her wear the colourful mismatched socks, the princess dress he'd bought for her birthday—complete with sparkly tiara—and fairy wings, regard-less of how uncomfortable he imagined they'd be to sleep in. If he could get her to sleep there was a chance he could slip the tiara and wings off at some point with-out causing too much of a fuss. At this point in time he'd agree to wearing a matching outfit if they could just bring this day to an end.

Gracie nodded, her lips pursed and brow furrowed as though she was prepared to fight some more for her fashion choices. Any such notion of another battle of wills left him feeling drained. 'Okay then.'

Except she still had no intention of going to bed as she bounced her way down the staircase to the lounge. Rafael had no option left than to leave her to tire herself out. He knew when to pick his battles with her and this wasn't worth the fight. At least the screaming had stopped and he decided if he wasn't permitted some time to sit back and chill, he may as well catch up on some paperwork. That was the part of his job he wasn't enamoured with and if he completed it during working hours, he'd never have a minute to see his patients.

He let the television babysit his daughter for a few minutes to retrieve the briefcase he'd left in the hall beside his bike, thinking he wouldn't see either again until the next morning. With Gracie sitting happily on the couch, legs swinging and humming along to whatever bright, noisy children's show she'd found, he seated himself at the dining table. It gave him sufficient room to spread out his notes and files and the open-plan style of the villa provided an unobscured view of his daughter at the same time. Although he would have to try and block out the noise or he'd never be able to concentrate.

He set the case on the table and flicked open the catches. The picture Gracie had presented him with at day-care was laid on top and he set it to one side to stick on the fridge door later, if he could find a space alongside her other artwork. He also lifted out an uneaten orange and a banana beginning to turn brown, leftovers from the lunch he hadn't had time to eat. His pen, his diary and various pieces of stationery lined the bottom of the bag but there were no case notes.

'Where are they?' he asked aloud to the now-empty elaborate lunch pail. His hand connected to his forehead in a slap of sudden realisation. The files were sitting on his desk at work. He'd intended to go back and fetch them from the office but he'd been so preoccupied with picking Gracie up from day-care he'd forgotten. The perfect day from hell.

They lived so close to the clinic it seemed silly not to simply swing by and pick them up, and another glance at Gracie, who was now jumping on the couch, confirmed there was no danger of her going to bed soon. If he could wrestle a coat on her she could accompany him and they'd be there and back in fifteen minutes, tops.

'Hey, Gracie, do you want to come with Papa to work?'

It should've been a quick trip in and out but he hadn't factored in the time spent chatting to passers-by enchanted by his daughter's quirky sense of style.

'Yes, she is quite a character.'

'No, I didn't dress her, this is all her own creation.'

An elderly woman being wheeled through towards the rehab ward hailed the porter to stop as though he was her personal chauffeur. This had to be the infamous Philomena Kerridge-Bates he'd heard was here to recuperate after a broken hip. No one other than a millionairess and a Society Grand Dame would have accessorised her hospital gown with matching priceless diamond earrings and necklace. 'This child should be in bed,' she decreed with a dismissive wave of her elegant hand.

'I agree, she should.' He didn't bother to argue or explain and hold them all up.

Everyone always wanted to offer him parenting advice so he'd become accustomed to it. The sight of a single dad drew pity from all corners, as though he was out of his depth without the child's mother in tow. Strangers weren't aware he'd been her only source of stability and love since birth and they'd been doing fine on their own since Christina had left. They'd probably been better off without her. Just as he was, without parents disappointed in who he'd become because he hadn't fitted in with their idea of how a son should behave and had wanted to earn a living in his own right. Away from family influences and the glare of the spotlight they were happy to live in.

Generally, people on Maple Island had good intentions so he didn't let it get to him and responded to comments with a forced smile. His private life, including his daughter's welfare and his wife's whereabouts, was his business and as such he refused to give anyone the satisfaction of dispelling rumour with fact.

He simply wished Philomena well on her way and reckoned their other feisty resident Theodore Harrington, or Old Salty as he was better known, might have met his match. The cantankerous fisherman was still recovering after his leg had been crushed when the ferry carrying twins on their way to the clinic had broken down in last month's storms and he'd gone to rescue them.

He'd already been discharged once, but he hadn't

looked after himself properly and had ended up badly aggravating the injury. In serious pain again, he'd reluctantly allowed himself to be persuaded to return to the clinic for a longer stretch of rehab, so they could keep an eye on him until he was fully healed.

He wasn't an easy patient to deal with, obviously used to living on his own, but he was now the local hero so they were forced to put up with him and his pearls of wisdom as he told everyone how to do their jobs.

The main problem with the attention Gracie was drawing tonight was that she hated it. She barely tolerated people she knew but strangers were a complete no-go area for her. Anything new and unfamiliar was a source of stress and could easily increase her anxiety level but she knew the clinic and he hadn't imagined there'd be as many people about at this time of night.

In the end he resorted to carrying her to stop the onslaught of head-patting and attempted hugs threatening to trigger his daughter into the mother of all meltdowns.

'We really should be going.' He excused himself from the latest admirer, a sweet old lady who had nothing but compliments about Gracie's big brown eyes, which, yes, were just like her father's. That prompted his koala kid to cling onto his shoulder with her fingernails digging into his skin, head buried in his neck so no one else could see her eyes.

'Sweetheart, I'm going to have to set you down until I find what I'm looking for.' Once they were safely behind the closed door of his office he thought he'd be able to prise her off but she was steadfast. His little girl was nothing if not stubborn. Rafael had no idea where that trait had come from at all and he resented any suggestion he should be the genetic culprit simply because he preferred to do things his own way too.

'No!' Gracie literally dug her heels in, right into his side.

'There's no one else here. Just you and me. See?' He prised her head from his shoulder to show her they were safe and alone in the small room and she relaxed her grip slightly.

Taking advantage of the brief reprieve, he disentangled her and set her down in his leather office chair, despite her protests.

'Hold on tight and I'll take you for a spin.' He did his best to make this fun for her, spinning her around the floor with one hand while the rest of his attention was focused on sorting through the stack of papers on his desk.

'More.' It didn't take long for Gracie to develop a love for the new game.

'*Uno momento*, Graciela.' He turned his back for a second to locate the file he needed.

'Papa!' Gracie screamed for him and he saw her spill out of the chair onto the hard floor a fraction too late to do anything about it. She'd managed to stand up on the seat without him seeing and had lost her balance in the process.

'Graciela! *Lo siento*.' Paperwork abandoned, he rushed to lift the chair, which now had her pinned to the floor, her feet twisted up beneath the seat. His heart was in his mouth, waiting to uncover whatever damage had been caused to her in a moment of distraction.

He held his breath, listening for any sound to give him a sign she was all right. He'd never known her to be this quiet. Then she let out a sob so he could breathe again. He moved the chair aside and set her gently onto his desk. 'Where does it hurt?'

She was wailing too loudly now to answer, or even hear him. He sat her on the edge of his desk, careful not to take his eyes, or hands, off her for a second and checked her all over.

He cupped her head in his hands—she was alert but there was a lump forming at her temple. Her arms and fingers were fine as he could manipulate them, with no sign of broken bones, but she let out a howl as he did the same with her feet. It was her right foot, he soon discovered, that was the source of her pain. As he carefully removed her shoe and pulled off her bright pink sock, he could see the ankle was badly swollen already.

Guilt bubbled in his gut. If only he'd jumped off his high horse for fifteen minutes and accepted some help to look after her, this might have been avoided. Now, because of his stubbornness, there was a chance she could have done some real damage to herself. The only consolation was that they were in the right place for immediate treatment and he wasted no time in rushing her straight to the emergency department.

While he was there he'd get them to extract the chip from his shoulder so he could start to trust those who genuinely wanted to help him when he clearly didn't always know best.

CHAPTER THREE

THE TERSE EXCHANGE with Rafael earlier had unsettled Summer; it worried her that she'd overstepped the mark and what the consequences could be if he made a formal complaint. He was a highly respected surgeon and she was dispensable in comparison.

The restlessness had sent her out for a walk to clear her head and remind herself how lucky she was to be on the island. It was safe enough here that a woman could go for a stroll along the beach alone at night and not be concerned about potential predators, the way she'd had to do in the city. Crime was practically non-existent here, making it part of the appeal of living on Maple Island. Everyone looked out for each other and she reckoned Sheriff Brady had one of the most coveted jobs on the force.

The only trouble they generally encountered was with over-exuberant tourists during the summer season. Here she was free to do as she pleased and sometimes she tended to get carried away by that novelty.

Gracie wasn't her daughter and, really, she had no business interfering in how she was raised.

Suddenly, she heard a scream from somewhere up in the rocky outcrop leading down to the sea. She ran towards the sound to find a sobbing mother and a shell-shocked father trying to soothe their son, who was lying spread-eagled on the sand, clearly having taken a fall from a considerable height.

Summer immediately swung into action and called for an ambulance before kneeling beside the boy and his parents. 'Hi, I'm Summer. I work over at the clinic. What's his name?'

'Ben. He just slipped… The rocks must've been wet… There was nothing we could do to catch him.' Clearly struggling with guilt, the father took off his jacket and covered his son as best he could.

'The clinic isn't too far from here and I've called for an ambulance. Help is on the way,' Summer assured them, although it was apparent they were dealing with a compound fracture that would require surgery as part of his femur was sticking out through the skin on his thigh. A splint simply wouldn't be adequate in this case. It was just as well she wasn't squeamish, having spent most of her working life around the sick and injured. Thankfully he would be given pain relief by the paramedics to cope until the bones were put back into alignment.

'Should we try and move him? It doesn't seem right to leave him lying here on the cold ground.' The mother's instinct to get him somewhere warm was understandable but Summer didn't want to exacerbate the injury any further.

'We might hurt him more by trying to lift him. Leave it to the paramedics, they'll be here shortly and will give him some pain relief before they attempt to move him.'

Although Summer deferred to the first responders

when they arrived shortly after, she did accompany them to the emergency room. Not only because the parents had been so shaken up but also because she had nowhere else to be. The accident had taken her mind off Marc, Leo and the reasons why she should continue to stay clear of single dads and their adorable children.

She'd been treated as an afterthought for most of her life, her parents never having taken her wants and needs into consideration before their own, and then Marc, who had rejected her in favour of his ex. Time and again those she'd loved had been taken from her without a thought given to how that loss would affect her. After Robbie and Leo, she couldn't face the heartache again. Her days would be better spent at the hospital, where she could make a difference, rather than mooning over someone she couldn't, and shouldn't, have.

There was some trouble in the hospital when Ben fought the nurses trying to fit an oxygen mask over his face to help him breathe and relax, obviously finding the whole experience overwhelming.

'Ben, the doctors will need to take you to Theatre to fix that leg for you. They're not trying to hurt you, just help.'

'Will I see the bone? Will I feel them moving it?' His bloodshot eyes were wide with horror.

Summer shook her head and showed him the oxygen mask. 'They'll put a mask like this one around your mouth and nose. You'll fall asleep and when it's all over they'll wake you up again.'

'I'm scared,' he admitted, fat tears rolling down his cheeks.

'There's no need to be afraid. Your parents can go down to Theatre with you if you like and be there when you wake up again. Now, we want you nice and comfortable before we get you to Theatre. This mask will help you breathe in some medicine to make you feel better.' Summer placed the mask over his face but the boy wasn't convinced, turning his head away.

She pulled out a couple of tubes of lip balm from her pocket. 'If you don't like the smell, you can put some of this inside. Would you prefer strawberry or chocolate?'

With some trepidation he pointed to the chocolate-flavoured balm and Summer proceeded to spread some of it inside the mask.

'See?' She held the mask up for him to inhale the scent, giving him some say in what was happening to him. Enough to convince him to co-operate.

'I just have to go and put on some special clothes so I can come to Theatre with you then we'll be on our way.'

She'd had a word with Cody Brennan, one of the clinic founders and the orthopaedic surgeon who was performing the operation, and he'd given the go-ahead for her to accompany Ben.

Although it was a relatively straightforward procedure for Cody, who did this every day of the week, it was a frightening experience for a young child. She'd be on tenterhooks herself until the whole thing was over because there were always risks associated with surgery. Not that she'd shown Ben any sign of her own nerves.

'This is a relatively new procedure called flexible intramedullary nailing but it's becoming popular to treat paediatric femur fractures,' Cody explained to her.

'Sounds...complicated.' There wasn't any gentle way of joining bits of broken bone back together and she'd heard of metal plates, rods, pins and screws being involved so she supposed nails were simply another piece of hardware incorporated in the mechanics.

Californian Cody could be a bit stiff at times, un-approachable if you were easily intimidated, but she'd persuaded him to share the process to educate her in what went on behind the scenes.

'It does the job. We insert flexible nails through the end of the femur and across the injury site. This holds the bones in place while they heal.'

'How long will that take?' Maple Island Clinic was renowned for its modern approach to rehabilitation and breakthrough techniques and Cody specialised in lower-limb surgery so she was aware there must be a specific reason they'd be adopting this new technique.

'It will take about four months to completely heal then we'll remove the nails. The advantage is that there should be no limb-length inequality or visible scars that can result from other procedures and the leg won't require a cast.'

'So he'll be as good as new?'

'All being well, yes, he'll make a full recovery and bounce back to normal.'

She shut up then and let the surgeon do his thing, observing in awe. One of the things she loved about her job was getting to work so closely with children and following their progress through injury and illness, though there was always a danger of becoming too close to some of her patients.

Perhaps if she'd had a family of her own around her it wouldn't leave such a void in her life when her patients moved on, as they inevitably did. That didn't mean she should involve herself with a ready-made father and child. The problem with getting entangled with someone else's family was that one day another woman might come to claim them back.

An image of Gracie and Rafael sprang to mind but she tried to blank it out. The operation was a good diversion for her and the empty house waiting for her at the end of the night.

Once Ben was safely through his operation, Summer was ready to fall unconscious into bed, although she knew her brain was bound to spend countless hours replaying the time she and Rafael had had together, preventing sleep from coming too easily. Even if she ignored the tension they'd shared in the corridor, there were still so many feel-good moments to choose from today. From the feel of his muscles under his shirt to that electric contact between their fingertips, she could spend all night reading more into those brief touches than had probably been there.

She left the recovery ward and rounded the corner to let the ER staff know she was leaving, only to be confronted by Rafael and a weeping Graciela sitting in the corridor.

The initial shock of seeing him here and the urge to go back the way she'd come in case he guessed she'd been thinking about him was quickly countered by the sight and sounds of his daughter's distress.

'Oh, Gracie. What's happened?' She dropped into the seat next to Rafael and leaned over to inspect the badly swollen ankle on view.

The exotic scent of his citrus and spice cologne teased her senses, so moreish it was making her hungry.

'Accident in the workplace,' he said with a grimace.

Summer surveyed the sight of Gracie's princess dress and her bent fairy wings and gave it her best guess. 'Trouble in Fairy Land?'

Was that a laugh she heard? The sound was so unexpected and devastating to her equilibrium she couldn't decide whether to crack another funny or render him mute for ever.

'I was picking up some files from my room and... er...we got a bit carried away spinning on the office chair.' Given how protective he was over his daughter, Summer could only imagine how much he was beating himself up over whatever had happened.

'Ouch. Poor baby,' she said, straightening Gracie's wings. Then she addressed Rafael. 'Has she been checked over yet?'

He leaned over to whisper to her, probably so Gracie couldn't hear, his black hair tickling the side of her face and conspiring to drive her senses crazy. 'I don't think she's broken anything but we can't get her to go in for an X-ray to be certain.'

It could be a scary place with all that machinery whirring in there. Gracie was already upset and under the fluorescent glare of the clinic lighting it was easy for her to become disoriented and confused. They needed to persuade her somehow so they could get a clear idea of what was going on with that foot and treat it accordingly, instead of leaving it to potentially worsen.

'I don't suppose... I mean I know we're not in daycare and it's not strictly your problem but you were able to work your magic with her this morning… Would you mind helping me get her in there?'

She knew it was taking everything in him to ask her as he fumbled to find the words. This was a huge step forward in her progress with him, which in turn might filter through to Gracie in accepting help. It wasn't obvious what had caused this turn-around and it could have been through sheer exhaustion rather than an acceptance that this was her area of expertise, but she wasn't going to question it.

'Give me a second.' An idea popped into her head about how they might be able to convince Gracie to co-operate and left them to go in search of the box of toys they'd have somewhere here to occupy the children in the waiting room.

A rummage around soon unearthed a raggedy-looking doll, a magnetic drawing board and a toy camera. Rudimentary perhaps but she often used toys to explain procedures to the children who perhaps required scans or X-rays, and it helped dispel some of that fear surrounding the unknown. She located a bandage, which she intended to tie around the doll's leg in exactly the same place as where Gracie had her injury, and she rushed back to the reluctant patient.

Rafael raised an eyebrow as he spotted the armful of toys she was carrying but for once he didn't question her plans or whisk Gracie away before she could implement them.

With him subdued, Summer seized her chance to present her finds and offer her assistance.

'This is Dolly. She's had a bit of an accident and she's hurt her leg.' Summer set the doll on Rafael's knee so Gracie could see her from her vantage point on her father's shoulder.

Curious, she peered down to see what was going on. A good sign that she was engaged in proceedings.

'She was spinning around in the garden and fell over. She bumped her head and I guess she hurt her leg too.'

Her face full of concern, Gracie shuffled down Rafael's torso to sit on his other knee. 'Will she get better?'

To hear a full sentence, have her attention so fully, was a feat not often mastered and a great achievement on both sides. Although Summer didn't want to make a big fuss about it and send her back into that world lost to everyone but Gracie, it took a moment before she could speak herself. Rafael's Adam's apple bobbing up and down as he gulped didn't escape her notice either.

'The doctor can fix her if she'll let him take an X-ray of her poorly leg. Do you know how to do that, Gracie?'

She shook her head.

'If I tell you how to do it then maybe you could be the doctor and help her?' Patient participation often helped the children understand what was going on and when she could she tried to make it as fun as possible for them.

Gracie looked to her father for guidance.

'You can do it, Dr Valdez.' Then he whispered in her ear, 'I think Dolly is a little frightened. She might need you to tell her it's going to be okay.'

Taking her new responsibilities very seriously, Gracie bent down to talk to her patient. 'Don't be scared. I'll make you better.'

'We have to lay her down to take a special photograph.' Summer's voice cracked with emotion at the focus Gracie was showing as she stretched the doll flat out on her father's knee.

'This is a special camera that will show the doctor where her leg hurts but she has to stay very still.' She handed over the camera and let Gracie push the button while she sketched a crude picture of a leg bone on the board.

'Could we get your opinion on the X-ray, Dr Valdez Senior?' Summer held up her artistic rendering for Rafael's scrutiny while they both tried not to laugh at it.

His eyes were twinkling with emotion and suppressed laughter, his scowl finally fading, and her pulse raced in response. She liked this softer side of him, it made him even more attractive and she didn't see it nearly enough. He always looked so deadly serious she often longed to be the one to help him smile again, and now she had she might start acting the clown around him more often to make it a permanent fixture.

'Well…it's not broken. A bad sprain, I would say. We'll bandage it up and prescribe plenty of rest.'

'Dr Gracie?'

The younger doctor proceeded to wrap the bandage around Dolly's leg and Summer fastened it so it wouldn't come loose.

'She'll be as good as new in no time. Now, we have to fix you too, Gracie. Do you think the doctor could take a special photograph of your leg?'

She thought about it for a moment. 'Can you and Dolly come as well?'

'We might have to go into the room where the lady takes the photograph but Daddy can go in with you if he wears a special apron. He can hold your hand and we'll wave to you through the window.' Summer was sure they could talk the radiographer into a couple of extra guests for a few minutes.

'Gracie?' Rafael coaxed her some more until she finally nodded her consent and they quickly whisked her off to the X-ray department in case she changed her mind again.

'Thank goodness it was nothing more than a sprain. That's bad enough but I'd never have forgiven myself if she'd broken something.' Rafael had thought as much but the confirmation was a hundred times preferable to sheer hope. Apart from the guilt that had lain heavily on his conscience, an immobile Graciela would have driven them both insane. The injury would temporarily slow her down but a cumbersome cast would have been much worse for a lot longer.

'Rafael, accidents are part of childhood. Are you telling me you've never broken a bone or had stitches through misadventure?' Summer's blue eyes glittered with something he couldn't quite put his finger on. He couldn't tell if she was teasing him or referencing something in her own background. Whatever it was, he knew she was only doing it to make him feel better when he'd been such an absolute horror to her earlier today.

He couldn't find fault with anything she'd said or done since coming across them in the corridor. Quite the opposite. She'd done everything in her power to help them through this without judgement, criticism or a clear desire to get on with her own personal life. She'd had nothing to gain from staying on here with them and she'd gone out of her way to persuade Gracie into having that X-ray. He was glad to have had her with them.

The doll idea had been genius. Gracie still had it now, clutched in her hand as she slept on Summer's shoulder. Rafael wasn't going to attempt to take it off her and if it came to it he didn't think the staff would mind if he replaced Dolly with a new one from the store. Small things such as a black-haired doll who looked a bit like her could make life a little less stressful for a while.

Summer was still watching and waiting for an answer so he had to switch his thoughts from the present to a time he didn't often wish to visit. Except her gentle teasing on this occasion did evoke a memory he'd forgotten and made him groan.

He ran his finger over the small bump on the bridge of his nose. 'Broken nose at fifteen when I came off a motorbike.'

Summer cocked her head to one side as though trying to picture the scene. 'No offence but I didn't have you down as the grungy biker type.'

'I wasn't that impressive. It was my first time on a bike and I slid halfway across the road on my backside.'

'Were you wearing leathers? I mean, to protect you, not because I'm trying to imagine you in black leathers or anything…' As she rambled on, apparently fascinated by his apparel at the time, the honeyed tone of her skin took on a scarlet hue. It was the first time he could remember ever seeing her rattled and he did get a kick out of her losing her cool for a second. He couldn't help himself from teasing a little more to glimpse further into this girlish persona beyond Summer's usual professional façade.

'Um… I think I had the pants at least.' He caught her eye, his smile broadening as hers narrowed.

'It's good to know you, uh, had some protection,' she said, cringing with every ill-chosen word.

'Some, but I'm afraid it didn't save my dignity and it definitely didn't succeed in pulling off the rebellious act I'd been attempting.' The local teenagers had seemed so popular and carefree compared to him, and though he'd longed to be part of that crowd, his first foray into normality had failed spectacularly.

'What were you rebelling against?' He'd stirred Summer's interest in his life before Maple Island and that was something he didn't want anyone poking their noses into. This was his new start and he didn't wish to be reminded of the past and those in it. It hurt too much. Especially now he had a child of his own and couldn't imagine turning his back on her the way his parents had done to him. He loved his daughter unconditionally and only ever wanted the best for her, not himself.

'The usual teenage angst—parents, school, peers—and feeling generally hard done by. What about you? Something tells me you have a story or two to tell.' His upbringing might not have been as conventional as most but he figured he'd encountered the same emotional turmoil as anyone else, only on a different level. Summer, on the other hand, was such a force of nature and so unafraid of taking chances he could imagine trouble following her everywhere she went.

She gave him the side-eye and he knew he'd hit pay dirt. 'I may have broken my collarbone playing soccer in the UK, fractured my wrist punching a handsy drunk in Rome and, oh, I cracked a rib tombstoning from the cliffs into the sea in Turkey. Just the usual gap-year stuff.'

Hearing snippets of her previous life before coming to the island only made her more appealing to Rafael, even though it should give him more reason to avoid her. Anyone who'd braved such adventures would eventually get bored with island life when it could be so limiting. He'd chosen to come here for that stability, secure in the knowledge nothing would really change, but there wasn't much thrill-seeking to be had around here unless you counted being tempted by a co-worker.

'You've done a bit of travelling, then?' None of it surprised him and not only was he impressed, he was kind of jealous of her conviction to her fearless spirit. He'd had many dreams over the years but the only one he'd seen through had been his desire to go to medical school in America, and that had cost him his family.

'A bit. When my mom remarried I went a bit wild but I've got that bug out of my system. I'm happy where I am now.' It suggested she hadn't always been content with her lot but she'd fought for more. That part of him he was trying to keep at bay hoped she really did intend to stick around for good.

He'd witnessed her fierce spirit for himself today and it had made him think that if she'd had a daughter like his, if Gracie had had a mother like Summer, she would've fought for her with every fibre of her being, instead of abandoning her at the first sign of trouble.

Tonight was a prime example. Here she was, long past the end of her shift, carrying his daughter through the clinic because she refused to let go. That was an endorsement of her character when Gracie very rarely showed any signs of affection to anyone and even less to complete strangers. Clearly Summer had worked hard to earn her trust and he was witnessing the benefits of her experience and expertise first-hand.

If he'd paid more attention to the relationship she'd developed with his daughter instead of pushing her away to protect himself, he might've saved them all from this upset in the emergency room. Summer would've minded Gracie, no problem, for the short time it should've taken him to collect his things from the office.

As they stepped outside the warmth of the hospital, the night air took his breath away, along with the realisation he had potentially harmed his daughter by rebuffing Summer's earlier proposal.

She carried the sleeping bundle over to the car for him and attempted to deposit her into her seat but Gracie refused to let go. They were all exhausted and rather than face another tantrum, Rafael suggested he take Summer home en route. It was the least he could do considering everything she'd done for them tonight.

'Thanks.'

Rafael closed the rear door and left Summer to belt them both into the back seat. He paused, watching her fuss around Gracie, not thrilled with the knowledge he made her feel uncomfortable around him. It wasn't fair to jeopardise her bond with Gracie when she was helping her to make such great progress. Hearing her chat away like any other three-year-old tonight and seeing her playing with the toys had brought a lump to his throat and a swelling in his chest that she'd made it this far despite her challenges.

'So, um, where should I drop you off?' he asked in the rear-view mirror as he started the engine. Not knowing which part of the island she lived on suddenly seemed ignorant on his behalf when she was privy to so much about his own personal circumstances.

'Don't worry about me, I can walk from your place to mine. It's not too far and I'd rather you get Gracie to bed. She's had a long day.' She was yawning herself and Rafael had to stifle his own. At least they didn't have miles to drive. The whole island could be circumnavigated in a lunch hour. That also meant the inhabitants practically lived on top of one another, though some might be completely oblivious to anyone else outside their own front door.

'You live near us? I didn't realise.' He met her eyes in the mirror and wondered how that had escaped him. The beach house where he and Gracie resided was more secluded than some of the properties nearer town and he thought of Summer as someone who'd prefer to be close to the action rather than existing on the outskirts.

She broke eye contact and looked away. 'A little further down the beach, I think. I've seen you running down there.'

That would explain why he'd never noticed her out there. When he was running he blocked out everything around him, using that precious alone time to work through whatever problems were uppermost in his thoughts at that particular time. It wasn't easy to indulge his sporty side, stealing breaks in between appointments or taking advantage of having child-care for a few extra minutes in order to do so. As well as providing him with time out, it was important he keep his fitness levels up for his busy lifestyle and to ensure he'd be around as long as Gracie needed him.

A familiar sense of calm descended on him as they reached home and the comforting sound of the waves breaking nearby soothed his stretched nerves. By the time he got out and opened the front door Summer was already there with Gracie in her arms.

'I can put her to bed for you so we don't wake her. It's no problem.'

Rafael was thrown by the innocuous offer simply because of the implications of letting her inside. He didn't have people over. This was his and Gracie's safe space where they didn't have to worry about anyone judging them. They shut themselves away here night after night, locking the outside world away to leave them in their happy bubble inside. He was the one person he could rely on to keep Gracie safe, having been let down by those he'd trusted. If it happened again, if Gracie was put in jeopardy because he'd shared his parental responsibility with someone else, it would be his fault for leaving them in that position again.

Yet if tonight had taught him anything it was to stop being so defensive about the idea of someone helping and to start being kinder to Summer, who had done absolutely nothing except be her usual wonderful self.

It was past experiences keeping him from trusting her, not his current instincts. If he didn't have the painful memories of betrayal lodging with him and went with his gut on this, he knew he should be throwing the door wide open for her. She wasn't on the clock, this wasn't a cash inducement, and she'd have been well within her rights to leave him to struggle in that hospital corridor with Gracie. He had to accept she had his daughter's best interests at heart and they were both on the same side.

Perhaps it wasn't only his insecurities turning this simple act into a life-changing decision. For him, he knew letting Summer into his house was a decision to let her into his life on a personal level too. Once she stepped inside he was allowing her access to parts of his life he'd cordoned off since Christina had betrayed him in the worst possible way. It had seemed the only way to keep him and Gracie safe. By crossing the threshold tonight Summer would become the first woman to enter their home who was anyone other than a paid childminder.

As his silence stretched to the point of becoming awkward for both of them, he eventually had to grant her admission. He couldn't live in the past for ever, and Summer was showing him he had to start trusting people, if only to benefit Gracie.

'First door on the left at the top of the stairs.' He led the way, opening the child safety gates at the top and bottom of the steps, unsettled himself by the disruption of their bedroom routine. It would be churlish to insist on carrying Gracie himself when transferring her would simply increase the odds of waking her.

'We'll have to get these things off our Fairy Princess,' Summer whispered, as she sat down on the mattress with Gracie on her lap.

Rafael took a seat next to her on the small bed and began to slip Gracie's arms out of her coat. The sound of his heart was thumping in his ears at the proximity of Summer next to him.

'Sorry,' he mumbled, fumbling to remove the fairy wings without bumping against her and failing. His hand brushed against the softness of Summer's body and he daren't look to see which part of her he'd connected with in case he combusted through sheer awkwardness. He wasn't used to being so close to a woman in his home and certainly not in such a confined space. It was almost as if he'd forgotten how to act normally, so aware was he of her presence beside him.

'It's okay. I can get it from here.' Her voice was a little breathy too as they struggled to undress the unconscious three-year-old merely millimetres apart. She managed to unhook the wing closest to her but as she stretched to slip the other down Gracie's arm, her fingers grazed along his thigh. Every muscle in him tensed and every hair on his body stood to attention in anticipation of her making contact with him again.

She didn't apologise but they exchanged nervous smiles and he knew she was as aware of touching him as he was. This electric tension between them was a strange sensation for a man whose job it was to physically examine people every day of the week. It was as though they were afraid to touch each other because of some unforeseen consequence that would make this about more than simply putting his daughter to bed.

He hadn't considered the possibility Summer might be attracted to him the way he was to her but it was there in the coy look she gave him and the spot where she'd brushed against him. It was a reflection of his own desire and recognition that there was something happening between them far beyond their control. That took them into even more dangerous territory than he'd imagined. This validated whatever feelings he'd been having towards her and somehow made it all real, more acceptable.

He broke out of the vacuum they'd created between their bodies, where logic and common sense had been forced out, so they could manoeuvre Gracie under the covers. Once he'd pulled back the comforter, Summer laid her down with the same tenderness he would've done. They both tucked her in and watched her sleep like two proud parents and that's when he knew they had to leave. It was one thing to bond over his daughter but they shouldn't get carried away that it meant anything.

He turned out the light and tiptoed from the room, leaving Summer to ease the door shut behind them.

'Hopefully tonight's excitement will help her sleep to a reasonable hour.' He kept his voice low so he wouldn't disturb her but he also found himself reluctant to move from the hallway. It seemed such an intimate act, putting his daughter to bed with her, and he was enjoying the closeness of sharing the moment after doing it alone for so long.

Summer rested her head against the door and smiled up at him. 'I don't know how you manage. I'm exhausted.' She covered her yawn with her hand.

'Through sheer determination and the help of clinic staff. I'm not sure we'd ever have made it home without you.'

'Nonsense. You're an amazing father. She's very lucky to have you.' The compliment wasn't having nearly as much effect on him as the way she was looking at him, eyes full of admiration and making him feel ten feet tall.

They stood in silence, Rafael being drawn closer and closer into her personal space and leaving no room for fear about where this could lead.

Summer tilted her mouth up towards him, so soft

and tempting and proving beyond doubt that none of these strange new feelings were one-sided.

Yet in that second he knew the next move would decide if she was to be in their lives for his or his daughter's needs. There was no competition.

He swallowed back any lustful thoughts and focused on everything she could offer Gracie.

'Summer, I… I'd like to take you up on your offer to look after Gracie permanently. We'll have to okay it with the clinic directors but I think it would be for the best after all.'

CHAPTER FOUR

SUMMER BLINKED, HOPING it would somehow bring things back into focus for her. For a minute she'd thought Rafael had been about to kiss her and she'd wanted him to. She'd had to put her fingers to her lips to make sure she wasn't still puckered up, waiting for it.

She knew she had been fantasising about him a lot recently but it couldn't have been all in her imagination because she certainly wouldn't have moved in for a kiss unless he'd leaned in first. He'd obviously had second thoughts in the nick of time, deeming his devotion to his daughter's welfare a higher priority than a spur-of-the-moment kiss. The lapse in judgement had most likely come from tiredness and gratitude and nothing personal that would warrant her jeopardising her position at the clinic anyway. An admirable move that she would appreciate more once she scuttled back out of his home to hide her embarrassment under cover of darkness.

She'd clearly done her job well enough tonight to convince him she could take care of his daughter. If they had kissed, their working relationship would've become untenable and she doubted the clinic management would've looked favourably upon her if they thought she made a habit of coming on to the dads at day-care.

'Sure. That would be great,' she said, much too brightly for someone whose ego was gradually shrivelling up the further Rafael backed away from her. 'I'll speak to the bosses tomorrow and we can work out a schedule as best we can.' One that entailed their only interaction from now on would be solely based around the handover of Gracie's care.

'Will you be okay walking home?' His polite, if unsubtle, query was his way of telling her he wanted her to get the hell out of his house.

'I'll be fine. I'll enjoy the walk.' She practically stumbled down the stairs in her haste to get away from him and the situation she'd found herself in.

He didn't even try to follow her and simply called out, 'I'll see you tomorrow.'

Summer let herself out onto the porch and the cold air seemed to sizzle against her red-hot skin. At least the non-kiss meant she could face him at work with a fraction of her dignity still intact. If they'd actually locked lips *then* thought about the consequences and pretended the moment hadn't happened, the rejection would've stung even more than it did now.

She pulled her coat around her to keep the chill from penetrating the rest of her body and stepped down onto the sand. It was dark but the sky was clear, the moon providing enough light for her to see where she was going. This was her peaceful place. The waves breaking on the shore always managed to calm the tangle of the thoughts in her head when she'd had a rough day and this one had been a doozy.

The Boston lights on the horizon reminded her of

the life and the people she'd left behind. Whilst she regretted the circumstances that had brought her out here, it was the best move she'd ever made and she didn't intend to make the same mistake twice. There was no way she was giving up a job she loved and moving because she'd got involved with the wrong man again. She was the one who'd end up alone and in pain.

'Are you sure you can't have the chef rustle up some eggs Benedict for me? I'm sure he's heard of it. That is if he didn't get his qualifications off the back of a cereal box.' Philomena Kerridge-Bates could be heard all over the rehab unit as Rafael walked through the main recovery ward on his way to the children's ward and witnessed her pushing away her breakfast.

'You don't want all that fancy nonsense. What you need is a bowl of good old oatmeal, thick enough to stand on. That'll soon build you up,' Old Salty yelled across at her, dispensing his prescription for her recovery.

'It sounds revolting. I thought this was supposed to be a first-class establishment? Why am I being subjected to this treatment?' She fanned her face with the bone-handled fan she'd apparently brought with her to deal with the shock of such eventualities. The harassed girl who'd brought the offending food offering scuttled off, no doubt to have a breakdown in the kitchen along with the other staff attempting to cater to her needs. She was a paying client so there wasn't much could be done about her attitude to the staff or the facilities except to try and pacify her. However, Old Salty was under no obligation to be polite and apparently regularly put her in her place.

'You have a bed, three hot meals a day and people at your beck and call. What more do you need, woman?' Her portly foe spoke with his mouth full of toast before slurping it down with his orange juice. The wink he gave Rafael made him think he was doing this on purpose to get under her skin but as long as they had each other to duel with, Rafael was keeping out of it.

'Some manners would be good, Mr Harrington,' Mrs Kerridge-Bates sniffed as she laid a linen napkin across her lap. Rafael had an inkling Salty would be making a point of ensuring she wasn't going to get everything her own way while he was around.

Rafael carried on to the children's beds to check up on his youngest patients, Peyton and Connor Walsh, who'd suffered severe spinal trauma after an accident with some scaffolding. He'd operated on them in Boston, removing shards of wood from Peyton's thoracic spine and performing the new mini-scaffolding procedure on Connor. The three-dimensional bandage should heal his cracked vertebrae and Alex Kirkland, who specialised in the leg and walking lab, was working towards helping the children walk again.

That pioneering operation had attracted the clinic's attention and he had these two to thank for bringing him and Graciela to Maple Island so he had a special attachment to the case.

'Morning.' He hadn't expected to find Summer in here with them.

'Morning.' Summer was clearly not as excited about seeing him as the Walsh children were, who greeted him with a simultaneous, 'Hi!'

Thank goodness they'd seen sense last night and avoided that kiss or things could've become awkward.

It was more important his daughter have stability and understanding with someone she trusted than giving in to a spur-of-the-moment temptation. It had felt like the most natural thing in the world to lean in for a kiss after tucking Gracie into bed for the night. The chemistry had certainly been there between them and she'd suddenly become part of their little bubble, isolated from the rest of the world outside. In his home, far from real life at the clinic, he hadn't been thinking about responsibility or the repercussions of what they had been doing. Only that he'd wanted to kiss her.

The irony had been when she'd made it clear the feeling was mutual, giving him pause for thought. He knew giving in to temptation would affect them both and so he had pulled them back from the brink of a mistake just in time. Since she'd agreed to his proposal about reconsidering Gracie's care on a more regular basis, they'd have to get over their personal issues pretty quickly. There was no room for embarrassment or attraction lest it impact on his daughter in any way.

'What have we got here?' The children were both sitting up in their adjacent beds with Summer between them, surrounded by art supplies and smiles. She split her time between the day-care centre and her patients here when she could to check on the twins' welfare, so it wasn't unusual to find her in residence. It was simply the timing which had thrown him.

'I thought we could try some art therapy today to see how Peyton and Connor are feeling about their time here and their progress.' Summer was perfectly civil as she addressed his curiosity but she couldn't quite meet his eye. Something he was going to have to work on if she was ever to trust he wouldn't make another advance towards her.

He peeked at the two canvases the twins were painting to get an idea of how they were feeling about their long road to recovery.

'May I?' He checked with them before taking a closer look in case these were private expressions not intended for anyone else to see, merely an outlet for frustrations they hadn't been able to communicate thus far.

There was no such hesitation in showing off their masterpieces so all credit went to their teacher for encouraging their efforts.

'Mine first.' Connor, the more confident of the two, held his up and waved it as if it was a winning lottery ticket.

Careful not to get any wet paint on his hands or his clean shirt before he did the rest of his rounds, Rafael took the canvas. The word 'WINNER!' was crudely written in thick black letters surrounded by an explosion of colourful splodges he thought might be ticker tape.

'I beat Peyton yesterday in rehab,' he explained with glee as his competitor stuck out her tongue.

'That's great. You're both doing so well.' Whilst some healthy competition focused in the right direction could aid a faster recovery, he didn't want Peyton to become self-conscious that she wasn't progressing as well as her brother.

'Yes, but my injuries were worse than yours. Weren't they, Doctor?' Peyton showed she was equally as feisty and there was no way she was going to be left behind.

'I'm a miracle of science.'

They competed to be crowned champion of the spinal unit but they were both winners in his eyes and he would never pick one over the other.

'Let's see what you've got, Peyton.' He deflected the beginning of an argument to see what she'd painted, praying they wouldn't force him to pick which one he preferred.

Although the colours—soft pinks and baby blues—weren't as in your face as Connor's, the word in the centre of the painting didn't have any less impact.

'Brave'.

They couldn't have described themselves any more accurately with a four-thousand-word essay. Especially when there were so many negative emotions they could've exhibited given their circumstances. It said a lot about their strength of character and the amazing staff surrounding them. Summer included.

'I didn't realise we had such talented artists in our midst, did you, Miss Ryan?' To maintain some sort of professional distance he'd decided to address her more formally and remind himself that due to her role in his life they should no longer be on familiar terms.

He was impressed today, not only with the twins' resilience but by the methods she'd used to gauge their states of mind. It was easy to forget how important her role was here as a child life specialist as well as in the nursery when she downplayed it so well, but the psychological welfare of the patients was every bit as important as their physical recovery.

As the children's wing expanded they'd have more need for her in this capacity when she provided such a positive experience for the children in between their medical procedures. He knew that would take her away from Gracie but she'd be starting school eventually and hopefully Summer would continue to job-share until then.

'They've done really well. I'll have to find somewhere special to hang them.' She began to pack away the art supplies, no doubt due in her other role at the nursery now since he'd already dropped Gracie off there.

'I think you both deserve a treat,' Rafael bent down to whisper. 'What about something from the bakery?'

'Yay! You mean Brady's, right, and not that vegan one my mom likes?' Connor shuddered and Rafael put his mind at rest with a nod. 'In that case, I'll have a crème doughnut.'

'Can I have a chocolate sprinkle doughnut, please?' Peyton added her request too and her obvious excitement at such a small gesture made him wish these kids could get back to their normal lives as soon as possible.

'Shh. Keep the noise down or everyone will want one.' He'd check with their parents but he was sure they wouldn't object to them having a small treat.

'What about Summer?'

'Yeah. Doesn't she deserve a doughnut too?'

They petitioned on her behalf for a share in their success and he couldn't deny such a request.

'Sure. Perhaps Miss Ryan would come and tell me which sweet treat she'd prefer and we'll let Dr Alex get on with your rehab.' As fair-haired Alex approached the children's bedside it became clear Rafael and Summer were no longer required and neither would want to step on his toes when Alex was the one now leading their case.

'Yes, I'll have to get in quickly before there are

none of my favourites left.' She was humouring him and the children but she did gather her supplies and follow him out into the corridor, leaving Alex to carry out his assessment.

'They both seem to be in good spirits, all things considered.' He debated whether or not to walk away and avoid a one-to-one with her but not only would that be immature, it wouldn't do much to improve their working relationship when they were about to become closer than ever thanks to Gracie.

Summer tucked the large sketch book under her arm. 'Yes. Obviously, our positive reinforcement is having an impact. At this stage I don't think they need extra counselling regarding their stay at the clinic.'

The twins would have needed therapy to overcome the trauma of the accident itself but often the long-term confinement to the hospital bed could be just as distressing.

'I think being here together has helped them settle in. I can see how Connor's competitiveness is spurring on Peyton's recovery.' That sibling rivalry would give them the determination to overcome their injuries, if only to get one up on each other.

'Yes, he's helpful in his unique way.' She smiled directly at him and Rafael took it as a sign she'd forgiven him and wanted to move past last night as much as he did.

'They've come a long way since I first treated them back in Boston, and as much as I love seeing them I'm looking forward to the day when they can walk out of here.'

'Me too. Well, I suppose I should get back to my

other job before your daughter comes looking for me. How is she this morning?'

'Still a bit sore and having trouble putting weight on the ankle, which is making her more challenging than usual.' Gracie had been particularly fractious this morning, to the point of refusing to walk at all, so he'd had to carry her into nursery. He had hoped Summer would've been there to calm her down until he finished work and had more time to pander to her. They'd both been disappointed to find her not there.

Since this meeting had proved his urge to see her wasn't apparently to apologise for last night or have her hurry back to the nursery, he had to conclude he'd simply wanted an excuse to see her. Not everything had been solved by resisting that kiss. Preventing it happening didn't automatically stop him from thinking about what might have been.

'In that case, I should get over there and see if I can take her mind off it.'

'She won't put that doll down so I think you've got two patients to contend with.' The only way he'd got her to leave the house had been to promise Summer would help make Dolly feel better, and he wasn't fond of making promises he couldn't keep. Even if they were made on someone else's behalf.

'I think I can handle it,' she said with a laugh to ease his conscience.

'Good. Are we still on for your future career as a Gracie shadow too?' He tried to convince himself that was the real reason he'd sought her out, that he hadn't stuffed things up and could still count on her to do the right thing by Gracie.

'Of course. I'll have a chat with my manager when I get a chance.'

'I'll hang on here and have a word with Alex too. See if we can make it official.' As a father himself, it might be beneficial to get his boss's thoughts off the record about if he thought this was a good idea. He'd leave out the bit about almost kissing another member of staff, although since Alex had got together with Maggie Green, a physiotherapist here, he couldn't very well complain about workplace romance.

'No problem. Let me know if he's on board before we say anything to Gracie.' They stared at each other a heartbeat too long before she added, 'All right, then. 'Bye,' and walked away.

Rafael was still there to see her face light up when she stopped for a chat with Kaylee. She was a different person with her friend, laughing and carefree and a world away from a deadly serious single dad with more personal issues than she'd probably covered in her psychology training.

It was then he realised he had nothing to offer her even if he did like her on a personal level. He wouldn't want to curtail her fun but a relationship with a single parent carried a lot of baggage that was bound to weigh her down. It wouldn't be fair to clip her wings with the responsibilities of a family when she had so much more living to do before she settled down. He couldn't whisk her away on spontaneous romantic breaks or take her clubbing into the early hours of the morning the way a single man could. Before he did anything, he had to consider Gracie and that meant Summer would always have to come second. She deserved to be someone's number one and be spoiled with time and affection.

The most he could give her was himself but even that came with stipulations. By entering into a relationship with him, Summer would be forced into a mothering role for Gracie that neither of them were probably ready for yet. It was best for Summer if they leave their one indiscretion in the past. She would get over it quicker than he would.

His chest hurt so badly at the thought of her moving on with another man he was sure that sadistic Cupid had taken a pot shot at him in a cruel prank.

CHAPTER FIVE

SUMMER PULLED A napkin from the dispenser and ripped it into tiny shreds, littering the table with tissue snowflakes. Fiona Brady, the co-owner with her husband, wouldn't be pleased she was making a mess in her spotless bakery and bistro or, worse, might come over to see what had her in such a flap, but she had to release some of this nervous energy somewhere. She daren't order a coffee before Kaylee got there or she'd be buzzing like a bug in a bottle on her second cup.

The waitress, one of the redheaded Brady offspring, was hovering but she hoped once her friend got here and they ordered, she'd give them some privacy. She needed to get some advice about this idea of working closer with Rafael, especially after what had almost happened last night. Since Kaylee had registered Summer's personal interest before she had, she seemed the logical choice for a confidante.

It was obvious Rafael wanted to keep things strictly professional. He'd made that clear last night when he'd avoided that kiss and all but thrown her out of his house. Then had reinforced his stance by carrying on as though nothing had happened. Working in the same clinic, sometimes with the same patients, including his daughter, it was probably for the best.

The waitress passed by and gave a puzzled glance at the confetti she'd shed all over the table. Summer brushed it into her hand and shoved it in her pocket before she reported it back to her mother.

Her heart and her stomach flipped as a familiar figure crossed the road towards the café but it wasn't the person she'd been expecting.

'Hi, Rafael, Gracie.' There was no way of avoiding them when she'd chosen the seat closest to the door to give her an unobstructed view of Main Street.

'Hey.' He walked past her towards the counter, allowing her internal body parts to stop somersaulting. Gracie, however, pulled out a chair next to her and sat down with Dolly.

Her father put in the doughnut order the twins had requested and Gracie's sugar cookie. 'Er, Miss Ryan? Can I get you something? I did promise.'

'Summer,' Gracie shouted without looking up from Dolly, who was hopping across the table on her good leg with some assistance.

'Pardon?' Rafael was noticeably perplexed by her response.

'Not Miss Ryan, Papa. Summer.'

Summer suppressed a smirk that one of the Valdez family was showing some maturity to ensure they remained on first-name terms and his eye roll at the correction didn't escape her attention.

'Sorry, *Summer*, would you like something from the case?' Under pressure from his three-year-old, he was being overly nice now.

'No, thanks. I'm waiting for someone. I'll order

when they get here.' She gave him a friendly smile and was surprised to see his features darken in response.

'Gracie, we should go and let Miss… Summer get her coffee in peace.' He snatched up the cake box from the counter and held the door open to leave.

'Did you get to speak to Alex about that matter we discussed?' She knew he hadn't, because her supervisor at the day-care centre had still been completely in the dark when she'd raised the subject of Gracie.

'Not yet. I got a little…distracted.'

'Let me know if you've changed your mind about the arrangement, or when you want me to start.'

He grunted some unintelligible response as he urged Gracie out of the premises with him. Summer waved them out, wondering what on earth had happened to put him in such a foul mood.

'Sorry I'm late.' Kaylee rushed in through the door and Summer was forced to drag her attention away from the father and daughter crossing back over the road. It was none of her business what was bothering him.

'Hello.' Kaylee waved a hand in front of her face to remind her she was there.

'Sorry. Dr Valdez was just here. He seemed upset about something.'

'What is it with you two? You always seem to rub each other up the wrong way.' Summer's coffee companion dumped her purse on the table and collapsed into the chair opposite.

'That's not strictly true. We both care about what's best for Gracie, that's all. In fact, we've been discussing the idea of me caring for her on a full-time basis.'

'Do you really think that's a good idea?'

'Why?'

'I've seen the way you look at him.' The raised eyebrows were enough to make Summer blush.

'He's a good-looking guy but we're both professional. Nothing's going to happen.' Despite planning to confide in her friend about the near-kiss, she decided there was nothing to tell and should simply put the matter behind her the way Rafael had clearly done.

'Is that so? In that case, it might be a good idea for the two of you to take a step back rather than get closer where there's more temptation. Now, we should probably order before they throw us out.'

'I guess. I'll have an Americano, thanks.'

'And to eat?'

'You choose.' Summer had zero appetite, her stomach in knots that her wayward feelings for Rafael were apparently so transparent. Kaylee was right, she needed a buffer between her and the man she hadn't been able to stop thinking about since last night, and he needed more people in his life than her.

She reached for her bag and the notebook and pen she kept there to jot down some sort of schedule for her and Gracie that would keep her too busy to think about Rafael.

It was only then she saw Dolly lying under the table and knew she couldn't go home until she'd returned her to her rightful owner.

'And you just complicated matters even more,' she muttered to her soft-bodied friend. If Gracie was as attached to Dolly as Rafael had indicated, she'd have to return her tonight. Against her better judgement her pulse was racing at the prospect of seeing him again so soon.

* * *

'We'll get Dolly now, Gracie.' Rafael had tried to placate her with every other toy in the house rather than walk back into the café and look as though he was using his daughter as an excuse to spy on whoever Summer was meeting in the bakery.

In the end he decided her wrath was preferable to his daughter's, which experience had told him could last for hours. He'd heard enough screaming, crying and smashing things for one night and right now all he cared about was making her happy.

He parked the car across the street from Brady's, unbuckled Gracie from her car seat and prepared to interrupt Summer's coffee date. She'd looked so nervous and guilty when he'd spotted her in there he was convinced she had to be meeting up with another man.

Jealousy was something he hadn't experienced in a long time and he couldn't say he enjoyed the realisations it brought with it. She had moved on after their near-kiss. That's what he'd wanted. Except he hadn't expected it to happen so soon. Not when the memory was still so fresh for him he could still feel her breath on his lips. Despite all the reasons he shouldn't be with Summer, that's exactly where he wanted to be. Envy of the man who would have that privileged position twisted through his body like fast-acting poison, eating away at his insides and turning everything toxic.

Then he saw Summer walk out the door, talking to Dolly and, taking Gracie by the hand, he strode straight towards her.

'We were just coming to find you.'

'Me or my friend?' she asked, waving Dolly's arm at him, her adorable playfulness only furthering his pain.

'Gracie wouldn't go to bed without her.' That was the understatement of the century and couldn't begin to convey the chaos that had ensued as a result of Dolly's disappearance. He'd torn the house and car apart looking for her to calm Gracie down before realising she'd been left as a gooseberry on Summer's date.

'Now she doesn't have to.' Summer handed her over with a smile that he only ever wanted to be for him.

'Thanks. Did you…uh…have a nice time?' He didn't know why he'd asked when the thought was physical and mental torture to him and the answer was written all over her face anyway.

Her frown disappeared as quickly as it had formed as she probably wondered why he thought it was any of her business who'd she'd been with, or what they'd done. 'I did, as it happens. Kaylee's good company.'

'Kaylee…yeah, she seems like fun.' Relief whooshed through him so quickly at the mention of her colleague at the nursery his head was spinning. The knowledge that she wasn't seeing another man after all revealed some home truths to Rafael. He'd convinced himself he couldn't be with her but the thought of her with someone else had eaten away at him at such a devastating rate it was clear this was more than simple attraction. There were feelings developing for her that went beyond superficial desires but understanding that didn't mean he was in any better a place to act on them.

'Actually, I was noting down a few ideas about some fundraising events we could do to pay for some more beds in the children's wing.' She rummaged in her bag and it was his turn to wonder why he should be involved.

'I'm sure it will be much appreciated. Let me know

what I can do.' The clinic already funded a couple of beds for those families who couldn't afford their children's medical expenses and he knew an extension to the charitable cause could only be a good thing.

'I was hoping you would volunteer to organise it,' she said with a grimace as he prepared to end his involvement with a donation.

'Me? Why?' He was stopped in his tracks by the suggestion and couldn't figure out where this idea had come from.

'In case you haven't noticed, a lot of the events on Maple Island are based around food. I was thinking perhaps we could promote a healthier option by having a sponsored triathlon. I know it's still too cold to expect people to go swimming in the sea, so we might be able to do something at the clinic. It shouldn't be too hard to get control of the pool for the swimming event and set up some exercise bikes and treadmills for the cycling and running.'

'Sounds good but I don't understand where I come in.' She'd obviously put a lot of thought into the idea and, although admirable, he didn't understand why she would then want him to take over the reins and claim the glory.

'That's a funny story… You have a bit of a nickname around here—Triathlon Dad.' She was trying to conceal a smirk and failing.

'Okay,' he said, not really understanding the joke.

'On account of all the sport you do around the island,' she explained, and this time he got it. The swimming, cycling and running he did apparently hadn't gone unnoticed.

'I had no idea.' He shook his head with a laugh. It

was kind of funny when he'd always imagined he'd managed to keep a low profile on the island outside the clinic.

Summer glanced at Gracie, who was too busy playing with Dolly to care what the grown-ups were talking about, and lowered her voice. 'Anyway, I thought it might do you good to integrate into the community more.'

He bristled at the thought of inviting more people into his life when he was still experiencing the fallout from bending his house rules for her. 'Gracie and I are quite happy as we are, thank you.'

'I just thought…well, have you ever considered that by closing yourself off you're also limiting Gracie's social skills even more?' She bit her lip, clearly knowing how close she was pushing his patience to the limit.

He didn't appreciate anyone telling him how to raise his daughter but Summer's opinion was one he was learning to respect. Everything she said made sense even if it sometimes felt like a slight against his parenting skills. Something he now knew she would never intentionally do.

It occurred to him that this exercise in public relations she was proposing might provide some distraction from his growing attraction to her. Their closeness could have been precipitated by his limited social circle since coming to Maple Island and he supposed it wouldn't hurt to extend it a little. If they had other things, other people to keep them busy, they might stop seeking each other out.

'I guess it's worth looking into and it's for a good cause after all.' The clinic, and those who came to it, would benefit from the fundraising. He glanced at Gracie as she clutched her second-hand doll and considered the possibility that in trying to protect her, he'd isolated her more. Something he wanted a chance to rectify for her sake.

'I'm not sure of your family circumstances, and do feel free to tell me to mind my own business, but do you have any family who might come over for the event? It might be a good excuse for them to come and visit, perhaps spend some time with Gracie.' She was fishing now, looking for someone else he could invite into his daughter's life, but that wasn't an option.

'No one local,' was all the information he was prepared to give.

He thought about his parents for the first time in years. When Christina had first left, when his life had been in utter chaos, he'd considered contacting his family. He'd needed to reach out to someone for that support most people took for granted in their lives, but by then Gracie's developmental issues had become apparent. With a future stretching ahead of them already full of uncertainty, he'd shut down any possibility of inviting his parents back into his personal business.

Someday he might forgive them for their lack of compassion towards him but he didn't want to leave Gracie susceptible to the same treatment. If they were to reject her for not fitting in to the mould of their perfect grandchild, he knew he would never forgive them. For now, he would rather leave things as they were so no one else got hurt.

Summer's apparent step too far into Rafael's personal affairs was disrupted by the sound of squealing brakes, followed by an almighty crash. They both paused, and the ensuing silence was as frightening as the initial din. It became clear someone close by might be hurt and requiring assistance. After rushing back round the corner, they saw a scene of devastation that was too close to home not to affect them.

The second she saw Rafael's silver sedan crushed between the two other vehicles she had to brace herself before her legs gave way. It had been shunted into the stationary car in front by the one currently wedged into the back of it. No one could have survived that double impact and she was grateful they'd been with her instead. The alternative didn't bear thinking about.

'It's okay, Gracie.' She comforted the little girl, who was understandably upset at the sight, and quickly moved to block the scene from Gracie's view.

A crowd had gathered around the station wagon slammed sideways into Rafael's car and once she'd convinced him she would look after Gracie, he sprinted across the road to help.

Every now and then he glanced up at her from his crouched position on the ground where he was talking to the injured driver, his face a conflicting mixture of emotions that weren't difficult to interpret. She knew him well enough to see he was thankful he and Gracie were safe but worried for everyone else involved. All of which he was setting aside to help the injured. Her heart swelled, full of admiration for the man he was, not only as a committed medical professional but also as a compassionate human being. So often she'd seen him put the needs of others first and not everyone she'd encountered in life was so noble.

He flashed her a brief smile, which was every bit as

brief and unsteady as hers but proof enough to Summer he was glad she was there for him and Gracie.

The assembled crowd worked on prising the mangled car door open on the driver's side to enable access for the emergency services. With this level of trauma they had to be careful to stabilise the patient until she was transported and assessed to prevent any further damage being caused. Rafael was trying to calm the woman, who was rambling and crying about the brakes failing and, most worryingly, that she couldn't move her legs.

The ambulance pulled up alongside and the paramedics dispersed the crowd so they could reach the injured party. Rafael relayed the events and it was only when the woman had been given urgent pain relief and stabilised with a backboard and cervical collar that he was able to take a step back and breathe.

'I'll come with you back to the clinic,' he told the crew as he came back to check on Gracie. 'Thanks for helping, Summer.'

'I'm just glad you're both safe.' Drop-down-on-her-knees-weeping-and-wailing glad, though she couldn't show it in public.

'I can't believe how close we came.' He ran his hands over his head, his hair and confidence visibly ruffled for the first time since taking charge of the incident.

'You couldn't have known that was going to happen and you weren't hurt, that's the main thing.' She knew he'd never have forgiven himself if Gracie had been injured, no matter how faultless he'd have been in what happened.

'On initial assessment I think I'm going to be required at the clinic to treat the family before we can transfer them to Boston.'

'It didn't look good.' Maple Island didn't have a major trauma unit and they'd have to be flown to Boston, but not before they at least knew the extent of their injuries.

Rafael shook his head. 'It's going to be a long night.'

'I could take Gracie back to yours if you'd like? Will we have a sleepover, Gracie?' This wasn't in her plans for creating more distance between her and their family but she knew that right now Rafael wouldn't let anyone else help and neither would Gracie. She was alone in that privileged position and this was more about the patient getting the treatment she needed than her private life.

'With Dolly too?'

'With Dolly.' She was grateful if that was the child's only concern and hopefully she'd managed to keep her far enough away from everything going on to bother her.

Rafael scooped Gracie into his arms for an understandably too-long hug and Summer had to look away, choked up by the unsaid words and unexpressed emotions filling the air.

'I'll check in with you when I can,' he shouted, and jumped into the back of the ambulance.

As the ambulance raced to the clinic Rafael wished he had more time to process what had happened. In all likelihood, and despite not having all of the equipment readily available in the major trauma unit of a city hospital, he was going to have to operate on the driver of the car, if only to stabilise her until they could trans-

fer her to Boston. As always, he'd leave his personal
problems outside the doors of the operating room but
for now his mind was a whirl of emotions that were
going to take a while to work through.

His first thoughts always belonged to Graciela and
how he could've lost her if she'd been strapped into the
back seat when the car had slammed into his.

That picture of twisted metal and shattered glass,
the vehicle crumpled beyond recognition, would haunt
him for ever. His shudder was a reaction to the thought
of the injuries she could've sustained and how empty
his life would be without her in it.

Summer had reassured him immediately in the aftermath. 'She's fine.'

Hearing her say it had released the pressure in his
lungs so he'd been able to inhale a shaky breath. She'd
interpreted his actions so easily he knew she'd felt as
concerned as he had.

The emergency room was a hive of activity as staff
buzzed around the new patients, the drama of which
he was sure hadn't been seen here before at the clinic.
It was more akin to the high-paced environment of its
city counterparts. Thankfully he was used to working
in this kind of situation and entered with determination to bring some focus to it. Although he was aware
this wasn't his department and the staff were more than
capable, he wanted to be there in case he was needed.

Rafael presented himself to the lead physician over-
seeing the initial assessment and shook his hand.

'Am I glad to see you here. I've ordered X-rays
but most of the pain appears to be centred around her
spine.'

There were a lot of serious problems associated with

high-impact accidents such as head, neck, chest or abdomen injuries and fractures. All of those would be referred to the relevant specialists but a further spinal injury could be prevented from causing more pain or deformity by initial surgery, and that was his area of expertise. Rafael wasn't in the habit of boasting but he knew there wasn't a better spinal surgeon to be found in Boston because he was here on Maple Island, and one of the first on the scene with first-hand knowledge of the traumatic event.

While waiting for the X-ray results, Rafael sought permission to do his own clinical evaluation on their adult patient. There was absolutely no hesitation from the attending physician in granting him access in the desire to expedite her treatment.

He applied progressive circular pressure to pinpoint where she was experiencing the tenderness but Paisley, the patient, was letting him know that everything he did hurt.

Potential injuries caused by the crash could include vertebrae fractures, disc extrusion, compression or carotid arterial injury. A cervical injury was often indicated by neurological discrepancy or obvious fracture or malalignment but it was too risky to perform a full range of motion assessment, given the high-impact collision she'd suffered and that she was experiencing neck pain, spine tenderness and was unable to even sit up.

She'd required a series of X-rays where all seven vertebrae had been visible and he'd consult Alex on this one too for a neurological exam measuring sensation, muscle tone and reflexes.

He was going to have to potentially stabilise the

spine, remove bone fragments and restore the alignment of the vertebrae to reduce compression in the spinal cord.

If the vertebrae in the spinal cord were unsuitable he might have to perform a spinal fusion with metal plates, screws wires and metal rods. In some cases it was even possible to use small pieces of bone from the hip or knee to grow and fuse vertebrae, but he wouldn't know until he saw the damage for himself.

Rafael was more aware than ever that his patient's quality of life had literally been in his hands. The trauma she'd sustained to her spine would take a long period of healing and he'd wanted to give her every chance of getting back to normal. If they'd transferred her to Boston immediately there'd have been a risk of causing more damage.

The excessive displacement of the spine had required a spinal fusion to stabilise the vertebrae. It had taken over three hours, using metalwork and bone grafts, to do the job so the body would eventually build bony bridges across those segments to prevent movement and the resulting pain.

As Paisley was wheeled into Recovery, with the drainage tubes protruding from her wound, the drip attached to replace lost fluids, and an oxygen mask to ease her breathing, he pictured himself in her place. A lapse in concentration and split-second decisions were all that had saved him from a similar fate.

What would've happened to Gracie in those circumstances? Paisley was going to be incapacitated for quite a while and there was all the follow-up treatment after that—physiotherapy to improve mobility, occupational therapy to manage daily activities once taken for granted, and a psychologist to work through the mental trauma she'd suffered throughout. In the same position, he was afraid he'd have to put Gracie into care.

Fortunately, the patient had family and friends in Boston able to step up and provide support for her. He had no one. His family had made the decision to cut him out of their lives when he'd chosen to live the life he wanted and buck tradition. However, when it came to friends he was entirely responsible for his own resistance to let anyone close enough to claim that title.

Now, imagining himself on that hospital trolley, perhaps with his daughter lying injured on another, he knew Summer was the only person he'd want by his side.

Here she was tonight, once again going beyond her duty to devote time to his daughter. She wasn't the sort of person who'd abandon Gracie without a second thought, the way her mother had. It was time he admitted the truth. That he was afraid another person he cared for would walk out on him again, leaving him to pick up the pieces of his broken heart and start over again. After being abandoned by his parents and Christina, he knew he wouldn't survive another.

When he'd first arrived in America, it had been a lonely experience as well as a cultural shock. Although fluent in several languages, including English, he'd had difficulty fitting into college life, unused to sharing his space with people who weren't family. It had taken time for him to acquire a small group of friends to socialise with, to confide in and generally spend time with. Up until then he'd had to wander the campus on his own, figuring out things for himself. Unlike other freshman students, he hadn't had the comfort of a familiar voice on the end of the telephone to reassure him things would work out. He'd been homesick without having a home to return to if things hadn't worked out.

Christina had been one of those who'd helped him fit in, always there to buck him up when he'd needed it, and falling for her had been inevitable when they'd spent so much time together. When she'd left he'd been taken right back to those early days, feeling abandoned and totally alone in the world. Except this time he'd had a helpless baby to take care of too. Since then it had been him and Gracie against the world and it was only recently he'd stopped thinking of himself as being alone.

Summer had shown affection for them both and had made a difference in his life and Gracie's. To lose her in any capacity would create a hole in his life that could never be filled. Not when he could sense the chance of happiness almost within his grasp.

Summer represented a danger to his status quo but that safety net he'd strung up around him and Gracie now felt more restrictive and suffocating than sharing his space with someone who cared for them.

He was exhausted from taking care of Gracie and working but they loved life on the island and he didn't want anything to spoil that. He'd thought he was protecting his heart by envisioning the worst-case scenario if he entered into another relationship. Now he was wondering if he wasn't doing them all a disservice by maintaining this detachment from the rest of the world.

CHAPTER SIX

RAFAEL LET HIMSELF into the house to find a sleeping Summer curled up on the couch. Seeing her waiting for him after the long, stressful evening was like a warm, comforting hug helping him to get over the stresses of the day.

How he missed having someone to come back to at night, someone who could help put Gracie to bed or to share a glass of wine with as he unwound at the end of a long day. It had been the simple things in a partnership that had often brought him the most joy and he'd forgotten that until he'd come home to Summer.

Her hair had fallen in a golden curtain hiding her face from view when he really needed to see her. He reached out and gently tucked it behind her ear, the slight contact stirring her into a lazy smile.

'Hello, sleepyhead.'

Her green eyes blinked back at him and she scrambled to sit up. 'Sorry, I tried to stay awake. I wanted to make sure you…er…everything was okay.'

She was brushing her tangled hair away from her face and trying to smooth out her crumpled clothes but she looked perfectly adorable the way she was. This tousled vision gave him a glimpse of what she'd look like first thing in the morning and stirred feelings inside him he'd thought he'd never experience again.

If he hadn't been so damaged by his previous relationship he could wake up to her in his bed looking just like this. It was a tempting thought and the conflicting emotions she aroused in him reminded him of the man he was as well as being a surgeon and father. He felt very protective of her when she looked so vulnerable but he also had an urge to kiss her until she was fully awake.

An act that wasn't appropriate when all she'd done was help him out during a very difficult time.

'The operation went well and she's in Recovery. It's going to take a while for her to heal completely and she'll likely have to come back here for rehab, but we've done everything we can for now.'

'I'm glad to hear it.'

'I'm so sorry for keeping you out all night.' He knew he should let her go and get some rest but since Summer was at the heart of a lot of the decisions and emotions he had to work through he appreciated having her with him. Logic and his self-imposed restrictions aside, he enjoyed being with her. With the sound of that crash still ringing in his ears and the what-ifs hounding him, he realised he didn't want to be alone, but he'd already asked so much of her tonight.

'It's not as though you were out partying, Rafael. There was an emergency. I was there, remember? You did what you had to do for that poor family and Gracie and I have been fine.'

'I know, and I'm eternally grateful you stepped up to help without hesitation. I just hate to impose on you, although if she's asleep it does make me feel a little less guilty.' It wouldn't have come as a surprise if Gracie had been howling until he'd come home to tuck her into bed, especially after the shock they'd had. It was comforting to know she'd been able to settle for Summer and it stopped him fretting about working away from his daughter.

'She did fuss for a while that you weren't here to read her a bedtime story and went to bed clutching one of your shirts. I hope that's okay? She took it from your closet and it seemed to give her some comfort.'

'That's fine. We don't really have anyone else to turn to at times like this. Her mother hasn't wanted to know her for the past two years and my parents, well, they kind of disowned me when I left Spain. They don't know who I am these days, much less their granddaughter.'

'It's their loss, on both counts.' It was meant as a compliment but it did make Rafael wonder if it was Gracie's loss, too, that she'd never get to know the rest of her family. He'd been so hurt and determined to succeed without their help that he'd forgotten about what was best for his daughter. She was the innocent party here and though he didn't want her to get hurt there was a possibility he had been projecting his insecurities onto her.

'I try not to dwell on it but today has opened my eyes. What if we had been in that car? What would happen to Gracie if I got hurt, or vice versa? I'm not sure either of us would survive without the other.' He was horrified to hear the slight crack in his voice, showing his one true weakness in front of Summer, but he hadn't planned for that eventuality. If he was ever seriously ill or injured, his daughter would be left at the mercy of children's services because he'd been too afraid to share her with anyone else.

'I'm always here for both of you.' She let her hand rest lightly atop his, a gentle reminder she was there, and he appreciated it more than she would ever know. It was a long time since he'd had that kind of support.

'Thank you. I'm glad she didn't give you too much of a hard time tonight in case I have to take you up on that.' A wrinkled shirt was a small price to pay for peace of mind tonight and now he had assurance that he wasn't on his own any more, everything he'd shared with Summer was worth it.

'Not at all. We were working on some posters for the triathlon idea.' She let go of him and rooted through the mess of paper and colouring utensils littering his coffee table to present him with their joint efforts.

'Well, these masterpieces should have people digging deep into their pockets.' He could just imagine the two of them, heads bent over the table, doing their best to illustrate Summer's ideas, and the image was heart-warming. They'd formed a real bond and he knew that wasn't something achieved easily with his daughter, or him. She was someone special.

'I showed her some of these so she'd understand what it is we're trying to do.' Summer grabbed her cell and came to sit on the arm of the couch beside him, scrolling through to show him a video of a triathlon.

'I'm not sure any of us are quite in that league,' he joked, trying to ignore the warm feel of her pressed against his arm or her hair brushing against his cheek and awakening every nerve ending in his body.

'I thought we could make it an annual event and perhaps make the first one for those hospital staff who are already in shape. Present company included, of course.' Her smile, so warm, so close, sucked all the oxygen from his lungs and it took some time before he was able to respond.

'And you'll be taking part too?'

'Not this time. Perhaps we could run a training course for those of us who need some practice for next year. Gracie even gave me some inspiration for running a nursery triathlon for a bit of fun. Nothing competitive. You know, some water play, trikes and a race, so the children could feel involved too.'

When he didn't reply she shoved the phone back in her pocket. 'It's probably a silly idea anyway...'

Rafael took her hand and laced his fingers through hers to show her he was there for her as she had been for him and Gracie. 'No, it's a great idea. You're amazing.'

'So are you. Gracie couldn't have asked for a better father and the way you dealt with that crash today was incredible.'

They locked eyes and it was then he realised there was more than mutual appreciation going on. He'd let Summer get closer to him than anyone since Christina because that's exactly where he wanted her to be.

'Summer...' Saying her name was an acceptance of his feelings for her that he'd been denying too long.

'Rafael...' She leaned in and as her lips met his in a soft caress, he was lost to the sensation. With the tip of his tongue he traced the outline of her mouth, dipped in to taste her sweetness, but when she gave a breathy moan he was carried away on a tidal wave of need. He shifted her over onto his lap and she made no protest. Instead, she wrapped her arms around his neck and gave herself over to the passion threatening to consume them both.

He hadn't been intimate with any woman since Christina had left but he didn't remember a simple kiss having such power over him, to the point nothing else mattered but maintaining that connection. It was only the thought of Gracie sleeping upstairs that eventually cooled his ardour before they were both swept away in the moment. He dotted kisses along the side of her neck, trying to wean himself away from her in small stages, afraid to break the spell and the possibilities that might be opening up for them.

He was still nursing his wounds from the divorce and he wasn't in the right head space to get involved with anyone. As illustrated by his toing and froing with Summer, unable to tear himself away but knowing he shouldn't get involved.

'Promise you won't hurt me, Rafael.' Summer was so moved by the unexpected kiss and her reaction to it, she knew she was in trouble. So much for her triathlon distraction. When he'd confided in her, showing that vulnerability she hadn't known was there, she'd been transfixed, captivated by his charms. Now she had sampled the evidence that his interest in her went beyond his daughter she would be at his mercy.

'I don't know what this is we're getting into, Summer, but I do have to consider Gracie in whatever happens. What I can promise is that I would never intentionally do anything to hurt you when I've endured that suffering myself. Christina did so much damage to us both when she left, I'm afraid of getting involved and leaving us both exposed to that pain again.'

It was the first time he'd mentioned his ex's name and it somehow made her existence more real, a possible threat. She understood Rafael's reasons for being guarded when her last break-up was the reason she was wary of another single dad. 'I would never hurt either of you. I hope you know that.'

'It's down to my own hang-ups, nothing you've done. Before Christina it was my parents who let me go without a fight. They didn't want me to leave my home country and when I did they saw it as a betrayal of my heritage. I guess I'm just afraid of losing anyone else in my life and I've been using excuses to push you away rather than face what's happening between us. You've been honest with me and I've seen how much you care for Gracie, for everyone in your life.'

'I don't play games, Rafael. I wear my heart on my sleeve. I like you, I want to be with you.' She knew how it felt to be so isolated from people she loved and she could never do that to someone else. He didn't have to worry that she would treat him as badly as his own family had.

'I know.' He leaned in and dropped a soft kiss on her lips to remind her he was still there.

'I couldn't bear to lose anyone else in my life, Rafael. My stepbrother is living goodness knows where with my father, and my ex-boyfriend went back to his previous partner, taking the son I'd helped him raise. Trust me when I say I'm not in the market for any more heartache.'

Rafael brushed away her silent tears with the pads of his thumbs. 'From now on we're only making happy memories.' He sealed the promise with another gentle kiss, so tender it was easy to believe he'd never hurt her.

'Look, I like you, Rafael, and I'm pretty sure you like me.' She touched her finger to her kiss-swollen lips as though she could still feel him. 'Why don't we just leave it at that for now with no expectations or worries about the consequences?'

Goodness knew, she wanted more of this, of him, but she knew he would never choose her above his daughter, she wouldn't expect him to. Yet a part of her wanted him to fight for her. The part of her that had been cast aside without a second thought when the mother of her ex's baby had come back on the scene as if she'd never been an important piece of his history. Her heart.

He looked surprised when she offered him a way out, and disengaged herself from his lap. 'Summer, I—'

'It's late. I should really get home and get some sleep.' She couldn't bear to hear empty promises when he'd probably come to regret this in the morning.

'It doesn't seem very gentlemanly of me to let you walk home alone.' He stood beside her, his ruffled hair and dazed expression a reminder of the passion they'd just shared.

Summer shook her head. 'I wouldn't expect you to when you have Gracie to look after.'

She left Rafael's house more confused than ever about how to proceed with him, knowing she'd shown her hand tonight. The life she'd created here for herself was a sign she deserved more than being a mere stopgap in someone else's love life. Maple Island was her home now. She was happy in her job and at peace with the decisions that had brought her here because she knew now that Marc hadn't been the right man for her.

That kiss with Rafael had been an expression of the

depth of her feelings for him, and having experienced the strength of his intoxicating passion in return had left her feeling weak. She was falling for him fast and she didn't know where that left her if he decided he didn't want her after all. She wasn't a book from the library to be borrowed and put back on the shelf at will, and cursed herself for getting involved with another man with complicated family issues.

'Wake up, Papa.'

Rafael's fevered dreams about kissing Summer were quickly doused as he was slapped awake by his three-year-old.

'Wh-what time is it?' He reached for his watch on the nightstand, trying to force himself awake in case he'd overslept again. Given last night's events, he wouldn't have been surprised. He and Summer had crossed the line into romantic territory and he still had to process exactly what that meant for him, and Gracie.

His effective alarm call climbed down off his bed and toddled off out of the room again. As the numbers came into focus, he groaned and lay back down on the pillow. It was way too early for this.

'Go back to bed, Gracie.' He closed his eyes, grateful he had another couple of hours before he really had to get up. Unfortunately, the sound of cupboards being opened downstairs in the kitchen and the sound of dishes breaking ensured he was jumping out of bed seconds later.

Apparently, she was big and smart enough that safety gates and cupboard locks no longer posed any threat, except to his mental health. There were so many potential dangers he bounded down the staircase without a thought to the hazards of being barefoot.

After finding the plastic building blocks she'd abandoned on the floor, he hopped into a scene of utter carnage in the kitchen.

'Are you okay?' Ignoring the trail of cereal across the floor and the milk waterfall currently pouring off the kitchen worktop, he was more concerned with the damage she could've done to herself.

'Breakfast, Papa.' She was so pleased with herself as she presented him with a half-full glass of orange juice and a bowl of soggy cereal, there was no way he could be cross with her. He could clear the mess up any time but it wasn't often his daughter did something so amazing for him.

'*Gracias, querida.*' He kissed the top of her head, tears springing to his eyes that she would even think of trying to make breakfast for him. It wasn't yet clear to what extent her autism would impact on her life when she was older, but this small act was a welcome sign she was aware of the world around her and was capable of displaying emotion. If this wasn't an expression of a child's love for her father, he didn't know what was.

He poured her some orange juice and cereal and pulled out a chair for her to join him. 'Did you have fun last night?'

She nodded whilst munching a mouthful of multigrain hoops and he decided to push a little further when she was being this co-operative.

'You like Summer, don't you?'

She gave another emphatic nod as she shovelled in another spoonful of cereal.

'Yeah, me too. We're going to be working on this triathlon together so you don't mind if she comes around sometimes?' It was true, even if he hoped she'd be here for other reasons too. He wanted Gracie to be happy with the idea before he would even contemplate getting in deeper with Summer.

This time she shook her head and Rafael ate the breakfast prepared by his daughter with a smile on his face. Sitting here in the midst of this chaos, puddles of juice, milk and cereal covering every available surface, it was the best meal he'd ever had.

As Summer made her way to Rafael's house, she knew the decision had been made on what part she was to play in his life. The invitation to join him and Gracie for dinner had been a personal one and not offered in any professional capacity. Still, she'd brought along all the stuff she'd been working on for the triathlon. It mightn't have done anything to stop their burgeoning attraction to one another but it would benefit the clinic nonetheless.

She worried that he would have had time to think about last night and regret kissing her, but he'd arrived at day-care this morning so eager to tell her what Gracie had done for him at breakfast it was clear he wanted her to be a part of their lives.

It was a leap of faith for both of them to begin a relationship, even if they'd been involved long before either of them had admitted it. If she left all thoughts of Marc and Leo in the past and simply let herself live in the moment, she knew she had to take the chance she could be happy.

'Hey.' She had to resist throwing herself at Rafael as he opened the door to let her in, so sexy in his charcoal-grey T-shirt and tight black jeans. Somehow his casual look did more for her than his dapper formal wear or the scrubs she knew a lot of women found attractive. Perhaps it was the novelty of seeing him relaxed or the hungry look in his eyes she knew was for more than food. Either way, he certainly didn't need to serve aphrodisiacs tonight to get her attention.

'Hey, yourself.' He closed the door, backing her up against it, and kissed her with such fiery passion she was sure her bones had melted.

She'd barely recovered by the time he led her to the dining room where she flopped into a chair. Her body was so weakened from that one kiss she daren't think about what else he could do to her or she might combust with want.

'Dinner smells lovely.' She took a sip of the wine he'd poured for her, hoping the alcohol would revive her from her swoon.

'Gracie helped me make the *patatas bravas*. I hope you're hungry.' Rafael set the dish of cubed potatoes in spicy tomato sauce beside the tray of herbed chicken and vegetables in the middle of the table so they could help themselves. Though her insides were fluttering in anticipation of the night that lay ahead, Summer tucked in along with father and daughter.

She enjoyed sharing dinner with them. It had been so long since she'd sat down to a family meal she'd forgotten what it was like to chat and swap stories of their day. The simple conversation and companionship was what she'd missed most when Leo and Marc had vanished from her life because they'd been the only ones to provide it since her own parents had split. Although she was afraid to get too used to it in case the same thing happened again, it was good to feel part of a family once more.

Once Gracie started yawning, both she and Rafael teamed up again to get her to bed. It was a routine the little girl seemed to accept, even with Summer there, and it wasn't difficult to imagine this could be something long term. The thought of that was holding more appeal by the second.

CHAPTER SEVEN

THEY LAUNCHED AT each other the second they closed
Gracie's bedroom door. With her arms draped around
his neck, Summer surrendered herself to Rafael's
touch and he took immediate possession. He tangled
his hands in her hair as his lips moved across hers, his
genuine feelings for her there in the urgency of his kiss.

The cyclone of lust twisting their bodies around one
another was in danger of whisking them off to the fan-
tasy land where this was possible.

'Where's your room?'

Rafael questioned her decision with a raised eyebrow but she was a woman who knew exactly what
she wanted.

He took her by the hand and led her to the room at
the end of the hallway, kicking the door shut behind
them before reclaiming her with his arms and lips. His
kisses were every bit as confident and sexy as she'd
been recalling all day, apparently without exaggeration.
Now they were alone and free to express the desire that
had been building since last night, clothes seemed an
unnecessary hindrance, although it had been a while
since she'd slept with a man and admitted as much to

him, so there was no confusion about the significance of what they were about to embark upon together.

'I...er...haven't done this for a while.' She was gulping feverishly as he kissed his way down her neck, opening the buttons on her shirt to follow the path into the valley of her cleavage.

He briefly paused his expedition to give her a smirk. 'Neither have I, Summer. I'm sure we can help each other remember what we're supposed to be doing.' The glint in his eye sent shivers of delight rippling across her skin and he continued to strip her while covering her in hot, sensual kisses.

By the time she was clad only in her underwear she didn't care about anything other than soothing that ache for him within. He slid the straps of her bra excruciatingly slowly down her arms, undid the clasp and let her breasts spill free. The shock of the air on her skin puckered her nipples and she gasped when his mouth found them.

'Rafael...' She was on the brink of incapacitating ecstasy, pleading for release when she hadn't even touched him or undressed him in return.

'I'm enjoying getting acquainted with you. If it's okay with you, I'd prefer to take my time.' Even in the dark she could tell he was grinning, relishing the fact that he'd rendered her speechless.

'Uh-huh.' She closed her eyes and left her body at his mercy.

He hooked his fingers inside her panties, slowly drew them down her legs and proceeded to trail his tongue down the centre of her torso until she was naked and he was kneeling at her feet.

She was breathless with want as his hot breath

skimmed over her inner thighs and he teased her open with the tip of his tongue. Her legs were trembling as he plunged deep inside her wet core, lapping the arousal about to consume her whole. She held onto his shoulders for support as he continued to drive her closer to the edge of oblivion.

With his hands squeezing her buttocks, his tongue a swirling tornado inside her, he whipped her into a frenzy of lust. His relentless quest for her orgasm sent her spiralling much quicker than she'd ever believed possible. She shuddered again and again, every aftershock of her climax leaving her limbs quivering with the effort of holding her upright.

Once Rafael had rendered her completely incapable of speech and mobility, he established control of her ragdoll body and carried her towards the bed. Although she'd have been happy to divest him of his clothes, she was equally content to watch him do the job himself, revealing the physique she'd been drooling over ever since he'd arrived on the island.

The evidence of all his sporting prowess was there in every toned, tanned inch of taut muscle, although his most impressive body part had been gifted to him by Mother Nature. Summer considered herself a very lucky woman indeed.

The way she was unashamedly staring at his naked form, her eyes dark with desire, was hardening him even more than bringing her to climax with his mouth alone. She made him feel wanted, desirable in a way he hadn't experienced since Graciela had been born.

She was lying here beneath him, beautifully exposed for his appreciation and panting with want for him, and he was going to savour every second. He slid slowly between her soft thighs into that slick, tight heat that made him jerk and almost abandon his vow. His groan chorused with Summer's as they finally forged that connection they'd been afraid of from the start.

Once past that initial, brief resistance as she adjusted to him inside her, Rafael began to move, both of them voicing their pleasure with every thrust and making a mystery of why they'd waited so long for this. Sex had always been about more than the physical act for him. For him the act was the culmination of his feelings for someone, not the starting point, and he wouldn't be here with Summer if he didn't believe she was someone special in his life.

He knew it was the same for her when she'd confided in him about how much her ex had hurt her. There was no way she'd have rushed into this with him based on lust alone, even if it felt like that when she was digging her nails into his backside and urging him deeper inside her. She was making it difficult for him to prolong their mutual satisfaction when she was sucking his earlobe into her mouth and grinding her pelvis into his.

His head was pounding with the rush of blood and endorphins coursing through his veins at breakneck speed. She leaned into him, her breath in his ear causing the pressure in his loins to build until he was no longer able to contain it. Then she contracted her inner muscles around his shaft and the dam burst in a spectacular roar.

He poured everything he had into her and with the last strokes of his climax he carried her there again with him.

They clung together, sweat glistening on their skin, chests heaving with the effort of breathing, and Rafael couldn't wipe the grin from his face. She was as amazing as he'd been afraid of because he knew he'd never want to leave her bed again.

When they finally extricated themselves from one another, bodies limp and breathing laboured, it was Summer who spoke first. She only managed one word but one that echoed his own thoughts.

'Wow!'

He rested his hand on his chest, feeling his heart beating fast and clear and making him feel more alive than he had since Christina had left, when he'd thought his whole world had ended. It was a reminder he still had a right to a life of his own outside his role of a parent. Not only was he a father and a surgeon but he was also a red-blooded man with his own loves and wants and he should no longer be content to set them aside.

He was almost afraid to recognise his current mood for fear of jinxing it but as he lay in the afterglow of their lovemaking he was content. Maple Island had provided him with a home, a job, a safe community for his daughter and a partner with whom he hoped to share all aspects of his life.

He turned onto his side but found himself too choked up to tell her how much she meant to him so he showed her with a kiss. Her lips were reciprocating all those emotions that went beyond great sex.

For what seemed the longest time they lay staring into one another's eyes, only breaking eye contact every now and then to indulge in some more sensual caresses and generally making the most of the little world they'd created for themselves in this room.

He smoothed the flat of his hand over the contours of Summer's body, mesmerised by her curves as his hand dipped in at the indent at her waist and over the flare of her hips, and wishing they never had to don clothes again.

'I'll have to leave before Gracie sees me.' Summer reminded him he had responsibilities beyond his libido and it showed how much she cared about his daughter that she even raised the subject.

'There's still plenty of time before she wakes.' He wouldn't want to upset his little girl by finding a woman in his bed but he'd give anything to be able to fall asleep here for the night with Summer in his arms.

She nodded to show her understanding of his situation but the worrying of her bottom lip with her teeth showed she didn't want to leave either.

Rafael didn't want to treat Summer as second best to his daughter but there would have to be a gentle lead in to their relationship around her. It would require specialist juggling skills to balance family duties with his love life now that he might have one.

Summer's selfless attitude and empathy for Gracie was the sort of unconditional love and understanding a mother should have. She would never expect him to choose between them, jealous of the attention he devoted to his daughter, but neither did he wish to confine her to the shadows.

'You know I'll be accompanying Paisley on her transfer to Boston?' She'd needed some time to recover from her operation but tomorrow they'd be moving her to the mainland. A gem of an idea had shone in his thoughts as he'd searched for a way to combine his time with those most precious to him without upsetting anyone. It would be impossible, not to mention painful, to expect the woman in his life to remain at arm's length now.

'Hmm…' She eyed him with caution but he wanted a concrete plan in place to see each other again.

'Why don't you and Gracie come over on the ferry and we'll spend some time in the city together?'

Her eyes grew wide at the suggestion and her ensuing response would surely set the tone for the continuing nature of their relationship.

Summer knew this was a big deal and in some ways a greater step forward for them than sleeping together. Although that had been spectacular in itself and she was thoroughly satiated from the experience.

Spending the day with Gracie, being given sole responsibility for her welfare and getting her to the city was a sign of Rafael's trust in her. A decision he would not take lightly when he'd spent so long trying to protect her from outside influences.

However, she didn't want his sudden keenness to integrate her into their family life to override everything else. Not only was it going to be a difficult transition for Gracie to get used to seeing her in a more personal capacity but Summer had a position at the clinic that extended beyond one adorable child and her delectable dad.

'Isn't that a lot to expect from Gracie at such short notice?' Summer could rise to the challenge if they were all in agreement but it could prove a step too far for Gracie to take her out of nursery to embark on a trip without her father.

'I know I can count on you to take care of her and

I'm sure she'll love the idea of visiting Boston again.' That level of faith in her when he'd fought against her for so long raised goose-bumps along her skin. She knew it came from more than sharing a bed but she couldn't help but think it was such a turnaround he could be making rash decisions based on his current euphoria. It also dragged her further into their family dynamic and she was afraid that would lead to more hurt if it all went wrong and she lost that mothering role to Gracie as well as being Rafael's partner. She'd be the one left with the gaping hole in her heart when he'd still have his daughter.

'What about nursery or, you know, my job? I can't just call in and inform them I'm taking the day off so I can play hooky with you.' It was what she wanted to do but she had to be an adult about this. Her position at the clinic was important to her and she wasn't about to blow it off simply for that first flush of excitement that came with a new relationship.

'Alex and Cody have asked me to be in that helicopter. I'll tell them I don't want to leave Gracie and you're the only one who can bring her across, which is all true. I'm sure the clinic can manage without us for one day.'

There was more chance of him swinging her the day off when his position here was superior to hers. 'I suppose one day off isn't going to kill me, or anyone else.'

'Our patients will still be here when we get back and there are plenty of staff to take care of them in our absence. That is, if the idea of spending the day with us appeals to you? I wouldn't want to railroad you into agreeing.'

'I'd love to spend time with you and Gracie away

from here. I just don't want to jeopardise my job in the process.'

'I would never ask you to do that, Summer. I promise I'll sort out the details first thing but it's important you know I'd never force these decisions on you. You will always be free to do whatever you're comfortable with. Including if you decide to walk away.' All the tension was back in his face, his jaw clenched, frown lines running across his forehead and his brown eyes almost black with the sincerity he was expressing to her.

He couldn't have been any clearer that he wasn't pressuring her and that she should want to be with them by her own volition. She could only imagine the burden of guilt he'd endured in the aftermath of his divorce if his ex had made him feel as though they'd been lead weights dragging her down.

'There is nowhere I'd rather be. Well, maybe one other place.'

She snuggled her naked body closer into his and hoped the morning wouldn't come too quickly when she'd have to sneak away before she was spotted.

'No Dolly.' Gracie lifted the doll Summer had been using to try and persuade her to get into the car and threw it on the ground.

They'd both spoken to Gracie about their plans, omitting any reference to personal developments. It had been a mutual decision not to rush her into the middle of that until she'd had time to get used to Summer sharing her father. Otherwise it would be overwhelming for her to accept that her nursery teacher was kissing Daddy.

He'd kissed them both—his passionate embrace

with Summer out of sight from impressionable young eyes—and set off for his helicopter transfer to Boston. Now, realising she was expected to get into a strange car and leave the island without her father, Gracie was understandably distressed.

The important thing was for Summer to remain calm and not get hung up on Rafael waiting for them. Gracie would pick up on her stress and it wouldn't get them on the ferry any quicker. What this would take was patience, reassurance and some ingenuity.

'That's a shame.' Summer brushed out Dolly's wool hair and Gracie turned down the volume of her screaming. 'Dolly was looking forward to her day out at the aquarium seeing the fish. She was hoping to make some new friends too.'

Curiosity shifted Gracie's focus from the absence of her father to the doll in Summer's hand. Summer waited patiently, silently with the car door open and let the child believe this decision was hers alone. After a time Gracie snatched back ownership of Dolly and climbed into the back seat with her.

Once both were safely belted into the car, Gracie's buggy loaded into the trunk in case her sprained ankle became too painful to walk on, Summer let out a long, steady breath. It was entirely different managing a child with challenging needs in a controlled environment such as the clinic or the nursery compared to out in the real world. She had no authority, no current support or even a right to be here. This was Gracie's world and Summer would have to adjust in order to fit in.

Rafael had been right to be cautious when it came to their relationship. A casual affair would never work when he was devoted to Gracie and anyone he got involved with would have to be equally as dedicated. Not all women would be prepared to take on the responsibilities she represented. Thankfully Summer had already formed an attachment to the little girl and was honoured Rafael had acknowledged that by inviting her further into their lives.

Although it was a tad daunting when she'd been here before with Marc and her bruised heart should've been a reminder to maintain some detachment. Impossible when she'd already fallen for the two brown-eyed beauties. She would never comprehend Christina's decision to leave her lovely family behind when they'd already become such a big part of her life in a relatively short space of time.

The calm crossing and long drive lulled Gracie to sleep for the duration of the journey so there were no more dramas between Maple Island and Boston.

The hustle and bustle of the city she'd been raised in came as a shock to the system after the sedate nature of island life she'd become accustomed to. Being plunged back into sensory overload with the bright lights and noise of city life could have an adverse effect on Gracie too. Rafael had commented on how the slower pace on Maple Island had lessened the frequency of her outbursts so it was a concern the reverse could happen back in Boston.

Although he'd taken that into consideration given the itinerary he'd planned, meeting them at the aquarium where Gracie would find some relief from the crowds on the bustling streets.

The guilt about taking time off at short notice to play happy families hadn't left her, even though Rafael had apparently smoothed it over with the big bosses. Perhaps it was because her job had become her whole life since leaving the mainland, the only relationship she'd had since Marc, and she was cheating on it with Rafael and Gracie. They were claiming huge chunks of her time and her heart, moving her away from being a workaholic avoiding emotional entanglements back into a fully functioning human being who was starting to think she could have it all.

Her phone buzzed with a message from Rafael.

I'll be there soon. Missing you. Xx

Every letter broadened the smile on her face further, knowing they'd be reunited shortly, he was missing her and sending virtual kisses, making her feel as giddy as a teenager with her first love.

'Good news, Gracie, your father is going to be with us soon.'

Gracie giggled, her attention elsewhere as the stingray came to the surface of the touch tank to let her stroke him. Every now and then he splashed some water over the edge of the tank onto her shoes, making her laugh like Summer had never heard before.

'I think he likes you.' The feeling was mutual, as illustrated by the inordinate amount of time they'd spent here, but Gracie was in her element. She'd been enamoured by all the exhibits and an absolute joy to be around. It was a shame Rafael had missed this part of the day but she'd taken plenty of photographs to mark the occasion. If it wasn't too far out of her jurisdiction she might suggest he get a pet for Gracie when she was as engaged as this.

'You two seem to be having fun together.' Rafael's voice, low in her ear, coupled with his arms sliding around her waist, made Summer every bit as happy as their budding marine biologist.

She kept her eyes on Gracie as Rafael kissed her neck and once she was sure they wouldn't be spotted she spun around to give him a much-too-quick peck hello.

'So far, so good.' It wouldn't do any good to recount the blip they'd had this morning before boarding the ferry when it was the same trying to get any small child to comply and she didn't want to spoil the rest of the day by mentioning any problems to him.

'*Hola*, Graciela.' He moved towards his daughter and she rewarded him with a toothy grin and sticking his hand in the cold water to meet her new friend.

'I think you could have trouble if you try to get her to leave. Her fingers will be wrinkled by now they've spent so long in there.' Neither of them minded when she was enjoying herself but Summer was looking forward to whatever else Rafael had in store for them today.

'That would be a shame when I'd planned another trip for us.' He spoke loud enough for Gracie to hear and she sidled closer around the perimeter of the tank to listen.

'I guess we'll just have to stay here until closing time.' Summer huffed out a sigh and played along.

'We'll save the boat trip to see the whales for the next time.'

Now she would be genuinely gutted if they couldn't go. It had been years since she'd gone whale watching and there was no one she'd rather share the experience with than current company.

The prospect of more sea life proved irresistible to an inquisitive three-year-old and she eventually whispered goodbye to the stingray and presented her wet palms to her father.

'I think this means she's ready to go.' He laughed and dried her off with the paper towels provided for the ray-whisperers.

Summer held out a hand and Gracie slid her fingers in to interlace with hers and grabbed her father with the other hand so the three of them strolled through the halls of the aquarium all linked together.

The transition from the clinic to Boston Harbour Hospital had been as straightforward as the team could've expected. Once Rafael was sure the patient was comfortable he'd hardly been able to wait to reunite with Gracie and Summer.

Nothing ever ran to plan with a child on the autistic spectrum and those not used to his daughter's *quirks* were often stressed at the end of their time with her. It hadn't been a test when Summer had previous experience with her but he was able to relax once he'd seen for himself how well they'd managed without him. There were bound to have been some hiccups along the way but Summer apparently didn't deem them significant enough to mention.

It was great for him to be able to delegate some of that responsibility and not be obligated to apologise or gush thanks for it but it would take some getting used to. For the duration of Gracie's young life so far he'd made every decision on her behalf, decreed he was to be consulted night and day on anything affecting his daughter, and it was a huge step to believe that Summer could manage without his input. He'd entrusted the most precious thing in his life to her and that wasn't something he did without considerable thought. It was a decision he'd taken in order for them to progress in their relationship and show her he was opening up his heart and his family because she was so special to him.

He'd have been devastated if Summer had declared she'd had enough after trying to wrangle Gracie on the journey, and would've spelled the end of the affair. There wouldn't have been any point in continuing if she couldn't accommodate his daughter and vice versa because there was no alternative available. He had no intention of embarking on a fling because it would be impossible to divide his time so completely between a partner and his family, even if he'd only been after a physical affair. He wasn't, of course, he was enjoying Summer's company, especially as she understood them better than anyone else ever had.

Deep down he hadn't expected her to let them down because he'd never have left Gracie in her care if he'd imagined she couldn't cope. Now he had definitive proof he could throw off the shackles of the past and live in the moment with both of them.

'Are you cold, *querida niña*?' Despite the appropriate layers of clothing they'd donned in preparation for their whale watching, Gracie wasn't always able to communicate to him if she was too cold.

'I can take you downstairs where it's warmer,' Summer offered, but Gracie clung tighter to the side of the catamaran, content to wait it out for the promised whale sighting.

The boat lurched on the choppy sea along with his stomach. For all his planning he hadn't figured motion sickness into the equation.

'How are you doing?' The gentle hand rubbing his back as he leaned over the rail was as comforting as the sound of her sympathetic words.

He couldn't remember the last time anyone asked him about his well-being. That warm glow inside that it gave him knowing someone cared immediately improved his condition.

'I'm fine. I wouldn't miss this for the world,' he said, hoping she realised that every time he took her hand, in his head he was kissing her. Hand-holding had suddenly become acceptable in Gracie's eyes, alternating between him and Summer, sometimes clinging to both, other times insisting he and Summer held hands too.

He didn't know what had brought this on other than it being a sign she was comfortable in the company of both adults and accepting their intimacy at hand-holding level. It was more than he'd expected but it was a positive boost for the bonds they were attempting to forge.

Summer responded with a squeeze that he chose to interpret as a lingering embrace. His pleasure at being close to her was matched by the joy of seeing and hearing his daughter pointing and shrieking at everything that came into view. From the harbour seal they passed, to the squawking gannets who'd swooped down to plunder his freshly caught fish and the frequent bombardment of gulls, she'd cherished every sighting. Both he and Summer took time to educate her on the species she spied while they had her attention.

'I think we'll have to do this more often. I mean if

you want to, or it could be something you and Gracie might prefer to do on your own.' Her assumption she'd be joining them on another family outing made him smile just as much as her attempt to take it back. She was already thinking of them as a unit and he didn't mind a bit.

'We will have to do it again. All three of us.'

She stopped rambling once he assured her she was welcome to join them any time. It made trips out fun for him as well as Gracie to have someone there he could have an adult conversation with and share the experience. Until Summer had entered his life he hadn't realised how lonely and empty his life was outside work and fatherhood. He had nothing of his own.

She lived up to her name, bright and sunny, lighting up the world around her when it was needed most. Rafael stepped in between the two females in his life and put his arms around them, making precious memories to last for ever.

All at once a chorus of shrieks went up around him.

'Look out there.'

He followed Summer's instruction and spotted a whale, which the on-board naturalist informed them was the elusive, and critically endangered, North Atlantic whale.

Further out in the water a humpback cast its fluke to wave as they passed. The amazing sights left them all spellbound. Watching Summer's eyes sparkle and cheeks flush with every new visitor was as exhilarating as the brisk wind and the glories of nature.

Some of the whales performed synchronised diving for their audience, drawing applause from the passengers. They soon had another species vying for their attention as a group of Atlantic white-sided dolphins began leaping in and out of the sea and showing off for anyone present. They captivated one particular fan.

'Oh, Rafael. They're beautiful. This is the best day of my life.' Summer clapped her appreciation for their acrobatic display, her enthusiasm mirrored by Gracie, who was holding up her doll so she could watch too.

Even with such a wondrous visual feast before him, Rafael was still drawn back to the face of the woman beside him, so excited by the spectacle she was in danger of bursting.

'Mine too,' he whispered, and felt her quiver beneath his touch. He was looking forward to some quality alone time with her once Gracie was in bed.

On their return to the harbour it became clear the fresh air had caught up with the youngest member of their party as she dragged her feet about getting off the boat again.

'We can't leave you here overnight, you'll freeze.' Summer tried to coax her into her pushchair as the rest of the other passengers disembarked. They'd waited until the rush to the exit had subsided in case the crush proved too much but Gracie was equally uncooperative on the almost empty vessel. His daughter's response was to stamp her feet, throw Dolly at Summer and refuse to budge.

That lightness Rafael had been experiencing dissipated, his body grounded once more by the prospect of one of Gracie's epic tantrums. It wasn't that he got embarrassed or that he wasn't used to dealing with them but because every time she displayed traits of her condition he worried it would cause Summer to have second thoughts about what she was getting into with them. Even though she'd been nothing but supportive so far.

'Gracie, we've got to get off so we can go home. You want to get back to Maple Island, don't you?' He tried to physically move her but that only resulted in further screaming and his shins taking a few well-aimed kicks from his surprisingly strong daughter.

Unfortunately, her meltdowns didn't run to any typical schedule and there was no way of predicting how long this would last or to what extremes her temper would reach. All anyone could do was let her work through it until she was ready to move on. That was difficult to explain to strangers, or those not sympathetic to the condition, who thought this behaviour was down to bad parenting. Summer might understand the circumstances better than most but it didn't make it any easier to live with.

When Gracie reached the stage of jumping on and off the seats, Summer simply took a seat on deck and waited with him for her to tire herself out.

The boat captain appeared and tutted. 'We have another party due to leave soon.'

It was Summer who tackled him on Gracie's behalf. 'I understand that, sir, but if you could leave us for a few minutes we'd have a much better chance of getting her to co-operate.'

The man screwed his face up in disapproval before turning on his heel and walking away.

Rafael was impressed with Summer's defence of his daughter and her acceptance of the situation as if it was the norm. It was a relief to have someone on their side, who wore her heart and her allegiance to his family for the world to see. She had their backs and he was thankful that he no longer had to do this alone any more. With her they were no longer outsiders pushed out to the peripheries of existence but very much participants who deserved their place alongside everyone else.

It was this unconditional support from her that eased open the final latch on his heart. Summer was the one and only person he knew he could trust with that fragile part of him when she'd proved time and again she loved his family as much as he did. He wanted a future with her in it and he could only truly have that if he gave everything of himself to her. Once they got home he would make sure she knew how strongly he felt about her and stop holding back because of what had happened in the past. She wasn't Christina, she was Summer, who had been there for him and Gracie since the day they'd met.

With the certainty she wasn't going to be put off by these outbursts from time to time, he took a leaf out of her book and reacted as though what was going on around him was perfectly normal. Well, it was for him, it was the rest of the world that had to get used to it and make exceptions for those who didn't fit perfectly into the norms of society.

He and Summer continued discussing everyday topics like what they were having for dinner and what time they'd make it home to Maple Island as though they were any other family. Something he'd thought he'd never have again.

Once Graciela had exhausted herself she climbed into her buggy of her own accord, as Summer had expected she would, eventually.

This time spent with Rafael and Gracie had re-minded her how much she enjoyed being part of a fam-ily unit. That sense of belonging and feeling complete only came for her when she was with them. Even on the rare occasions she ventured home to visit her mom it left her with the same emptiness inside she'd had when half of her family had been taken away from her. With-out her brother and her father in her life she'd thought she'd never find that missing part of her again. Marc and Leo had filled that gap for a while but in hindsight that might have been what had attracted her to him in the first place—a ready-made family who'd taken her in and let her play make-believe.

This was different. Past mistakes should have made her steer clear of Rafael, but if today had shown her anything it was that she genuinely cared for him. She wanted to be with him and Gracie for no other reason than who they were and what they meant to her. They certainly hadn't been looking for a replacement wife and mother any more than she'd been planning on get-ting involved in someone else's complicated family matters. It had just happened and now she was con-tent to let fate do its thing when it seemed to know better than she did what would make her happy. Ap-parently, that was no longer hiding away from a life outside her job.

Rafael insisted on one last stop before they left to catch the ferry. 'I know how much you loved the rays, Gracie. Why don't we go to the gift shop and see if we can find a new friend for Dolly?'

'You go on ahead and we'll wait outside. It's pretty busy in there.'

'If you're sure?' He didn't wait for a reply but simply kissed her on the cheek and disappeared into the aisles of souvenirs and novelty gifts.

Summer turned Gracie's pushchair away from the shop so she didn't notice him slipping away and took a seat opposite the entrance. It was easy to keep track of him as his dark head bobbed above the throng of tourists eager to spend their money. She watched his progress across the floor towards the cash registers as he wasted no time in selecting his purchases. The next time she glanced up the crowd had thinned out and Rafael was deep in animated conversation with a glamorous, dark-haired woman.

He walked away scowling but the stranger tugged his arm, urging him back. It was clear she knew him and though Summer was aware he'd had a life before Maple Island it was a slap in the face to be reminded of it. Seeing him with someone else, despite his reluctance to be engaged in conversation, made her realise it was the strength of her own feelings for him that made it so painful to watch.

She'd fallen for him and couldn't bear to think of having to share him with anyone except his three-year-old sweetheart. It was impossible to change his past any more than she could her own and she had to accept he had exes out in the world. However, Rafael was different from Marc and committed himself wholeheartedly to everything important to him. She had to believe she was included in that list and he wouldn't be so cavalier about her feelings as to cast her aside as she had been in the past, or she would never be able to move forward with him.

* * *

'Time to go,' Rafael said on his return, putting a protective arm around her and propelling them all towards the exit in a hurry.

'Who was that? Is something wrong?' Of course, Summer had witnessed his run-in, she missed nothing, but he refused to let anything ruin their day.

'I'll tell you later. Let's go home.' If Summer had any further questions she didn't raise them. Not that he gave her much of a chance he was in such a rush to get back to the island, away from the ghosts of relationships past, but he didn't want to discuss it in front of Gracie.

Seeing his ex-wife in Boston had been a shock, and a nasty one at that. There might have been a time when he would've been pleased to see her, begged her to come back and try again, but not now. Gracie was his family and Summer was a bigger part of her life than her mother had ever managed.

Given the choice, he'd have preferred never to have set eyes on Christina again. One brief moment back in his life and she'd already wedged herself firmly between him and Summer. The secret of her identity made the silence on their journey home unbearable.

CHAPTER EIGHT

'HOME, SWEET HOME,' Summer declared as she pulled up outside Rafael's house, the engine still running making it clear she wouldn't be staying.

It was his fault things had cooled off between them. Or Christina's, actually. Up until then he and Summer had been closer than ever and now, with Gracie accepting her presence on a personal level, it gave him hope for their future together. That could be in jeopardy if her mother came back on the scene and he wasn't prepared to lose Summer when he'd only just found her.

'Why don't you come in and we'll have a coffee or a nightcap after I get Gracie settled?' He didn't know if, or how, to broach the subject of his ex-wife but he was sure he didn't want their relationship to suffer as a result. Summer had gone out of her way for the two of them and proved her commitment beyond a doubt. She deserved an explanation, or at least some display of gratitude for everything she'd done today. If Christina hadn't spoiled things they'd have ended the perfect day cuddled up enjoying some quality time together.

'Is that what you want?' Her question was so full of uncertainty it killed him after their day together should've cemented her position in his life, not made her doubt it.

'Yes.' He hoped that definite answer would assure her things remained on track for them. Whatever was going on with Christina had absolutely nothing to do with Summer and she shouldn't be tainted by it.

Once he'd convinced her to stay she parked the car and followed him and Gracie into the house. The fresh air and excitement had caught up with his little whirl-wind who, for once, put up no resistance at bedtime so he could put her pyjamas on her with minimal fuss. The only obstacle in getting her settled was when she insisted Summer tuck her into bed.

After reading her a quick bedtime story, Summer made sure she had Dolly in beside her to keep her com-pany. 'Is there anything else I can do for you, Gracie?'

'Can we have a sleepover?' Gracie's request came out of the blue and Rafael wasn't sure she knew what it was she was asking.

'What do you mean, sweetheart?' The room was too compact to host any guests other than her cuddly toys.

'Can Summer stay?' It dawned on him then that she'd enjoyed the novelty of having a woman around. Summer stopped fixing the bed covers, looking to him for some guidance on the issue. Gracie had accepted her so readily, moving their relationship forward much quicker than he'd expected, he had to be certain Sum-mer was comfortable with it too.

'Summer has her own house to go home to and I'm sure she's tired, but she's very welcome to stay. I'd really like that.' He tossed the final decision back to her, mak-ing her know he was keen on the idea himself and this wasn't simply Gracie's fancy.

'Will you be here for breakfast?' Gracie yawned, forcing herself to stay awake until she got the answer she was waiting to hear.

'I…er…' Summer looked towards him again but this had to be her call. If she stayed the night it had to be because she wanted to, not because she'd been pressured into it.

'I make a mean omelette.' He added another incentive in case she'd be more tempted with the offer of food too.

'In that case, how can I resist? I'll be here when you wake up, Gracie.' She kissed her newest admirer on the forehead and when she locked eyes with Rafael he felt the heat of desire flare between them, the night full of possibilities.

'Goodnight, Graciela.' Rafael kissed his daughter too and she made no objection tonight as he exited the room and closed the door.

'Are you sure it's all right for me to stay?' Summer whispered when they were alone in the hallway.

It had been way too long since he'd been able to hold her the way he'd longed to so he gathered her in his arms and took his time answering her with a slow, sensual kiss.

'I'll take that as a yes,' she said with a laugh once they took a breath.

'Thank you for today. You're a very special lady, Summer Ryan.' Now he had her in his life, he didn't intend to lose her.

'Don't you forget it,' she said, poking a finger into his chest.

Regardless of her playfulness now, her usual chatter had been MIA since leaving Boston and he could tell she was bothered by what she'd witnessed earlier.

'The woman in the shop was Christina, my ex-wife.' He didn't want his ex to have any place in their lives but Summer deserved the truth. The colour drained from her face and this was exactly why he hadn't wanted to tell her.

'I see. What did she want?' Although she sounded calm, the news must have come as a huge shock. If she ever ran into her ex he knew he'd find it difficult to be the outsider when they'd had a whole life together he knew little about.

'I didn't give her a chance to say whatever was on her mind. She suggested going somewhere to talk but I didn't want her to see Gracie. So I did the only thing I could think of in the moment. I handed her my business card and told her to call me, to get rid of her.' Her sudden reappearance had cast up all sorts of negative emotions he wasn't ready or willing to revisit, and he wouldn't have gone with her even if he'd been there alone. It hadn't been the time or the place for a confrontation when he wouldn't have been able to stop himself telling her some home truths about what he thought of her for deserting them.

'She must want to see her daughter. Why else would she need to talk to you?'

'She hasn't felt the need to do either for two years. Not even when the divorce papers were served.' He'd long since got over the upset and Gracie didn't remember her at all. All he was bothered about was the impact this was going to have on the life he'd made for himself now with his daughter and Summer.

'Do you...do you think she wants custody?' Summer broached the subject he'd been in denial about ever since he'd crossed paths with Christina today.

'Over my dead body. She isn't a mother to Graciela. She is nothing to her.'

'You'll have to consider that possibility, Rafael. Perhaps she's had a crisis of conscience and decided to make it up to you both. People change.'

'Not in Christina's case. I think she's simply seen me in Boston and tried to stir up trouble. We shouldn't waste any more time thinking about her. I just didn't want to keep any secrets from you. There mightn't be any reason to get worked up anyway when she isn't known for her reliability.' He'd spent too long second-guessing Christina's actions and for the sake of his sanity he'd learned to detach himself from the decisions she made when they were out of control. If he let today's encounter dominate his thoughts he'd go mad at the potential threat she posed to his status quo here when she mightn't ever show her face again.

Christina had no place in his life on Maple Island and he certainly wasn't going to let her spoil his quality time with Summer when they were so early into a possible relationship. The best way to put his ex-wife far from his thoughts was to focus on the woman with him now, who would never do anything to hurt him or Gracie.

By engaging her in another breath-stealing kiss, it wasn't long before he was led astray by the taste of her and knowing she was his for the entire night. With one hand tangled in her hair, the other possessively around her waist, he backed her towards his bedroom.

'Dr Valdez, I'm afraid I don't have any pyjamas to

wear for our sleepover,' Summer murmured against his lips.

'That's okay. For what I have in mind you're not going to need any.'

Summer knew he was trying to take both their minds off the woman she'd seen him with today. It was working. When he was sucking her bottom lip into his mouth, undressing her painfully slowly and taking his time to kiss every inch of skin he uncovered, she didn't want to think about any other woman. Especially not the one he'd thought he'd spend the rest of his life with. He'd assured her he hadn't been interested in anything his ex had to say or offer, and she had to believe him because the alternative would break her heart. Tonight she wanted to enjoy time with *her* man and there was no room for another woman in their bed.

Summer slid her hand over his crotch and staked her claim on the hard evidence it presented that it was definitely her he wanted.

Rafael exhaled a hot breath in response. 'Summer, we've got all night.'

'You promised we weren't going to be needing clothes.' She undid his fly. 'So I'm simply making sure you stick to your word.'

Her bold move prompted a flurry of mutual undressing until all she was wearing was a coy smile.

The invitation to spend the night marked a progression in their dynamic. He didn't do anything without a lot of thought behind it and he was showing her he was thinking of her as part of his family.

The thought should have terrified her after the loved ones she'd lost in the past, but Rafael wouldn't have let her get so close if he wasn't serious about them having a future together. Their relationship had evolved so naturally she hadn't seen it coming. She mightn't have intended it to happen, or been ready for it, but she was becoming part of this family and she didn't want her insecurities spoiling it now.

They tumbled onto the bed, desperate to make that final connection. Looking into Rafael's eyes, she could see the moment he entered her was as gratifying and meaningful to him as it was to her.

It was too early to say she loved him, or to expect it in return, but she felt it every time their bodies joined together. As he made love to her, Summer was powerless against the waves of pleasure carrying her ever forward towards paradise. She clamped her hand over her mouth, knowing she couldn't hold back voicing her pleasure when the final wave hit.

Rafael peeled her hand away from her mouth but didn't slow his quest for her orgasm. 'I want to hear you.'

That demand was all it took to tip her over the edge, her body shuddering simultaneously with the cry of ecstasy ripped from her. Again and again Rafael hit that sweet spot and triggered a succession of repeated responses until she had nothing left to give before he finally indulged his own satisfaction with one last vocal thrust.

As they spooned together atop his bed, her body satiated and her mind at peace, she let herself drift towards slumber. She'd tried the single life, told herself she'd be happier on her own safe from the pain of risking another relationship, but it simply couldn't compare to lying here with Rafael's arms wrapped around her.

Today he and Gracie had shown her all she had to gain from having them in her life, everything she'd missed growing up and had thought could hurt her after Marc. The fun of a family day out ending with sharing a bed with her lover was no match for going home to an empty house.

If this was a dream she never wanted to wake up. Unless it was to a naked Rafael and the promise of a home-cooked breakfast.

Opening her eyes to see Rafael next to her with the early morning sun shining through the window was bliss compared to those mornings lying in bed staring at the ceiling until it was time to get ready for work. She'd be content to lie here all day.

'Morning.' He scooted close enough to her that she could feel his erection pressed against her.

'Morning.' She didn't open her eyes and simply snuggled back into him.

Rafael cupped her breast in his hand, rolling her nipple between his thumb and forefinger until her body stirred with arousal. She gave a happy purr and let him continue the wake-up call, his hand travelling down to find the warmth between her legs. He slipped a finger easily inside her and Summer sighed as he began stroking her, stoking the embers of last night's fire back into life.

As he increased the rhythm of his ministrations she was writhing against him in ecstasy, desperate to find that welcome release. With great effort she finally opened her eyes and turned around so she could see his face and kiss his lips. His erection grazed against her as she shifted position and it was apparent he was in need of some relief too.

She straddled those muscular thighs she'd fantasised about so often and sank slowly down onto his thick shaft, revelling as he filled her so completely. With her hands on his chest she ground her hips into him, savouring the feel of him inside her. Hands on her buttocks, lips at her breast, Rafael thrust into her, filling her to the brim until she was ready to burst. As sensation overtook her, limbs trembling with her impending climax, Rafael took charge, rolling her onto her back and pumping into her relentlessly. Their lazy morning in bed quickly became a frantic pursuit of mutual gratification. Her cry was drowned out by Rafael's primal growl as he gave himself completely to her.

With heaving chest and panting breath, Summer smiled at him. 'I wouldn't mind that kind of wake-up call every day.'

'It certainly beats my usual exercise routine.' Rafael laughed through his laboured breathing, equally exhausted by their early morning workout.

'I hope that doesn't mean Triathlon Dad is hanging up his running shoes and swimming trunks. I wouldn't want to disappoint your legion of female admirers waiting to see you in all your glory. For some of us the sight of you in very little is the highlight of our day.' Now she had intimate knowledge of what lay beneath his clothes she had a lot more to be thankful for.

She danced her fingertips around his nipple, delighted he'd found another outlet for all that energy.

'I can think of much better ways to get sweaty.' His throaty growl travelled all the way down Summer's body, immediately reawakening that need for him.

'You're insatiable.' She giggled as he slid his body

over to cover hers, apparently already sufficiently recovered from the last event.

'Only for you.' He covered her face and neck in
swoony butterfly kisses to drive her wild.

The baby monitor on his nightstand suddenly crack-
led into life with the sound of a certain three-year-old
getting restless to start her day.

Rafael groaned. 'Perfect timing as usual, Gracie.'

'We can't complain. She's been very good. As has
her father.' Summer gave him a playful slap on the bottom, aware their sexy time was over. Gracie expected
to see her at breakfast but not in her father's bed.

As she moved to get dressed, Rafael lay back to
watch. 'We don't have to commit to anything formal
but I would like you to stay over here whenever you
can.'

He was being deadly serious and though the suggestion made Summer's heart pick up an extra beat at
the thought of sharing his bed on a regular basis, she
remained wary. The last time she'd jumped in with
both feet she'd had to change jobs and move to an island to get over it.

'Let me think it over and I'll have my people get
back to you.' She kept the tone light so he wouldn't take
offence that she wasn't leaping at the chance.

'You do that.' Thankfully he appeared confident
enough in his prowess to know she wouldn't be able
to resist.

'In the meantime, I think your daughter and your
house guest are expecting some breakfast.' It was going
to be a rush to get home, showered and changed in time
for work but she wasn't going to miss sitting down to a

cosy family breakfast together. Something she hadn't experienced in a very long time.

'You're in a good mood.' Alex interrupted Rafael's whistling to comment on the huge grin he hadn't been able to wipe off his face today.

'It does happen occasionally.' Rafael closed the patient files he was reading at the nurses' station, unwilling to get drawn into a conversation about the reasons behind his current exuberance. Usually after battling to get Gracie ready and fit in a swim he had a fraught start to the working day. It was a completely different experience having Summer there in the morning.

Her presence hadn't made his daughter any more co-operative but with Summer's help and calming influence he hadn't found it as stressful as he normally did. The memory of their incredible night, and morning, in his bed had probably helped his mood too. He didn't want to scare her off, and it was early days, but he'd meant what he'd said about having her there on a regular, hopefully even permanent, basis.

He'd spent the last couple of years being careful, guarding his heart along with his daughter's, and it had very nearly cost him the best thing to happen to him since Graciela. Yes, he'd been burned before but so had Summer and she wouldn't have embarked on this affair to play games with his affections when she knew how that felt. He'd give her whatever time and space necessary to be sure he and Gracie were truly what she wanted because he already knew she was the one for him.

He was living, enjoying life, rather than simply surviving, which he'd been doing ever since he'd left

Spain to come to America. Medical school had been his dream but it hadn't been easy, cut off from everything he'd ever known. He'd had to work hard to achieve his success with no emotional or financial support along the way.

He'd loved Christina but their time together had been marred by arguments and their clashing views on what married life should entail. For him it had been about settling down and having a family but she hadn't believed it should curtail her love of partying. When Gracie had come along Rafael had been overwhelmed by love for their child, but bringing a baby into their marriage had only added to their problems when Gracie had demanded more attention than her mother had been prepared to give her.

Looking back now, he could see she'd only agreed to start a family for his sake. He was thankful for the joy it had brought him but it had come at the price of their marriage. Christina hadn't been ready for motherhood, if she'd ever really wanted it. This time spent with Summer had shown him what family life could be like with someone supporting them both. Someone they both loved in return.

This wasn't post-sex daydreaming. Summer was everything he could ever want in a partner—she was smart, kind, caring and had proved she'd be there for them come what may. It was natural she should be cautious about rushing into this but he was prepared to wait, content with his life on the island. In the meantime, he'd woo her the old-fashioned way, with hearts and flowers and whatever it took for her to believe the strength of his feelings for her.

He pulled out his cellphone to text her on his way to his next clinic.

Thinking about you. xx

A reply pinged back before he could switch his phone off.

In that case you should take a cold shower ;)

He laughed out loud then had to check and make sure he hadn't disturbed anyone nearby. Thankfully everyone else was too busy to notice him sexting Summer.

Why don't you take one with me later? Dinner at mine tonight. Don't forget your toothbrush. xx

What? No PJs? :)

Rafael smiled at the screen, the image of Summer, naked in his bed, burned into his brain for ever and putting him in danger of spending the rest of the day in physical discomfort until he was able to do something about it.

Perhaps for the bedtime-story-reading part of the evening but not for the adults-only section. I want you naked.

He groaned. He was going to have to end this flirting by text before he got into trouble wishing the day away.

Ooh, very demanding, Señor Valdez. Now break's over. We'll have to save the rest of our fun for tonight. xx

He turned his cell off and put it in his pocket or there'd be no chance of focusing on work this afternoon.

He was still smiling as he walked into his office. Although the good mood wore off pretty quickly when he saw who was waiting for him there.

'Christina? What on earth are you doing here?'

'*Hola*, Rafael. I thought it would be better if we spoke face to face instead of over the phone. Your work address was on the business card you gave me.'

She knew him too well. He'd had absolutely no intention of answering her calls or continuing a discussion with her. He didn't believe they had anything to say to each to her after all this time. They were strangers now. The Christina he'd known would never have followed him here but run in the opposite direction from the life he represented.

'I don't think there's anything you could possibly say that I want to hear.' That time had passed. Whatever explanation or feeble apology he'd expected two years ago literally didn't matter to him now. The deed had been done and he and Gracie had managed fine without her.

'Don't you think we have things to discuss?' She was sitting in his chair, her perfectly manicured hands resting on his desk as though she had every right to be there.

'Such as?' He wasn't going to play games and the sooner she got to the point the sooner he could get her out of here. She wasn't going to steal away his chance at happiness for a second time.

'Our daughter.'

All that warmth that had been spreading through his veins from his exchange with Summer now turned to ice. There was no way she was going to drop in now and upset things when she'd shown no previous interest. He wouldn't let her.

'I thought you'd forgotten you had one.' The bitterness he could still taste in his mouth suggested he hadn't quite got over her abandoning them.

Christina flinched at that one and displayed a hint of a conscience. 'I know I treated you both appallingly but I've done a lot of growing up since then. I did try to find you. I've missed you. Both of you.'

If she'd thought she could walk in here and he'd drop to his knees begging her to come back, she was deluded. Seeing her here today at least confirmed one thing, that he didn't love her any more. There had been that lingering doubt in the far recesses of his mind that he might harbour feelings for her—after all, he hadn't been the one to end their marriage—but there wasn't one part of him that was even slightly pleased to see her again.

'Up until a couple of months ago we were still living in the same house in Boston so you couldn't have missed us that much.' Life could've turned out so differently if she'd come back before he'd met Summer and discovered what true love felt like, but he was happy here. He'd moved on.

'You've every right to be mad at me, Raf. I wasn't a good wife to you, or a good mother to Graciela. I've only figured that out now when I see all of my friends getting married and settling down.'

Rafael sank down into the seat usually reserved for his patients during consultations, experiencing the same sort of dejection they probably did when he had to give them life-changing news. Whatever his personal views about her, Christina was still Gracie's mother. It was just a shame it had taken her so long to realise it.

'What exactly is it you want, Christina?' He would fight tooth and nail to keep his daughter with him when he was all she'd ever known. There was no danger of him letting Christina take her away from him only to dump her when she got bored playing house again.

'To be a good mom to Gracie.' She ignored his snort of derision. 'She doesn't know me and I want to rectify that. I'm hoping she's young enough not to remember the past so we can start over again.'

'I'll need more than that to convince me this isn't simply a whim and you'll walk away from Gracie when you get bored again.' This was exactly what he'd known she would do when he'd seen her again—rock up and ruin everything he had going here.

'Okay, cards on the table.' He could see her swallow hard, looking uncomfortable about whatever she was about to divulge, but he took no satisfaction in it when it could be potentially life-changing for all of them. 'Recently, I've found out my chances of conceiving again are small. Graciela was something of a miracle, although I didn't know it at the time. Seeing you again, well, it made me think of everything I'd lost.'

'You didn't lose us, you tossed us aside like trash.' He didn't want to get taken in by her crocodile tears if this was nothing more than an exercise in self-pity.

'I'm sorry. You'll never know how sorry I am for my behaviour. All I can say is that I wasn't mature enough to handle the responsibility of having a family.'

'And now you are?'

'I like to think so.' She gave him a watery smile. 'I realise how precious it is these days. Since seeing you, I haven't stopped thinking about Gracie and wondering what she's like. She'll be a proper little person now.'

Thinking of what a real character his daughter was did make him smile. 'Yes, she is.'

'Who does she look like?'

'Me.' It had made it easier for him that she'd clearly inherited his family features rather than being a clone of her mother and reminding him every day of the woman who'd broken his heart.

'I don't suppose you have a photograph?' Suddenly this was becoming all too real, with Christina showing an interest in the child he'd raised on his own all this time.

'Look, this is a lot to dump on me. We have a good life here without you.' It was all he could do not to tell her he was with someone else now. Not to save Christina's feelings but to stop Summer getting caught up in this whole mess of his failed marriage when she was the symbol of the bright future available to his family.

'She's my daughter too, Raf. I don't want to get into a custody battle with you, but I do have rights as her mother. I'd prefer it if we could come to some sort of arrangement between us.

She might have a right to see her daughter but discussing custody of the child he'd raised alone for so long was something so momentous it deserved more time than he had in between appointments at work. Not only would he need time to think through the implications of letting her back into their lives in any capacity, he'd have to get some legal advice too. Introducing any change into Gracie's world would be a huge undertaking and even letting Christina have access was only something he would do when he was one hundred percent sure his ex-wife's intentions were long term.

He got up and opened the door to indicate he wanted her to leave. 'Not here and not now. I have work to do and patients to see.'

Christina sighed. 'Can we make an appointment to continue this discussion later? I'm not leaving the island until we do.'

He'd forgotten how stubborn she could be when she didn't get her own way, and an ex-wife stalking his every move wasn't going to make him an attractive prospect for Summer.

The breath he huffed out as he returned to the desk to scribble down his address was born of frustration and resignation that he was going to have to see her again no matter how unappealing that was to him. 'I'm not promising anything but if this is the only way I can get you to leave—'

'It is.' Christina took the scrap of paper with a triumphant grin but at least it prompted her towards the exit.

If she intended staying on Maple Island for any length of time it was going to be awkward for Summer. Christina wouldn't take too kindly to someone else taking her place in the family, regardless of her absence, her fiery temper a contrast to Summer's stable influence, which he'd come to cherish. Too bad.

If it came to choosing sides he'd always take the path best for his family and that would lead him directly to Summer. Christina didn't stand a chance.

CHAPTER NINE

SUMMER COULDN'T WAIT. If she didn't manage to sneak in a quick Rafael fix to satisfy the craving she'd worked up with those text messages, there was no way she'd be able to concentrate on anything.

She'd managed to grab five minutes out of the nursery on the pretext she had to consult him on the matter of Gracie's pick-up today. It wasn't a complete fabrication since he hadn't given her a definitive time frame for their romantic evening and it might be easier for her to bring Gracie home straight after work.

She knew she couldn't keep on this way, texting and snatching moments with him during working hours. Sooner or later people would notice and start to talk and they couldn't keep their relationship quiet for ever on this small island. They couldn't exactly gag Gracie either if she chose to tell anyone about their *sleepover*.

Besides, she was fit to explode with happiness at the turn their relationship had taken and that wouldn't go unnoticed for long with her co-workers, who didn't think she had a life beyond her job. She was beginning to believe that all this time she'd spent alone was so she'd appreciate having Rafael and Gracie all the more. It was amazing how much joy there was to be had in simple things like a day out or having a meal in company.

Despite voicing her concern about spending too much time at their house, she knew she was too far gone to help herself. She wanted to spend every waking moment with Rafael, as well as the sleeping ones. He was so protective of his daughter he wouldn't have issued the invitation if he didn't whole-heartedly believe she would be a permanent feature in their lives.

That thought was both exhilarating and terrifying. Whilst she considered herself lucky to have found someone so loving and willing to share the most precious thing in his life with her, opening her heart left her more exposed to harm, compared to the protected life she'd led these past months on her own.

Hopefully, they'd have an opportunity to discuss what it was they both expected out of this relationship later and put her mind at ease that getting into something serious with him wasn't simply a step closer to heartache. For now, she'd be content to catch a minute or two alone with him. A quick kiss would be enough to carry her through the rest of the day on cloud nine.

Her pace increased with anticipation the closer she came to his territory, her heart beating that much quicker and the smile on her face becoming broader. It was amazing the effect a new relationship could have on a person, though she was sure he'd always possess the ability to send her body into raptures without having to lay a finger on her.

As she turned the corner into his department she paused to check her reflection in one of the glass panels lining the corridor. He'd seen her at her worst with bed head and yesterday's mascara smeared under her eyes.

Her hair tied up in a ponytail and minimal make-up was essential for work and would have to do for now, but if she had some time later she'd prefer to go to a little more effort for their first *official* date.

When she found him waiting in the doorway of his office she was tempted to push him back through the door and ravish him on the desk she was so overcome with lust at the sight of him.

'I couldn't stop thinking about you.' She had her arms open, about to throw them around her man, when she saw a tall figure over his shoulder and composed herself again. The second she recognised Christina she could feel every painful splinter as her heart shattered.

'Who is this?' Although Christina addressed Rafael, she was clearly referring to Summer. As she looked her up and down, assessing her with a critical eye, Summer couldn't help but feel inadequate compared to this well-dressed, flawlessly made-up beauty. Rafael had dismissed their encounter altogether but she'd followed him here, proving she had some serious unfinished business with him.

'This is Summer Ryan. She's our child life specialist and nursery assistant at the clinic.'

Not 'my girlfriend', 'partner', or even 'friend'. A matter that wouldn't have bothered her if he was introducing her on a professional level, but they were supposed to be in a relationship now.

The unwelcome embodiment of her fears held out a hand for her to shake. 'Christina Valdez. Rafael's wife.'

The white noise was so loud in Summer's head she barely registered Rafael's correction. 'Ex-wife.'

'Sorry. I didn't realise you had company.' She turned away, tears beginning to blur the edges of Rafael's frame in the doorway. When he didn't reach out to try and stop her leaving, they fell in earnest.

'We'll talk later.' His words were a promise he'd see her again but not any more than that. She was clearly an outsider here, not included in their discussion of the future.

This should've been the start of their life together but with Christina back in the picture Summer's own position in his life was in jeopardy. She'd been here before, and knew she couldn't possibly compete with the mother of a man's child. It was a bond she could never hope to replicate or interfere with. Not that she ever would.

That threat she'd feared most was real now but she was in too deep to come out of this without adding a few more scars. She knew how this played out. Once the ex made it clear she was open to a reconciliation Summer would become a cuckoo in the nest. Christina was a real part of the family she could never call her own.

Even if they didn't get back together she was going to be gradually pushed out of her relationships with Rafael and Gracie when Christina claimed higher priority in the pecking order.

She didn't know why Christina had come back but she did know it was bad news for her. Summer was the poor substitute for a missing wife and mother, second best, and faced with a choice a single dad would choose to save his family.

She couldn't blame anyone for that decision when a child was involved. If she hadn't come to the island and her ex had wanted to try again she might have chosen familiarity over the unknown quantity of a new relationship. With Christina back on the scene she didn't know if she would have a future for herself with the Valdez family. It was a difficult decision to make but she wondered if it would be best to end things now, instead of waiting for Rafael to come to the same conclusion when she was in too deep to ever recover from the loss.

Although the idea she was saving herself from more pain than she was currently experiencing wouldn't soften the blow of letting him go now.

'What are you painting for us today?' She forced some brightness into her tone so Gracie wouldn't pick up on the fact something was wrong when she went back into the nursery unit. This was for her father to explain, not her, even if she had a clue what was going on.

'Boat,' the little girl said, as though it was as plain as day what the splodges on the paper represented.

Then it became clear that the three multi-coloured splats on the paper were supposed to be the three of them yesterday on their trip. Summer swallowed back the wail she wanted to release at the injustice of the new loss she was to suffer.

Rafael was walking on shards of glass, pacing the room as he waited for Summer to arrive. She'd barely glanced in his direction when he'd gone to pick Gracie up from nursery. Not that he blamed her. There was so much they had to talk about but at the time he'd simply wanted to put some space between her and Christina.

That's why he hadn't been in any hurry to inform his ex about Summer's real identity as his new partner. He wouldn't put it past her to try and make trouble through pure jealousy. Her pride would decree it if Christina thought she'd been replaced. Which she most certainly had.

Tonight was supposed to have been romantic, something for Summer and him to look forward to when they could simply enjoy each other's company in private. Now he knew they were going to have to spend the evening discussing his ex-wife, what she was doing here, and how he was determined not to let her interfere in their personal business. That was before they came up with a plan of how to introduce her back into Gracie's life with minimal disruption.

All of this could only be achieved if Summer forgave him his earlier brusqueness to show up here for dinner. With Gracie already in bed they'd be able work through any problems in peace and quiet, and pick up from where they'd left off this morning. Preferably back in his bed, leaving the rest of the world outside the door.

His confidence in their relationship had been knocked by Christina's arrival, as he was sure Summer's had. An ex-wife was a reminder of all the ways in which he'd failed as a husband and a partner. Whatever her reasons for leaving, he hadn't been enough for her to stay and he couldn't be sure it would be any different with Summer.

In an effort to convince her that despite the evidence of one failed relationship he was worth a chance, he'd pulled out all the stops tonight with a home-made seafood paella and sangria for his seduction attempt. He wanted Summer to remember there was more to him than work and emotional baggage.

He lit the candles in the centre of the dining-room

table and when the rap on the door finally came, he poured two glasses of fruit-infused red wine to help them both unwind. Until then he hadn't been sure she'd keep their date.

'I'm so glad you came—' His relief was short-lived when he found Christina standing on the doorstep instead of Summer.

'Hello, Rafael.'

'Christina, now is not the time,' he said, making no effort to hide his disappointment.

'You're the one who gave me this address.' She shrugged and pushed past him into the house. He followed her, without even bothering to close the door because as far as he was concerned she'd be going straight back through it once he caught up with her.

'We're going to have to discuss boundaries and the importance of sticking to a schedule if you want this to work,' he said with a frown.

She helped herself to a glass of sangria and made herself comfortable on his couch. 'So, you do agree we need to sort out an arrangement for me spending time with Gracie?'

If she'd arrived a week ago he would've said under no circumstances but events had made him re-evaluate decisions like that and how they would affect Gracie. It shouldn't be down to him to deny them from getting to know each other. Perhaps it was about time Christina realised how wonderful their daughter was but not right now when Summer was supposed to be on her way over.

'I'll agree to think about introducing you but not tonight. She's in bed.'

'Can I at least pop in and see her?'

'No. If you wake her it'll take all night to settle her again. I promise I'll sort something out so you can meet her but I really need you to go.' She had no clue about Gracie's needs and it was going to take time to understand them, if she was willing to put in the effort. That wasn't something that could be taught, and so far Summer had been the only one who'd truly understood what it took to make a difference in Gracie's life, and his too.

'I'm so happy you've decided to give me another chance, Raf.' Christina bounced up from her seat to plant a kiss on his cheek and he could feel the glossy imprint of her lipstick stain his skin.

'Sorry, am I interrupting something?' A pale Summer stood at the door, watching their interaction, and Rafael immediately sprang away from his ex-wife, feeling guilty for even having her in the house.

'Christina just stopped by to talk about Gracie. She's going now.' Rafael stared daggers at Christina, willing her to take the hint that she'd outstayed the welcome he'd never issued in the first place.

'No, you stay, Christina. I'll go.' Summer turned on her heel and walked back out the door without any further discussion. This was not the seduction he'd had in mind.

'I had no idea she was coming here tonight,' he said, chasing after her.

'What is it she wants? What is it you want, Rafael?' This time she did meet his gaze but all he saw in her eyes was uncertainty, replacing the desire he'd seen there earlier today.

'She says she wants to be part of Gracie's life again

and to make up for her mistakes. I have to think of what's best for my daughter.' He didn't want anyone to get hurt and believed the only way to handle this was if they all worked together.

'Two parents.' Summer agreed with the conclusion he'd come to too. He didn't want or need Christina in his life but it wouldn't be fair for Gracie to suffer because of their issues.

'How's that going to work when you're here and Christina's in Boston?'

'We haven't figured that out yet.'

'You're seriously thinking of moving back? For Christina?'

'I want to do whatever's best for Gracie.' He didn't want to uproot her but the arrangements were going to prove tricky. The first step was at least to agree she could meet her mother.

'I see…' Summer reached up and rubbed at the spot where Christina had kissed him earlier.

'Summer, it's not how it looks.' He scrubbed at the lipstick evidence of his ex-wife's over-exuberance and cursed his bad luck. It was understandable Summer was upset when their supposed romantic evening had ended up with Christina firmly in the middle of it but he had no interest in any other woman. He thought she knew that.

'You're Gracie's parents. It's probably best if I let you two work things out between you.' With that, she walked out of the house and disappeared off into the night.

'Summer, come back. There's nothing going on between us. Summer…' he called out into the darkness, hoping his word was enough for her. It wasn't as though he could rush out and explain things, leaving Gracie here by herself. Summer knew that and by walking away she wasn't leaving any room for discussion.

He felt bereft standing in the doorway, waiting for her to come back once she'd cooled off, but she didn't. He wasn't sure if her parting words pertained to cancelling their dinner or their whole relationship. Christina was Gracie's mom and it was inevitable Summer would feel slighted by her arrival when she'd done so much for the little girl, but it shouldn't have affected their relationship.

He tried to find comfort in the fact that he hadn't actually done anything wrong. Summer meant so much to him he wasn't going to let things end like this. If she wouldn't talk to him tonight he was going to make sure she heard him out tomorrow. On an island this small she couldn't avoid him for ever and he would track her to the ends of the earth to give their relationship a fighting chance. He just hoped she felt strongly enough about him to put up with the hassle of having his ex in the picture.

He'd opened his home, his family and his heart to her, believing she was the one who could love him and Gracie without conditions, and prayed this wasn't a sign she'd turned tail and run at the first hurdle, rather than tackle it with him.

Perhaps a painful break-up had been inevitable. That wouldn't make it any easier to accept losing the woman he loved.

Summer stumbled down the steps blinded by the tears she worried would never stop. Rafael had sworn he'd never hurt her and he was doing the same thing Marc had done by putting his ex before her. Despite his in-sistence nothing was going on, she'd heard Christina thanking him for giving her a second chance and seen the evidence of her kiss on his cheek. He hadn't come after her or put up any sort of fight for her, much less considered her feelings about any of this. Perhaps he was hedging his bets by keeping both of them onside but she'd already been pushed out of the decision-making that would affect her life as much as every-one else's.

If she threw away everything she'd built for herself on Maple Island on a man who could cast her aside when the mood took him then she obviously hadn't learned her lesson well enough the first time around.

CHAPTER TEN

'DO YOU WANT me to clean that off your fingers, Gracie?' Summer tried to get her to communicate her needs verbally as she held up her hands, crying about the pieces of modelling dough sticking to her skin, but recently she seemed to be having trouble to adequately express her feelings.

She picked off the bigger pieces herself and took a cloth to wipe off the rest. Tears pricked her eyes as she tended to the little girl who was now only her ward on a professional basis. It had been a tough couple of weeks for them both but at least Summer had an idea of what was going on. She had no clue what Gracie had been told about why she'd stopped coming around or about Christina's arrival in her life, but the disruption had set back her progress. Something she knew neither she nor Rafael would have wanted for her.

'All clean for your father coming.' The words almost stuck in her throat as she saw Rafael and Christina walking towards the nursery unit, coming to get their daughter to complete the happy family picture.

She had known Christina was still on the island as the rumour mill was working overtime about the mysterious woman spending time with Dr Valdez. It didn't give her any satisfaction that she was the only one aware of her real identity when it was the reason for ending her relationship with Rafael.

She hadn't seen her face to face since that last night at Rafael's place when her whole world had come crashing down around her. If she'd had any doubts she'd done the right thing it had been confirmed by the fact he'd chosen to stay with Christina rather than come after her. She'd lain awake the whole night crying, tormented by the image she had of the two of them sharing the candlelit dinner meant for her.

Since then the only contact she'd had with Rafael had been here at the nursery during Gracie's handover, which had been limited to stilted conversation over his child's progress and nothing more. That was entirely her doing. Rafael had tried calling, texting and had attempted to explain his actions, but she'd blocked him at every turn. She didn't need to hear excuses when Christina was still here and very much part of their lives.

Although she would admit to missing him, spending time with him and Gracie and generally being part of the family. There should be some relief to be found that they had never got around to signing contracts regarding Gracie's full-time care when it would be excruciatingly painful watching them bond as a family from the outside and see them sail off into the sunset.

She'd felt so alone all of a sudden she'd even made attempts at rebuilding her relationship with her mother. They spoke on the phone most days now and she was thankful she had someone who would still be there for her no matter what. If things here finally got too much she might think about taking an extended vacation to spend some time with her mom and her stepdad, getting to know them again. It seemed to have worked for Christina.

By all accounts Christina was renting a property on the island so she wasn't in Rafaèl's house full time, probably to ease Gracie into the idea of her being there before they made anything permanent. Summer believed it was just a matter of time and the thought they might even consider moving back to Boston was enough to keep her awake at night. It was torture watching them all grow closer as she faded from memory.

'Hey, how's my girl?' He forced a hug on his daughter but she kept her eyes firmly on Christina, who was standing hesitantly beside him.

'We've had quite a day, playing with the modelling clay.' Summer pointed towards the table where she'd been rolling and cutting out multicoloured butterfly shapes before mashing them all together and starting again. That creation and destruction had held her attention for most of the day and she'd protested when Summer had attempted to introduce her to a new activity. In the end she'd capitulated and joined her at the table, the repetitive action surprisingly calming. She might take the mini rolling pin, clay and cutters home to keep her too occupied to wonder what the Valdez family were up to elsewhere.

'Your papa and I thought we could take you for a nice treat. I hear there's a lovely bakery down the street. Would you like to show me where it is?' Christina was crouched down and holding out her hand in the hope Gracie would want to go with her. To her credit, she didn't seem as though she was steamrollering her into a mother-daughter relationship. At Rafael's insistence she was slowly but surely building up that trust and easing her way into her daughter's life. The way Summer had been doing up until Christina's arrival on the island.

Gracie glanced at her for reassurance. 'Can Summer come too?'

The request twisted the dagger deeper into her heart when she wanted more than anything to remain part of this family, but her reasons for putting some distance between them hadn't changed. Even if her idea of self-preservation was painful now, it would save her in the long run.

'Yes, you're very welcome. Gracie talks about you a lot and we're very grateful for everything you've done for her.' Christina's thanks, though well meaning, did nothing to make Summer feel any more included. She didn't say that Rafael talked a lot about her and she was thanking her on their behalf, as a couple. Even Rafael looked awkward about the invitation.

What could she do but smile through her heartbreak when this was Gracie's mother and Summer knew what it was to go through life with that void left by absent family members. 'Thanks, but I'm needed here for a while longer. Enjoy your treat.'

When Gracie slowly reached out to take Christina's hand in hers and they walked off down the corridor, the moment was bitter-sweet for Summer.

'Thanks for doing that. Gracie's finding this a little difficult to come to terms with. As am I.' Rafael held back to speak to her and despite the appearance of having his family back on track he looked as miserable as she felt. If it wasn't all unicorns and rainbows at Casa Valdez, it made her sacrifice all the more tragic.

'It will take time. You know that. Wait and see. In another few months it will be as if you and Christina never split up and you'll be one big happy family.' Where that left her she didn't know because if this was any indication, she couldn't cope with seeing them all together on a daily basis. It was like rubbing salt in the open wound where her heart used to be. She was the ultimate loser in this game of happy families.

Rafael frowned at her. 'I don't want to get back together with Christina. I never did. I'm only tolerating her because she's Graciela's mother. It's not her I want, it's you. Nothing happened that night with her, or any other night, I swear. We've only ever talked about Gracie.'

'We've been through this, Rafael. I'm no longer part of the equation and the sooner you realise that the easier it will be for you to move on as a family.'

He wasn't making this any easier for her by telling her he wasn't over her when she'd been consoling herself with the idea that she was somehow saving his little family and giving Gracie the stability she herself had never had growing up.

When she'd walked in on that intimate moment between Rafael and Christina she'd seen the reunion between parents she'd always wanted as a child herself. Although it had almost killed her so soon after she and Rafael had got together, she had hoped something good would've come out of this whole sorry mess for Gracie.

Of course she wanted to believe him that he wasn't interested in Christina when there was still a candle burning for him in her very soul, but how long would that last when his family was growing closer by the day? She'd done the hard part in walking away and it would only reopen the wound if she let him close again.

'Gracie misses you too. I've tried to explain to her that you're giving her some space to get to know her mama but I can't expect her to understand when I don't know myself what the hell happened.' He made a move towards her but Summer immediately backed away. Not because she was afraid someone would see but because she didn't trust herself not to weaken if he touched her.

'That's not fair. You know I love Gracie but she's not my daughter, is she?' Outside this nursery Gracie was no longer her responsibility. That privilege was entirely her parents', and she wouldn't allow Rafael to use emotional blackmail to get around her defences. Not when she was on the verge of telling him she loved him too. That really would jeopardise Gracie's chance of growing up in a stable home with someone who wasn't paid to look after her interests.

Over his shoulder she could see the two figures coming back down the corridor, probably wondering what was keeping him.

'I think someone is waiting for you.' Summer pointed him in the direction he was most needed. Already she was making plans to run into the staffroom for the emotional breakdown that had been coming since she'd walked out of his house, her voice wavering with the sob she was trying to hold back. It was all too much today, seeing them together, the uncertainty in Gracie's face as she'd taken her mother's hand, and Rafael no less attentive towards her than he'd ever been.

If she'd done the right thing in letting him go to protect her heart then why did it feel so wrong?

Rafael waved at them then turned back towards her with one final comment before he left. 'I'm not giving up on us, Summer. Even if you have.'

She'd completely detached herself from him and Gracie since Christina had arrived at his house that night and she felt a huge sense of loss. They were professional and courteous to one another at the clinic but it was awful pretending that was all they'd ever been to one another. Any time he'd tried to apologise for what had happened or explain what had happened, he was met with the same response. That he shouldn't worry about her and to concentrate on his daughter. It was in his nature to do both when he wanted to find a way to have them both in his life.

Based on her relationship history he could understand why she was so convinced he and Christina were trying to get their relationship back on track, but he liked to think after everything they'd shared Summer would give him a chance to prove his feelings for her.

He wasn't simply going to abandon what they'd had together over a misunderstanding, or because the damage their exes had done was getting in the way of them having a future together. They'd resisted their feelings for each other for far too long and things had only come to a head when they'd started working together outside the clinic. If she wasn't going to speak to him at work, there was one last reason she would have to see him and that was for the triathlon.

There was still a lot of red tape to sort out for the event and Summer had been the main driving force, courting publicity and participation since their parting of ways. She'd insisted she could manage on her own, regardless that it was supposed to have been about integrating him into the community as well as supporting the clinic.

Well, if it would force her to face the feelings she had for him and realise how much she meant to him, he was going to step up as co-creator of this enterprise. Whether she liked it or not, he loved her and he was going to make sure she knew it.

'Where did you put all the signed sponsorship forms and insurance papers?' Summer was trying not to let her temper get the better of her but she was stressed to breaking point, not only with the task of putting on this event, which seemed to have captured the interest of the entire island, but because Rafael was insisting on doing it with her.

They were in her house on the eve of the triathlon, making sure they had all eventualities covered because she thought it would be easier meeting at hers than at his, where Gracie and all the lovely memories she had there would be tarnished with Christina's presence. However, she hadn't accounted for the claustrophobia of having him under her roof and not being able to walk away from all the emotions that brought bubbling to the surface.

'They're right here.' He leaned over her shoulder and sifted through the mass of print-outs and schedules to uncover the items she'd accused him of misplacing.

'Sorry, I must've set them down there earlier. I... er...have a lot on my mind.' Particularly how good he smelled, like soap and cologne, as if he'd just got out of the shower. She tried to stop her brain venturing there, giving her a vivid memory of what a naked Rafael looked like, and failed. There he was, muscles, abs and everything else on display as he soaped himself up…

'Too much on my mind,' she muttered. Once this triathlon was over that was it. She was putting a ban on him getting within hot-breath-on-her-neck distance.

'You need to relax.' He placed his hands on her shoulders and started to massage the bunch of knots her nerves had become. She hoped he didn't hear the little whimper that escaped as his strong hands kneaded her flesh for the first time since their break-up. It felt so good to have him touch her, firm, tender, and always with the goal of seeking her pleasure. She closed her eyes and let him work his magic until she knew she was in danger of getting carried away and forgetting they were supposed to be working. Rafael was no longer hers and her body was no longer his to manipulate. Even if she enjoyed it.

She shrugged him off. 'Okay, I'm relaxed now.'

'Everything's in place. You should really take some time out before you work yourself into the ground. We could open a bottle of wine and have a chat like old times if you'd like. Christina's keeping an eye on Gracie tonight.' He was still hovering beside her, putting her body on high alert as though it was waiting for another touch to send her back into raptures. Not even the mention of Christina could apparently dissuade her treacherous libido that this man wasn't any good for her, and she swore Rafael was doing this on purpose. It wasn't as if she didn't have any furniture for him to sit on.

'I don't think that's a good idea. You should be in

training and I think we're done for the night anyway. If I think of anything else before tomorrow, I'm sure I can manage on my own.' She turned around with the intention of dismissing him and pointing him in the direction of the door but he was there, in her space again, so close her mouth was dry with anticipation over his next move. The flick of her tongue to wet her lips only succeeded in drawing his attention further and turned his eyes black with desire for her.

If she didn't still have that one little part of her refusing to let her forget every time someone had hurt her in the past she'd have melted right onto her dining-room table and let him take her there on top of all the hard work she'd undertaken to try and distract herself from thinking about him.

'Please, Rafael.' The teary plea was for him to stop because she knew she couldn't. It was enough for him to take a step back and let her breathe again.

'I know you still care for me, Summer, and I have never loved anyone the way I love you. Just remember that.'

He left then, leaving her gasping for air in between the sobs of frustration and pain. How could she ever forget when it was the first time he'd said the words and made her realise more than ever what it was she'd lost. Everything.

Rafael no more wanted to take part in this triathlon than he wanted to follow Christina back to Boston but it was his last shot to get close to Summer.

He watched her now at the far side of the pool, homing in on her in the midst of the whooping crowd as she corralled her day-care charges into the stands to watch the race. He waved to Gracie, who was holding her hand, but the only person waving back was Christina, sitting a few rows back. It was all he could do to nod an acknowledgement of her support when it wasn't hers he sought.

The starting pistol sounded and he launched himself into the water along with his other competitors. He knew he was up against it with the super-fit Alex and a determined Maggie Greene, a physio at the clinic and a gold-medal-winning ex-Paralympian athlete. Not to mention Rick Fleming, the English doctor in the rehab team and all the other members of staff keen to compete today. Although he didn't care about winning. It would be all he could do to simply get through this today. Swimming, or any of his other leisure pursuits, was no longer the alone time he'd once looked forward to. Now he had too much of it.

He'd tried to remind Summer what they'd had together but even that hadn't been enough to change her mind when she was clearly still hurting over what had happened. That fear gripped his heart again that he might not ever win her back and he had to remind himself to breathe before he drowned himself in front of everyone on account of his troubled personal life.

With a rolling turn at the end of the swimming lane he launched himself into another lap, wanting to get this over as soon as possible. He didn't realise he was first to finish until he hoisted himself out of the pool and turned to see the women in his life on their feet, cheering. Even Summer was giving him a sad sort of smile. One that said she was proud of him but was wary of letting him know.

It occurred to Rafael in that second how miserable

they all were without each other. Summer was such a caring woman who wanted the best for Gracie as much as he did and would put the little girl's happiness before her own. She was determined they should be happy together as a family. What she had yet to realise was that she was their family. He needed to show her in some way, make a commitment to her so she could see she was as important to him as his daughter.

'Come on, Raf, give the rest of us a chance,' Rick called to him with a laugh as they jumped on the exercise bikes to complete the cycling. There weren't enough to go around all of the competitors so their times were being added to their other scores later. That didn't stop the crowd following to cheer them on, gathering around the competitors so there was no escape from the scrutiny. The 'Triathlon Dad' nickname didn't make him laugh any more when it summed up the man he'd been before Summer and the man he'd return to if she wouldn't take him back. When all he had outside work was Gracie and his leisure pursuits, and though he loved his daughter, he loved Summer too. He wanted to be known as her partner, lover and companion, along with the other roles he had.

If the only way she was prepared to talk to him or acknowledge his existence was through this sporting spectacle, he was going to give it his all. He wanted her to see he was doing it for her, that he wanted this to be a success, but most of all that she was his motivation to win.

His legs were pumping, racking up the miles on the clock, sweat beading on his brow with the effort, but his focus was only on one thing. Summer. She'd managed to position herself near the front of the throng with Gracie in her arms and he knew she was there for him. He locked eyes with her and neither of them looked away until the bell sounded to signal the finish. It was obvious there was no one else for either of them, they'd simply been too scarred by the past to face up to it. Once this race was over he was going to confront her once and for all and make her acknowledge those feelings she had for him.

Now all he had to do was complete the running stage of the triathlon and reach the finish line, where he knew Summer and Gracie would be waiting for him.

Summer couldn't help herself. She just had to be close to him. They'd both put so much effort into getting this event organised, in bringing the community together, he deserved her support. After checking that the rest of the children were being supervised, that's how she justified shoving her way through the crowd at least.

He had accrued quite a fan club, who'd followed him from the pool to watch his progress in the other events, and she was sure it wasn't entirely down to his athletic ability. She was as aware as every hot-blooded woman in the room how handsome he was in or out of the water, in or out of her bed. Even now, drenched in sweat after his exertions, people were swarming around him in an effort to be close to him. She, on the other hand, had remained at a distance until now, telling herself she had no right to celebrate his achievements when they were nothing to do with her any more.

When he fixed her with that intense stare and rendered everything going on around them invisible she knew it was pointless to continue denying her true feelings for him. She was sure even Christina had realised since she'd backed away, leaving her and Rafael staring lustfully at each other.

If his ex-wife hadn't remained in the picture it would all have been so much easier. She would've forgiven Rafael by now if she wasn't still afraid he'd leave her for his ex. As they all made their way to the running track she made sure she had another prime viewing spot, close enough to see Rafael but somewhere Gracie wouldn't get jostled by the other spectators. Although she was so busy waving the little Spanish flag Summer had helped her make in nursery, the noise and the crowd didn't seem to be bothering her.

The competitors lined up in the starting blocks and she could see Rafael searching the faces to find her. A smile brightened his face once he found her and a blush crept over her body at his renewed attention. He'd had a couple of weeks without her, plenty of opportunity for his feelings for Christina to resurface, but it was always *her* he was looking for, saving his smiles for. Rafael wasn't a player who'd do that simply because he knew she'd turn to mush every time he looked at her.

She had to face the fact that he loved her, not Christina, and she was damn sure she loved him right back. The hardest thing to come to terms with was having Christina as a permanent fixture in their lives if she did get back together with Rafael. There was no way around that when she was Gracie's mother. Summer had to accept that, and the only thing stopping her then would be her own hang-ups about being second best. Something Rafael had repeatedly told her wasn't true. She had to trust him if she was ever going to be happy again.

When the starting pistol went off, a roar went up around her as everyone cheered on their favourite amateur athletes.

'You can do it, Rick.' Fleur Miller, Dr Fleming's other half, was doing her cheerleader bit beside Summer, and she automatically wanted to prove her allegiance to the man she loved too.

'Come on, Rafael,' she shouted, hoping he could pick her voice out among the rest when Rick seemed to be closing in on his lead. It wasn't clear if he'd heard her or not but he did begin to pull away and Summer's heart was in her mouth as the two sprinted to the end.

'Your daddy won, Gracie!' Summer celebrated with Gracie as her father crossed the finish line, arms held aloft in triumph.

'I want my papa.' The little girl twisted in her arms, demanding to be set down so she could run to him. Summer did so but took her hand to lead her there safely. An excited Gracie was the only thing he'd want to see at the end of that gruelling challenge.

'Well done.' She gave him a verbal pat on the back as they went to meet him.

'Thanks.' He was doubled over, trying to catch his breath, but at the sound of her voice he looked up and gave her a smile bright enough to light up that black hole where her heart used to reside.

Gracie threw herself at him and regardless of his obvious discomfort he gathered enough energy to celebrate his win with his daughter.

'I'm not sure it's official yet, is it? The others couldn't have been too far behind.' As he said that, Rick crossed the line but Rafael had won every event so comfortably there was no doubt who was in first place overall.

'Trust me, you've got this,' Summer assured him, but even when they gave out the official announcement he was insisting Maggie should have been crowned the first triathlon winner. Due to a teenage bout of meningitis, the popular physio had lost both of her legs and had come a close second despite her prosthetics. However, the fiercely independent redhead had insisted that she shouldn't be given any special treatment or advantage over the others.

She seemed quite happy with simply finishing, kissing and hugging Alex and pulling his little boy into their celebrations as though they'd won the Olympics. Summer envied their happiness in contrast to the awkwardness between her and Rafael as he was awarded his gold medal. She wanted to do all those things too but she'd forfeited that position in his life, even though he had no one else to fill it. Christina, who, it seemed, was learning the patience and understanding it took to secure a place in her daughter's life, was also hovering uncertainly in the background.

'I'm giving this to the person I love most in the whole world,' he said, as he unhooked the medal and hung it around Gracie's neck. Summer wanted to be so much more than a spectator in their special moment. Her throat was raw with the effort of holding back the emotions she wanted to unleash.

'Congrats again. Sorry, I'll have to go and set up the course for our own mini-triathlon this afternoon.' She left Gracie with her father and the rest of the nursery staff, worried that she'd left it too late to patch things up with him.

* * *

'Good girl, Gracie!' Summer was supposed to be im-
partial for these things and this was supposed to be
more about participation than competition, but she'd
gravitated towards Rafael and Christina on the side-
lines rather than taking an official role. It was impossible not to cheer Gracie along beside the other proud
parents because that's exactly how Summer felt, watching her blossom. She'd grown from that anxious child
who couldn't bear to be parted from her father to this
absolute force of nature who was following the example she'd seen this morning and going hell for leather
across the course. Even if paddling in a pool to collect
a rubber duck and riding a tricycle across the grassy
play area outside the nursery wasn't quite on the same
level as the clinic triathlon.

'I can't believe how well she's doing. Her focus and
co-ordination alone are amazing.' Rafael came to stand
next to her, clapping and cheering his daughter on as
she moved confidently from one stage to the next as
directed by the staff.

'She has a great role model.' Summer had no doubt
this display was in direct correlation to the one Gracie
had watched her father triumph in and was eager to
replicate it. Rafael had double the reason to be proud
of his achievements today.

'I'd say she has two. You've done so much for her
since we came to Maple Island. Summer, I—' He
turned his attention away from his little athlete to look
at her, the sudden wrinkle in his brow indicating he
wanted to speak about something serious, and Summer swallowed hard at the thought she was going to
have to stop avoiding the subject of their relationship.

Rafael took Summer's hand and made it obvious to anyone who was watching that he wanted to be with her. She had to stop pretending she believed otherwise and abandon her fears if she was ever going to find happiness.

She took a deep breath. 'It's been a joint enterprise in getting Gracie to reach this milestone and I want to be at your side, watching her grow and flourish. Today has reminded me that wherever you are is exactly where I need to be too. You've both taught me to grab life by the horns and go for what I want most in life, and that's you, Rafael.'

'You mean that? You have no idea what it did to me when I thought I'd lost you for ever. Please don't ever do that to me again.' He cradled her hand against his cheek and she knew she'd hurt him by trying to protect herself, thinking she knew what he wanted better than he did. Today he'd shown her beyond all doubt what it was he wanted and it was about time she stopped comparing him to Marc.

She was more than a convenience or a glorified babysitter to Rafael—if anything, she'd definitely been an inconvenience when she'd butted into his life. Even when they'd been on a break he hadn't given up on her. Thank goodness he could be as stubborn as she could when it was called for. 'I promise.'

'I want that in writing.'

Summer couldn't blame him for being wary when she'd denied those feelings for so long but she never wanted to be apart from him again.

The cheers went up as all the children completed the challenge but there was special recognition from Gracie's supporters that she'd been so adept at everything set before her. Since the participants were too young for the concept of competition they were all awarded medals, but Gracie stared at hers forlornly.

'What's wrong, Gracie? You did so well. We'll have to display your medal next to mine on the mantelpiece.' Rafael did his best to lift her spirits but she was still staring at her prize, lost in thought. Summer supposed that she was smart enough to realise it was a plastic replica and not the real deal like her father's.

'I think someone might have to stop at Brady's Bakery for a celebratory treat today.' She tried to raise a smile too without success, then Gracie said what was really on her mind.

'Can I have another medal?'

'Sure.' Summer retrieved the bag of leftover prizes and handed over an extra reward since she deserved it. 'Is this for Dolly?'

Gracie frowned at her. 'No. Papa said you give medals to people you love most.'

With that she gave Rafael the one hung around her neck and gifted the other right back to Summer. The sob was out of Summer's mouth before she could stop it, the gesture so unexpected and lovely that all three adults had tears in their eyes. She crouched down so Gracie could hang it around her neck and Summer couldn't have been happier with real gold. This was priceless, bestowed with such love she really felt like part of the family.

As she glanced across at Christina she realised her joy had come at the other woman's expense. She was gulping and dabbing her eyes, fighting the opposite emotions Summer was experiencing with the gesture.

The rest of the parents and children had filtered back

inside the nursery for the refreshments that had been laid on, leaving them to work out their complicated family issues with some degree of privacy.

'Christina, no one wants to hurt you.'

'Gracie just needs time to get to know you better.' Summer followed up Rafael's attempt to console his ex-wife but they'd used the phrase so often it sounded lame even to her. There was nothing that could be said to take away the pain of what Gracie's mother would take as a rejection when it was how Summer had felt when she'd thought Rafael was leaving her. Only the strength of Christina's feelings for her daughter would determine what she would do next.

It was a surprise, and unnerving, to see Christina smiling at her. 'You're lucky, you know. I was married to this guy and we both know how great he is and my daughter loves and trusts you. I was a fool to let them go but it's you they love. I know they're both miserable without you, Summer. I guess I'll have to work on my relationship with Gracie some more. She's thriving here and, believe it or not, I want what's best for her.'

She shrugged her shoulders and led Gracie inside with the others for refreshments but Summer could sympathise with everything she'd lost when she'd come so close to losing it herself.

'Are you okay?' Rafael checked with her, though it was Christina whose heart was probably breaking.

'I'm fine. I just feel bad for her. After all she's Gracie's mom, she's always going to be part of your lives. She was right, though, that you're the best thing to ever happen to me. Did you mean it when you said you loved me?'

'Yes. I am totally, absolutely, crazily in love with you.'

'Good, because I love you too. Now make my dreams come true and tell me that in Spanish.'

'*Te amo*. Which is why I want you to marry me, Summer.'

'Pardon me?' She blinked at him, wondering if he'd taken a knock to the head during the triathlon.

'I know we haven't been together long but I'm happy to have a long engagement if that's what you need. You're the only woman I want to spend the rest of my life with and if you feel the same way I don't see why we should fight it. I want you, me and Gracie to be a family. For ever.'

The proposal of marriage was unexpected and wonderful and risky to even consider after all their troubles. But it was also the best reason she could think of to show how much faith she had in the relationship and the strength of her love for him. From now on she was focusing on the future, and the past was no longer going to dictate the decisions she made.

'Yes, I'll marry you, and Gracie. You're all I've ever wanted.' Summer had never imagined that coming to Maple Island would've been the answer to her prayers, but finally she felt complete. Now she was part of the loving family she'd always dreamed about.

EPILOGUE

'DO I NEED to curtsey or anything?' The prospect of meeting her in-laws for the first time was nerve-racking, not least because she'd come to learn how much of a big deal the Valdez family was in Spain. Rafael had almost been embarrassed by the column inches they'd taken up over the years in the Spanish glossy magazines when she'd done some research over the internet.

He was noticeably absent from the photographs of glitzy parties they'd thrown and attended over the years, but it was understandable when the man she knew was a world away from that kind of flashy life-style. She was nervous about meeting them when she was just a normal working woman and wondered if they'd consider her up to scratch for their son, and their family.

Rafael rolled his eyes at her as he loaded the cases into the car. 'I've told you, this is going to be all very low-key. They've been warned we don't want any fuss, especially for Gracie's sake.'

He was trying to downplay the significance of this but she knew it was an important step for him, intro-ducing them to Gracie. Even though they'd been video-calling over the internet these past few months at her insistence, she could tell he was still worried that they might not accept their granddaughter.

'I suppose we have Christina to thank for this belated honeymoon.' She threw her arms around her husband's neck and kissed him, safe in the knowledge she'd never tire of kissing this gorgeous man for the rest of her days.

'We'll send her a postcard,' he said, and hugged her close.

Although they'd imagined a long engagement, things had kind of fallen into place when they'd realised what was important in their lives and both had come to the conclusion it was each other and a particular little girl.

They'd travelled back to Boston to get married in a private ceremony and surprised everyone with the news on their return. Life with Rafael and Gracie was chaotic and wonderful and she loved every moment of it. Since Christina had decided to stay on the island too, they had shared custody and it gave Summer and Rafael plenty of quality time together alone, making everyone happy.

The clinic had hired travelling nurse Stacey Ryder, who was softening Cody's hard shell with her arrival, so there was enough staff to cover their leave for a while. The only thing missing had been Rafael's family in Spain and, with Christina having already opened a dialogue, Summer had persuaded him to get in touch with them again.

He'd been surprised how emotional they'd been to hear from him and she thought perhaps a little sad at the time he'd lost with them. She understood that because of the half of her family she knew she'd probably never see again. However, she'd been making inroads into reconnecting with her mother, who doted on Rafael and Gracie almost as much as she did. She'd never expected to end up with such an extensive family but it was doing them all good to get to know one another again.

'We mightn't get time. After all, this trip is technically our honeymoon and Gracie's grandparents are very keen to babysit…' She trailed a finger down his chest and flicked open one of the buttons with her nail.

Rafael groaned and stilled her hand with his before she could tease him any more. 'It's a long flight, you know, and saying and doing things like that are going to make it very uncomfortable.'

'Sorry. I'm just looking forward to some alone time with you.' Although they'd packed everything they could think of to keep Gracie entertained on the journey, they both knew it was going to be challenging so she was already thinking ahead to the good part.

'I thought you might want to do some sightseeing and touristy stuff?'

'We could do that or we could get some baby-making practice in,' she said, biting her lip. They hadn't discussed the idea of having children of their own but she thought having a sibling for Gracie would make their little family complete.

Thankfully Rafael looked delighted at the idea. 'Really? You want us to have a baby?'

Summer nodded.

'In that case, what are we waiting for? Let's hit the road!' He hurried her into the car, a great big smile plastered over his face, and the love she had for him almost bubbled over. She already knew what a great husband and father he was and another baby would be the icing on the cake for her perfect little family.

Coming to Maple Island had been the best move she'd ever made.

* * * * *

NURSE TO FOREVER MUM

SUSAN CARLISLE

MILLS & BOON

To Anna, the niece who is so much like me.
I love you.

CHAPTER ONE

"LIZZY, HONEY. STAY STILL." Dr. Cody Brennan squatted on his heels in the hallway in front of the day-care suite to re-tie his daughter's hair-bow. He couldn't keep his frustration out of his voice as he fumbled at forming a loop with the slick ribbon. Suturing he'd learned in medical school, not securing bows.

"Dadd-yyy, it has to be right," Lizzy's whine echoed off the hallway built of glass.

"Hey, mind if I give it a try?" a sweet-sounding feminine voice beside him asked.

Cody looked over his shoulder. Two large, sympathetic green eyes with thick dark lashes met his gaze.

"Dadd-yyy," Lizzy moaned.

Not giving him a choice, the woman moved in close. A hint of peach tickled his nose as she tugged the ribbon from his hand, hers brushing over his. With a quick side step he moved aside, giving her better access to Lizzy's ponytail.

As if by magic Lizzy went statue still and the woman in a deft twirl of fingers secured the bow.

"There you go," she announced with such fanfare that she might have been giving Lizzy an award.

"Thanks," he muttered.

Lizzy pulled on his hand. "Let's go, Daddy."

"You need to tell the lady thank you first." He used his stern father voice.

"Thank you." Lizzy obeyed with uncharacteristic shyness.

"No problem." The woman smiled.

The beautiful upturn of her mouth captivated him. Her full lips surrounded white straight teeth, creating a unique sunbeam that pulled him toward her, making him feel good. A sensation he'd not experienced in a long time.

Lizzy tugged on his hand again. Seeing she had regained his attention, she towed him into day care. When he walked out a few minutes later he looked for the woman. There was no one in sight. She'd been wearing a knit top and jeans, so she must be making an early morning patient visit. Why she had grabbed his attention so, he couldn't fathom.

He'd been off women for what seemed like ages now and that suited him fine. After the years of anguish and constant distress his ex-wife Rachael had put them through, his children and he had finally found contentment. Throughout his life he had admired his parents' marriage.

He'd always wanted one like theirs but that dream had been destroyed by the reality of a wife struggling with a drug addiction. Supporting her and raising two small children while at the same time completing his medical training had made him want to find a simpler life. Moving to Maple Island had given him that. It had taken years but he now had the peace he'd hoped for and the ability to give his girls the attention and security they deserved. Bringing someone into their world would only disrupt what he had so carefully built.

After a car accident, his ex-wife had become hooked on painkillers. He seen the signs, had done everything he could think of to try to help Rachael. She had gone in and out of rehabilitation but nothing had seemed to work. Life had become a round of clinics, counseling, begging and shouting. After finding one of his pre-scription pads missing, he'd known the crisis Rachael had created had to end. He'd finally accepted defeat. Their marriage was over. He had the girls to consider. Unable to save Rachael, he had to think of Jean and Lizzy and his own sanity.

He'd filed for divorce and full custody. With years' worth of documentation against Rachael, her parental rights had been permanently revoked. Being a solitary parent and a surgeon with a demanding job hadn't been part of his life plan, yet here he was.

Soon after the custody trial he'd met Alex and the answer to his problem had been born. Every day he was grateful for that serendipitous bar conversation he'd had with Dr. Alex Kirkland about the perils and the pitfalls of solo parenting. During their mutual commis-eration, the dream of a first-class, cutting-edge clinic with an equally state-of-the-art day care for employ-ees was created. Faster than Cody had imagined, he'd become Alex's partner and co-founder of the Maple Island Clinic off the coast of Massachusetts.

The day care had been a lifesaver, but Cody's prob-lem this morning had been that children were supposed to show up already dressed for the day and in his five-year-old daughter's mind that included a properly tied hair-bow. Lizzy didn't consider herself dressed without a ribbon in her hair.

Like this morning, Cody sometimes worried he might not be enough for Jean and Lizzy. He often felt they needed that special attention that only a woman could provide. He shoved that thought away, his teeth clenching from the force of his resolve. He couldn't risk a repeat of the hell Rachael had put them through. What if he chose wrong again?

Enough of those thoughts. He didn't have time to review ugly memories. Besides being a single parent, as an orthopedic surgeon specializing in knees and legs, he had a busy clinic and a full surgery schedule this Monday morning to occupy his mind. Some attractive woman visiting a patient shouldn't even be a concern.

Heading down the hall, he soon entered his office and habitually checked the time. He could complete some paperwork and make a couple of phone calls before he was needed in the OR.

An hour later, dressed in green scrubs and matching surgical gown with mask in place, he pushed through the OR doors. He had a meniscus repair to perform. It always troubled him that he was intelligent enough to do such delicate surgery but he still hadn't been able to save Rachael.

His team was waiting for him. The patient was on the table with his left knee surrounded by blue sterile drapes.

Cody looked at Mark, the anesthesiologist.

"All set," Mark confirmed, without being asked.

"Everyone ready?" Cody glanced around the table.

All eyes focused on him then a feminine voice from across the patient said, "Yes."

His scrutiny fell on her. Dressed in the same surgical garb as he, all he could see of her was her enthralling green eyes. They were familiar but he didn't know why. "And you are?"

"Stacey Ryder, your new clinical nurse specialist. I thought I'd stand in today and see your technique. It makes it easier to sound confident in front of the family when I've seen the doctor in action."

Normally Cody would have met his replacement nurse before she started. Instead he had trusted the personnel department to handle it. His regular nurse would be out for a month, taking care of her aging mother after a surgery. He had just vetted this new one on paper, seeing she came with the highest recommendations. However, her straightforward approach hadn't been noted.

There were suppressed murmurs behind the masks of his team members. Were they as shocked by her boldness as he? As a rule, the people he worked with didn't use such an imperious tone with him.

Cody caught and held her attention. "You're welcome to stay but don't get in the way."

"Understood, Doctor."

Giving her a curt nod, he crisply announced, "Let's get this tennis player back on the court."

"Yes, sir," Stacey Ryder quipped with a note of humor in her voice as if she had given him a mental salute. He narrowed his eyes. She didn't blink.

Dismissing her, Cody looked at the knee, making sure it was the one he'd written his initials on. The patient's leg already had a tourniquet in place and was secured to the table in a padded leg holder. Cody made a small incision to prepare for the diagnostic camera that would give him a view of the joint. He located the damaged meniscus and probed it with a tiny metal hook.

"This is going to be a pretty extensive repair. I hope no one has early lunch plans. Shaver."

The surgical nurse handed the instrument to him. He trimmed the edges of the tear. "This isn't going to be enough."

"Why not?" his new clinical nurse asked.

"Because I'm not pleased with the blood flow."

She looked at him. "So, what're you going to do?"

He glared back at her. "Ms. Ryder, I don't usually teach procedure during my operations."

"I'm sure you don't but I'd like to know enough to help the families understand and also save you time when you talk to them."

Cody couldn't fault her logic. "I'm going to make the lining bleed and then suture it together. First I need to make another incision to work through to do that." As he did so, blood oozed into the field, making his visibility poor. Without him having to ask, Stacey used already prepared gauzes on forceps to wipe it away.

"We need to get that under control before I continue," he stated. "I'm ready to suture."

His surgical nurse handed him the equipment required.

"Nurse Ryder, I need you to keep the area clear while I work."

"Yes, sir." She replaced the gauze and dabbed the area.

Cody watched. "Good." He worked the thread into a neat stitch.

"Doctor, since you seem to have improved your tying skills since this morning, I'm going to speak to the family now. They must be anxious."

Cody frowned at her. Her eyes snapped with humor. That second he realized why he recognized those eyes. She was referring to his inability to tie Lizzy's bow. They would have a talk about her OR decorum later. His voice tight with disapproval, he said, "Please tell the family I'll be out to see them in soon."

"Yes, sir." She quietly left.

For some reason the room suddenly felt cooler.

Stacey was still sitting with the family when Dr. Brennan strolled into the waiting room with a smile on his face. She had to admit it was a nice one. For a while there, she hadn't been sure if he knew how to form one. It was so congenial she was sure if he turned it on her, her stomach would flutter. Stacey wrinkled her nose. Why would she think that?

Had she overstepped in the OR when she'd teased him about "tying" his stitches? By the steely look in his eye she might well have. Sometimes her humor was misplaced. She was so used to working in laid-back, often difficult conditions where levity was required. This wasn't one of those situations. In fact, this was the nicest, most upscale medical facility she'd ever been in.

When the director of the World Travel Nursing Agency had told her about her next assignment, she'd shared with Stacey information about the fabulous care given at the Maple Island Clinic. It turned out it was true, right down to the beautiful island and the top-notch physicians.

Dr. Brennan certainly knew his stuff. She'd seen

enough good and bad surgeries on her journeys to recognize a surgeon with exceptional skills. Not just the
abilities acquired through training and experience, but
that special touch inherent in someone devoted to his
patients' welfare. Did that quality extend to other areas
of his life?

He'd been great with his daughter, despite his charming ineptness with her bow. It probably came more from
being in a hurry rather than incompetence. Something about Dr. Brennan's manner made her believe
he worked hard at being confident and competent in
every aspect of his life. She also had the idea he was
driven to keep any weakness or flaws well concealed.

"Here's Dr. Brennan now," Stacey said to the middle-
aged mother of their patient seated beside her. Releasing
her hand, Stacey stood. "I'm sure he can tell you more."

Dr. Brennan had pulled a long white lab coat over
his scrubs. His thick chestnut hair was still mussed
from removing his surgical cap. She guessed he'd only
run a hand through it because a lock hung over his forehead. The effect gave him a less polished look than he'd
had that morning in front of the day care. Deciding she
liked this version better, Stacey stepped out of his way.

He sat on the edge of the chair she had vacated and
turned to the mother. "Your son's doing very well and
is in Recovery right now. He'll be in some pain, but
I promise we're handling it. You'll be able to see him
in about an hour."

"Oh, Dr. Brennan. Thank you for taking care of him.
Do you think this'll get him back on the tennis court?"

He nodded. "I have complete confidence it will.
Now, why don't you go get something to eat and meet
him in his room?" He turned to Stacey. "Nurse, would

you please direct his family to the room where Mr. Washington will be?"

Stacey wasn't sure where that would be, but she'd find out somehow. She wasn't about to make her ignorance of that detail obvious to him so she answered with confidence. "I'll be glad to."

His attention returned to Mrs. Washington and he placed a hand on her shoulder. "If you need anything, will you let me or Nurse—"

"Please make it Stacey." She looked at the woman with warmth before giving Dr. Brennan a pointed stare.

A thin smile curved his lips and he nodded once before leaving the way he'd come.

Stacey settled the Washington family in the patient's room before returning to the waiting room to speak to the family of Dr. Brennan's next surgery patient. When she checked in with him during surgery he gave her a brief, concise pronouncement that the patient was doing as expected. She left with a "Thank you, Doctor." Again, she was with the family when he came in to speak to them.

Finished he stood, stepped away from the group and said, "Stacey, may I speak to you a moment?"

A shiver of uncertainty went through her. Yep, she'd overstepped. "Yes, sir."

In the hall, he slowed long enough to say, "I'll be doing rounds in thirty minutes. Meet me at my office in ten. Do you know where that is?"

"I'll find it."

He nodded. She was quickly learning it was his signature acknowledgment.

Stacey made sure she was a minute early when she knocked on his door.

"Come in."

His accent wasn't the typical clipped, sharp, New Englander one. What was his story? It didn't matter. She wouldn't be around long enough to really get to know him, or anyone else well. Four short weeks didn't leave much time to create friendships. That's how she'd spent most of her life. She never stayed in one place long enough to get close to people and start caring about them on a personal level, on purpose. She made sure to leave before she could be left. If you cared you got hurt. She'd had enough of that in her life.

Early in life after her father had left and then again when her mother had divorced her second husband, she'd learned not caring meant that you didn't feel pain. The ache had been so great when she'd been a child she never wanted it to happen again. She'd do anything to make that not occur, to the point of remaining distant. People disappointed her if she let them close enough. When her mother had brought home her third husband, Stacey hadn't even bothered to call him by his real name. Instead she made up a name for him, one she could easily forget. She'd spent most of her time in her room.

The only permanent person in her life was her mother and Stacey hadn't seen her in over a year. In fact, she was due for a visit that Stacey planned to make before she left for her next assignment in Ethiopia. As soon as this placement was done she would spend a couple of days with her mother then not bother again for another year. She couldn't rely on her mother, who had always had her own screwed-up life to worry about. The one time Stacey had let her guard down and let someone get too close romantically, he had disappointed her as well. Once again her heart had been crushed.

She'd been engaged. Had believed she had found the guy who would treat her as if she were special, one who would always be there for her, share the family with her that she'd never had. Instead she'd found out he'd been cheating on her. Their life together had been over before it had even properly started. Once again she was of no value to anyone. She'd ended their relationship with one of the same ugly scenes she'd witnessed her mother having when one of her relationships had ended.

That's when Stacey had decided seeing the world and devoting herself to professionally caring for people was safer than nurturing the terminally ill hope that someone would someday actually want her, see her as essential to their life. Now she didn't stay in one place long enough to allow a bond to form beyond what was necessary. It was better, simpler, and easier on her heart that way.

Dr. Brennan, sitting behind his desk, raised his dark head, his eyes studying her. She was sure his intent scrutiny wasn't missing a thing. That shrewdness must be part of the reason he was such a well-respected physician in his field. She had researched him on the internet before agreeing to the job.

"I want to apologize for my comment in the OR. That wasn't the place to tease you." She walked further into the room.

One of his brows rose slightly. "I'm not used to being teased, in or out of the OR."

Oops. She had no doubt that was true.

"We need to get to rounds. The girls have dance practice this evening."

Thankfully he'd changed the subject. "Girls? As in plural?"

Standing, he moved around the desk. "My daughters."

He was tall, her head only reached to his shoulder. His large open office seemed small with him in it. She'd only seen one child that morning. But he had another.

"Lizzy has an older sister, Jean. She's isn't quite so demanding and is far more independent. She'd already gone into day care when you came along." He twisted his lips. "And didn't require a bow."

Stacey grinned. There was affection in his voice when he spoke of his children. That alone made her admire him. She'd never heard that from a man while growing up. Mostly she'd just been in the way.

He led the way out the door.

Prone to chattering when she was nervous, Stacey said, "This is an amazing clinic. Nothing like what I've been working in while I was in South America."

"Thanks. It was a real answer to our prayers. Alex and I created a great place to work while still giving our children and the staff a quality place to stay while we do that." He stopped at a patient's door. "This is Mrs. Fitzpatrick. She had her surgery a week ago." Dr. Brennan was back in doctor mode as he knocked on the door.

At the sound of "Come in" they did, him leading the way.

A woman in her mid-sixties with vivid white hair cut in a fashionable style sat regally in a chair next to the windows. Across from her in a matching wingback was an older man, who complemented her appearance. They had the aura of wealth.

Stacey took a quick glance around the room. The bed alone said that the Maple Island Clinic was a cut above other medical facilities. It looked like a typical one that might be found in anybody's bedroom, but she was pretty sure that beneath the floral spread it functioned like a hospital bed. The view beyond the windows was of a spring-green grassy area leading to ocean waves. Stacey could well understand why people would want to come here to recuperate.

"Hello, Dr. Brennan," the woman said proudly. "I've been up and moving around today."

"That's good to hear." He stepped closer.

The older man stood and the two men shook hands.

Dr. Brennan turned toward her. "Mr. and Mrs. Fitzpatrick, this is my new nurse, Stacey Ryder."

Smiling at them, she said, "Please call me Stacey." Then she addressed the woman. "I understand you had a knee replacement."

"I did. Thanks to Dr. Brennan I'll finally be able to get on the floor with my grandkids."

Stacey's smile widened. Mrs. Fitzpatrick didn't seem the type to want to do that, but now she could. "That's great to hear."

"I'd like to check your incision, if I may?" Dr. Brennan asked.

Mrs. Fitzpatrick pulled her right pants leg up over her knee. Dr. Brennan went down on his heels to examine it closely. "It looks good. Now let me see you bend it."

The woman lifted it up and down. Stacey didn't miss how her lips tightened, but she didn't make a sound.

Dr. Brennan stood and put his hand on her shoulder. "I'm impressed. I can tell you've been working hard in physical therapy. I think you're about ready to go home."

Mrs. Fitzpatrick's smile was a bright one. "That's sooner than you had said."

"It pays to be a good patient," he responded, grinning.

Stacey enjoyed the moment. Dr. Brennan had a nice rapport with his patient. She hadn't seen much of that in her work in medical facilities in developing countries. There the patients came and left the same day. None of the doctors, and certainly none of the temporary nurses, had an opportunity to really get to know the patients. It was lovely to see that personal interaction in this clinic but at the same time it made her uncomfortable. She wasn't looking to become involved with anyone on any level.

Over the next few hours Stacey found out that Dr. Brennan's bedside manner didn't just extend to the Fitzpatricks. He treated all his patients with the same respect and concern. Each time they saw someone new he took the time to introduce Stacey, making her feel she was part of his team, significant. That was an odd thought.

They were passing through the activity room where the afternoon sun beamed in through the windows when a weathered man sitting at a table lifted a hand in acknowledgment.

"Hey, Salty. Good to see you," Dr. Brennan greeted him.

"Who's that with you?" Salty wanted to know.

"This is my new nurse. Stacey Ryder. Stacey, this is Salty, our local hero."

Stacey couldn't miss the pink spreading across the older man's cheeks, the wrinkles that gathered beside his eyes and the straightening of his shoulders. "Aw, 'twas nothing. Anyone would have done it." His gruff voice was filled with pride.

"Done what?" she couldn't help but ask.

"We had a ferry accident a few months back. Salty went out in his boat and helped save people."

"That sounds impressive." And she was impressed.

Salty shrugged his shoulders. "Glad I could help."

"We've got to be going. See you around." Dr. Brennan strolled on through the area.

"Nice to meet you." Stacey hurried to catch up with the long-legged doctor.

They hadn't made it into the hall when Salty called, "Hey, Doc, find a good woman and you've found a jewel."

Dr. Brennan raised a hand and kept walking. "Thanks. I'll remember that."

Stacey had seen the slight flinch of his shoulders before he'd waved off Salty's unsolicited advice. "What was that about?"

"Nothing. Salty is always dishing out his idea of wisdom."

Dr. Brennan didn't appear to think that particular piece of advice was very impressive. Were he and his wife having trouble? Whatever it was, it had nothing to do with her and so was none of her concern.

A few minutes later as they walked out of a patient's room a tall, sandy-blond man wearing a lab coat came toward them. "Hey, Cody. How's it going?"

"Well. Your staff has done wonders with Mrs. Fitz-patrick." Dr. Brennan passed her his hand computer on which he was making notes. "As uncooperative as she was before surgery, I'm impressed by how far she's come in such a short time."

"What can I say? We're good!" The man chuckled, then gave her a questioning look. "Hi, I'm Alex Kirk-land, your medical director."

"I'm Stacey Ryder, Dr. Brennan's temporary nurse."

"That's right, Marsha's out taking care of her mother. Welcome. We're glad to have you," Dr. Kirk-land said. "Feel free to call me Alex."

She liked him. He wasn't quite as stuffy as Dr. Bren-nan. "Alex. I'm glad to be here. Didn't I read some-where that it was you and Dr. Brennan who started this clinic?"

"Yeah, that was us." Pride filled his voice.

An attractive woman with a riot of red hair headed their way with a bounce in her step. She called, "Hey, Alex, you have a minute?"

Alex's eyes lit up before he turned. "I always do for you."

"Aw, you do care." She joined them.

Stacey suspected there was a deeper meaning to their greeting by the way Alex lightly touched her elbow to direct her attention to Stacey.

"Maggie, this is Stacey Ryder, Cody's clinical nurse for the next few weeks."

Maggie extended her hand. "Maggie Green, one of the physiotherapists around here. I specialize in hydro and equine therapy. Glad to have you. I hope you enjoy your stay." She turned to Alex. "I hate to drag you away but I need to talk to you about one of the twins for a sec."

Alex shrugged. "Duty calls. Good to have you, Stacey. Don't let Cody overwork you while you're here." He followed Maggie down the hall toward the hydro area.

Stacey looked at Cody "She seems like fun."

"That's not what Alex thought for a while. Now he'd agree with you."

They continued down the hall.

Uncharacteristic curiosity had gotten the better of her and Stacey had researched the founding of the clinic. After meeting a few people, she'd already figured out the internet didn't tell the entire story of Maple Island Clinic. Doing the research in person with one of the founders, especially a particularly handsome one, was an invitation to get personal. Taking a breath for courage, Stacey asked, "So how did you and Alex decide you wanted to start this facility? By your accents you don't come from the same part of the country."

He looked at her for a moment as if he was deciding whether or not to answer. "We don't. We met at a conference. Single guys with childcare issues in common. Next thing I knew we were coming up with this clinic idea." He turned the corner and started down another hall. "I'm originally from California."

"That makes sense. One coast for another." That seemed a pretty dramatic move for a specialty surgeon of Brennan's caliber. Was there more to it than a chance meeting at a conference? Had something else pushed him into the move? She shouldn't pry further yet she couldn't stop herself. "Was that a hard sell to your family?"

"No. The girls were so small they were good with it."

"Your wife?" Stacey winced silently. She had already asked too many questions.

"She was already out of the picture." His words were flat and final.

Stacey let go a private sigh of relief. He'd closed the door on that subject, slammed it shut.

They walked back to his office in silence. There he said, "I'll see you in surgery at six in the morning." Then he literally closed the door in her face.

So much for Mr. Charming.

CHAPTER TWO

TWO DAYS LATER Cody picked up the girls from dance practice. It wasn't his favorite night of the week because it was always so busy. To make it less stressful he usually took them out to dinner. Tonight they were going to Brady's Bistro and Bakery for pizza. They all loved the thin slices and best of all he didn't have to cook.

As often as possible he tried to give the girls nutritious meals. He was trying to make up for the time when they hadn't had them. By the end of his marriage, Rachael hadn't cared enough to prepare meals. Every cent she'd been able to get her hands on had gone toward her next fix.

Cody had promised himself that his girls would have home-cooked, locally grown, wholesome food as much as possible. For the most part he'd managed to achieve that. Still, it was nice to get out of the kitchen and concentrate on having more quality time with his kids.

He held the door to the bistro open. The place was full, noisy with the sounds of talking, laughter and dishes rattling. He looked around the space with its red chrome tabletops and yellow chairs covered in plastic. The black and white tile floors added to the fifties vibe.

With a moan and a hunger pang, he resigned himself to the fact they would have to wait. He scanned the dining area with irritation. It wouldn't be a short wait. Stepping to the left a pace, he searched again. There was a booth with some empty seats. Looking closer, he saw Stacey sitting in one corner of it.

The thought that it wasn't a good idea to join her was interrupted by Jean's plaintive announcement, "I'm hungry."

Cody drew a fortifying breath for reasons he couldn't put a finger on. They had worked well together over the last few days. Stacey had a great rapport with the patients, could anticipate many of the things he needed done, and she took direction without complaint. Most of all she was friendly and always wore a smile. So why did he have an issue with her? Could it be he found her attractive and that made him uncomfortable? Even if that was the cause of his hesitation, he had an immediate problem to solve that overrode his feelings.

"This way, girls." He weaved between the tables, glancing back to make sure they were following.

When he reached Stacey's table she looked up in surprise. "Dr. Brennan."

"Hey, do you mind if we join you? There don't seem to be any more seats and the girls are *very* hungry."

"Please do." She waved her hand toward the open places and smiled at the girls.

"Daddy, do you know her?" Jean asked in a suspicious tone.

Lizzy gave Stacey a look of wonder. Finally, she burst out with, "You're the woman who fixed my bow."

Stacey smiled. "Yes, I am. You're Lizzy, right?"

His younger daughter bobbed her head up and down.

"Yes, I know her," he said to Jean, then looked at Stacey. "And this is Jean." He placed a hand on his other daughter's shoulder.

Jean gave Stacey the sulky look that had become her standard greeting to unknown women. His elder daughter was having the most difficulty with the loss of her mother. She could remember Rachael being a part of their lives, but had been too young to understand her mother's problems.

"Hey," Jean said belatedly, with zero enthusiasm.

"Hi, Jean. It's nice to meet you." Stacey gave her an encouraging smile. "I work with Dr. Brennan…uh… your father. Why don't you sit over here beside me?" She patted the bench beside her.

Jean offered her father a doubtful look. He nodded and gave her a light nudge of encouragement. Jean slid in beside Stacey. He said to her, "And you can call me Cody."

Stacey instantly produced the smile that made him want to return one. "Cody it is."

He appreciated the way she pronounced his name, as if it were a sweet she was tasting for the first time and finding she liked it.

"You go first," Lizzy said, leaving Cody no choice but to scoot in until he faced Stacey. His knees bumped hers. Their looks caught. "Sorry."

"No problem."

His fascination with Stacey's green eyes was broken when Lizzy scrambled into her spot beside him.

The awkwardness he was experiencing disappeared when Brigid Brady, their waitress today, walked up to the table. "Hi, Jean and Lizzy. Cody."

Her look lingered on him a little longer than mere politeness allowed, much to his annoyance. More than once she'd made unmistakable overtures. He wasn't interested in a relationship with her now or even later. He glanced at Stacey. She watched them with a quizzical smile. No, she definitely hadn't missed Brigid's extra attention.

"Uh… Brigid, we'd like a medium pepperoni and cheese pizza." His gaze returned to Stacey. "I'm sorry. Have you already ordered?"

"No. But pizza sounds good."

"Then make that a large," he said to Brigid. "And four sodas." He looked at Stacey again.

"That work for you?"

"It does."

"It'll be out in a few minutes," Brigid said with a huff of disgust in her voice.

As she left a soft chuckle came from across the table. "Charming in and out of the OR, I see."

He twisted the corner of his mouth and shrugged.

Her attention went to Jean. "I heard you're a dancer."

"I take dancing. I'm not very good, though." Jean stared at the tabletop.

"I take it too," Lizzy proudly announced.

Stacey acknowledged her with a look of wide-eyed wonderment and asked, "You're a dancer too? Awesome!"

Stacey's focus was completely on his girls and it was genuine. They needed that in their lives. Their mother had never been there for them. The few women he'd had anything to do with in the years since his divorce had been more one-night stands than anything. He certainly had not brought them home to meet his daughters.

"That's great. I never had a chance to learn." Stacey leaned toward them as if enthralled with what Jean and Lizzy were telling her.

"Why not?" Lizzy asked, but Jean appeared uninterested.

"I moved around a lot and my mother didn't put me in any classes."

"You could come to ours," Lizzy offered so emphatically that Cody couldn't help but chuckle. The action felt good. He could only imagine Stacey in an eight and under class of girls in tutus.

"I think that would be fun but I don't think I'll be on Maple Island long enough to take lessons now either." Stacey hadn't taken her eyes off the girls, especially Jean.

"Where're you going?" Jean asked, frowning at the tabletop.

"In a few weeks I'll be going to Ethiopia after a quick stop to visit my mother for a couple of days."

Jean sat straighter in her chair. "Ethiopia. We've been studying about that country in geography. It's in Africa, isn't it? That's a long way away."

For once his oldest was engaged in the conversation. Stacey had a carefree manner about her. That unique congeniality came from living life on the move with the ease of the wind. Her life was a complete contrast to his. Still, he liked her ability to interact with people as if she'd known them forever. He'd seen her use that skill with his patients and now with his girls. She never treated people as though they were strangers. That was a talent to admire.

"It is, but I'm looking forward to going," Stacey said.

"Why?" Lizzy asked.

"Because I'll get to help lots of boys and girls."

"How?" Jean wanted to know, finally turning to study Stacey's face.

"I'm a nurse. So I'll help them feel better."

Jean lowered her gaze again but stopped short of the table surface. With a tentative touch, she fingered the wooden bead bracelet on Stacey's wrist.

"You like it? It's from Bolivia."

"Boo-liver-a," Lizzy said.

He and Stacey tried not to laugh.

"Bo-li-via," Stacey said slowly. "It's in South America." She turned back to Jean. "A girl about your age made it for me." She took it off and handed it to Jean. "You can have it. I bet she'd like to know that a girl in America is wearing it."

Jean looked at her father in silent question. He nodded. "If Stacey says it's okay."

"It is. I don't get to wear it enough. If you have it, Jean, I'll know it'll be cared for."

"Thank you." Jean's words were almost inaudible as she placed the bracelet on her slim wrist.

Stacey continued patiently engaging his girls in conversation until the drinks and pizza arrived.

"I hope you didn't feel forced into eating this just because it was what we were having." Cody put a slice on each of the girl's plates.

"Not at all. I don't always get pizza in the places I go." Stacey gave Jean and Lizzy a conspiratorial look. "I have to fill up when I have a chance." They nodded in simultaneous agreement.

Cody asked the girls what they'd done today, particularly how school had gone.

"I thought you stayed in the day care," Stacey said.

"We do," both replied at the same time.

"They go there before school opens, and then are transported to school and back again when school finishes." Cody took a bite of his pizza.

"Nice and convenient." Stacey pulled a second slice from the pizza sheet. Cheese strung out, breaking as she turned its triangle edge into her mouth.

Cody held his breath as the cheese landed on her chin. "That was the plan when Alex and I came up with the idea. So far it has worked out great."

"You have cheese on your chin," Jean pointed out.

"I do?" Stacey wiped her napkin across her cheek.

Lizzy yelped. "It's still there."

Stacey dabbed the napkin over her face again.

"You didn't get it." Lizzy giggled.

"Here, let me help." Cody reached across the table with his napkin in hand. As he removed the cheese, his gaze rose to find Stacey watching him. Her eyes were a forest green, and there was a twinkle in them. They looked like an inviting place where he could go and forget his cares.

"Hey, Daddy. Can we go get an ice cream?" Jean asked, dropping a crust on her plate.

Jerked back to reality, Cody quickly returned his hand to his side of the table. "Yeah, sure," he said before he'd thought about it.

"Yay," both girls yelled.

He put a finger to his mouth. "Shush. Not so loud. We're inside."

"You want to go with us?" Jean asked as she and Lizzy turned to Stacey.

She looked at him briefly. He did his best not to react one way or another but he didn't think that was a good idea. For him or the girls.

Finally, Stacey said, "I don't believe so this time. I've had too much pizza. Maybe next time."

To his amazement, Jean looked as disappointed as he felt. Why? he questioned himself on both accounts. Stacey had managed to forge some kind of relationship with his elder daughter who normally didn't warm up to strangers, especially female ones. So, what was it about Stacey that had him and Jean doing and saying things they didn't ordinarily do?

He paid for their meal despite Stacey arguing that she needed to cover her share. "Because of you we didn't have to wait to eat. The least I can do is get your meal."

"Thank you, then."

They were exiting the bistro when Jean pointed out the poster about the island's Founder's Day Weekend taped to the glass window. "Daddy, Fleur has been teaching us dances at day care. She wants us to do them on Saturday of Founder's Day Weekend. We have to have costumes."

"Costumes. That sounds like fun. I love to dress up," Stacey commented as she held the door open for the girls to exit.

Cody almost groaned out loud. Putting together costumes was his least favorite thing to do. Imagination wasn't his strong suit. They'd had to have outfits for the library's Fright Night a couple of months back. They had gone as trolls only because those had been the only costumes he could find in the store. He believed he should at least be allowed a full year before he had to come up with more. The side of his brain he used most held facts and numbers. He had to stretch to the other to be creative *and* inventive. Hopefully, Fleur, a recent patient and now the soon-to-be wife of Rick Fleming, a doctor at the clinic, would provide some guidelines or ideas.

They were out on the sidewalk when Stacey asked, "Founder's Day Weekend. What's that?"

"It's so much fun," Lizzy said, hopping with anticipation. "I like the pony rides."

Cody rubbed the top of his younger daughter's head and chuckled. "You like anything that has to do with a pony." He regarded Stacey. "We celebrate the settling of the island. The story goes that after a long and very hard winter a few early settlers traveled from the mainland over to the island, seeking food. They found the maple trees and tapped them. The maple syrup helped restore the strength of the people. No one really knows whether it is true or not, but we remember those early settlers and focus on maple syrup by having a Founder's Day Weekend. With all the trimmings—food, entertainment and fireworks. Everyone turns out for the event."

"I've never been to a Founder's Day anywhere," Stacey said.

"You'll come see us dance?" Lizzy stopped twisting to and fro long enough to ask.

"Of course I will." Stacey assured her. "If I am still here."

Jean and Lizzy grinned from ear to ear.

"Well, we'd better be going. Thanks again for sharing your table with us." He was uneasy on some level with what was happening between Stacey and his girls, as well as his reaction to her. The whole meal had seemed far too family-like for his comfort.

"No problem. I'll see you in the morning. Bye, Jean and Lizzy." Stacey glanced back at him as she turned. "Thanks again for the pizza."

He nodded. She lifted a hand and strolled away, looking in shop windows as she went. Why did he feel some of the pleasure in the evening was walking away from them?

Two days later, Stacey fixed a cup of hot chocolate in the employees' kitchen and pulled on her sweater. She loved the ocean and didn't always get an assignment near one, so she planned to take her afternoon break on the sundeck.

She eased into a chair. Being early April, the days were still cool. Raising her face to the sun, she closed her eyes. She'd been at the clinic for almost a week already. To her surprise she'd relished every minute of it. After living in little more than huts most of her professional life, she enjoyed staying in the tiny cottage called Paradise, facing the harbor. It was a slice of heaven. The village was pretty and she was slowly working her way through all the eating places. People were friendly and she was at ease here. She would miss it when she left.

Inhaling the damp salt air deeply, she released it slowly. The seagulls squawked nearby as the waves rolled in. Oh, yes, this was a great place to recharge her batteries. She needed this downtime in her life. This would be her first weekend on the island and she planned to do more of this.

A hand touched her arm. Her eyes jerked open.

Cody's dark coffee gaze looked down at her. Determination, along with a touch of something else, etched his features.

"I've been searching everywhere for you. I need you to come with me."

She'd been so absorbed in her thoughts she'd not heard either him approaching or apparently her phone ringing.

"Where're we going?" She thought through the fog of surprise and tried not to react to his touch, which had left her forearm tingling, tiny hairs raised by goosebumps. Her reaction to him had to stop. She was too old for a crush.

"Boston. We have an emergency. I need you at the helipad in ten." He was already walking away.

Stacey rushed into the clinic behind him. She spoke to his back when she asked, "Do I need to prepare a bag, take anything?"

"They'll have everything we need there. I'll see you at the pad. I have to check on the girls."

She was waiting at the helicopter pad when Cody arrived. His lips were moving rapidly as he spoke into his phone. A furrow creased his forehead. The blades of the machine were already humming as they climbed aboard. She was a nervous flier. She gulped and climbed aboard. A high level of trepidation zipped through her.

She fumbled with her seatbelt. Cody reached over and clipped it into place. She gave him a weak smile. "Thanks."

He cupped his ear, shook his head and mouthed, "Use headphones," then pointed to them hanging above her.

Stacey placed them on her head.

"This the first time you've ever been in a helicopter?" He spoke through the headpiece.

She looked at him and nodded. Over the years she'd ridden in jeeps and in the back of trucks over rutted, washed-out roads, and once in a small plane, which she hadn't liked any better than the helicopter. Apparently, her fear was showing.

"There's a button on your headphones just above your right ear. Push it when you talk and release it so you can hear me."

She found the button and did as he instructed. "You can hear me now?"

"I can."

The helicopter shifted, and the wind swooshed before the machine started to lift. Her hands gripped the edge of the seat as she stared out the front windshield. Seconds later her right hand was prised off the seat. Cody took it in his, holding it. His hand was large, enveloping hers and radiating a promise that he was there for her. Unsure what was more disconcerting, Cody holding her hand or the flight, she gripped his fingers tightly like the lifeline they were.

She dared to glance at him. His eyes were intently focused forward. Was he already envisioning the surgery ahead of him? She'd gotten to know many of his facial expressions over the last few days. More than once she had seen those worry lines on his brow, the twinkle in his eyes when he talked about his girls and the rare but always breathtaking event when he laughed. Which happened usually when he was talking to Alex.

She relaxed somewhat and Cody released her hand.

Her growing security was gone. Placing fisted hands in her lap, she looked out the side window. The view of the island was amazing. It was green, a luscious ornament in the middle of a vibrant blue dotted with tiny spots of white.

As they sped out over the water she peeked at Cody again. He looked much as he had earlier. It was as if he were somewhere else. Her attention moved to the approaching coastline. The tall ship moored in Boston harbor was clearly visible along with a few of the historical buildings. They flew by them and over the modern structures. Suddenly the helicopter went into hover mode.

Panic tightened her chest. As she reached for the edge of her seat Cody took hold of her hand once more. Gratefully she clung to it.

There was a crackle in her headset before his voice fill her ears. "The take-off and landing are always the worst."

She gave him what she hoped was a look of gratitude, but she worried that her actual expression appeared pained. Not soon enough for her, the helicopter settled on the top of what she assumed was the hospital. Too soon Cody let go of her hand. With his simple action he had shown more awareness of her needs than her mother or fiancé ever had.

He climbed out of the helicopter and stopped long enough to help her down. After they were out from under the blades, he was on the phone. His questions were clipped and his responses short.

Soon they were on the elevator, going down.

Cody leaned against the opposite wall from her as they rode. "Our case is a seventeen-year-old boy involved in a car accident. His knee has been crushed and both his tibia and fibula are broken. When the general surgeon is done with some internal injuries I'll get to work. To add to the trickiness of the surgery, the boy is the son of a state senator. I understand the kid was running from the police when the accident happened so make sure you don't speak out of turn to anyone. The family should be in a private waiting room. I'll talk to them before I go into the OR."

"I understand." She had no experience dealing with high-profile cases, but she had no intention of disappointing Cody.

She hurried to keep up as he took long strides toward the surgery department. She waited to the side while he quietly conferred with another doctor. Done, Cody stepped to the hallway door. He said to her, "This way."

They walked down the hall side by side. Soon they came to a closed door. He opened it and she followed him through. Inside was a room with cushioned chairs that didn't match. She was sure they had been pulled from various places. People in suits sat and stood, all talking on phones.

"Mr. and Mrs. Clark?" Cody said, loud enough so he could be heard over the din.

"I'm Mr. Clark." A man with graying temples stepped toward them. "This is my wife. Senator Ann Clark."

A woman with a stately bearing and bloodshot eyes rose from the chair in the corner.

Cody stepped forward and offered his hand. "Senator Clark, I'm Dr. Cody Brennan. I'll be taking care of your son's knee and leg."

She nodded. "I understand you're the best at this type of surgery."

"I'll certainly be doing my best for your son."

"His name is James." The senator leaned against her husband.

"This is Stacey Ryder, my clinical nurse. She'll be keeping you updated on how things are going in surgery. If you have any questions or concerns you let her know."

Stacey nodded and gave the parents a professional smile of reassurance.

"How long should James be in there?" The senator sniffled. "It's already been hours."

Cody's grave look didn't waver. "My guess is it'll be after midnight before you can see James. Now I have to go. I'll be out to speak to you as soon as I'm done in the OR."

The terrified parents just stared at him hopefully.

Cody lifted his chin toward the door. Stacey followed him out.

"I'll show you the OR I'm using. Sit with them for a few minutes then come check in with me. I want to give them as much reassurance as possible. Based on what I've been told over the phone, the surgery is going to be a tough one."

They entered the surgical unit. Cody was greeted by a couple of people in surgical scrubs. At the OR unit desk he introduced her to the clerk. While they were there a man hurried up to them. Again, Cody introduced her. It was nice he remembered to do so because it would have been easy for him to get caught up in the case and forget she was there. It made her feel valued. The man was the surgeon's assistant who would be aiding Cody.

The two men went into a deep discussion about the amount of damage to the boy's leg.

Cody finished with, "Then we'll plan to stabilize everything tonight and go in again in a day or two to complete the repair. The swelling needs to go down and James needs to be stable first."

"The general surgeon should be through in about fifteen minutes. They'll be ready for you then." His surgical assistant was already headed down the hall.

"Sounds good. That'll give me time for something to drink and a granola bar."

The striding assistant called over his shoulder, "The dinner of champions."

Cody looked at her. "Come join me?"

Stacey followed him to a small break room a few doors down containing a couple of vending machines.

"May I offer you dinner?" Cody waved his hand toward the machines. She couldn't help but smile at his levity. "I suggest you have something. It'll be a long night." He pulled some bills out of his pocket and looked at them.

Stacey had left the island without even thinking about getting her purse. She was at his mercy in more ways than one. "My, Doctor, you do know how to turn a girl's head with a meal." She tried for her best nineteen-forties seductive-movie-star voice.

He looked over his shoulder and gave her a dry smile. "I'll try to do better in the future."

"In that case, for now I'll have a protein bar and a bottle of water, please."

Cody nodded. "Good choice. I'll have the same." He fed money into the slot.

With their food in hand, they sat at a small table with only two chairs.

"Are you sure this meager fare will be enough to get you through surgery?" She didn't hide her concern. When had she taken on worrying about him? Surely it was just one human being feeling concern about another and not something more.

Chewing, he studied her a moment. "I've gone on far less."

"I'm sure that isn't healthy."

"Maybe not, but necessary sometimes." He took a long draw on his water. She watched his throat as it went down. A day's worth of beard growth gave him a sexy edgy look. A little less buttoned up and more uninhibited. She liked it. He needed to let go somewhat.

"Is something wrong?" He stared her back to reality.

"Uh…nothing. Just thinking." To her dismay, her cheeks grew warm.

"About what?" Cody watched her much too closely.

Yeah, like she would admit she'd been thinking about how sexy he was. Her eyes didn't meet his as she spoke. "I was just wondering about who's watching the girls." *That was such a lie.*

Cody gave her a suspicious look as if he suspected she hadn't spoken the truth. "When Alex and I set up the clinic we knew we would have to occasionally be away for emergencies, so we set up an after-hours plan through the day care. Someone who works there is always on call. That person will come to my home and make sure the girls are taken care of. Even see they get to school. Because the girls are familiar with the person, they don't usually mind."

Stacey pursed her lips in thought, seriously impressed with such planning. "Nice thinking. Maple Island Clinic is really special."

"Thanks. We tried to think of everything." He shrugged. "If we didn't, we've figured it out as we've gone along." Cody stood. "I've got to head to surgery."

She needed to check in with James's parents.

"Just ask the unit clerk for anything you need. Give me half an hour to assess what I'll have to do, then you can come and get a report."

"Will do."

He gave her a wry smile and went out the door.

Cody was in the process of resecting the damaged skin when one of the surgical nurses said, "Doctor, I'm not feeling well." She ran for the door.

"Get some help in here!" He already had his hands full with the mangled leg and now he was short a nurse.

Another nurse in the room said, "At this time of night we'll have to call someone in."

"I need those hands now." The case was tough enough without this issue.

The ill nurse hadn't been gone a minute when the phone rang. No one could stop long enough to answer it. A few minutes later, with a mask over her mouth, Stacey stuck her head in the door.

"Dr. Brennan—"

"Scrub in. I need you in here," he barked, not even taking the time to look at her.

The door closed and a short time later Stacey entered. "Where do you want me?"

"Stand beside me. I need you to resect and clean the blood away so I can see." He had no more time to give directions. If any more tissue was lost then the boy would require skin grafts.

"Little to the left, Stacey. That's right."

As they worked he noted that he had to give her fewer instructions. Stacey anticipated his next move. "All right, let's get these bone splinters out of here."

His surgical nurse held a metal bowl as he picked bone pieces from the muscle.

"That looks like all of it." Now he could start trying to repair the jumbled mess.

"Doctor, I think I saw one more." Stacey pointed to a spot and dabbed it with gauze.

"Where?" He searched the area. "Ah, got it. Nice catch, Stacey."

She cleared the area again while he used the tweezers to remove the sliver before blood covered it again. "Excellent. Now, let's get this boy's leg pieced together."

Everyone worked patiently and efficiently over the next few hours arranging veins, ligaments and putting screws into bones as they put the human puzzle back together.

It was almost morning when he, Stacey and the other staff walked out of the OR. Cody pulled his surgical gown and hat off, dropping them into the cloth bin beside the door. He was acquainted with tough surgery but this one had definitely been in the top three he'd ever done. The boy had damaged his leg almost to the point of no return. He would have additional surgeries ahead of him, painful rehabilitation and a limp.

"Job well done, all." He turned to Stacey. "Nice

work in there. How much surgical training have you had?"

"Very little."

She sounded exhausted but there had been no complaints from her. She'd done what needed doing without question. He couldn't have been prouder of the work they'd accomplished.

Stacey stripped off her surgical clothes in record time and was headed out the door. "I need to speak to the parents. They must be crazy with worry since I just disappeared on them."

Cody hadn't thought of that. "Please tell them I'll be right out."

Hours later he and Stacey were standing at the ferry port, watching the vessel dock.

"I'm sorry the helicopter couldn't come get us. It's out, bringing one of Rafael's patients in." Cody watched the water froth as the ferry, its massive engines rumbling, eased beside the dock.

Stacey shrugged. "Part of the price of living on an island is living by the ferry schedule. It's better than swimming."

Cody chortled deep in his chest. "That I can agree with. Especially since the water isn't all that warm here. And it's too early and too far for a morning swim."

"I like the beach but I'm too darned tired to enjoy it today. All I want is my bed." She stepped onto the ferry.

"I couldn't agree more." He was by her side once more. "You were good in the OR and with the senator as well. What's a nurse with those skills doing traipsing around the world?" As a general rule he didn't ask women personal questions, but for some reason he wanted to know more about this one, who was such an enigma. The need to learn what made her tick was beyond his control.

"Much the same thing as here, nursing."

Something in her tone, or lack of it, made him believe there was more to it than that. "But why the traveling part?"

Her slight frown suggested she was reluctant to answer yet she lifted a shoulder nonchalantly. "With a mother who has been married three times and is currently working on her fourth, I never really lived in one place very long. Being a traveling nurse was just an extension of that. It also gives me a chance to do all types of nursing in innumerable types of circumstances."

She was about going from one place to another, whereas he was about staying put. He wanted stability and calm in his life. He already knew what it was like to live daily with the anxiety of uncertainty. He pressed his lips together. Was Stacey's reluctance to settle down generated by fear as well?

They made their way inside to one of the bench seats. The engines rumbled as the ferry pulled away from the port. The sky was an orange pink over Maple Island, making it appear on fire. The best thing he'd ever done had been to move to the island. "So on-the-job training gave you those surgical skills."

She yawned behind the back of her hand. "Yes, even in developing countries a general practitioner will do major surgery if it's in the right place at the right time." She gave him a pensive look. "I know the clinic is great and all, but to move all the way from California seems a little extreme."

She'd deliberately changed the subject. Did she not

want to talk about herself? He sure didn't. "Yeah, but it was a necessary one."

"How's that?"

Now he was the one hesitant to answer. But she'd responded to his difficult question so it was only fair that he do the same. "I'd gone through an ugly divorce and the girls and I needed to start over. Have a change." He leaned back, trying to get as comfortable as possible on the hard bench.

"Their mother didn't care that you took them so far away?" She watched him with disconcerting intensity.

He shrugged, trying to appear as uncaring as possible. "It didn't matter. She's no longer in their lives."

Stacey covered another yawn. "I see."

Cody doubted that she did, but he wasn't going into it any further.

"I don't want to be rude but I've got to close my eyes for a few minutes."

He stretched his legs out and crossed them at the ankles. "Not rude at all. It was a long night."

The ferry gently rocked. In minutes Stacey's breathing turned even. When her head tipped forward Cody put his arm around her shoulder and brought her to him. Her head rested on his chest. It had been a long time since he'd held a sleeping woman. Unable to resist, he brushed his cheek against her hair. It was as soft as it looked and smelled faintly of the peaches he remembered.

She murmured, shifted toward him then settled.

Cody closed his eyes. It seemed only seconds later the push of hands on his chest woke him.

Stacey's eyes were wide and her hair wild as she

stared at him in alarm. She had such expressive eyes. Cody couldn't imagine her telling a convincing lie.

"I'm sorry I went to sleep on you. I hope I didn't drool on you." She brushed at his chest, the tips of her fingers leaving hot spots through the fabric of his shirt.

He grinned. "I didn't mind. Your head was bobbing, and I felt sorry for you. Especially after I'd already woke you once today…uh…yesterday. I didn't want to do it again."

"I wasn't asleep on the deck. I was thinking. Enjoying the sunshine." She stretched, showing a hint of skin at her waist before she tugged at her clothes, adjusting them.

His body reacted in ways that had been dormant for far too long. This was his nurse. He had no business ogling her. He couldn't help himself, though. Something about Stacey made his blood warm. He grinned. "Looked like sleeping on the job to me."

She stood over him, her hands on her hips. "I do not sleep on the job. Ever."

He winked at her. Even after a long night Stacey looked amazing. She had a knack for making him smile. There was a brightness to her that somehow made life look sunnier. He wanted to capture that. Hold it close. He reached for her but stopped himself, letting his hand fall to his thigh. "I was just kidding."

Kidding. He wasn't a kidder. What was she doing to him?

CHAPTER THREE

STACEY CONTINUED DOWN the path leading to the harbor. The day was beautiful. The sun shone brightly, seagulls swooped and squawked. Sailboats and small fishing craft bobbed in the sparkling water. Had she found paradise?

She'd slept well past noon the day before, exhausted from her all-nighter with Cody. To her horror she had actually fallen asleep on him. Yet she had to admit it had been nice to wake up in a man's strong arms. Especially his.

Cody was far better natured, more tender-hearted, than she'd assumed, given her initial assessment of his character. Just thinking about being so close to him raised goose-bumps on her arms. She liked him too much. What would it be like to have a few weeks of fun with him?

No, she couldn't act on that idea, even if he wanted to. Cody and his daughters didn't need someone flitting into their personal lives, disrupting them and then leaving. More than that, he was her boss. Mixing business and pleasure often didn't turn out well.

He didn't strike her as a fling kind of guy. He had two little girls he adored, and was incredibly protective of them. All Stacey knew about relationships was that when the going got difficult then people left and never looked back. Even her ex-fiancé had followed that philosophy. At least she'd found out about his affair before they had married. Now she did all the leaving. She didn't wait around for it to happen to her.

Long ago Stacey had concluded it was easier not to even attempt marriage and parenthood. Stay loose and laid-back. Enjoy what came, but not get too involved. She was happier that way. While everything about Cody screamed commitment. That alone should make her keep her distance. She needed to focus on enjoying her time on Maple Island and not go anywhere near Cody Brennan outside the clinic.

From the harbor she made her way into town. Though she'd only been on the island for a week, she could tell the population was increasing. The tourist crowd had started creeping in as the spring weather warmed up quickly. She took a seat on an empty bench in front of the library so she could people-watch for a few minutes.

She looked across the street to see Lizzy coming her way with her hair pulled back at the nape of her neck. The child wore a sweatshirt, jeans and sneakers.

"Hey, Stacey," the little girl called out.

So much for staying out of Cody's life outside the clinic. "Well, hey, there."

Lizzy plopped down. "What you doing?"

Stacey searched the area. "Does your father know where you are?" Surely she wasn't by herself. It wouldn't be like Cody to let Lizzy run around the island unsupervised. He was a better parent than Stacey's had ever been. She spied Cody and Jean coming out of a store. Her heart skipped a beat.

Cody's dark looks and air of authority made him a fine-looking man. Dressed in a button-down plaid shirt with a navy zippered fleece vest over it and jeans, he couldn't have been more island casual or handsome. Tall, with those broad shoulders she knew well, he drew responses from all the women passing him. He captivated her for sure. Somehow she needed to get beyond this infatuation with him.

She regarded the charming cherub next to her. "I was just out for a walk."

"Hey, Daddy. I'm over here." Lizzy waved.

His tight look of worry eased into one of relief. He started across the cobbled street in their direction with Jean beside him. As soon as he was within hearing distance he spoke sharply to Lizzy. "I told you to wait outside the store."

"I saw Stacey and I wanted to say hello." Lizzy seemed to miss how concerned her father was.

Cody stepped closer and leaned down, gaining the girl's attention. "Next time you ask me before you go somewhere. I need to know where you are."

"Yes, Daddy," she said meekly.

Stacey tried to lighten the mood. She smiled. "Hey, Jean, Cody."

"Hi." Cody stepped back and looked at her. His voice hadn't lightened much.

Jean just watched her, not saying anything but obviously curious.

"Well, we need to be going." Cody looked at Lizzy and offered his hand. "Enjoy your day, Stacey."

Lizzy took hold of it and jumped to his side. She

smiled at Stacey. "We're going to catch lobster and eat it and build a fire on the beach."

"That sounds like fun." And it did.

"It is, so much fun. The best." Lizzy almost hummed with excitement.

"Come on, let's not bother Stacey anymore." Cody tugged on Lizzy's hand.

"Daddy, can Stacey come lobster hunting with us?" Lizzy craned her neck to see her father's face.

Cody looked unsure as his eyes cut to Stacey. "Lizzy, I don't think Stacey—"

Lizzy yanked on his hand. "Daddy, we can show her how to set the trap, and row the boat, everything."

Getting more involved with Cody and his girls was the last thing Stacey planned to do. "Thanks for asking but I really should go home." She stood, intending to step away.

"Don't you want to catch lobster with us?" Lizzy asked, giving Stacey a serious frown.

"It's so much fun." She turned to Cody. "Tell her, Daddy."

It took a moment before he asked, "Have you ever put out a lobster pot?"

Stacey considered him, then Jean, then Lizzy. "No."

He placed his hand on Jean's shoulder. "Everyone should have the experience at least once."

"You need to come." Jean offered her first words since she and Cody had walked up. "It's my favorite thing to do too." Lizzy grinned at her. Cody's gaze met Stacey's. She watched his chest expand then he released a breath as if he had made a huge decision. "You should definitely join us."

Going with them wasn't a wise move, but it would

only be for an evening and it wouldn't be just Cody and her—his daughters would be with them. Against her better judgment and because she couldn't resist their urging she said, "Okay."

Decision made, she planned to enjoy herself.

She joined Cody and the girls on their walk to his house. It turned out that he lived in a home not very far from Paradise Cottage. It was built in the saltbox style that was so common in that area. Yellow with a red door, it implied everyone was welcome. She loved it immediately.

The girls entered ahead of Cody and her, leaving the door open. He pushed it wider. "Welcome."

The hallway, laid with gleaming wood, went the length of the house. There was a staircase near the front door and large rooms off the hall. It was gorgeous.

"Head on back to the kitchen." Cody indicated down the hall to the back of the house.

As they made their way there Stacey could tell that it was a functional home with little extras for decoration. It screamed that no woman lived there. In the kitchen, she found a large bar and picture windows through which she could see a porch running the length of the house. There was also a great view of the ocean beyond.

"Girls, let's get what we need together before we go out to check the lobster pots. Jean, you get the fire supplies. Lizzy, the pot, napkins, plates and bowls."

Both went into action. Stacey couldn't help but be impressed. Cody was teaching his girls important lessons like teamwork. "What can I do to help?"

"Uh…how about getting the butter and drinks out

of the refrigerator and the bread off the counter?" He pointed to the other side of the room.

A few minutes later the girls headed out the back door, down the steps of the porch and along the path to the water. She and Cody followed with their hands full. He had pulled matches out of a high cabinet, put a roll of brown paper under his arm, located a butcher's knife and picked up a bag of tiny potatoes before he was ready to go.

They continued down the path through the rocks to a small sandy beach where a wooden rowboat sat beached and tied to a pole.

"You run a smooth operation, in and out of the OR, Doctor."

He grinned. "It helps to be doing something they want to do. I can't say that it's always that way."

"They're nice girls. You should be proud." She watched Jean and Lizzy place the things they had on a rock.

"I am. It hasn't always been easy for them." There was a sad note in his voice.

"My guess would be not for you either."

He gave her a wry smile and continued ahead of her. He called, "Girls, get your lifejackets on."

Both girls scrambled to the boat.

Cody put his things down beside the others and turned to her, taking what she held. "Thanks for asking me along. I could tell your heart wasn't in the invitation."

"The girls are right, everyone should experience a lobster bake when they have a chance. I'm glad you agreed to come. Really."

He sounded sincere. "I'm looking forward to seeing how this all works."

"Have you ever been out in a rowboat?" he asked.

"Nope."

"Thankfully it's a calm afternoon so we should have a good trip out and back. We aren't going far. You'll need to put on a lifejacket as well."

They walked to the boat. Cody reached inside and pulled out a lifejacket, handing it to her. While she put hers on, he did the same with one of his own and checked the girls. Stacey was glad she'd worn her windbreaker, her old jeans and canvas shoes. Her evening walk had become an unexpected adventure.

Jean and Lizzy scrambled over the side of the boat and took a seat on a bench in the middle.

"Get in," Lizzy called. "Daddy will push us out."

Stacey looked at Cody. "You don't need my help?"

He gave her a pointed look. "Just have a seat."

She did, taking the small one up front, facing the girls and the back of the boat. They were soon sliding into the water. Cody hopped in with the litheness of an athlete at the last second, keeping his feet dry. He took the bench seat in the back of the boat and picked up the oars. Moving into a rhythmic pull, with determination, he had them out in the water in no time. With skill he turned them around so that he was facing out to the horizon.

Since Stacey faced him she couldn't stop herself from appreciating the flexing of his body as he heaved the water forward. The tendons in his neck rose, making him look more masculine. This type of exercise must have something to do with creating his firm chest. She was staring, but she couldn't help herself.

"We're going out there to where those red and green floats are. Our pots are tied to them. Those are our colors so the lobster fishermen know not to pick them up."

Stacey pulled her attention away from Cody long enough to crane her neck around to see the bobbing buoys behind her, which were large enough to see clearly.

"Hey, you okay?"

She met Cody's gaze, hoping her expression revealed nothing.

"You're not scared, are you?" He was watching her closely. "You do know how to swim?"

Stacey swallowed. "Uh…no. I mean yes. I'm just enjoying the scenery."

His eyes widened slightly, holding a questioning gleam before his lips curved at a rakish angle. "Really?"

Realizing what she'd said, heat as hot as a summer day shot up her neck. Had he thought she'd meant something else by the way she'd been looking at him? Maybe she should jump overboard! She stared at Maple Island behind him instead of his impressive chest. "Yes, really."

Cody's soft chuckle carried over the sound of the water lapping against the boat.

Soon he pulled alongside the first float and Jean grabbed it. Cody quickly brought the oars into the boat and took it from her. Hauling the rope attached to the buoy hand over hand, he brought the pot to the surface.

Stacey held her breath in anticipation. The girls' eyes were glued to the water.

"I bet we've got a big one." Lizzy's voice was filled with excitement.

"It's a little early in the season so I hope we have at least one." Cody continued to work.

"We'll get one, Daddy. You know where to put the pots."

Stacey watched him, grinning. It was nice to hear a child have that much confidence in her parent. Stacey hadn't felt the same about hers. If her father had been around, would she have adored him? She'd never know. "Why, Dr. Brennan, you're a lobsterman as well as a surgeon. Who would have thought?"

He gave her a quick acknowledging look before his attention returned to the job at hand.

The girls were inching toward the side of the boat the pot was on.

"Girls, stay put. We don't want to turn Stacey over. Better yet, move to the other side while I'm getting this up."

"Where do you want me?" Stacey asked.

"You just stay put. If you see the boat dipping too far to one side, then adjust a little."

Stacey had next to zilch experience with boats but she could do that.

Cody continued to lift the square metal cage until it sat on the rim of the boat, with water sloshing through the holes until it was completely out of the water. Cody's thighs were wet now, defining the strength of them.

"Daddy, we got one. We've got one," Lizzy squealed, half-standing.

The greenish-brown crustacean remained secure in the middle of the pot.

Stacey reached over and placed a hand on Lizzy's shoulder, easing her to the bench.

"Well, it looks like at least one of us is going to eat tonight." Cody's broad smile beamed at them each in turn. He placed the pot in the bottom of the boat, sat and picked up the oars once more. The girls' attention remained on the lobster as Cody rowed to the next buoy. Minutes later he came alongside it.

"I'll get it." Stacey reached over the side. Grabbing the buoy then the rope, she hung on as the boat continued to move forward. When the slack was gone it jerked her forward and onto the bottom of the boat, but she continued to clutch the rope.

"You all right?" Cody's concern was clear in both his voice and face. He started over the girls' bench toward her.

"I'm fine. Give me a second and I'll have this trap… uh…pot out of the water." She righted herself by sliding into a sitting position. Tugging, she felt the pot lift off the sea bottom. Slowly she drew the rope up. Her shoulders burned.

When she started to stand Cody called, "Don't! You might go over. You're doing great. Just keep at it. It should almost be up."

Seconds later the top of the pot surfaced.

Jean leaned over the side. "You have two. Two!" Her smile went from ear to ear.

"Our best catch ever." Cody sounded as excited as his daughter as he sat as far to one side as he could as a counterbalance to the extra weight. Stacey grabbed the pot.

"Let me see." Lizzy moved to Stacey's side of the boat.

"Hold on a minute. Let's let Stacey get it into the boat. Give her some room."

Stacey pulled it up and over the side until it sat on one end in the bottom of the boat. The process wasn't nearly as effortless as Cody had made it look. She had gotten wetter than him. Yet she smiled triumphantly. "I'm going to get to eat tonight after all."

"That you are." His smile was the one that she liked so much.

"We all are." Jean moved the pot around, laying it down as she gave the lobsters a closer look.

"You're right." Cody picked up the oars again and started pulling them toward the shore.

The return was much faster with the help of the current.

When they reached the sand, Stacey jumped out with the rope in hand having given up on trying to keep her shoes or clothes dry. She hurried to the pole to secure the boat. Cody hopped over the side, pulling the boat up on the shore. He then lifted Lizzy out. Jean handed him one lobster pot then the other before he assisted her.

"We need to get the fire going, girls." Cody tied off the pots so that the lobsters remained in the water. "Go out and scrounge up some driftwood. Think small pieces first."

Jean and Lizzy scampered away in opposite directions.

Stacey watched them with a smile. "What can I do?"

"All we're going to need is a good fire. Have you ever built one?"

She threw her shoulders back and let him see her indignation. "I'll have you know I'm a professional at that. When you live part of your life in different spots all over the world you learn some survival skills."

"Well, all right, Ms. Professional Fire Builder, let's see what you've got."

Getting down on her hands and knees, Stacey scooped out a hole in the sand. With that done, she pulled some paper off the roll Cody had brought down. By that time both the girls had returned with kindling-size driftwood. "Now run and get some larger pieces and we'll soon have this fire blazing."

Jean and Lizzy took off.

"Hey," she said over her shoulder to Cody, "do you have those matches?"

He sat the large boiler he'd filled with water down next to the fire pit and dug into his vest pocket, bringing out a small box of matches. Her hand brushed his as she took them. Awareness shot through her. Her hands shook as she tried to strike one.

"If we're going to have cooked lobster then we're going to need a fire, Ms. Professional Fire Starter. Do you need my help?"

Stacey took a stabilizing breath. She could do this. Leaning close to the paper, she struck another match and the paper and kindling caught fire. "I've got this."

Cody grinned. "I see that."

The girls returned with their arms full and dropped the wood on the ground. Stacey added pieces and they soon had a roaring fire. Standing, she stretched the kinks out of her muscles. She glanced at Cody. Their gazes met for a moment.

Jean called, "Daddy, put the pot on."

He hesitated a moment before turning away to pick up the boiler and carefully place it over the fire. "It'll take a few minutes to boil."

"What do we do now?" Stacey was enjoying this adventure more than she had anticipated.

"We need to set the table." Cody picked up the roll of paper and opened it across the ground.

"We're going to eat on that?" Stacey looked at his arrangement in amazement.

"Yep. Jean, you want to help me with the lobster?" He handed Stacey a small metal bowl and the stick of butter on his way to the boat. "Will you put the bowl near the fire so it'll melt?"

Stacey did as he asked, aware of Lizzy watching.

Soon Cody and Jean returned with a lobster pot carried between them. "We'll get this one in then go get the other two." Pulling heavy gloves on, Cody removed the lobster.

"Watch the pinchers, Daddy. You know what happened last time." Jean moved to stand beside him as if she planned to protect him.

"What happened?" Stacey really wanted to know. To be included in the shared story within this close-knit family. She had so few stories of her own with her family. What family? She only had her mother. They had never really been a family like Cody and his girls were. She always missed that.

"Daddy forgot his gloves and tried to get the lobster out without them. It pinched the end of his finger and he danced around."

Both girls giggled while Stacey laughed.

"It hurt." Cody sounded pitiful, but he smiled.

"It was so funny." For once Jean appeared happy and her age instead of older than her years.

"You can see I didn't forget them this time. I left them in the boat, so I'd have them close."

Stacey grinned. "I can see it now in the papers: *'Eminent surgeon loses finger to lobster.'*"

"Funny, very funny. If you're not careful, you might not get to eat."

Right now, Cody was nothing like the uptight, humorless and far too serious doctor she'd first met. She liked this guy. Really liked him.

Lizzie came to sit beside Stacey, crossing her legs. When Cody held the lobster over the boiling pot, Lizzy clutched Stacey's arm. "Oh, this is the part I don't like."

"Why not?" Stacey searched Lizzy's stricken face.

"Because the lobster cries." She put her hands over her ears.

Cody lowered the lobster into the pot. Soon a small keening filled the air.

Stacey wrinkled up her nose and twisted her mouth. "That is bad." She covered her ears.

"Well, well, well, such a tender heart." Cody had leaned close so that she had no trouble hearing him. "You don't flinch at the sight of blood but you're sympathetic to a lobster." His low chuckle rolled through her, leaving behind a lovely warmth.

They all watched the pot for a few minutes then Cody pronounced, "It's time for this one to come out."

"How do you know?" Stacey asked.

"When it turns red." Jean's tone implied that anyone should know that.

Cody picked up tongs, reached into the pot and pulled out the lobster. Giving it a gentle shake, he placed it on the paper. "Don't touch. It'll still be too hot." He opened the bag of tiny potatoes and dumped them in the pot. "Jean, let's go get the other two."

His daughter didn't hesitate, slipping her hand into

her father's larger one. It was a sweet picture, one that Stacey had never experienced with her own father. Shaking off the morose thought, she watched them return with the second pot. Was Jean afraid she might lose her father like she had her mother? What was the real story about Cody's wife?

They returned and set the trap down. She and Lizzy considered the lobsters. One of them was missing a claw.

"What happened?" Stacey asked no one in particular.

"They get in fights when sharing space." Cody picked up the lobster. "This one lost." He unceremoniously dropped that one and then the other into the water.

Once again Lizzie covered her ears, and Stacey joined her. Cody was wearing one of those spectacular smiles she rarely had a glimpse of. The one that made her stomach flutter. When the lobsters were done he lifted them out. He then dumped the water, saving the potatoes. Those he poured out onto the paper. "Stacey, would you please get the butter?"

She did and placed it on the paper as well. He sat on the ground and the girls joined him around the paper "table." Stacey took her spot. Cody reached for the cans of drink and handed one to each of them. Next, he picked up one of the lobsters, removed its head then, using the knife, sliced it down the middle of the back. Pulling the meat from the tail, he halved it and gave a piece to Jean and the other to Lizzy.

He picked up another and waggled it at her. "Do you want to do the honors or shall I?"

"Let me have a try." Stacey reached for the lobster.

"Figures. Is there anything you won't try?"

Stacey looked directly at him. "I try to stay open to new things."

He raised a brow, his gaze not leaving hers as he handed her the lobster.

She clenched her jaw as she twisted the head off, following his example. Handing the body to Cody, she waited while he sliced it open and returned it.

"Here, dip it in the butter." Jean pushed the bowl toward her.

Stacey did as Jean suggested then put the white meat into her month. "Mmm…" A rivulet of butter ran down her chin. "Wipe." She waved a hand in a *give me, give me* motion.

"Be still and I'll get it." Using a napkin, Cody caught the stream before it dripped onto her jacket.

Her gaze jumped to his. Her breaths came in jerks as if she had been running. Among all the men in the world, why did this one affect her so? Why did she let him? It had to stop. "May I have my own napkin?"

Cody pulled back as if rejected. Dismay filled her. She hadn't meant to sound so harsh. But they were becoming too easy with each other. She was being sucked into his world. Even worse, she liked it. But she didn't belong here. Had no experience with a real family.

Reaching beside him, he snagged a napkin and thrust it in her direction.

"Thanks."

"Daddy, my hair is getting in the way." With a messy hand Lizzy pushed the mass of hair that had slipped from the band.

"Scoot around this way and I'll fix it for you," Stacey offered.

"I'll get it." Cody moved to stand.

"Stacey can do it." Lizzy turned her back to Stacey. Cleaning her hands with her napkin, she brought the girl's hair under control.

Lizzy twisted around and studied her with unnerving intensity. "You'd be a good mommy."

"We already have a mommy," Jean announced in a flat tone.

The painful silence was broken when Cody said, "Girls, you need to eat. It's getting dark."

The rest of the meal revolved around finishing it. Done, they all pitched in to clean up.

Amazed, Stacey watched Cody roll what was left of the meal and any garbage in the paper and throw it on the fire. The rest of the stuff he dropped into the pot, including the empty drink cans. "Best clean-up job I've ever seen."

Looking pleased with her praise, he confessed, "I'll admit this is the easiest meal I cook. Jean, Lizzy, grab an armload and head for the house."

The girls did as he requested and were soon on their way up the path.

Stacey picked up the pot. "You're making great memories for them." What had made her say or think something like that? She knew nothing about making family memories, especially good ones. There were only a few in her childhood that would even measure up to the worth-remembering mark. Still, it was nice to know that even though the girls didn't have their mother, they could still have a happy life. Cody was doing all he could to make that happen.

"I hope so." He kicked sand over the fire, putting it out and filling the hole.

They walked in the direction of the house. "I know this is none of my business…" Stacey glanced over her shoulder to judge his reaction to her next words "… but I can't help wondering what happened with their mother."

Cody wasn't surprised Stacey had asked about Rachael. If he had learned anything in the last week it was that Stacey was forthright. She wouldn't go behind his back and ask others about his life. When there was something she wanted to know she would go to the source and she didn't beat around the bush.

That didn't mean he wanted to talk about Rachael. The subject still left him feeling sick and unsure. Guilt nagged at him when he thought of her. Still, there was something about Stacey that made him want to confide in her. Wanted her to understand him. Why he was the way he was.

"My ex-wife and I were college sweethearts. We had planned the perfect life together. She'd take care of the home and children and I would be a great surgeon. Give my children what I'd had as a child. A secure home with two parents who loved them. During our senior year she was in a horrible car crash that damaged her ankle and foot. After the initial surgery she went through physical therapy but was still in a lot of pain. There were more surgeries but she finally began to recover. At the end of my med-school years, she walked down the aisle on our wedding day without a limp and I believed that our world had righted itself."

He hated to voice this next part out loud. The misery of that time strangled him. "But for a long time she hid a huge secret. She was addicted to painkillers."

Stacey sucked in a breath. She stopped walking and faced him. "She must have hidden it well."

"She was a functional addict. Jean had already come along when I found out. I got Rachael help and I thought things were better. By the time I found out differently, Lizzy was on the way." He hesitated, the memories making him feel momentarily queasy. "During my residency I was working twenty-four and sometimes forty-eight hours straight. I couldn't keep an eye on her all the time. Mother helped out but it was still hard. What really brought things to a head was when I found a prescription pad missing. Rachael denied she took it but I know she did."

"Oh, Cody, what a nightmare."

He nodded his gratitude skyward, only to focus on Stacey's compassionate face. "Yeah, and I had this perfect life all planned out. Nothing about that time was perfect. My career was on the line. My marriage was dying a painful death and my girls needed at least one good parent. Rachael was crying out for help I couldn't give her."

"What about rehab?"

"Oh, she would break her heart, swearing she would stop, then go to rehab but check herself out early. That happened more than once. It took me over a year of documentation and being overseen by strangers to get full custody of the girls. A few months after that happened, Alex and I met and shared our woes. You know the rest of that story."

Stacey put a hand on his forearm. Thankfully there was no pity in her words when she said, "I'm sorry. I had no idea. I shouldn't have pried."

For some reason it had felt good to tell her. Outside

his parents and Alex he'd never discussed what he'd been through. Maybe it was knowing Stacey would only be around for a short period of time that had made the difference. She was here, he had spilled his ugly secret and she would carry it off with her to Ethiopia in a few weeks. Whatever the reason, it felt good to give voice to it. His shoulders felt lighter than they had been in years. He could take a breath.

"Do the girls ever see their mom?"

Cody moved toward the house again. "No. She's in California somewhere. Not even her parents are sure where she is."

"Oh." Stacey slowly followed.

"You can tell Jean has some memory of her. Lizzy doesn't. After I got custody we moved here for a new start. Jean is working through her issues with a help of a therapist. Soon she'll be old enough to fully understand about her mother."

"I'm sure you'll do the right thing when the time comes."

"Don't give me credit where it isn't due. I failed my wife and my girls for a time."

"But you're making it up to them." She continued up the path and climbed the porch steps before she looked back at him. "You're an okay guy, Dr. Brennan."

Cody joined her.

She patted his shoulder. "You're a good dad. You do what you can to give them a nice safe life. They're happy, sweet girls."

"I appreciate you saying that, but it doesn't make the ugliness they started out with go away."

"No, but you're slowly replacing those ugly memories with good ones. Not all children are given a second chance like yours have had." She headed into the house before he had a chance to ask about that wistful note in her voice.

The girls were waiting for them in the kitchen. "It's time for a bath and bed," Cody told them.

Not surprisingly, Lizzy whined, "Do we have to? I wanted Stacey to stay and play a game."

Stacey shook her head. "I can't tonight. I need to be going home. Bye, Jean."

"Bye." There was no warmth in Jean's response.

It didn't matter. She wouldn't be around long enough that Jean should care. But would she treat every woman Cody brought around the same way? Would Jean always yearn for something she didn't have, like *she* had?

"Now head on up," he ordered. "I'll be along to check on you in a few minutes."

"That's my cue to find the door." Stacey put the pot in the sink then walked down the hall to the front of the house. Cody followed her. At the door, she turned to him. "Thanks for the lobster experience. It was fun. I'll have a nice memory too."

"You're welcome. I'm glad you joined us." He meant that. Without thinking, his hands went to rest lightly on her waist. It felt really good to touch her. Their gazes locked.

She inhaled sharply and went stock still.

Did it really surprise her that he would want to kiss her? Was she honestly unaware of how appealing she was? "I know this is a bad idea on so many levels," he murmured, his head moving closer. "You are a colleague. I promised myself I wouldn't bring anyone into my girls' lives who wasn't staying for the long haul. Yet along came you."

His lips met hers. So delicious. Tender, yielding. Perfect. He wanted more.

Stacey pushed him away. "Don't," she commanded. "We can't do this." She opened the door and hurried out.

He watched her blend into the evening shadows. Their kiss had been too short, only leaving him longing for more. A feeling, heavy like a cold wet blanket, hung over him. He wanted Stacey but he'd learned the hard way that there were other considerations in his life that frequently overrode his own wishes.

CHAPTER FOUR

ON WEDNESDAY MORNING, Stacey took a deep breath and knocked on Cody's office door. It was time for rounds. She hadn't seen him for the last two days. He'd been in Boston both mornings, doing small repair surgeries on the senator's son. He'd said she wasn't needed there, but he wanted her to see the patients at the clinic for him.

After her rejection of his parting kiss, she wasn't sure what her reception would be. She shouldn't have gone with him to the beach. Shouldn't have put either one of them in that position. More than once she'd tried to say no but had given in anyway. Now things would be strained between them. She didn't need that, even if she was only around for two and a half more weeks.

The time she had spent with Cody and the girls had been the best she'd experienced in a long time. For just a little while she'd been a part of a family. And she'd liked it too well. It wasn't a good idea for her or for Cody and his girls to get too involved with each other. Still, she couldn't help herself. Growing up in a family had been all she'd wanted, to really belong somewhere.

Trepidation filled her. Would Cody want to talk about their kiss? She was likely making too big a deal out of it. After all his lips had barely touched hers. So

why couldn't she get it out of her mind? She briefly
brushed her bottom lip with a finger. She remembered
every second of his touch, the press of his firm mouth
against hers. It probably hadn't been as memorable for
Cody. In spite of herself, she wanted a chance at trying it again. She'd bet he could really curl her toes if
she gave him half a chance. But she wouldn't let that
happen. Couldn't.

At the sound of his "Come in," she stuck her head
around the door. Cody sat behind a large oak desk that
looked as if it was an antique.

"I'm ready to do rounds when you are." She couldn't
step any further into his space for fear her resolve
would slip.

He glanced up. "Okay. Give me another sec here."
Cody looked down again. "Come in and sit down. We
need to talk anyway."

Great. That wasn't what she wanted to do. But she
had no choice. How foolish would she look if she refused to talk to the man she worked for? She was trying to forget their kiss and them hashing it out wasn't
going to help that happen.

She took one of the two overstuffed chairs in front
of his desk. It should be against the law for a man to
look so attractive when doing nothing more than sitting
at his desk. Heaven help her, she was losing her mind.

Cody clicked a key then looked at her. "I just wanted
to let you know what's going to happen."

Her heart pounded. *Happen?* Between them?

"The senator's son is going to be moved out here
the day after tomorrow."

Relief, quickly followed by disappointment, washed
over her. She needed to focus. If she'd worried Cody

might have felt something after their kiss she had just been assured he hadn't. "Um, okay. I'll see that the paperwork is in order."

"Good. See it gets to Harborside Hospital. The boy will be doing physical therapy here and will need a couple more small surgeries when he has healed enough. I'll also need you to run point with his parents as well as any reporters they require you to respond to."

"Shouldn't you be the one to speak to the reporters?" She didn't do well with being in front of people. The thought of talking on TV struck her heart with terror.

Apparently that was evident on her face because Cody asked, "You don't like that idea?"

"Not at all."

"Why not?"

"I don't do public speaking." She wrung her hands in her lap.

Cody crossed his arms, leaned them on his desk and watched her with those amazing all-seeing chocolate eyes.

Stacey squirmed.

He said with slow emphasis, "You mean there's something in this world that you're afraid of? Who would have thought?"

Was he making fun of her? She sat straighter. Gripping the arms of the chair, she said, "I'll have you know I'm afraid of a number of things." *Like you not kissing me again.*

"I haven't seen it. If you're uncomfortable with anything to do with the reporters just let me know. As a general rule security will handle almost anything. The reporters know we put a high priority on protecting our patients' privacy. For the most part they leave us alone."

Cody sat back. "That being said, if the senator's son's history is any indication, I don't anticipate him being one of our easiest patients. So don't say I didn't give you fair warning."

"I can handle him."

"There's that confidence I was looking for." He grinned. "If there's anything you question or are not one hundred percent sure about, you can certainly run it past me first. I'll be putting him in a semi-private room instead of a private one. His parents probably won't like the idea, but he'll be busy feeling sorry for himself and I want him to work at getting better while he is here. If for no other reason than he wants to get away from his roommate. No lying around in his bed all day."

Stacey was impressed. Cody wasn't only thinking about his patient's physical well-being but his mental health as well. "I'll see that he gets a particularly ir-ritating roommate."

Cody smiled. "Good thinking." He pushed back from the desk. "Let's get the rounds done. It's dance night for the girls."

"Don't sound so excited." She stood and headed to-ward the door.

He joined her. "I have to admit it's the hardest night of the week. You really saved me last week. If you hadn't shared your booth with us at the bistro, I would've been there waiting for ages with two whiny girls on a school night. Not my idea of fun. I owe you."

They walked up the hall toward the patients' rooms.

"I had payback with that lobster dinner you gave me on Sunday." She pushed her hair out of the way to see him better. "You want me to go to the bistro again and save you a table tonight?" She was kidding but what if he took her seriously? Her goal was to put space between them, not see him more often.

He stopped at the room door of Alonso, the tennis star whose knee he had repaired the week before. "I don't think that'll be necessary."

She was glad to hear it.

Knocking, he then pushed the door open to see the room empty of tennis stars. He looked back at her. "Where is he?"

"This time of the day I bet he's in the community room. He likes to listen to Salty tell the twins stories."

They moved on up the hall.

"So, you have met Connor and Peyton Walsh?"

"Yeah, they're hard to miss. Cute kids. Really nice parents."

"It has been tough on them with their children both being hurt. But the twins are recovering well and should be going home soon. They've kind of become the clinic mascots."

"Well, it's testament to you and Alex that you guys decided early on that you'd save some beds for those who couldn't afford the clinic and take care of the locals. You two are good guys."

"Hey, don't be putting me on a pedestal because I can guarantee I'll fall."

Did he really think that little of himself? From what she'd seen, he was almost perfect. Almost too good to be true. "I'm sure it wouldn't be far if you did."

Cody glanced at her in a doubtful manner. "Thanks."

She shouldn't have said that. Her mouth was always getting her into trouble. Even their conversations should remain impersonal.

As if he didn't like the direction of their exchange either, he said, "Alonso decided that he would recover faster here at the clinic. That way he would be able to stay out of the media spotlight for a while longer. It's also easier to do the rehab without coming over daily on the ferry."

She whispered, "I've heard that more than one famous person has hidden out here. Want to share who?"

"Nope, and we like to refer to it as recovering." He mimicked her low tone.

The sound made her shiver inside. What would it be like to have him whisper to her like that as they made love? No, that was no place for her mind to go. She swallowed. "Aw, got it."

He stopped and looked at her before he said, "I thought Alonso might be the person to put the senator's son in with but I've thought better of it."

Stacey gave him a wry smile. "I'm thinking Salty might be the best choice."

Cody nodded. "I think you might be right. He will certainly be able to hold his own with the unhappy teen. And since Salty's here for only a few more days of observation and IV antibiotics, neither one of them will have time to kill the other off. Philomena will be here to referee. She isn't going to let anything happen to Salty."

"It's sweet."

"Salty isn't sweet."

"No, but the fact that Mrs. Kerridge-Bates and Salty can find love after all these years is. Especially since they're so different."

Cody gave her a narrowed-eye look. "I wouldn't have ever taken you for a romantic."

Was she? She didn't believe in happily ever after for herself, but she did like to see others achieve it. She shrugged. "We all have our off days."

They visited two more patients before going to the community room in search of Alonso. He was there. Salty was surrounded by him, the twins and a few other patients.

"Hey, there, Connor and Peyton. You two look like you are doing well." Cody greeted them.

"Hi, Dr. Brennan."

"So, what's this group up to today?" Cody looked from Salty to Alonso and then to the twins.

"We've just been listening to stories." The twins looked at Salty with nothing short of hero-worship.

"Your mom and daddy coming in this evening?" Cody asked.

"Mom is. Dad has to work again." Peyton fiddled with a string on her shirt.

Stacey couldn't help but feel sorry for the twins. They had been at the clinic for too long.

"How're you feeling, Salty?" Cody asked.

"He'd feel much better if he'd stop holding court and rest more," a gruff but caring female voice said behind them.

They all looked toward Philomena, who was shuffling in using a walker.

"Philly thinks she should run my life," Salty grumbled. "Where I'd really like to be is off on my boat."

"Not until you're completely well this time." Philly sat in a chair beside him. "I'm too old to worry all the time."

Stacey didn't miss him touching her hand for a second. They cared about each other more than they let on. What would it be like to have that type of connection with someone? She glanced at Cody. A girl could dream.

"Sorry to interrupt but, Alonso, can I have a look at your incision sites?" Cody asked.

The young man turned in his chair and pulled up his knit pants above his knee.

"They look good," Cody confirmed. "How's the physical therapy going?"

"Well, I think I'll be better than ever on the court." Alonso sounded pleased with his progress. "Thanks, Doc. I wouldn't be this far along without you."

Cody lowered his head in a humble gesture. "You've done most of the work."

How like Cody. It was nice to work in a place with quality care and excellent doctors who weren't full of self-importance. Stacey glanced at him again. Also, with devoted doctors. If she wasn't careful she'd move from admiration straight into the hero-worship he had already warned her about.

A few minutes later she and Cody left the community room. He headed down the hall in the opposite direction from the one she took. "Stacey."

She stopped and turned. Had he forgotten to tell her something? "Yes?"

He stepped closer. "I…uh…wanted to apologize about the other night. I stepped over the line. It won't happen again."

Here it was. What she'd been dreading but had thought by now wouldn't come up. "It's okay." She lowered her voice. "It's nothing against you. I just don't think it's a good idea for us to get involved."

"I agree."

He did? Her chest ached with regret. She shouldn't feel that way. Didn't she want him to agree? Protecting her heart was the priority. She was a short-term girl and he was a forever man. They would never work as a couple.

Neither of them spoke as a nurse passed by.

"Then I guess there's nothing more to say." Stacey forced a smile to her lips.

He watched her for a moment before he said, "I have to get the girls."

Cody had mulled the problem over for a couple of days now, trying to figure out what to do. He was attracted to his nurse. So much so that Stacey consumed almost all of his thoughts. Maybe it was because he couldn't have her. Or it could just be because he'd been without a woman so long that anyone who showed him any attention appealed. Whatever it was, it had to stop. Seeing her every day didn't help. He'd taken to counting the hours until Stacey left the island. At least then he would have some peace of sorts.

She wasn't a woman he needed to bring any further into his life. She already fit too well. His girls liked her too much. Like sunshine after the dark, Stacey added light to his world. She had been open and giving with his girls and they didn't need to grow attached to someone who would be leaving them soon. Still, the need to get to know her, have her, gnawed at him. He just had to live through it for a couple of more weeks and then the problem would be solved for him.

He'd just finished surgery and spoken to the family when she came up beside him. Without speaking, they walked to his office to finish some paperwork she needed to discharge a patient. Once again, he would be alone with her.

She'd remained all business since his apology, which both helped and maddened him. He couldn't think straight when she was around, especially when she came close enough that he caught her scent.

She gave him a curious look. "Hey, what's bothering you?"

Cody glanced at her. Did she really know him well enough to recognize when something was disturbing him? Was he that transparent or had she been watching him closely enough to learn his moods? He wasn't sure he liked either idea. Should he tell her? He sighed. No, that wasn't going to happen. He'd find something else to say.

"It's not that big a deal."

"It must be something because you've been… I don't know…preoccupied the last two days."

He huffed, giving her the only excuse he could come up with. "The girls need costumes for Founder's Day. And the worst part is they need to be home-made. They have a dress rehearsal on Wednesday." It might sound stupid but it was a very real problem he'd been struggling with whenever he could get his mind off her. Even better, he didn't have to admit the real reason he was acting out of the norm—his battle to not kiss her whenever they were alone, which was far too often for his peace of mind.

"And this is a problem why?"

His arms went wide with his palms up. "Because I have nothing. Nothing. No ideas. No capability or even the desire to do it."

She actually laughed at him. Doubled over with it.

Between gasping breaths, she said, "The super-dad is undone by costumes."

"It's not funny." He stalked into his office. At least being mildly irritated with her made him stop thinking about grabbing her and kissing her for all of a minute.

"No, it's not. I'm sorry I'm making fun of you. Would you like me to help?"

Stacey had actually offered that after their "discussion." She had made it clear they shouldn't get mixed up in each other's personal lives. Had she changed her mind? Whether she had or hadn't wasn't important. He could use her help. Should he accept her offer? She had said she liked to dress up. Surely she had some skills in that area. The girls had to have outfits.

The only women he knew who might help were already busy. Maggie had her hands full with Jake. Fleur was running the show so she didn't have time to take care of his girls. He probably could ask Brigid Brady from the bistro, but she'd expect more from him than he was interested in giving. Stacey was offering, and he was definitely interested in what she might expect of him in return.

He hesitated a moment longer but couldn't think of another choice he had. "Would you, please? Getting costumes together is not in my wheelhouse. Even buying them in a store gives me the hives but the idea of coming up with them on my own makes me want to pull my hair out." He sounded pathetic even to his own ears.

Stacey continued to grin. "Little dramatic, aren't you? You've convinced me, if not for you, then for the girls. What are they supposed to wear?"

"They need to dress like children of the historical

period. You know, dresses or just something that's easy but along that line. Remember me, that 'no ideas' guy?"

She chuckled. He didn't appreciate being laughed at, but he did enjoy the sound of her laughter. When it subsided she nodded. "Okay. When's a good time for me to see the girls?"

"I don't expect you to do it by yourself. I can help." He winced. "With some guidance." He pushed the door to his office open. "I hate to take up your time off but being Saturday tomorrow, the girls are also free—afternoon would be the best."

"I'll be at your house at three. Does that work for you all?"

"It does. I'll try to have what the girls already own out for you to look at. Give you somewhere to start."

With great relief on two levels, Cody watched her leave his office a few minutes later. One, that someone else would be organizing costumes for his girls and, two, that Stacey was no longer standing so intimately close to him. He fisted his hands. Her scent still hung in the air.

Stacey arrived at Cody's house the next day right on three. She was sure she was making a mistake by becoming further involved in Cody's life. For a moment there yesterday she'd feared he would swoop her up into his arms when she'd offered to help him.

She knocked on the front door. Seconds later there was the sound of feet running before the door opened and Lizzy stood there with a grin. Behind her was Cody. He wore a pullover sweater with a T-shirt beneath, jeans and socks. An unsure smile covered his lips.

She shivered. Was she missing something?

Lizzy pulled on her hand. "Come on. We have to go upstairs."

Stacey looked up to see Jean standing on the stairs. "Hi."

Jean quietly said, "Hi."

"Lizzy, let's give Stacey a chance to come in." Cody brushed Stacey's back with his arm as he reached to close the door. She had no doubt it was unintentional but that didn't stop her body from reacting. She'd made a huge mistake by coming here. Why had she opened her big mouth and suggested she help them? Because Cody had looked so pitiful and she'd been unable to stop herself from volunteering her talents. Or resist the opportunity to be a part of his family just once more before she left them behind forever. It was nice to feel needed, valued.

"How're you?" he asked, as if he really wanted to know.

"I'm good." She looked at Jean again who had come further down the stairs. "I'm ready to get started on costumes. How about you, girls?"

"Better you than me," Cody muttered.

Stacey smiled. "I figured you'd think that."

"The girls have already gone through some of their clothes and put out things that you might be able to use. I apologize for the state of their rooms."

Stacey started toward the stairs. "No problem. We'll see what they have."

"Let's go." Lizzy pulled on her hand. "This way."

Jean climbed the stairs and she and Lizzy followed. Stacey looked back at Cody, who followed them up. His brows were in a V of concern at the bridge of his nose. She grinned. "Don't worry. I've got this."

He gave her a quizzical look. "You sure?"

"Positive."

On the landing at the top of the stairs, Stacey stopped. "How about we start with you, Jean?"

She stood inside a doorway. "Okay."

Stacey followed her into the room. It was decorated a bright yellow. "Wow, what a pretty room."

Cody moved to sit in a chair in the corner, out of the way.

Jean gave her a slight smile and looked at Cody. "Daddy let me pick the color."

Stacey wasn't surprised. Cody loved his girls and wanted to make them happy. "Let's see what you've got here. I found a picture of what you need to look like on the internet. Do you girls have any boots? Maybe rubber ones? You know, the kind you wear in the snow?"

"They do," Cody said.

Jean ran to the closet and returned with black boots.

"Perfect."

"I have some too," Lizzy confirmed.

"Great." Stacey ruffled her hair. "Then you can wear yours as well. Now for dresses. Let's see what we have here." Stacey looked through the clothes that were all topsy-turvy on the bed then turned to the closet. There she found a dress with long sleeves and would hang below Jean's knees. Stacey held it up. "I think this might do. Jean, would you put it on with your boots?"

The entire time she was working with the clothes she felt Cody watching her. She glanced up to confirm it. His dark look didn't waver. "Jean, have your dad help you." Maybe with Cody having something to do he wouldn't have time to make her feel self-conscious.

"While you do that, Lizzy and I are going to see if

we can find something for her. Lizzy, how about show-ing me to your room?"

The child skipped out of the room and down the hall. Stacey couldn't help but like the girls. They'd had a hard start in life but were pleasant children. Jean still hadn't warmed up to her but that didn't matter. It was even better that way. If she did, it would just make it that much harder for both of them when Stacey had to leave.

The girls' bedrooms were side by side and they shared a bathroom. Lizzy's room was blue and done in what Stacey guessed was a theme from her favor-ite cartoon show. Clothes were spread everywhere in there as well.

On the floor Stacey found a dress similar to Jean's and held it up. "This should do. Lizzy, will you put this on? And your boots."

She was in the process of removing her shirt when Stacey turned around. Jean had entered the room. "Why, Jean, you look great. All we have to do now is find you an apron, collar and head covering." Lizzy was having trouble pulling her dress over her head and Stacey stepped over to help. "Now, what can we use for collars? Do you girls have any white scarves?"

"I might have a couple," Cody said from the door-way.

Lizzy gave her a perplexed look "Scarf?"

"You know, Lizzy. The kind Daddy wears when he's going to an important meeting when it snows."

"I know where those are." Lizzy shot out of the room, her boots slapping against the wood floor.

"Wait, Lizzy, I'll get them," Cody called.

Jean shot by her, going after Lizzy and Cody.

Stacey followed more slowly. She stopped in the doorway of a spacious bedroom overlooking the back of the house. A wide bed faced a picture window framing a beautiful view of the ocean. There was a sitting area that included a TV and desk. On another wall was a chest of drawers.

Cody was looking through the top drawer of the chest. He pulled out a scarf with an air of triumph. He looked at her. "Will this do?"

"I believe so."

Jean joined Lizzy beside Cody. "Is there one for me?" She considered her father expectantly.

Cody pulled out another one. "Back up, girls, and let Stacey do her thing. She's the one with the plan."

All three of them turned to her with *now what?* expressions on their faces.

"They go around your neck. The ends can be tucked inside your dresses." She hadn't moved from the doorway.

"You *can* come in." Cody's voice held a hint of humor.

Still Stacey hesitated. If she did, she was entering his personal space, the forbidden land. Even with the girls there it filled her with naughty anticipation. As if she were entering a place of excitement and danger. She refused to let him see that. "I know." Taking a deep breath, she walked toward them. As innocent as the reason was, she was still in Cody's bedroom. She looked around. It would be the one and only time.

Cody's gaze remained on hers as she came toward him. What was he thinking? Anything near her own thoughts? No, she'd made it clear the other night and again in the hallway of the clinic that she wouldn't allow anything to happen between them. But had she really meant it? Had he accepted it?

Jean handed her a scarf. "Do mine first."

Stacey blinked, her focus shifting to the eight-year-old. That was good. She had to quit thinking about Cody. Taking the scarf, she wrapped it around Jean's neck, tucked the ends into her dress then fluffed it out around her neck. Standing back, she looked at her handiwork. "You're starting to look like a real Pilgrim girl."

"My turn," Lizzy cried.

Stacey did the same with her scarf. Done, she said, "Now we need to find you each an apron." She turned to Cody. "Do you have any aprons in the kitchen?"

"Are you kidding?" he croaked. "Never use them."

"Figures." She looked around the room. "What can we use?" She pursed her lips in thought. A slow grin formed on her lips. She snapped her fingers. "Got it." She looked at Cody. "I'm not sure you're going to like this."

He took a step back. "What?"

"I need a couple of your white dress shirts."

"Are you going to cut them up?" He sounded horrified at the idea.

She grinned. "No, but they may take some wear and tear."

His chin drew back and he narrowed his eyes, looking unsure. "Okay, I guess."

The girls whooped and ran for the door. They soon returned, each with a shirt in hand.

Cody's eyes widened and his brows rose.

"There a problem?" Stacey asked, standing beside him.

"Those look like my very best shirts."

She giggled. Cody looked at her. His eyes sparkled and she wasn't certain why but a hot spot formed in her belly in response.

"Here." Lizzy thrust the one she held at Stacey. Jean did the same.

"What're we going to do with them?" Jean asked.

"Come over here and I'll show you." Stacey moved to the bed. Not one of her better ideas but she was left no choice but to follow through. Laying the shirt across the bedspread, she buttoned it up completely. She then flipped it over and smoothed the wrinkles out. What would it be like to do this while Cody was wearing it? She shook that pulse-raising idea out of her head. Folding the collar down, she rolled the shirt tightly past the shoulders.

Cody groaned.

She glanced at him.

"My shirts will never be the same."

Stacey grinned. "You're the one who asked for my help."

He winced. "I did."

"Okay, Jean. Turn around." When she did so, Stacey adjusted the shirt so that the buttons faced inward then tied the sleeves at Jean's back. "Okay, you can turn around." Jean did so, and Stacey said with arms wide in a theatrical pose, "Ta-da."

Jean had a genuine smile on her face.

"Do mine now," Lizzy said.

Stacey started on the other shirt.

Cody watched over her shoulder. "I have to admit this is pretty creative. I'm impressed."

"You doubted me?" She looked at him.

"Not really."

Having male support was a new experience for her.
Stacey rather liked Cody's faith in her. She tied Lizzy's
"apron" on. "I believe we have two original settlers.
Stand over there so your dad and I can see you."

The girls did as they were told with smiles on their
faces.

Stacey twirled a finger. "Turn around for us."

The girls did.

"You two look great." Cody nodded, his relief evident. "Thanks, Stacey. I would have never come up
with this."

"You're welcome, but we still have something missing." She snapped her fingers. "I meant to bring my
old hat. I can go get it."

"I'm afraid that will have to wait for now. I have a
Founder's Day meeting in a few minutes." He clapped
his hands. "Girls, we've already taken too much of
Stacey's time. Lucy is expecting you at her sleepover
party."

Jean wrinkled her nose. "But we need to finish our
costumes first."

Stacey put a hand on her shoulder. "I'll work on your
head covering while you're gone and have it ready for
you. Now, let's take those outfits off and keep them
safe. It sounds like you have a party to go to."

With her help and Cody's, they changed.

"Go put your regular clothes on, girls. We've got to
go," Cody encouraged.

Stacey helped Cody lay the clothing neatly on the
chair at his desk. He placed the "aprons" just so and
the boots beside them with great care. "I don't want
anything to happen to these between now and when

they need to use them. I hope I can get it all on them correctly."

"I'm sure you can but if you need me to come help, let me know." The offer came out of her mouth as though it had a mind of its own. She had to stop saying things like that. Getting more and more deeply involved in Cody's life wasn't her plan. It wasn't until they were done that she registered she was alone with him in his bedroom.

His voice dropped and he touched her hand briefly, sending a ripple throughout her body. "Thanks for helping me out. For that I'll always be indebted to you."

She stepped out of touching distance. "I'm not helping you to make you feel you owe me anything."

"I know that. You're not that kind of person. Still, I'm grateful." His eyes filled with an emotion she didn't want to put a name to. "Stacey, I—"

"We're ready to go," Lizzy announced from the doorway. Jean stood behind her, watching closely.

Cody retreated, his unfinished statement lingering in the air. Stacey desperately wanted to know what he'd been going to say while at the same time feared it. "Girls, what do we say to Stacey?"

"Thank you," they chorused.

Stacey smiled. "You're very welcome."

"Jean and Lizzy, get your overnight bag and go get in the car. Buckle up." The girls followed his orders. Soon the stomping of their feet filled the air as they went down the stairs.

Cody stopped her from following them with a hand on her arm. "Stacey—"

"You don't have to thank me again. I was glad to do it."

"That wasn't what I was going to say."

She made herself meet his unwavering gaze. "What?"

Cody studied her for a second as if unsure. "You know, you really are special." With that he left her alone in his bedroom.

Heat rushed through her. What would it be like to hear those words from his lips all the time? That wasn't a dream she should be having. Cody's life wasn't the one for her. This was just a temporary interlude.

CHAPTER FIVE

CODY ARRIVED HOME a few hours later to a house that was too quiet. The girls didn't often spend the night away and when they did he was usually gone himself. He'd never thought much about being lonely until now. Lizzy and Jean had been his whole world for years but somehow Stacey had stepped into it and he was starting to ask himself if he needed more in his life.

She brought warmth and laughter to his world. Being around her had him feeling things he'd not felt in a long time. He was excited to wake in the mornings. Not until Stacey had he realized he had been living on autopilot. He would miss her teasing and quick smiles when she left for Ethiopia. That left him feeling oddly dejected.

A knock on the front door brought him out of his musing. He opened it to find Stacey standing there.

"Hey, I hope I'm not interrupting but I finished these and I thought Jean and Lizzy would want them as soon as they got home in the morning." She held up two strips of white.

He gave them a peculiar look, trying to figure out what they were. Had she stopped by to see him knowing the girls wouldn't be there?

"They're bonnets. Don't you remember?" She sounded as if she wanted to shake him to get him to answer.

He was still wrapped up in the surprise and pleasure of seeing her again. "Yeah, but isn't there more to them than that?"

She harrumphed. "Sorry. Not. Pilgrims didn't wear much headgear."

He nodded. "If you say so."

She extended her hand, offering the fabric to him. "Well, I'd better go."

He took them from her, his fingers brushing hers. Awareness rippled through him. The impulse to grab her and pull her into his arms ran through his mind but he didn't want to scare her away. The girls weren't there so he didn't have to worry about them becoming any more attached to Stacey. This was just a chance for some time alone with her when it didn't involve work or his children. As a grown man he could deal with the fallout when she was gone. "I was just going to have a bowl of ice cream. Would you like to join me?"

She gave the question more thought than it required. He began to worry she wouldn't accept. "That sounds good to me. Sure."

"Good. Then why don't you come in." He stood back, giving her space.

Stacey grinned at him. "And I was starting to think you might make me eat it on your front stoop."

"Are you questioning my manners?" He narrowed his eyes at her as he grinned before he closed the door.

"It's not my place to question the doctor," she cooed.

He laughed. "Yeah, right. You do that regularly."

She led the way to the kitchen. "I don't think we remember things the same way."

"I think my memory is just fine." He'd like to give her something to remember him by. Mercy, he needed to get his mind out of the bedroom and back in the kitchen. He hung the bonnets over a doorknob. Maybe he should stick his head in the freezer instead of taking the ice cream out of it.

Stacey took a seat on one of the bar stools. Cody was aware of her watching him. He was sure she wasn't missing a single move he made. It had been a long time since he'd been this unsettled by a woman. He found it both exciting and disconcerting. "Chocolate or vanilla?"

"Both, please."

"Both it is." He took the cartons out of the freezer then retrieved bowls from a cabinet and spoons from a drawer. "Scoop of each?"

"Two scoops chocolate and one vanilla." He looked at her and her gaze didn't waver.

Cody smiled. He was having fun. "You do like ice cream."

"Yes, I do. You offered just the right dessert."

His gaze caught hers. "I have others as well." She blinked. He let her off the hook and filled a bowl and pushed it over to her. Stacey eyed it. "Don't wait on me to get started."

She didn't hesitate before she filled her spoon. "Mmm…this hits the spot."

Cody watched her. He wished he could be the one who had put that look of pleasure on her face. He shook his head. If he didn't get control of his raging emotions he would jump her right here in the kitchen!

He filled his bowl and put the ice cream away before he joined her on a stool next to hers. They ate without any conversation for a few minutes with nothing but the sound of spoons against the bowls. It was a comfortable silence, the kind he'd not shared with another adult in a long time.

"You know, my mother and I always ate ice cream after one of her husbands left," Stacey said, as if she had forgotten he was there. She lifted another spoonful of ice cream to her lips. "I hadn't thought about that until now. I ate a lot after the second one left."

"You did?" Cody held his breath, hoping she would continue. He wanted to know more about her. Why she thought what she did. Why she had never settled down.

"Yeah. And cried a lot too."

"You loved him?"

"I did, but it didn't matter. He left anyway. I never saw him again." Hurt surrounded each of her words.

A boom of thunder and then a flash of lightning filled the air. The lights flickered then went out.

"We're in for a strong storm tonight. Springtime in New England." Cody went looking for the flashlight he kept in a drawer just for these occasions. There was another roll of thunder and then more lightning. "I'll have to check the roof shingles after this one."

He lit one of the candles, setting it on the bar. Even in the shadowy light he could see Stacey's stricken look and pale skin. Her eyes were squeezed closed. At the next flash of lightning they opened wide and held a wild look. She was terrified.

Taking her hand, he led her to the living room, encouraging her to sit on the sofa. He took a seat beside her and pulled her into his chest. Stacey didn't hesitate to bury her face in his shoulder. She shuddered at the next flash of lightning.

For a moment Cody's heart caught. This was what it should be like all the time. He needed someone he could share his life with, where he could be her safe port in a storm. Could that person be Stacey? Would she let him be that for her?

The flash of lightning, the boom of thunder and rain pelting the house made Stacey jerk and put her arms around Cody. She trembled, her heart pounding. From childhood she'd never been a fan of storms. Too often she been left alone during them. Her mother had forbidden her from coming to her room. Many nights she'd huddled in her bed, trembling with fear. More than once during her travels she'd had to deal with her anxiety over bad weather alone. She curled farther into the security Cody offered.

"Are you okay?" He snuggled her tighter.

The rumble of his deep voice where her ear lay against his chest somehow eased her panic. Would he think she was silly? A grown woman worried over a storm? "I don't like storms."

Lightning flashed again. She shook.

"I've got you. I won't let go."

She felt safe and secure next to Cody. For the first time in her life she could say that. Peeking out the window, she said, "You sure know how to give a girl a show."

He kissed her temple. "I can't take credit for putting this one on but thank you anyway."

Sometime later the lights flickered on again. Stacey slowly pulled away from Cody. "Hey."

"Hi. You better?"

She moved to stand but he held her back. "Yeah. I should go. I've embarrassed myself enough."

"You still look scared and it's still pouring. You're not going anywhere."

"I'll be fine. I've been taking care of myself in worse places and weather for years." She really should get out of Cody's arms. If not, she'd want to stay...too long.

At a distant roll of thunder he gave her a stern look. "Maybe so, but not when I've known about it. You're staying here tonight. You can have my bed."

What was he suggesting? Her eyes widened and she jerked back, shaking her head.

"I'll sleep down here on the couch," he assured her, bringing her back against him once again.

"I can't let you do that."

"Sure you can. You've been helping my girls all afternoon. I think it's the least I can do."

"I'm not sleeping in your bed!" She wanted to make that clear. Fear of the outside kept her there even discussing it.

He raised his hands in a gesture of defeat. "Okay. You can stay down here. I'll get you a blanket and something to sleep in. You know where the bath is. There should be clean towels under the cabinet. For now I'm going to stay right here with you until the storm eases."

"I'd like that." She burrowed closer to him.

Later, when nothing was left but heavy rain, Cody went to his room and returned with one of his T-shirts for her to sleep in, a blanket and a pillow that must have come off his bed. She silently groaned that she would be sleeping on where his head might have been.

He dumped his armload on the sofa. "Here you go. I still wish you would take my bed and let me sleep down here."

"I'm good here. Thanks. Goodnight."

Stacey woke to a bang in the kitchen and the smell of bacon. Her intention had been to be gone before Cody woke, but apparently she'd been more tired than she had thought. There was another cling-clang. *What was he doing?*

She had to admit it was nice to wake to the sounds of someone nearby. She'd spent so much time in private housing she rarely awakened to people. There was something soothing about knowing Cody was close. Her eyelids lowered.

A large hand cupped her shoulder and shook her gently. "Stacey, your breakfast is ready."

What? She'd gone to sleep again? Her eyes sprang open. Her gaze lifted to see Cody's smiling face. "Good morning, sleepyhead. Your breakfast is on the table when you're ready."

He left her. She untangled herself from the blanket and followed close behind him.

Cody headed for the kitchen and went around the bar to the stove. There he poured batter on the griddle. She looked at the table and found a plate stacked with perfectly round pancakes, a bottle of syrup and another plate with strips of bacon on it. There was also a pitcher of juice nearby.

"What did I do to deserve this?"

"This is my thank-you for helping with the costumes," Cody announced as he flipped pancakes. He was dressed in a tight T-shirt, well-worn jeans and wore no shoes. She'd never seen a sexier man.

"Haven't you already done that by letting me sleep on your couch?"

Cody looked at her and shrugged. His focus dipped to her chest. Heat shot through her. She'd forgotten she was wearing his thin T-shirt with no bra. Her breasts tingled as her nipples tightened, pushing against the soft fabric. She turned and headed out of the room but not before she saw the flash of disappointment in Cody's eyes. "Hey, Doc, your pancakes are burning."

Stacey grinned at his uttered oath as she grabbed her clothes from the living room and hurried to the bathroom. She quickly washed her face and used the new toothbrush he'd put out for her last night, put on her clothing and ran her fingers through her hair. Checking the mirror, she saw she'd done the best she could do.

When she returned he asked, "Did you sleep well?" His voice had gone deeper, and held a gravelly note.

"I did."

"You should have been in a bed." His gaze held hers.

She looked at him. Had he wanted to say *my* bed? She tingled low at her center. How would she have responded if he had asked her to sleep with him? He wouldn't have. He wasn't the type of man who would take advantage of a woman when she was scared. They said nothing more for a few seconds, just watched each other.

"Your breakfast is getting cold."

She went to the table and Cody pulled out her chair. "Thank you." When was the last time a male had done that for her? Stacey took her seat. Cody sat. She glanced at him. He was watching her and winked. The flutter in her stomach had nothing to do with hunger.

What would it be like to have breakfast with Cody all the time? To be treated as if she were special? Even her ex-fiancé had never made her feel as important as Cody did. What was she thinking? Cody was just being nice. Her life consisted of living all over the world and his was all about hearth and home.

They finished their breakfast with Cody having a second cup of coffee and her another glass of juice.

"I have to pick up the girls in a few minutes. I can drop you off at your cottage on my way to get them." Cody put his mug down and stood.

"Sounds like a plan."

He began removing dishes from the table. Stacey joined in. When he ran water in the sink she bumped him out of the way with her hip. "You cooked. I'll clean."

He nudged her back with a grin. "My kitchen. You don't get to tell me what to do."

She snatched the dishrag from him.

He reached around her, enclosing her within the circle of his arms. He smelled of man and coffee. She squirmed and his hold tightened, bringing her back against his chest. It was large, firm and secure. His warmth enveloped her. She stilled. For a moment they just stood there. Stacey held her breath.

"Stacey..." He kissed the top of her head.

She turned to face him. Expectant. He leaned into her, pressing her against the counter, making his intention clear. His gaze bored into hers. A flame of desire burned in his before he blinked and it was extinguished. Seconds later she was alone, staggering to remain standing. Cody had stepped around the breakfast bar, putting it between them. "I can't. No matter how much I want to."

Stacey couldn't respond to that. It was no surprise. She'd not been wanted enough before.

"I'll go get some shoes on and take you home," Cody muttered.

Before she knew it, he'd left the room.

On Saturday, nearly a week later, Cody searched the Founder's Day event area for the girls. They had been running from tent to tent excited to finally be attending. He couldn't help but be pleased with the turnout. It was the largest event of the year and people from the mainland had come over to join in the fun. The vendors ranged from face painters to arts and crafts to local food, all centered on maple syrup. Everyone appeared as if they were enjoying themselves. The committee had planned long and in detail to make the occasion a success. Cody was proud of their efforts.

During the past week he'd had to make a couple of last-minute meetings to handle specifics and issues. In the end every aspect of the weekend was going off smoothly and he hoped it would continue that way through to Sunday evening. The weather had even co-operated by being spectacular.

He couldn't say the same about his relationship with Stacey. She'd been conspicuously absent from his life outside the OR and the daily rounds to see patients. By appearing at the last possible moment then slipping away the second the job was complete, she had curtailed any chance to talk other than on medical-related issues. Cody couldn't blame her. He didn't like knowing he'd hurt her, no matter how justified the reason. What he should say he was well aware of, but what he wanted to say he wasn't so sure of.

That night she'd stayed at his house he'd climbed the stairs alone. All he'd been able to think about had been Stacey in his home and the what-ifs. What if he kissed her? What if she let him cup her breast? What if he asked her to join him in bed? He'd taken a shower. A cold one. Having Stacey so close had played havoc with his libido.

As was his habit, he'd gone downstairs to secure the house for the night and passed the living room. Stacey had been sound asleep. Her fear of the storm must have zapped her adrenaline, taking all her energy. She'd pulled his pillow to her chest and had been under the blanket. He'd had to move on, fighting himself not to wake her and make sure she slept in his bed. With him.

Now he was longing for her. For what could have been. When his pillow had been returned it had smelled of peaches. His T-shirt hadn't fared any better. He'd made more than one move to wash them but couldn't bring himself to do so.

He been doing the right thing by not getting too involved with Stacey. That statement had been on audio repeat all week, echoing inside his head. His mind might understand but his body wasn't agreeing.

He only had to hold out for a little while longer. She would be leaving soon but he missed their talks, even her teasing remarks. More than once he'd tried to convince himself his concerns stemmed from his girls' constant questions about her but he knew better. He wanted Stacey with a driving need that almost overwhelmed him.

She'd been so sassy and happy during their breakfast together last Sunday morning. It hadn't been until he'd touched her that things had started to get out of control. He knew when a woman wanted him and her eyes had said that clearly. For a minute he'd taken advantage of that, almost kissing her but stopped himself. He knew hurt, deep hurt, and wasn't setting himself up for that again. His girls deserved to have someone who wanted them more than anything else. He did too. Stacey had made it clear she couldn't offer them permanency—moving on to the next exciting place was what she wanted more.

It wouldn't have mattered so much if he hadn't recognized there was something extraordinary between them. He couldn't put a name to it but he did know his entire being simmered whenever he was near her. Stacey had to feel it too. Knowing her time there was short didn't change his desire to get to know her better, touch her, kiss her. In fact, it intensified it. At the same time, he needed to protect his girls. He and they were a package deal. Being an adult, he could deal with the void Stacey would create in his life when she left, but he wouldn't put Jean and Lizzy through that kind of loss again.

"Don't the girls need to be getting to the stage soon?" his mother asked.

"We have a few more minutes," he assured her. His parents had arrived the day before.

"Have you thought any more about letting them go with us up to Maine for a few days?" his father asked as they continued along the crowded aisle between the rows of tents.

"You need some time to yourself," his mother commented. "You haven't really let those girls out of your sight in years. It's time to let go a little."

He and his parents had had this discussion more than once in the recent months.

"I'm thinking about it." Cody still wasn't ready to commit to such a big step.

"Stacey!"

The chorus of Jean and Lizzy's voices above the crowd of people jerked his thoughts to where they were. Both girls ran and wrapped their arms around the dark-haired woman who filled his dreams. She wore a pink T-shirt, jeans and tennis shoes. She'd never looked better.

Lizzy and Jean clung to her. It had taken Jean a while to warm up to Stacey but putting together costumes seemed to have done the trick. Perhaps a little too well.

Stacey hesitated a tad long before she knelt and hugged them in return. As she did she peered over their heads, looking around in alarm. Uncertainty darkened her green eyes as their gazes met. She clearly hadn't planned to run into them.

That moment of uncertainty went against the grain and left him with a bad taste in his mouth. She was dodging them. *Him.*

By the time he reached them, Jean and Lizzy had pulled away and were excitedly telling Stacey about their week and how much Fleur had liked their costumes.

"She said we looked the best!" Jean said to Stacey with hero-worship in her eyes.

Stacey smiled down at her. "I'm glad."

She sounded as if she was.

"Are you ready to dance?" Stacey asked Lizzy.

She nodded. "I know all my steps."

Her joy at seeing the girls appeared genuine. Stacey looked at him again, having to tilt her head back to do so. This time the cloud of anxiety was missing in her eyes. Had it been replaced by hopefulness? He was more conflicted than ever.

"So this is 'super' Stacey," his mother remarked in a congenial tone, stepping around him and extending a hand. "Hi, I'm Cody's mother, Jeanette."

Wearing a stunned expression, Stacey stood and accepted his mother's hand. "Hello. It's nice to meet you." She glanced at him. "Cody didn't tell me you were visiting."

He gave her a pointed look, not caring that his exasperation showed. "You didn't give me chance to."

Stacey had been skirting him all week so he had her there. Cody had made it clear what he wanted and she would respect that. She wanted the same thing. Separation. Space.

No, she didn't. She wanted him.

For the benefit of both of them they needed distance between them. With a great deal of effort she'd accomplished it but loneliness filled her free time. She hadn't been plagued by that despair in a long time. Since childhood. She'd learned long ago how to be self-sufficient. Depending only on herself for happiness. In a few short weeks she'd backslid into expecting to find happiness with another, but it was a mistake she had been trying to correct and would continue to right. If only she could get her heart to co-operate.

"The girls can talk of little but you," his mother continued with the captivating smile that Cody had inherited.

Stacey wasn't sure how to respond.

Cody clearly took pity on her when he said, "Stacey Ryder, this is my father, Roger Brennan." Cody patted a man on the shoulder who had similar features to him but with silver hair.

She shook Cody's father's offered hand. "It's a pleasure to meet you."

"And you too. I understand you work with my son."

"Yes, sir. I'm Dr. Brennan's clinical nurse, or at least I am for seven more days." A sadness deeper than she'd ever felt settled over her at that thought.

"You *are* going to come see us dance, aren't you?" Jean asked.

Stacey's plan had been to arrive just before the girls were to go on stage, stand in the back long enough to see them dance and then leave without being seen by them or their father. Now all she could do was answer with conviction, "I wouldn't miss it."

Both girls beamed at her.

"It's time we should be getting your costumes on, girls." Cody put a hand on each of their backs, heading them in the other direction. "Fleur said you needed to be dressed and ready to go on time."

His mother put a hand on Cody's arm. "We'll get a seat up front and save you one. Stacey, you will join us?"

It wasn't really a question. Stacey watched Cody and the girls walk away. She was stuck now.

Cody's mother said, "Let's go get those front row seats."

There were no rows of chairs in front of the stage. Instead there were picnic tables. Cody's mother picked out one off to the right of the front of the stage. Mr. and Mrs. Brennan took one side of the table and she sat on the other bench.

"Why don't I go get us all a drink while we wait?" Cody's father asked.

"That sounds wonderful. Thanks, honey." Mrs. Brennan smiled at her husband. She then turned her attention to Stacey. "I understand that you worked nothing less than a miracle with the girls' costumes."

"I wouldn't call it a miracle." Stacey didn't want to carry that responsibility. Why did she feel the sudden need to escape? She'd just been tapping into her creative side.

"That's not how Cody described it."

Stacey smiled. "He only saw it that way because he didn't know how to handle it himself."

Cody's mother's face turned serious. "He's had to be father and mother for most of the girls' lives. Those more creative touches he sometimes has difficulty with."

"That has to be frustrating for him. He's such a perfectionist with his patients."

"It is. Very frustrating." Her look met Stacey's as if Mrs. Brennan wanted to make sure she clearly understood. "Cody and the girls have survived a very difficult few years."

"He told me."

Mrs. Brennan's eyes went wide, her surprise obvious. "Really? He never talks about Rachael."

"I asked him and he told me."

"Interesting. Because of what happened with Rachael he's always trying to make up for those bad times. He is very overprotective where the girls are concerned. Of himself as well. I wasn't sure I'd ever see the genuine smiles of happiness on Jean and Lizzy's faces like I saw today. It's wonderful. Even Cody has a look in his eyes that I feared was gone forever." Her eyes glistened. "Thank you for that."

Stacey's stomach fluttered with joy, only to turn sour from acute apprehension. She would be leaving soon. Of that there was no doubt. Life seemed unfair to her, to Cody, and even to his girls. It was the wrong place, wrong people and wrong time. She wasn't right for Cody. If they moved past being friends and co-workers there was nothing but pain out there for all of them.

Cody wouldn't keep her. Even if she wanted him to. One day he would push her away. Her father had done it, her stepfather had and then finally so had her fiancé. All the men in her life left her eventually. She wasn't staying around for that to happen again. So there was no reason to start something that had no future. Knowing what it felt like being left behind and the pain it brought, she wouldn't do that to Cody. Or let him do it to her either.

"I don't know if I'm who you should give that credit to. I've not done anything special."

"Maybe just being you is what makes it special." Cody's father approached. Mrs. Brennan added in a low voice, "I'm sure that I've said more than Cody would appreciate." She placed a hand over Stacey's. "Just know that you are special to them."

Stacey fiddled with a loose sliver of wood on the tabletop. When had she last felt special to anyone? Or had someone tell her that she was? It was nice to hear, even if it was coming from Cody's mother.

While they had been talking, people had been settling at the tables around them. It wouldn't be long before the program started. Mr. Brennan joined them and they talked about the island and the festival for a few minutes in between sipping their iced drinks.

Mrs. Brennan's attention moved to somewhere behind Stacey. "I think Cody needs you."

Heat burned her cheeks. What was his mother saying?

She smiled. "I don't mean that, hon, though it might be true. I mean he's waving that he needs you to come to him."

Stacey turned to find Cody standing at the corner of the stage, gesturing for her to join him. She started that way. Once again she was being pulled in despite her vow to remain detached.

There was a desperate note in Cody's voice when she reached him. "I need some assistance with the girls' bonnets. They say I'm not doing it right."

Stacey couldn't help but be pleased. It was nice to feel needed.

"I'll owe you even more than I already do if you could get them on for me."

"I can do that. Where are they?"

Cody took her hand. It was large, solid and secure. Steady. Something about having her hand in his felt right. He pulled her through a gaggle of little girls, around a couple of mothers talking and passed another group of girls to where Jean and Lizzy stood.

"Daddy couldn't do this right," Lizzy said, handing Stacey her bonnet.

She took it from the girl. "To be fair to your father, this does have a degree of difficulty. He doesn't know what I had in mind. Turn around and let me get this on you."

Lizzy turned her back to Stacey.

"Who put your hair in a bun?" Stacey worked at positioning the cap and tying it under Lizzy's chin.

"Daddy."

"He did a nice job on that." She glanced at Cody. He mouthed, "Thank you."

"All done. Okay, Jean, it's your turn."

Jean stepped up and turned her back to Stacey, who soon had the cap secured. "Okay, now let me look at you both."

The girls grinned up at her. "Perfect. Now go dance as good as you look."

Jean grabbed her by the waist and hugged Stacey so tightly she swayed. Cody placed a steadying hand in the small of her back. Trying to ignore the intimate sensation his touch generated, Stacey returned Jean's affection. Lizzy joined them.

"Okay, girls. Let Stacey go. Fleur is trying to get you to come to her."

They took off to where other girls stood dressed in similar clothing to them. She and Cody walked back to join his parents. This time he didn't take her hand and she missed the contact. Too much.

When they sat down Cody's mother said, "What was the problem?"

"I didn't put their bonnets on like Stacey did."

"I see."

Stacey was afraid she might see too much.

"How did you make those bonnets anyway?" Cody asked.

"I cut the brim off a white hat I had, then cut it in two. That way I had the curve that was needed. Then

I used sewing glue on the edges. I hand sewed shoe strings on to tie them with."

"That's impressive." Cody's mother gave her a smile of admiration.

Cody put his hand on her shoulder. "I know. I couldn't have done it without her."

His praise was nice to hear but wasn't making it any easier for her to keep her resolve to remain detached.

The program started and soon the girls and boys were dancing across the stage. Cody sat beside her, close enough that she could feel his warmth. She was so aware of him she had difficulty paying attention to the children in Native American outfits, as English soldiers, and then Pilgrims. He squeezed her hand then let it go when Jean and Lizzy came on stage. They did a beautiful job with their dance.

As soon as the program was over Stacey made a production of checking her watch. For her own good, she needed to leave. "I've got to go."

"Right now?" Cody's disbelief filled his voice.

"I…uh…told Summer that I'd help her with something at two. So I have to go. Please tell the girls for me that they were great."

"I bet they would rather hear that from you." The dark disapproval on Cody's face came close to snuffing out her determination.

"I'm sorry, but I really must go." Why couldn't he leave it alone? She looked at his parents, who were watching her closely, then back to Cody. "It was nice to meet you, Mr. and Mrs. Brennan." She threw those words over her shoulder as she hurried away. She was no longer counting the days but the hours until she could leave the island.

* * *

Sunday afternoon, after his parents and the girls had left, Cody made his way to Stacey's cottage. He'd had enough. He had to see her. Put things right between them. Somehow.

He had no intention of bringing anyone disruptive into his world. Stacey was that type of person. The kind that unsettled people. She had certainly had that effect on him. Yet he still couldn't stay away from her.

After Rachael he'd accepted he wasn't a good judge of character. He couldn't make that mistake again. Yet here he was on Stacey's cottage doorstep. Even if there couldn't be anything real between them, he still wanted her. She needed to know that. He had to make the hurt in her eyes go away. She wasn't unaffected by his family. He'd seen Stacey's pride and pleasure in Jean and Lizzy's dancing. Some things she couldn't hide.

He knocked. There was no sound. Knocked again. Was she at the festival? Something made him think she wasn't. Maybe out for a walk? He didn't want to do this at the clinic but if that was the only way, he'd take it. As he turned to leave, the door opened.

"Cody, what are you doing here?" Stacey asked around the door. "Is there an emergency?"

"Of sorts. We need to talk."

"Why?" She pushed at her hair.

"I want to tell you I'm sorry."

She looked away. "You have nothing to be sorry for."

"You're wrong. Do you mind if I come in? Or you could come out here." For a second, he feared she was going to say no to either option. For some reason he needed her to understand how he'd been feeling.

"I'm not really dressed for company."

He could tell she had her hair up on top of her head in a messy arrangement. She wore a long T-shirt and shorts. "I think you look fine." Too fine, really. Even in that outfit he wanted her. He stuffed his hands into his pockets.

"I'll come out." She pushed the door just wide enough for her to exit and stood on the porch.

"Why don't we sit on the steps?" He'd figured this might be hard but had had no idea she'd be so stand-offish. Why was he putting this much effort into their relationship or friendship or whatever it was? He'd had enough emotional upheaval in his life without adding more. "Look, on second thoughts, just forget it. I'll leave you alone. I'll see you at work tomorrow." He turned to head down the steps.

She grabbed his arm. "Don't go."

He sank to the porch, his feet on the first step and his elbows on his knees. Stacey sat beside him but not too close. Neither of them said anything for a while.

"I'm sorry I hurt your feelings the other morning." Her slight hiss didn't miss his attention. "I want you to know it isn't about you. It's about me." She shifted beside him, but he didn't look at her. Instead he focused on a knot in the board between his feet.

"What do you mean?"

"Come on. You know exactly what I mean. This thing between us." He waved his hand between them.

Her voice went higher as she said, "There's nothing between us."

Cody sighed but tried again. "Sure there is. I feel it. I know you feel it too. I've seen the way you look at me. How you react when I touch you. The other morning at my house I could see the excitement in your eyes when you thought I was about to kiss you. I know why you are putting up a wall between us. I get it, but I don't like it."

Stacey hopped up and was almost to the door before he could make a move. He stood, preparing to leave. He'd gotten his answer.

"I can't do this," she muttered.

"Do what?" Were they even talking about the same thing?

"I'm not staying on the island. I know you're looking for more than that. I can't give it. It's not fair to you. I won't hurt you or the girls."

"I'm not looking for more than what you can give. What I do know is that I've missed you."

"I've been right—"

He gave her a pleading look. He wanted her to understand. "I mean you being yourself. You making me laugh. You being around. You teasing me."

"I don't do that."

He glared at her. "Yeah, you do."

He took a deep breath, choosing his next words with care. "Look, I like you, Stacey. It's been a long time since I could say that about any woman. And I'm guessing by your actions up until this past week that you liked me too. That alone makes you special. I know we work together and that can complicate things but I want you like I've not wanted anyone in a very long time. Can't we just explore what's between us? Enjoy each other for the time we have left?"

Had he completely lost his mind? Was he that lonely? This was nothing like what he'd promised himself. He'd vowed to protect himself, and his girls, by not getting too involved with the wrong woman. But his vow be damned. He wanted to get to know Stacey better, far better.

He gestured with both hands to emphasize his next words. "I know it's crazy, with you having just a week left, but I can't help myself. I want to spend as much time with you as possible before you leave. Can't we do that?"

Stacey turned to face him, watching him, judging him. She took a step toward him. Her voice was steady with no hint of indecision or hesitation when she said, "I'd like that."

Relief washed through him. "Good. I know this is short notice and I apologize, but the Founder's Day weekend is almost over and I was wondering if you'd like to go with me and get some dinner?"

A slow smile formed on her lips. "That sounds like fun. What about Jean and Lizzy?"

"They left this morning for Maine with their grandparents for a few days. So it'll just be the two of us. Is that okay?" Would she want the buffer of the girls between them?

"More than okay. Give me a few minutes to get dressed."

Cody swung on the porch swing while he waited, pleased with himself. His powers of persuasion were so refined should he consider going into politics?

Stacey didn't keep him waiting long. Her hair was still up on her head but she wore an exotic-looking dress that he guessed she'd gotten during her travels. It caressed her curves and flowed around her legs. A bright beaded bracelet circled one wrist. Sandals protected her feet and she carried a sweater.

He offered her his hand. She took it. His heart soared. She smiled sweetly. "I'm ready."

CHAPTER SIX

STACEY COULDN'T BELIEVE how quickly she had changed her mind about spending time with Cody. All it had taken was for him to show up at her door and all of her firm resolve had crumbled. It hadn't taken her even a minute to decide she wanted her short time on Maple Island filled with wonderful memories of him. She could have those, and take them to Ethiopia or wherever she went for the rest of her life.

The past week had been miserable. Avoiding Cody outside work had been doubly difficult because her common sense had constantly been at war with her undeniable desire to be with him. She had never felt lonelier in her life. Despite living on a beautiful island during springtime, she wasn't enjoying it. Even the opening celebrations of Founder's Day Weekend had been spoiled because she'd been so wary of running into Cody.

With the air cleared between them it was like they were truly friends. They said little on the ride but there was nothing uncomfortable about the silence. It was as if they were both determined to make the time they had left positive.

The sun shone brightly and the sky was blue as they

walked into the festival. She looked forward to really experiencing it. Today she planned to soak it all in. Being with Cody made it even better.

Stacey stopped for a second to tie her sweater around her waist. "Wow, there're a lot of people here today as well."

"With more hours of daylight, people are making the most of the event. It has been a good year. It helps when the weather is nice." Cody looked around with a smile. "There's a band tonight and many folks will stay late for that."

He took her hand but gave her a quick, questioning glance as if asking for permission. Stacey squeezed it, and he gently tightened his grip. As they moved from tent to tent he didn't let go of it. More than one person spoke to him as they strolled along. With each one he introduced her right after returning their greeting.

They were busy looking at handmade weathervanes when someone called, "Cody."

They both looked around to see Dr. Rafael Valdez, who was pushing a stroller, and Summer Ryan coming their way.

Stacey knew them from the clinic. From what she understood, Rafael was a relatively new addition to the staff, only having arrived on the island a few months ago.

"Hi, there." Cody offered his hand and the two men shook.

"You two enjoying the festival?" Summer asked her and Cody.

"Yes, we are." Stacey smiled at Cody, who returned it. She looked into the stroller. "Who do you have with you? I don't believe we've met."

"This is my daughter, Gracie." Pride filled Rafael's voice.

"Hi, there," Stacey said to the girl.

"We're just going for a bite to eat. Want to join us?" Rafael asked.

"Thanks, but we have a few more tents to visit. Maybe another time," Cody said.

"Then we'll see you tomorrow." Rafael waved over his shoulder as he and Summer moved on, Gracie preceding them in her shaded stroller.

Stacey watched them leave. "They make a nice couple."

"Rafael is a topnotch addition to the staff." Cody turned to her. "I hope you don't mind me not accepting their offer. I wanted it to be just us tonight."

Stacey's heart did a pitter-pat. "I like that plan."

They continued walking while looking at the arts and crafts.

He tugged gently on her hand. "I'm getting hungry. How about you?"

"Starving."

Cody steered her toward the food court. "Good. How does a lobster po'boy sound?"

"I don't know. I've never had one."

"It's lobster meat on a bun. I think you'll like it. Willing to give it a try?"

Stacey was confident she would give anything he asked a try. "Sure."

A few minutes later they had their sandwiches and drinks. Luckily, they found an empty table among those set up near the food trucks.

"Goodness, this is so big. I don't know if I can get

my mouth around it." Despite what she'd just said, Stacey opened wide, managing it with little trouble.

"Doesn't look like you're having a problem to me." Cody chuckled.

Stacey glared at him. "And to think I thought you had no sense of humor when I first met you."

"Maybe you bring that out in me."

She liked that idea. Cody should smile often. She loved his smile. "I'm glad I can be of some help."

"That's all you've been since you arrived. Help with my patients, help in the OR, help with the girls, and the list could go on."

"You once told me not to put you on a pedestal, I'm going to say the same." She too was afraid she would fall.

"Then we'll agree to be less than perfect." He took another bite of his sandwich.

"That I can certainly agree to."

When they were finished Cody asked, "Would you like to stay and listen to the band or I can offer you the view of the sunset from the point near the lighthouse?"

"I'd love to see the sunset." For the day to start off so depressingly, with her sitting alone in her cottage, it was fast turning into a perfect one.

Hand in hand they walked to his car. Dusk crept in as they rode along the windy road toward the lighthouse. Just before they got there Cody turned off on a smaller road that led toward the beach. Across the water was the Boston Harbor. Lights were blinking on in the buildings.

Cody pulled the car to a stop and turned off the engine. He didn't say anything but took hold of her hand. In silence they watched the play of colors in the western sky. The blend of red, orange and yellow melding into black became the backdrop of their view of Boston.

Stacey had never seen anything more beautiful or been in a more romantic setting. "Wow, you sure know how to show a girl a good time."

He laughed. "You do have a way with words. Would you like to stay a while longer or for me to take you home?"

"Truthfully?" Could she really tell him what she would like to do?

"Yes."

"I'd like to sit on your porch, look at the stars and listen to the waves."

"That we can do." He sounded pleased with her request. "How about a hot drink to go with the view?"

"Sounds wonderful."

He started the car, turned around and headed up the road. "You know, if we're not careful we'll do everything there is to do on this island on our first date."

"Maybe we can think of something new." She had a few ideas already.

The drive to Cody's wasn't far but he didn't hurry. A light burned over his front door, welcoming them as they entered and walked to the kitchen.

"You go on out and make yourself comfortable. I'll get us something warm to drink." Cody put a kettle on the burner.

Stacey pulled on her sweater before she chose the cushioned settee, sat and slipped off her sandals, tucking her feet under her. Leaning her head back, she closed her eyes and listened to the ocean. Every day should be like this. Since coming to Maple Island, it seemed as if she had stopped running and had started taking time to appreciate the smaller things in life. Many of those Cody had introduced her to.

For years she'd been living six months here, three months there, and another nine months to a year elsewhere. She'd forgotten what it was like to stay in one place any length of time. As if she had ever known. Even as a child she'd moved often. She didn't know how to stay in one place. This sensation of belonging was surely just temporary. She would soon get restless and be ready to move on. Why did she even think she would be happy settling down?

Soon the kitchen light went out and Cody joined her. "Don't panic. I turned the lights off so we could see the stars better."

"I'm not going to panic." After her erratic actions of late she wasn't surprised he'd believed she might overreact. "I wondered if you were trying to be Mr. Romance."

He handed her a mug and took a seat in a chair nearby.

Was he afraid to crowd her? She wanted him close.

"I can be that with or without the lights on." His deep, rich voice was made more so under the blanket of darkness.

"I like a man with confidence." She enjoyed teasing him. He was far too serious.

"Did you ever doubt it?"

Stacey could only make out his silhouette but she clearly heard the inflection in his voice. It mattered to him what she thought.

"No." She hadn't. How could she? Her body hummed with excitement whenever he was near. Like now. She felt the power of his male magnetism continually.

They quietly sipped their drinks. Stacey had never had a relationship with a man in which she was content to just share time with him. It was calming. They remained there while the stars slowly disappeared behind clouds.

"It will rain tonight. But no storm like the other night." Cody's voice came out of the darkness, his hand taking hers and giving it a squeeze.

"It's a good thing the Founder's Day Weekend is over." Her voice sounded soft and relaxed.

"It is." They were talking about nothing significant yet she enjoyed the moment. There was contentment, a feeling of rightness that filled her just being around Cody.

A few minutes went by and the air between them simmered with awareness.

Would he make a move? He'd said he was interested but acted as if he was unsure about asking her for more. Stacey stood, searching for her shoes with her toes. "I'd better go."

"Please don't." There was a note of urgency in the statement as he stood. "Will you stay with me tonight?"

She stepped closer to him. "What took you so long to ask? A girl might think she isn't as irresistible as you led her to believe." She grabbed his shirt, pulled him to her and gave him a kiss she hoped he would remember.

Cody crushed her against him, taking control of the kiss. His lips sauntered across hers as his hands roamed her back before wandering over her cheek to kiss her neck then returning to her mouth. Teasing the seam of her lips with his tongue, he asked for entrance. She gave it and his passion set her on fire. Her hands pulled his head closer as she returned his ardor with a twirl of her tongue. Cody groaned and brought her hips against his, making his desire thickly obvious.

Heat pooled between her legs. Desire had her blood hot and humming. She needed Cody more than anything else in the world.

Cody had been waiting for an invitation, any invitation, just some indication Stacey wanted to stay. He'd gotten his answer.

He'd purposely chosen to sit in a chair across from the settee to avoid the temptation to pressure her. He enjoyed her company, the peace of just being with her. If that was all she'd offer him then he would accept that. Stacey had brought him back to life. Still, the drive, the desire to touch her had his fingers twitching. There was electricity in the air whenever they were together. Waiting had been agony. He now planned to enjoy every pleasure she offered, for as long as he could.

Stacey's arms circled his neck and she returned his kiss with all the hunger he'd imagined during sleepless nights. His tongue ran along the seam of her lips and she opened like a bloom waiting for sunshine. Her eager greeting turned the kiss into a heated tango.

His pulse pounded in his ears while blood, hot and pulsing, ran to his manhood, making it thick and tall. Her fingers tunneled through his hair in provocative exploration as if she'd been dreaming of touching it. He cradled her butt, pulling her against him. Those curves he'd admired were now in his hands. His fingers traveled up along them until they framed her breasts.

Cody cupped one, lifting it. Full and firm, the only thing wrong with her breasts was that they were still covered. His thumb brushed her nipple and he was rewarded with it standing to sharp attention.

Stacey moaned and wriggled against him.

His length throbbed, begging to have her. If they didn't slow down he would take her on the bare boards of his porch. Stacey deserved better than that. Their first time should be less hectic and far more tender. Reluctantly, he dragged his mouth from hers. "Wooh, woman, you've got me hotter than a firecracker."

She gave him an enticing grin. "I like the sound of that."

Cody let out a low pained chuckle. His mouth gently met hers. Stacey's hands cupped his face and held him there as she deepened the kiss. Her tongue teased his as her hands moved to his shoulders. She kneaded them as she pressed harder against his aching manhood. How like Stacey to let him know exactly what she wanted.

His mouth moved away from hers to leave kisses across her cheek. He stopped to nuzzle the dip behind her ear. She tensed then squirmed, giving him easier access. So she liked that. He flicked the tip of his tongue over the spot he'd just kissed and she quivered.

Stacey, just as he'd suspected, was ultra-responsive. So vitally alive. He'd been dead for too long. This age-old rush of raw desire she sent through him made him feel alive once more. "Like that, do you?"

"I like everything you do to me," she murmured against his temple as her hands ran down his chest to his waist. She pulled his shirt from his pants and slipped her hands beneath. They set his skin on fire as they skimmed across his waist around to his back.

His attention returned to her breasts. He filled his hand with one. Her nipple, pushing against the material of the dress, called to him. He had no intention of disappointing. His mouth covered it. Cody tantalized and teased as Stacey leaned toward him. He had to see her bare flesh, truly touch her.

Giving her another lingering kiss, he whispered, "Let's go upstairs." It was more of a question than a statement. Cody still wasn't sure she would agree. Stacey had kept him standing on an edge for days now and she might keep him there. What if she overthought what they were doing, like he had the other day? It might kill him to let her go, but he would if that's what she wanted.

"There isn't anything that I'd rather do, but you must understand that I'm still leaving next Sunday. You know that, don't you? I won't change my mind."

His chest constricted. He didn't want to think about that now. "I know. Let's enjoy tonight and worry about later then."

Her lips met his before she took his hand and pulled him toward the door. "It just happens I know the way to your room."

Cody chuckled. "Yes, you do. You didn't seem that eager to be there last time."

Even in the dim light he could make out her sassy look. "That was actually the problem last time, I *was* eager to be there."

Cody pulled her close and gave her a hot kiss that promised things to come.

On their way through the kitchen he flipped the light switch off. Stacey tugged on him in her impatience, making him stumble. He couldn't remember a time when a woman had been this ready for him.

His ego soared, as his heart pounded with excitement against his ribs.

At the stairs, he flipped the light on. Stacey took advantage of the pause to stand on the first step and helped him remove his sweater. She dropped it and took his hand again as they climbed further.

She stopped again. This time she kissed him. As she did so her hands went to his belt, released it and tugged it free. She let it slip through her hands with a grin and started up once again. At the top, she confronted him once more. Cody caught her hands. "Two can play this game. It's my turn."

Her eyes narrowed as she teased him with an enticing grin. "You think so?"

His hands went to her shoulders and pushed her sweater off one of them. He placed a kiss on the soft skin he had exposed. It was as smooth as he had dreamed it would be. Stacey shivered. He continued to remove her sweater until her arms were bare. Starting at one shoulder, he kissed down her arm. He continued to love her until he'd sucked each one of her fingers. He then moved his attention to the other side.

As he slowly released her last digit between his lips Cody glanced at Stacey to see that she had her head back, exposing her long neck. Her eyes were closed. Her breasts stood erect while her nipples peaked against her thin dress. She looked like a goddess in the throes of rapture. Kissing the curve of her neck, he promised himself he would make her look like that as often as he could. Her dazed look met his and he grabbed her hand, leading her into his bedroom. Enough of that game.

In his bedroom, he left her alone beside the bed

long enough to turn on the lamp on his desk. Stacey stood watching him with hooded eyes. He returned to her, bringing her into his arms and giving her a tender kiss as his fingertips lightly brushed the backs of her arms. She trembled. He'd never had a woman respond so profoundly to his touch.

Her hands moved to the buttons of his shirt. She made slow, tantalizing work of removing a button from its hole. Her fingers were like the best-quality down as they traveled over the skin of his chest again and again. With each touch his manhood jerked. He watched her movements, the efficacy of her fingers and their length, despite her small hand. Even that simple action on her part filled him with awe.

When the last button came undone she pushed his shirt wider over his chest and studied him with a small smile. The palms of her hands came to rest on his pectorals. She teased the hair there, before she leaned in and placed her lips over his heart.

He pulled her face up and captured her mouth, unable to resist kissing her. His hands went to her hips and he gathered her dress up until he found her silken panties. Cupping her bottom, he squeezed gently, bringing her against his hard, hot length. Could anything be more perfect than the feel of Stacey against him?

Finding the bottom edge of her panties, he slowly traced it around to the crevice of her legs. Slipping the tip of a finger under the elastic band, he brushed it over her skin, moving inexorably toward her center.

Stacey trembled. He loved drawing a reaction from her. Widening her stance a fraction, she offered him access. Unable to resist, he ran his finger over her mound, then slowly slipped between her folds. She stilled, as if anticipating his next move. Cody had no intention of disappointing. He tightened his hold at her waist before his finger entered to find her center wet and waiting.

Instantly Stacey released a held breath and pressed into his hand, moaning. He pulled away. She groaned in complaint.

"Panties have to go." He pulled them down to her knees. She kicked them off and he raised her dress again. He didn't hesitate to cup her center. Stacey squirmed. Cody's finger entered her again. Her hands gripped his shoulders while her head fell back as his finger pushed and pulled, teased and titillated her. Her gaze found his, held. Stacey's green eyes were wide and misty with pleasure. His chest tightened with pride. Soon she shattered, and shivered, having found intense satisfaction.

He held her as she leaned against him.

"My, Doctor, you have magical hands," she muttered against his chest.

He chuckled low in his throat. "Thank you, but I have other parts that are just as magical. You haven't seen anything yet."

Stacey, still weak in the knees and holding on to that feeling of floating away, pulled back and met his gaze. "Promises, promises."

Cody swept her off her feet and dropped her on the bed with a bounce. "That sassy mouth is going to get you into trouble one day. You'd better be careful who you tease."

She grinned. This Cody she could learn to love. No. She wouldn't let that happen.

He'd pulled her dress from beneath her and continued until he had it off over her head.

Standing above her, he studied her. She lay bare to him except for her bra and sandals.

Bringing a foot up, she unbuckled her shoe. Simmering desire sparkled in his dark eyes. It flared the glowing embers low inside her into roaring flames that only he could extinguish. She dropped the shoe to the floor and started on the other.

Cody's look flickered to what she was doing then slowly traveled over her. "You are so sexy. Even more so than I dreamed."

He'd been dreaming about her? Shoe discarded, her fingers moved to the clasp of her bra between her breasts.

"Don't. Let me." He came down on one knee beside her. With a nimble flip he had her bra opened.

At the hiss of his inhaled breath her body went on full alert. Did he actually like what he saw? She dismissed that insecurity when he cupped her naked breast, weighing and caressing it as if it was precious.

"Perfect," he breathed, before his lips claimed her nipple.

Stacey involuntarily arched, offering him all.

Cody's tongue tugged, curled and enticed her nipple until her core became a tight fist of need. After a soft blow across her damp skin that only made it more sensitive, he moved to the other breast and cherished it in turn.

Stacey feared she couldn't take much more. A craving burned in her like a live thing.

Cody's lips found hers as his hands explored her body. She pushed at his shirt until there was nothing between them. They touched chest to chest, heated skin to heated skin. Breaking off the kiss, Cody came to a half-seated position and jerked his shirt the rest of the way off. When he returned to her, Stacey's hand went to the front of his pants and caressed his solid ridge.

The hot length of him bulged against his zipper. She freed the button from its hole. She had to touch all of his strength. Pushing at his pants, she murmured, "These have to go."

He rolled away and kicked off his loafers. While he did that she untangled her arms from her bra. Standing with his back to her, Cody dropped his pants.

She'd never thought of herself as being a woman who admired a man's backside but Cody's was worth admiration. Rounded and firm, it was a perfect specimen above his thick muscled thighs. His was the type that could fill pants or hands just right. He turned, and she gasped. He was all glorious, gorgeous and generous male. Knowing he was hers for the night enhanced his masculine beauty.

Stacey offered her hand. He took it and she drew him to her. He slowly sank over her until he completely covered her. His mouth found hers for a tender kiss that hinted at barely held restraint.

Cody pulled back and looked at her, his fingers stroking her cheek. "You are the most amazing person I know."

His words flowed soft and sweet as water over rocks in a stream. Helplessly spellbound by his possessive gaze, she felt as though for once she stood out in a crowd. No one had ever said anything like that to her. She would cherish those words forever. She'd always dreamed of being special to someone.

"I want you so bad I hurt with it," Cody groaned.

She slid her hand around the nape of his neck and brought his lips to hers. Nipping the bottom one, she licked the spot soothingly. "I want you too."

With a quick movement he rolled away from her. He opened his bedside table drawer, pulled out a small foil package and opened it. Seconds later he was covered and he returned to her. His hands tightened on her waist. He gave her a kiss that started out gentle until he increased the pressure. Meanwhile, his hand skimmed over her hip, following the line of her body to her thigh. He shifted to the side, his hard length pressed against her.

Blood roared in her ears. She kneaded the muscles of his back with an impatience that made her breaths uneven. He ran his lips along the seam of her mouth with the tip of his tongue as his fingers tangled in her curls. She opened her mouth in welcome as did her legs. Every fiber of her femininity silently begged him to join her.

Cody adjusted once more, bringing the tip of his manhood to her center. He nudged her begging heat but held in place. She flexed toward him.

"Shh." He softly kissed her as his palm brushed her nipple. "Easy. We have all night." He prodded her entrance.

She couldn't bear it. Every nerve in her body was tight with anticipation. Stacey squeezed her eyes shut in order not to beg. Need twisted and throbbed within her.

"Stacey." Her name was a barely audible whisper coming from deep within him. "Open your eyes. I want you to know it's me here with you."

"Like I could ever forget," she moaned, but she opened her eyes.

His intense gaze held hers without blinking as he deliberately, inch by precious slow inch, sheathed himself inside her to the hilt. He'd done it so gradually she feared she might die before he found home. Cody paused as if savoring the moment, her.

No one had ever done that before. Others had been so quick that the act had been far more about them than her. Even her ex-fiancé hadn't taken the time or made the effort to really make love to her. That should have been her first sign he hadn't been right for her. There was more than sexual passion between her and Cody. They were making an emotional connection. That realization both excited and disturbed her.

He leisurely arched his hips, pulling away until he almost left her before returning in the same excruciating motion. Stacey wanted to scream, *Go faster!* but at the same time his actions were so sweet she never wanted them to end. All the while Cody watched her, his dark eyes almost bottomless. His skin was drawn tight across his cheeks as if it took enormous effort to control himself.

She ran her hands over his chest, shoulders and arms, testing and memorizing the texture of his skin and the muscle mass beneath it. Still he eased in and out of her, making her wiggle with frustration when she feared he might leave her. She bit her bottom lip as the knot of burning need grew. Lifting her hips, she silently pleaded for…what she wasn't sure.

Cody's lips found hers as the tangle of need and want contracted. He increased the pace. She joined him, encouraging him. They participated in a game that was theirs alone. The knot at her center grew, expanded and throbbed. Grasping him, her fingers raked his skin. She cried for him to stop then begged for him to continue. Finally, the twisted white-hot need gave way. Quaking, she soared into heavenly oblivion, keening Cody's name.

He remained deep within her while she drifted back to reality. He kissed her on the forehead before he stirred again. He soon shifted into a driving rhythm. Confident she didn't have it in her to catch up and match his pace, Stacey surprised herself. Wrapping her legs around Cody's waist, she pulled him to her. In a frantic final shove, Cody groaned his pleasure long and low.

He fell away from her. One of his hands remained at her waist and a leg was still thrown over hers.

Cody wasn't new to lovemaking. For heaven's sake, he'd been married, but he had never experienced anything as soul shaking as what he'd just shared with Stacey. He'd poured everything in him into the act and been rewarded with Stacey's ego-affirming response. Would he live through another joining? And there would be another.

When his breathing finally evened out, he rolled to his side, propped his head on an elbow and smiled down at her. He received a grin in return as she caressed his chest.

"It's nice to know you keep your promises." A fingertip followed the line of his hair going south.

"I told you not to doubt me."

"That you did." Her hand drifted lower.

Cody placed one of his over hers. "Don't be teasing me. I'm not as young as I once was. You'll have to give me a few minutes to recuperate."

Stacey pushed his shoulders to the bed and straddled him. Her lips wore a devious smile. "What if I do all the work?"

CHAPTER SEVEN

STACEY WOKE TO the gray light of day. Rain lightly tapped against Cody's large bedroom window and the sound of waves crashing were a faint reminder the ocean was near.

"Good morning." Cody's deep raspy sleep-laden voice sent a ripple of desire through her. Could she ever get enough of him?

She turned so she could see his face and smiled. "Good morning to you too." It seemed as if it had come quickly. After their night together she was exhausted, while at the same time invigorated. Her nerves still quivered with awareness of the sexy man beside her.

Cody shifted so that her head rested in the hollow of his shoulder. They were quiet. She watched the rain. When she'd come to Maple Island she would never have thought a morning like this was possible. She'd never felt more complete than when she was with Cody, but that would be over soon. Too soon. Mentally shaking her head, Stacey pushed that thought away. She refused to let anything ruin this moment.

She moved until she was lying over Cody's chest. She cupped his sexy stubbled cheek and kissed him tenderly. "Thanks for last night." She grinned. "The middle of the night and early this morning."

"My pleasure. Anytime." His kiss wasn't the frenzied type of the night before; instead it was passionate, as if he wanted to tell her something he couldn't voice.

They both drifted off to sleep again in each other's arms.

The next time Stacey woke it was to Cody fondling her breast. Instantly desire shot through her. It was still gloomy outside but warm and cozy next to Cody.

He rolled over her, his lips finding hers. "Mmm... this is a nice way to start a day."

She brushed a finger along his extended manhood.

"Woman, you're going to kill me."

Sometime later they made their way to the bathroom for a shower. It turned into a long one, with her washing him then him her. Before they knew it the water had turned cold.

Stacey kissed his chest as they dried each other off. "We'd better get going or we're going to be late for work. My boss is a demanding one."

Cody grabbed her butt and pulled her against him, giving her a deep erotic kiss. "You bet he is, but why don't you ask him if you can come in late today?"

One thing she had learned about Cody was that he was super-dedicated to his job. He was never late and didn't miss any time. She looked at him with disbelief. "You actually want to play hooky for a few hours?"

"I do. I don't have any surgery scheduled this morning and only paperwork to look forward to. I thought maybe we could have a leisurely breakfast here or at the bakery."

Stacey looked at him askance. "So what you're

saying is that spending time with me is preferable to doing paperwork?"

He stopped her hand from toweling off his chest and looked at her. "Something like that. But the real truth is that I just want more time with you."

"What's happened to the Cody I know?"

"Possibly you." His words whispered across her shoulder as he turned her and dried her back.

That sounded too close to caring for her comfort. She needed to get things back to a lighter note. "I'd rather stay here and eat."

Cody stood confidently in front of her in all his male glory and said, "Pancakes or bacon and eggs?"

She was tempted to take him back to bed. Her addiction to Cody Brennan must be cured. It wasn't healthy. "Bacon and eggs."

Pulling her against his warm naked body, he said, "Sounds almost as tasty as you." He nibbled at her neck.

She broke the embrace. "I'm hungry."

"Me too." He gave her a wolfish grin.

"None of that until you have fed me." She'd brought his shirt into the bathroom with her. Pulling it on, she buttoned it and rolled up the sleeves.

"Mmm… I don't know if I can keep my attention on frying bacon with you dressed like that."

"You know, I could just make it into an apron." Giving him a wicked expression, her hands went to a button.

He groaned. "As much as I appreciate the possibilities…but I promised you food."

She brushed her fingertips across his chest on the way out of the door. "And I want you at full strength."

Cody joined her in the bedroom dressed in just jeans and nothing else. She was going to have a hard time keeping her hands off him. If she wasn't careful, things would get out of hand. Still, she couldn't bring herself to leave. She wanted all of Cody she could get in the time remaining to them.

They went downstairs, picking up their discarded clothing as they went. She hung hers on the newel post and Cody placed his on top of hers.

"While I fry the bacon, would you butter toast and beat the eggs?"

"Sure."

A little while later she was busy with a bowl and whisk when Cody came to stand behind her. "Where did you learn to beat eggs?"

"I'm not really very good in the kitchen. My mom always ate out or bought in food. There was a cafeteria in college, and at the hospitals. When I went to work there were always cooks to see to the crew's meals. So I never had a need to learn."

"Then let me give you your first lesson." He wrapped his arms around her. The heat of his chest warmed her back. Cody placed his hands over hers. He then tilted the bowl slightly and briskly whipped the eggs.

She rubbed her butt against him. "I think I would be a good cook if all my lessons were given like this."

Cody chuckled. It vibrated all the way up her spine.

"Is there anything you're not good at, Doctor?"

"There are a few things, I assure you." There was a note in his voice that made her suspect he referred to his past. Would he ever let what had happened go? As far as she was concerned, he was just about perfect. Her heart squeezed. She would miss him when she was gone. Unwilling to let anything harm their beautiful morning together, she turned and put her arms around his waist, laying her cheek on his chest. "You couldn't convince me of that."

"Something wrong?" Cody sounded concerned, the eggs forgotten.

"No, I just needed a hug."

He squeezed her tight for a second then released her. "I'd better get these eggs on."

Stacey moved to stand close to him, leaning against the counter. "Did your mother teach you to cook?"

"No, I learned out of necessity. Taking two young children out to dinner every night turned out to be a bigger fiasco than me trying to prepare a meal. Plus I didn't want to raise them on fast food."

Like she had been.

"I was determined to learn how to make at least a few solid meals. I still have disasters every now and then, but basically I can put together a nutritious meal in a fairly short time."

"Once again you're an amazing man. Everyone should be so lucky to have you as a daddy." Cody was the type of father she wished she'd had. This morning would be one of those precious memories she would take with her when she left.

It was around noon when there was a knock on Cody's clinic office door. He called, "Come in.

Stacey strolled in with a smile on her face. He liked that look much better than the one that had been there the entire week before. His preference really was the expression of bliss Stacey had when she found her pleasure beneath him.

"Hey, I wanted to talk to you about the senator's son, if you have a few minutes."

"I always have a minute for you." Even to his own ears he sounded like Alex when Maggie was around. Surely he wasn't that lovesick. *Love?* He and Stacey had both agreed in not so many words that emotions weren't part of their arrangement. If they weren't, he was afraid he'd taken a large step over the line. She'd made it clear she wouldn't be staying for any reason.

"That's nice to hear." She started around the desk.

"Stop right there."

She jerked to a stop. Her brows rose and she gave him a questioning look.

"I just want to make it clear before we start talking that I'm going to stay over here, keeping this desk between us, because I don't think I can get through the conversation otherwise."

Stacey gave him a wicked grin. "Got the hots for me, do ya?"

"Yeah, that would be an understatement." He was already thinking about having her again. About kissing that spot behind her neck that made her squirm.

She didn't blink when she said, "Sounds good to me."

Would she ever stop surprising him?

Taking one of the chairs in front of his desk, she crossed her legs and gave him a self-satisfied smile. "No comeback, Doc?"

He had one but it wasn't something he should be doing at the clinic in the middle of the day. "You'd better watch that mouth. I keep telling you it's going to get you into trouble."

Her voice went low and seductive. "What kind of punishment did you have in mind?"

He gripped the edge of the desk to keep himself from hurling himself over it and grabbing her. "You come to my place tonight for dinner and I'll show you."

"Will I be expected to participate?" Stacey leisurely swung her foot. She was enjoying this.

"Oh, you can count on that."

"Then I wouldn't miss it. What time?"

"Seven?" He needed time to do some special grocery shopping.

Stacey nodded. "I can't wait." Then she actually winked at him.

When was the last time he'd traded bedroom talk with a woman? And not in the bedroom. He'd never done so. What was happening to him?

She straightened in her seat and her look turned serious. "I think Salty is getting the best out of the senator's son. He's doing all of his therapy without complaint now."

"I hear a *but* coming."

Stacey's lips pursed and she nodded. "He's still seriously grappling with the idea of a limp for the rest of his life. I'm worried about his emotional stability more than anything."

"I'll have Rick look in on him. He worked wonders with Fleur. Maybe it'll work again."

Stacey stood. "Then I guess that's it. I've got a hot date to get ready for so I'll see you later." She gave him a grin and a little wave over her shoulder on the way out.

* * *

A few hours later Cody was putting the final touches on the small table on the porch where he planned they would eat their meal. His romance skills were so rusty he was nervous about the evening.

The doorbell rang. She was here. He hurried to the door.

Stacey stood on the stoop looking adorable. Her hair was down and swung freely around her shoulders. The slight breeze lifted a few strands and blew them across her face. She brushed them away. The simple but feminine dress she wore fit tightly to her body then flared out around her hips. It was a short one this time that showed an amazing amount of her breathtaking legs. A pair of almost-not-there sandals were on her feet. Her smile gave her both a vivacious and beautiful appearance. He was completely captivated.

Cody pulled her inside and took a deep inhalation of her peach scent before he kicked the door closed. He kissed her with all the pent-up passion he'd been tamping down all day. Her arms came around his neck and she leaned into him. When they broke apart they were both breathing heavily.

A buzzing came from the kitchen. He released her and hurried down the hall. "I have something in the oven."

She followed. "You'd better not burn my supper."

He pulled the hot pot out of the oven.

"It smells wonderful." She was the one who smelled like heaven. He had to get a grip on himself or he'd be groveling at her feet.

"What do we have there?" She tried to look in the pot when he removed the top.

"Brennan pot roast."

Pursing her lips, she nodded. "I feel important. Not just pot roast but Brennan pot roast."

"Are you making fun of the cook?"

"I'd never make fun of someone feeding me." She smiled amiably at him.

He gave her a narrow-eyed gaze. "Good, because you'd have to watch me eat and do without if you had been. Why don't you go on out on the porch while I finish up here? We're going to eat out there."

"You don't need my help?"

"I've got it. I'll be out in a minute." He stirred the beans in the pot on the stove. When he went to join her she was standing at the rail, looking out at the ocean as if she was contemplating a puzzling problem. He placed their plated meals on the table.

She turned to him. "This looks amazing."

He held her chair for her.

"The girls would love to see you now." She sat.

"I can hear them giggling. They're not used to their father romancing a woman."

"Are you romancing me?" She studied him as if she couldn't believe herself worthy of his actions.

"I like to think so. That was the plan." He took his seat across from her.

Their meal was slow and easy. They talked of movies they had seen, places they had been and their favorite meals. Cody enjoyed every minute of it. Stacey was intelligent and engaging, in his eyes the perfect dinner guest.

Stacey placed her fork on her plate. "Uh… I've been thinking."

His chest constricted. About what? "I'm not sure I like the sound of that."

"I'd like to take a walk on the beach."

Relief eased the tension in his shoulders. He had been afraid she might want to call a halt to their relationship.

"Then come back and show you just how sexy I think you are."

His manhood immediately sprang to life. He could forgo the walk for the latter but he would go along with her plans. Anything to keep her in his arms and bed for as long as possible.

The last few days and nights had been the most amazing, exhilarating and fascinating Cody had ever known. Stacey was everything he'd ever dreamed of in a woman. She was as exciting and entertaining in bed as out.

They worked side by side during the day, exchanging small smiles when nobody was watching. In the evening they had dinner and then sat on the porch until after dark. Hand in hand they would climb the stairs to his bedroom. Stacey satisfied all his desires and more. She continued to surprise him. Aggressive and demanding at times, she could be just as tender and giving at others.

Today those days and nights of heated pleasure would end. His mother and father were bringing the girls home. He expected them at any moment. Their return was bitter-sweet. He had missed his girls but tonight he would miss Stacey too. His heart was made even heavier by the fact that in just three days Stacey would be gone for good.

Their lovemaking the night before had been slow, deliberate and utterly poignant. Stacey seemed as aware their time together was nearly over as he was.

A sick feeling filled his gut. He had to start adjusting, accepting it must end. Now he was waiting at the ferry for his family to arrive. So why did it feel like part of it was still missing? That idea he refused to examine. It would get him nowhere.

He hadn't asked Stacey to come along, believing them being together to meet the girls might send them the wrong message. Before he'd left the clinic he had told her he was leaving to meet the ferry. She smiled but it didn't reach her eyes and she said, "I'll see to things here."

He watched as the ferry pulled into port, the ramp came down and cars started to unload. Soon he saw Jean and Lizzy waving excitedly at him. He returned the greeting, spying his parents behind them. The second the girls were off the ferry they ran to him, wrapping their arms around him.

"Hey, Daddy. We missed you," they each said to him.

"I missed you too," Cody said. He had, yet he was confident that the separation had been good for all of them. He had needed to let go temporarily.

"We had the best time." Jean beamed up at him.

He went down on one knee and wrapped them in his arms. "I want to hear all about it." A few minutes later, after he had spoken to his mom and dad, he herded them all off to his car.

Lizzie said, "We brought something home for Stacey."

His chest ached. "You did?"

Excitement filled Jean's voice as she said, "We got her a bracelet to replace the one she gave me. Now she can remember me when she leaves."

"I'm sure Stacey will like that." He had no doubt she would.

"Can we call her? Go see her?" Lizzy asked.

He drove out of the parking lot. "We'll get in touch with her soon. Right now we need to get you home. So, Mom and Dad, how was your trip?"

Stacey tried to push away her feelings of being left out. She didn't belong with Cody when he met his family. She wasn't a member of that group. She understood that in her mind but her heart tugged her to the harbor. Knowledge didn't make her heart hurt any less. She'd known she was getting in over her head, had tried to stop it, but couldn't. Cody's magnetic pull was just too strong. She and Cody hadn't discussed the fact she would be returning to her cottage that night instead of being in his bed. They both knew the score.

Going home to an empty cottage held no appeal so she worked late. Stacey updated all the patient charts and had done some work that wasn't necessary until the next week. She even made a second round to check on the patients. She didn't want Cody to have to come in for an emergency on the first night of the girls' return or while his parents were visiting. At least, that was the excuse she used.

Instead of going home, she chose to go to Sunbeam Victuals and Delectables for a cup of hot tea and a vegan sandwich. Not her favorite fare but a change from Cody's high-calorie meals. There she wouldn't have to worry about running into him.

The last few days had been the most contented of Stacey's life. She and Cody worked together during the day occasionally sneaking a kiss when no one was around. In the evenings she went to his house. Some-times she helped him prepare dinner and other times she sat and talked to him while he worked. They most often talked about his childhood which was almost idyllic compared to hers. Sometimes she would share one of her experiences in a different country.

She'd never before shared this type of connection with another human being. Cody hadn't only become her lover but her friend. Those were more difficult to find. She'd always looked forward to leaving one post and been excited about the next but this time she was dreading the change.

She was climbing into her car when her cellphone rang. To her surprise the phone ID told her it was Cody. "Hi."

"Could you come over?" He sounded as if he wasn't sure about asking or was afraid she might refuse. Still, her heart skipped a beat.

"Aren't the girls there?"

"Yes, they're the ones who asked me to call."

It hurt that it wasn't him who'd wanted to call. Even though she felt compelled to go, it wouldn't help her start detaching herself from Cody. It had been years since she'd let someone get so close to her. "I don't know. I'm tired. I'm just heading home." She had been up most of the night with him so it was a sweet tired.

"Just for a minute." His flat tone implied he was uncomfortable about insisting.

"I don't think it's a good idea." She was confident it wasn't. It would only make it harder for her. Possibly them.

His voice lowered. "The girls brought you a surprise or I wouldn't insist."

She couldn't not go now. Everything in her wanted to see Cody anyway. If just for a moment. She sighed. "Cody."

"We're adults. We can do this." He sounded as unconvinced as she felt. "The girls are refusing to go to bed and it's a school night."

He was laying the bricks of guilt on her.

"My mother and father are here also. They would like to say bye before they leave."

"They don't really know me." Her being friends with his parents was just one more level of involvement she didn't need.

"They feel like they do after they've spent a few days with the girls. I understand you were the topic of conversation for most of the trip. You make an impression on people." His voice dipped lower. "You sure have on me."

Warmth poured over her. He had on her as well. "Okay, but I'm only staying for a few minutes. I'm just leaving Phoenix's now."

"Thanks for doing this."

The pathetic thing was she wasn't even fooling herself. Everything in her drew her to Cody.

When she pulled up to Cody's house the porch light was on. What would it be like to come home all the time to someone who cared enough to leave a light burning for you? She tapped lightly on the door and it was immediately opened.

Jean and Lizzy said in unison, "Stacey!" They wrapped their arms around her waist for a hug. She returned their embraces. Her heart swelled. She could learn to love this type of reception.

"We watched the fishing boats come in, hiked to a

waterfall and went to the national park," Jean said, so fast Stacey almost missed some of it.

She smiled. "It sounds like you had a wonderful time." Stacey glanced up to see Cody standing in the hall. Longing filled his eyes. Did he see it in hers as well?

"Girls, let Stacey come in," he said gruffly.

They let go of her and scurried down the hall into the living room. Stacey closed the door behind her and followed them. As she passed him, Cody took her hand, raised it to his lips and placed a kiss in her palm. His gaze held hers. Stacey quaked. A hot response pooled at her center. Just as quickly he released her. They continued down the hall. His parents stood when she entered.

Mrs. Brennan said, "Hello again."

"Hi. Did you have a good trip?"

She nodded, giving Stacey a studying look. "We did. Maine is beautiful."

Did his mother see what was between her and Cody? "It is. I worked in a hospital there for a month. Hello, Mr. Brennan."

He smiled at her. "Nice to see you again, Stacey."

"We brought you something," Jean announced, holding out a box.

Lizzy snatched it from her hand. "I wanted to give it to her!"

"Let's be nice, Lizzy." Stacey stopped herself and her eyes jerked to where Cody stood in the doorway. She'd just disciplined his child in front of him.

"Stacey's right, that wasn't very nice, Lizzy," Cody said in a calm tone.

Jean said, "You can give it to her."

"That's nice of you, Jean," Stacey praised her. "May I see what's in the box?"

"It's something so you will remember us," Jean stated.

That wouldn't be a problem for Stacey. The reverse, in fact. She took the box, removed the top and inside found a multicolored stone bracelet. "It's beautiful."

"Now wherever you go you'll think of us." Lizzy looked at her eagerly.

"Thank you so much." Stacey slipped it on her wrist and placed the box on the coffee table. She then went down on one knee and opened her arms wide. The girls stepped into her embrace for a hug. "I love it. Thank you for thinking of me. You have my promise I'll always think of you both when I wear it." She looked over their heads at Cody and blinked to keep the moisture in her eyes from spilling over. This was just the type of emotional upheaval she'd been guarding herself against.

"Okay, girls, it's time for you to get ready for bed. You have school tomorrow." Cody placed a hand on each of the girls' shoulders.

Stacey let them go. "Better do what your daddy says."

The girls went first to one then the other of their grandparents and told them goodnight before they left the room.

"I'll be up in a few minutes to tuck you in," Cody called from behind them.

Stacey stood then shifted from one foot to the other, unsure what to do next. "Uh…it's time for me to get going as well. I've had a long day. I understand you're leaving tomorrow." She spoke to Cody's parents.

"We are. We're taking the earliest ferry off the island," Cody's mother said.

"Then I'll say goodbye now. It has been nice to meet you. I wish you a safe trip home."

Mrs. Brennan gave her a thoughtful look. She acted as if she wanted to say more but stopped herself. "It's been nice to meet you too."

Mr. Brennan nodded and smiled.

"I'm going to walk Stacey out," Cody said to no one in particular.

Stacey started toward the door with Cody close behind. She stepped outside and Cody came with her, flipping off the porch light and closing the door behind him. He pulled her into his arms. His lips joined hers in a sizzling kiss that slowed to a tender one. He continued to hold her close as he nuzzled her neck. "I'm going to miss you tonight."

This wasn't making it any less stressful on either of them. She put her hands on his chest and stepped back. "I have to go. See you tomorrow."

This was painful on a level she'd not experienced before. Grateful that the darkness hid her tears, she made her way to the car. Half an hour later she pulled a pillow to her and curled around it, hoping she could get at least a few hours' sleep.

CHAPTER EIGHT

LEAVING CODY'S HOUSE had to have been the most difficult thing she'd ever done. Every fiber in her being had wanted to stay. Had wanted him, wanted them, but more than that wanted to have a place where she belonged.

Family had been something she had grown up wishing for. Being a member of a loving group that cared about each other, no matter what. At one time she'd thought that would be a reality of hers but not now. She'd lost that dream. Still, it pulled at her at times, like the scene she had just been a part of at Cody's.

She had it bad. Had jumped over the line. This was just what she had fought against. Since her fiasco with her ex-fiancé she'd managed to remain unattached to anybody. Not this time. But she understood the score. Cody wanted someone who would stay on Maple Island, be there for him and his girls. Or did he really? Anyway, that wasn't something she was capable of doing. What if she screwed it all up and he left her?

All she knew was to keep moving. It was safe. Her visit on Maple Island had proved what staying in one place too long did to a person. She'd become attached to him and the girls, and would carry the pain of leaving them with her forever. It was a hurt she'd said she would never let herself bear again. And yet…

Even if Cody asked her to stay, she couldn't. But he wouldn't ask. He wouldn't let go of his fear that the marriage he wanted wasn't possible. He'd been hurt too deeply before. She wouldn't take the chance she might fail him. Cody had already suffered through one demoralizing marriage. She couldn't do it to him again. He deserved better.

Determined they would remain friends and on good terms, she would square her shoulders and find the fortitude to focus on work until it was time for her to leave. After all, nothing had really changed except they had stopped sharing a bed. But that was the change she hated most.

Despite two sleepless nights from being without Cody, she decided when Saturday morning arrived sunny and warm she would go to Boston and do some sightseeing. She took the midmorning ferry. She'd not seen any of the city except for the inside of a hospital. Today she would play tourist, for tomorrow she would be gone.

Refusing to dwell on the turn her life had taken, she put all her efforts into walking the Freedom Trail. She followed the painted directions on the street leading to all the important historical buildings that had been built before America had gained its independence. She saw the site of the Boston Tea Party, went inside Faneuil Hall to explore it, listening to the ghosts of the American Forefathers debating declaring independence from Great Britain. She stopped in the bustling market for lunch before returning to her walk that ended at the North Church that had been an integral part of

Paul Revere's night ride. She even took time to climb through the tall ship the *USS Constitution*, which she'd seen from the air when she and Cody had flown to the hospital. She made it a full day.

The only thing that marred her visit was the occasional thought slipping into her head that Cody would like this or she wished the girls could share that. The one concession she made to missing Cody's family was buying Jean and Lizzy a copy of *Make Way for Ducklings* at the Old Corner Bookstore. She couldn't help herself. The classic tale of the mallard ducks taking a stroll in the park was one she was confident the girls would enjoy.

With time on her hands and the next ferry still a few hours off, she decided to go to an afternoon movie. It would be months before she would have a chance to see a new release again. Ethiopia was a long way from home. From Maple Island. From the clinic. The girls. Cody.

She'd been back at the cottage long enough to shower and pull on one of Cody's T-shirts that she'd brought home with her when there was a pounding on her door. She pushed the curtain to one side. Cody stood on her porch. Concern filled his face. His hand rose as if he was going to knock again.

When she opened the door he stepped in and grabbed her, lifting her off her feet. It was heavenly being held by him again. His words rushed out, his worry surrounding each of them. "I've been trying to get in touch with you all day."

"Is something wrong?" She searched his face. Her

heart raced from just being so close to him. She would miss him every day for the rest of her life.

"No. I just couldn't find you. I've been calling you for hours. I thought you might have left without telling me goodbye. Why haven't you answered your phone?"

"I turned the volume down when I went into the movie and I forgot to turn it back up. I would never leave without saying something to you." She knew too well how it felt when someone you cared about just disappeared without warning.

Cody set her on her feet but didn't let her go, his gaze meeting hers penetratingly. "Movie? Where have you been?"

She wasn't used to someone keeping tabs on her. "I went to Boston for the day."

Disbelief covered his face. "Alone?"

"Yes." Before coming to Maple Island she'd done everything by herself. She'd not checked in with anyone in years. No one had cared enough about her to ask her to do so.

"I wanted to invite you to lunch. But I couldn't find you and kept calling. I got worried. I even lied for the first time in my professional life and said I had an emergency so that someone from the day-care center could come stay at the house with the girls. Then I came hunting you."

It gave her a warm fuzzy feeling deep down to know that Cody had been that anxious about her. Stacey couldn't remember the last time a person had shown any concern about her whereabouts or worried if anything had happened to her. No man since her first step-father had shown that much emotion for her and in the end he hadn't either. "I'm sorry I scared you. I hadn't seen Boston and so I thought today was a good day to do so."

"Why didn't you say anything to me about going?"

She hesitated a moment. "I didn't want you to feel pressured to go with me. The girls have just gotten home. I knew you would want to spend time with them. And I know you don't want them to know about us."

"I don't think they need to know we're sleeping together. And about that…" He kicked the door closed and walked her backward as he looked around. "By the way, where's your bedroom? I've missed having you beneath me."

"Do you think that's a good idea?"

"Probably not." He gave her a hot, wet kiss that made his intentions clear.

She gripped his shoulders and returned his kiss. Her center throbbed with need for him. No, it was probably not a good idea but she couldn't help herself. She would worry about how to recover from leaving Cody later. Right now she was going to enjoy every sweet moment she would have with him.

He pulled her hard against him, his desire long and ridged between them. "See how I've missed you."

She pulled back and said as seriously as she could, "You have? You only saw me yesterday."

Cody continued walking her backward as he nuzzled her neck. "Shut up. You know what I mean," he growled. "Now, where is your bed? I need you."

"I like the way you're showing me how much." She wiggled against him, making him moan as she gave him better access to her neck. Her hand slid between them to run along his hot, hard length.

"Stacey, as much as I enjoy trading quips with you, I'd much rather be doing something more meaningful."

She leaned back, giving him an innocent smile and batting her eyelashes. "And you have what in mind?"

He groaned. "You're doing it again." He backed her against the wall. Leaning in, he kissed her passionately before his hand skimmed up over her thigh and slipped beneath the hem of the T-shirt. "I'd hoped for something softer for you but I'm good here."

She giggled. "I like it when it's hard."

Cody groaned as he pressed her more securely to the wall and his lips found hers. He dipped a finger under her panties, making her jerk as he entered her. "There's that sassy mouth again."

She closed her eyes to savor the moment. This was the Cody she would miss the most.

Cody finished the last of his cheese omelet then put his plate down on the planks of Stacey's small porch. They were sitting in her swing with the only light coming from a lamp inside. He raised both hands above his head and took a large, very satisfying stretch. Done, he gave a little nudge with his toe and started the swing. He had no idea that he could be so…happy.

When had he last thought of happiness? Years? Obligations, his job, his girls, those, yes. The shoulds, musts and need-tos of his life—yes. But happiness? That hadn't entered his mind in so long he wasn't sure he could have put a name to it until this moment. Yet wasn't he fooling himself here? As good as he felt now, he knew he'd feel equally bad when Stacey left. She shifted where she sat crossed-legged beside him, finishing her meal.

"Thanks for the omelet."

"No problem. You got the extent of my culinary skills. And my refrigerator. You were lucky I had eggs and cheese."

"I noticed things were kind of sparse in there." He took her plate and set it on top of his.

She laid her head against his upper arm. "I've never kept much because I don't cook for myself often and since I'm leaving tomorrow I was trying to use up what I do have."

A lump formed in his chest. There went his happiness at the reminder she was leaving. Cody watched her. Could he let her go? Did he have a choice? What if he asked her to stay? Would she? He studied Stacey a moment. She looked so amazing with her disordered hair, her make-up-free face and dressed in what he'd learned was one of his T-shirts. He was such a love-sick calf. "Have you ever thought about staying in one place?" He held his breath, waiting for her answer. Maybe, just maybe she would answer as he hoped.

"I did one time but it didn't work out." She stated it as a fact, lacking emotion.

His heart fell. "What happened?"

"My fiancé left me for his old girlfriend a month before the wedding." Her voice sounded hollow, devoid of all emotion. Would she speak of him that way one day? That idea cut like a knife.

Now he had a better idea of why she moved around so much. She'd been hurt. Badly. They were more alike than he'd given her credit for when they'd first met. He'd run from his troubles in California and she was running around the world to hide from hers. "It was his loss."

Stacey stood and looked down at him in the dim light. "Thanks for saying that. A girl likes to hear things like that. Okay, no more talk about the past or the future. Right now is all I'm interested in."

He sighed. He could refuse her so little. He'd been kidding himself for days. This had to come to an end. It might kill him when Stacey got on the ferry but he wouldn't give up what time they could still share.

She clasped his hand, tugged him up and led him into the house. This time her eyes shone bright with seduction and desire. She led him to the bedroom he couldn't find earlier. They removed the few clothes they wore, saying nothing, just looking into each other's eyes. Their lovemaking was deliberate, delicious and passionately deep. Everything about it said they were aware this would be their last time together.

Sometime later Stacey asked while Cody was dressing, "May I come over and say bye to Jean and Lizzy tomorrow? I'm planning to take the midafternoon ferry off the island. I don't want to just disappear on them. I had that happen to me more than once and I won't do it to them."

He looked at her, indecision obvious in his eyes. "Why don't you come for a late breakfast?" Cody asked as he buckled his belt.

"I don't think that would be a good idea." It would surely make it more difficult for her.

"At this point nothing about this is going to be easy."

She couldn't disagree with that statement.

"The girls would really like to be with you for a while one last time." What he left off was how he would feel about it.

He put his hands on each side of her where she lay

on the bed and gave her a long tender kiss. "I'll say my goodbye now. It has been nice knowing you, Stacey. Good luck."

Stacey didn't like the sound of finality in his voice. Cody was already distancing himself. She didn't want that. Not yet. She reached around his neck and tried to pull him down to her but he stayed propped on his palms above her. He gave her one more searching look. As if he were memorizing her. He straightened. She groaned her complaint.

"I've got to go. I still feel guilty about lying to the sitter."

She stretched like a cat in the sun, arching her back so that her breasts were thrust high into his chest.

Cody muttered a word under his breath that wasn't repeatable in polite company. "You aren't playing fair."

Stacey pretended to giggle, trying to lighten the mood. "Is there a problem, Doc?"

"Yeah, there is." With that he turned on his heel and left.

Her smile dropped and she looked at the empty doorway. She had a problem too. Oh, yes, she would leave part of herself on Maple Island. A part she was sure she would never recover.

When she arrived at Cody's the next morning she was confident the idea of her having a meal with his family was a wrong step but she'd agreed to do it and wouldn't turn away. For once in her life she was willing to chuck out her major rule in life and not make sure she had said her goodbyes. It would have been so much easier to just get on the ferry and not look back. But she couldn't bring herself to do that.

Jean and Lizzy were giddy with excitement over seeing her. As Cody once again cooked pancakes, each girl took turns to share stories about their trip with their grandparents. They also got out the things they had brought home with them. A rock, a pine cone, a special cup, and every one Stacey treated as if it were made of gold.

Stacey presented the girls with the book she had bought them. They were happy to get it, even wanting her to read it to them. She did so while Cody continued to work on the food. She shared the inscription she'd written on the inside cover: "'To two very special girls. I'll always hold you and our time together in my heart.'"

They wouldn't understand that at their young ages but they would as adults. Maybe they would think about her when they read it to their own children. Wherever she was, it would be nice to think someone was thinking about her on occasion.

She looked at Cody after she'd read it. He was watching them with shadowy eyes. What feelings was he hiding there? Did he think it was too much? He'd been cool, even standoffish when she had arrived.

He seemed as resigned to her leaving as she was determined she would go. That was good. She didn't want a scene. There shouldn't be one anyway—she had told him all along that she wouldn't be staying. Why she was even worrying about it, she didn't know. Not once had he suggested that she should stay. There was no job here for her now. Cody had certainly not offered her a position in his life.

They'd had their fun and games while they'd had the chance and now it was over. They could part as friends and their time together would be a nice interlude she'd remember fondly. Sadly, despite trying to pretend, she wasn't sure it would be that simple for her.

Cody looked across the table at Jean and Lizzy. They were growing up fast. Right now they were all smiles and lively conversation, each one trying to talk over the other in an effort to hold Stacey's attention. She, as always, was listening raptly to each word. She would make a wonderful mother.

He had to stop that line of thought. It would get him nowhere. He wasn't even sure he could offer anyone that role ever again. Bringing her into their life permanently was another issue completely but, heaven help him, he would ache for her for a long time to come.

Cody had to stop himself more than once from holding her hand under the table. He just wanted to touch her for as long as possible. Instead, he resisted and tried to keep the meal moving on a light note.

It wasn't until they were all through with their meals that the atmosphere became gloomy. Stacey reached across the table and took the hands of Jean and Lizzy. "I wanted to come here today to tell you both I was leaving this afternoon."

The girls' smiles dropped.

"Can't you stay longer?" Lizzy asked mournfully.

Stacey's lips drew into a thin line and she shook her head slightly. "No. Remember I told you that I have a job waiting for me. They need me."

"But who is going to help us with our dance costumes? Daddy is no good at it." Jean looked from her to him and back again.

Stacey glanced at Cody giving him a weak smile

before her attention returned to the girls. "Maybe you can use your imaginations and help him."

This was just what Cody had tried to guard against. Once again someone Jean and Lizzy cared about would no longer be in their lives. He'd been unable to stay away from Stacey and now Lizzy and Jean were caught in the fallout.

"But we like you," Lizzy announced.

"And I like you both too. Me leaving won't change that."

"Do you have to go today?" Jean asked.

"I do. My mother is expecting me for a visit and then I'm off to Ethiopia." Stacey sounded as if she was trying to put an excited note in her words but it was falling flat.

The girls' eyes glistened with tears.

"Will you come back?" Jean asked.

Cody was devastated. This was the daughter who had taken time to warm up to Stacey and now that she had, Stacey was leaving. This was far worse than he'd imagined. He had to defuse the conversation. "Girls, we want to wish Stacey well, don't we? So let's smile and be happy for her. Since you have finished eating, how about putting your dishes in the sink. It's a nice day so why don't you go outside and play? Stacey doesn't have to leave for a little while. She can come out and say a final goodbye later."

As the girls scrambled to do as he'd asked, Stacey gave him a resigned look. "I didn't think it would be this hard. Never has been before." She said the words more to herself than to him.

Neither one of them said anything for a few minutes.

His phone ringing interrupted the silence. "I've got to get that."

Stacey nodded.

Cody picked his phone up off the counter and went into the next room to talk.

"Dr. Brennan," Cody answered. He hoped he didn't have to go in. He wanted all the time he could get with Stacey, even if it was rocky.

"Cody, it's Marsha Lewiston."

His clinical nurse. The one Stacey had been filling in for. "Marsha, it's good to hear from you. I'm looking forward to having you back tomorrow." That wasn't exactly accurate. If Marsha was his nurse again then Stacey would be gone. The knot that had formed in his stomach grew. "How's your mother doing?"

"That's the thing, Cody. She's recovering well from the surgery but she isn't getting any younger. I know this is short notice but I'm going to resign my position. I need to live and work closer to Mom."

Cody couldn't miss the extra thump of his heart at Marsha's announcement. There would be an opening for Stacey to stay. "I understand. You have to do what's best for you and your mother. I will miss working with you."

"I'll make it a formal note by email in the morning."

"That sounds fine. Let me know if you need a reference. I assure you it will be a glowing one."

"Thanks, Cody. I appreciate that. Again, I'm sorry for not saying something sooner."

"Don't worry about it." As far as Cody was concerned, the timing was perfect. He could offer Stacey the position. Maybe it would give her an excuse to stay. They could build from there.

CHAPTER NINE

WITH HIS PHONE call completed Cody returned to the kitchen, hope making his step lighter. There he found Stacey standing at the sink, doing the dishes.

"Leave those. I'll do them later." Cody moved around the counter near her and leaned a hip against it.

"I don't mind. It gives me something to do." She placed a plate into the dishwasher. "I have to go in a few minutes anyway."

He tried to tamp down the excitement that Marsha's phone call had generated in him. Would Stacey go for it? He couldn't help but be thrilled about the idea. Maybe it would be enough to get her to stay longer. Still, he wasn't clear on how he really felt about Stacey agreeing to what he was about to ask. Would she see it as him asking for more between them?

The fear that something he couldn't get back was leaving his life enveloped him and helped him make up his mind. He had to ask her. He couldn't let her go without at least trying to get her to stay on some kind of terms. Even if right now it was for work reasons.

"That was Marsha. You know, the nurse that you've been filling in for. She has decided to hand in her resignation."

Stacey stopped in mid-motion, the dishcloth dangling in her hand, to look at him.

"Effective tomorrow. She wants to work closer to her aging mother." He smiled at her. "It looks like I have an opening for a good clinical nurse." His eyes searched her face. "Interested?"

Time hung, unmoving. Cody's eyes searched her face. Stacey said nothing. Panic burned through him. Acid rose in his throat. She was taking too long to answer for it to go his way.

With a sad look in her eyes, Stacey finally shook her head slowly. "Cody, I can't. I've already committed to the job in Ethiopia."

"Can't or won't?"

"I told you when we first met that I don't stay in one place long. That's just not who I am. Let's not make this into something unpleasant after what we have shared. We both knew when we got together it was just for fun. Would only last for a few days."

"I thought that's what you would say." He had to admit he was disappointed but he'd known her view before he'd asked the question. Cody couldn't help himself; he had to know. He stepped closer to her and asked in a low flat voice, "When you leave here, you won't look back, will you?"

Her eyes filled with pain and uncertainty. Her lips thinned and she shook her head. "Cody, I told you how I am. Let's not ruin what we've had."

Cody hated the idea that she could leave him and that he'd mean nothing more to her than some man she'd met and bedded while on Maple Island. He wanted her to care more than that. "What have we had, Stacey? Just sex? What exactly?"

"Isn't that what we agreed to? What you wanted? I don't remember you offering me more."

"Yeah, but I had the impression that it might be more than that now." He shouldn't have let himself get involved deeply enough that his heart hurt at the thought of never seeing her again. Why hadn't he protected himself more? If she really cared for him and the girls, she would want to stay. At least try taking the job. He tamped down the anger that welled in him.

Getting frustrated with Stacey would only make the situation worse. Why didn't she act as if she was hurting over her choice to leave as much as he was? She was just like Rachael after all. Only cared about herself.

Stacey hadn't counted on there being this much emotional baggage when she left. It had never existed before. When she had become physically involved with Cody she'd feared this might happen but had never considered it would be like carrying a car around on her back. Yet she was determined to put a smile on her face and soldier on. Just because there was a job opening at the clinic, it didn't mean that she was going to dump all her plans and stay here.

Anyway, given some space, these developing feelings for Cody would probably pass. They had when her fiancé had left her, as well as her stepfather. Now she could talk about those times without even flinching. Given enough time, she would be able to treat thoughts of Cody with the same disregard. She would move on. That's what she did. Kept moving.

She was kidding herself. This time it was different. She would tie all the sweet memories of Cody and their time together with a pink bow in her mind and take them out to pore over every day forever. She almost groaned out loud.

He studied her a moment. "You know, you are the last person I'd have sworn I would ever think this about, but you really are a coward, aren't you?"

She dropped the dishcloth into the sink and rounded on him. Her face flushed. How dared he! "What?"

"You are scared."

"What are you talking about?" Stacey considered herself fearless. She had lived in the jungle, the desert and places with no running water. She wasn't afraid of anything.

"You can't even live in the same place for more than a few months at a time because you're afraid you might care about someone. So what's the plan? Live in fear all your life?"

"You have real gall to say that to me when you have closed yourself off on an island? You have some nerve." For a second he felt as if she had struck him.

He bared his teeth. "You don't know the hell that I…" he pointed outside "…and my girls have lived through. I can't just open the door and let *anyone* in."

"No, I don't know what you have been through but what I do know is that you can't put your life on hold because you are afraid of it happening again. Somehow you're going to have to learn to let go enough to let people in and, when they're old enough, let your girls go. When I got here you were so closed off that I was afraid if you smiled your face would crumble. You couldn't even take a joke!"

"I let *you* in!"

"You did." She shook her head. "But only enough to

have sex with me. I was easy, though." She raised her hand to stop him from speaking. "Not that kind of easy. Easy for you because I was only going to be here for a month. That way you didn't have to give too much of yourself or make a commitment. I was a safe bet. You didn't have to worry about me being the wrong choice because you knew I wasn't going to stay around." She harrumphed. "I was both the right and wrong choice. Right for a fling and wrong for you in the long haul. Which made me perfect." She chuckled dryly.

"Why do you think you're wrong for me for the long haul?"

"For starters, I don't know anything about being a mother. I probably had one of the worst. She spent all her time worrying about keeping her man or getting the next one. I mostly raised myself. You need a woman who would be attentive to your girls. I don't know how to do that."

He pointed toward the table. "That's bull. I just watched you with them a few minutes ago. And when you were helping them with their costumes. You're a natural. That's just one more of your excuses."

"You told me once you wanted a marriage like your parents have and hadn't got it. That doesn't mean it isn't out there for you. The right woman will come along. You just have to open up enough to let her in." The idea of Cody having another woman permanently in his life made Stacey almost lose her breakfast.

"Now you're giving me marriage advice," he stated incredulously. "The woman who won't stay in one place long enough to have a relationship. That's laughable." But he wasn't laughing.

"You are right. I have no business telling you how to run your life. Really I don't."

His shoulders slumped as if he were defeated. "I grew up believing marriage was forever. Permanent. Then addiction destroyed it all. Now I'm gun-shy. Afraid to trust or believe in anyone. Particularly where the girls are concerned."

He paused and looked lost for a moment. Under any other circumstances she would have felt sorry for him. A stricken look had come over his face and he straightened as if he were ready to go to battle. "But I'll have you know I don't lightly invite people into my life or my girls'. I took a chance with you."

If she'd let herself admit it, she knew she wanted what Cody offered. All of it. But she couldn't take it. History told her that it would be snatched from her just when she started to feel secure. She couldn't take that chance. Stacey's voice softened. "I know you did. Only because you knew I would soon be leaving."

Cody had had enough. What had started out as a job offer had turned into an ugly personal argument. "All I'm saying is that if you take my job offer then we could explore what's between us. Maybe I could let go some, trust more. Trust you. But you'd have to stop running. Could you do that? Let me in enough that you could trust me not to leave you? Look around you. You've made friends here, have a job you say you love. The girls and I are here. Why can't you accept you're good enough to deserve all of that?"

"Maybe because I've never felt wanted before and I don't know how to handle it!"

Cody stepped closer to her. There was a plea in his voice when he said, "I could help you."

"Yeah. I know how that goes. You'd have me around until I do something you don't think is right. Then you'd not want me anymore. You'd leave me or I'd have to leave!" She shook her head as if she was trying to dislodge the past. "No, I can't. I won't go through that again. I won't be left behind again. Ever."

"I would never do that to you." Cody reached for her but she backed away, out of touching distance.

If she allowed him to touch her, she'd never be able to leave. "You left your wife. Why wouldn't you leave me?"

Air whistled from Cody as if he had just been sucker-punched. "I stayed to the bitter end. I didn't want to give up. I was just left no choice."

"You say I ran away. But you have run in your own way as much as I have. You've moved all the way across the country to get away."

"To protect my children. My move from California was different from hopping from place to place around the world because you're scared to give anyone or any-place a chance."

Stacey scowled at him. "That's not true."

He cocked his head and gave her a narrowed-eyed look. "Are you sure about that? Are you happy with your life? Being alone all the time?"

She flinched.

"You do know you don't have to go." He let the words sink in.

She stepped toward him. "I have already made a commitment."

He met her glare head on. "Yeah, but I also offered

you one here. With me." That sounded too close to a proposal.

"To be your nurse and your night-time booty call whenever the girls happen to be elsewhere. Sounds like the perfect life for you."

That time she'd cut him to the core. Even to him it sounded one-sided. Sleazy and self-centered.

"Daddy, why're you and Stacey fighting?" came Lizzy's small voice from the doorway.

She and Cody whirled in her direction in shock. He hoped Lizzy hadn't heard Stacey's last statement.

Stacey went down on one knee and brought Lizzy into her arms. "Your daddy and I were just talking. I was telling him it's time for me to go now." She looked over Lizzy's shoulder at Cody. "How about a big hug before I do?"

Lizzy had a sad little smile on her face.

"Bye, sweetheart." Stacey pulled her close.

Standing, Stacey moved toward the back door. "I'm going to speak to Jean on the way out. Bye, Cody." She gave him a little wave.

His lips drew into a thin line and he closed his eyes. When he opened them she was gone.

CHAPTER TEN

CODY HAD BEEN working through his pain and loneliness. Not well, but he tried. The days since Stacey had left had been long and seemingly endless as the ocean he spent too much time looking out at. The nights made the days feel short and sweet. Without Stacey next to him he couldn't rest. When he did sleep, he dreamed of her. He was just existing and didn't know how to come out of the fog. His heart was broken and Stacey was the only cure.

The day she had left and his back door had closed between them he'd been confident that all the joy in his life had gone out that door with her. He'd not been wrong.

Nothing about living whilst being deprived of Stacey was easy. In fact, it made what he'd lived through earlier in his life seem stress-free. He was tied in a knot with no idea how to unsnarl it. Somehow he had to recover from Stacey. Help his girls do so as well.

They spoke of her almost daily, which only increased his pain. Stacey had made such a strong impression on them in such a short time. To make matters worse, he was grumbling at the girls. He was muddling through life and doing a very poor job of even that. The happiness he'd been so surprised to have was gone now. He hadn't been able to hang on to it. Having so briefly tasted it, the loss of it was almost too much for him to bear.

He went through the motions of working. Most of his medical care was done by rote. Nothing interested him. Each patient had become a case instead of a person. The fact that he was doing it all on little or no sleep didn't make matters any better.

The nurses already on staff were taking turns filling Stacey's position. They were efficient enough but there was no real rapport between them and him. He missed Stacey's humor, the way she anticipated his next move or need. Heck, he missed her in his professional life almost as much as he did in his private one. She had managed to permeate every corner of his world. He'd been caught up in the tsunami that was Stacey and it was now tossing him around.

Two weeks after Stacey had left he passed the day care as Alex exited.

"Hey, buddy, you got a minute to talk?" Alex asked, putting a hand on Cody's shoulder.

"Uh…sure." Cody wasn't fit company for anyone. "Is there a problem?"

"I think so, but you'll have to confirm it."

That was a cryptic remark for the usually straight-forward Alex. "Is something up with a patient?" Cody couldn't think of who it might be.

"Let's go to my office." They entered and Alex said, "Close the door."

Cody did so then slumped into a chair in front of Alex's desk. "What's going on?"

Alex continued around the desk to sit behind it. "That's just what I was going to ask you."

"What do you mean?" Had Alex noticed what a mess his life had become now that Stacey was gone?

"Come on, Cody, you're talking to me. Neither one of us has any dirty laundry that the other doesn't already know about. Something's eating at you. You've not been yourself since Stacey left." Cody started to deny it but Alex raised his hand. "Don't say there wasn't something between you because this is a small island and an even smaller clinic."

"Great. I thought I was covering better than that," Cody muttered.

"Sorry to disappoint you, buddy. So what happened?"

A big fat fight. Too much said. Too little said. Not the right things said. Cody shrugged. "Nothing. It was time for her to leave and she did."

"Did you want her to stay?" Alex watched him closely.

Cody hated to admit how much. "Sure I did. I offered her Marsha's job but she said no."

Alex nodded his head a few times and pursed his lips. "You offered her a job. I see."

Sitting a little straighter, Cody asked, "What do you mean by that?"

"Well, if I have learned anything from Maggie it's that a woman wants more than just a job offer from her man. Did you tell her you loved her?"

He hadn't even dared to think in that vein. If he did he might fall down the hole of despair and never come back out again. It took him a few seconds to answer. "No."

"You do, though, don't you?"

There he was on the edge of the hole. Did he? Yeah, he did. Why had it taken this conversation to make him admit it to himself? Because it was the first time he'd ever really loved a woman enough that he couldn't live without her. He'd never felt that way before.

"I know what it's like to start again. The fear of opening your heart again. It's scary but you need to know, from what I learned about Stacey she has a huge heart and she's nothing like Rachael. From what I saw she was a better mother to Jean and Lizzy in just a few weeks than their biological mother was, can be or ever will be. That said, I need you in top working order around here."

Cody squared his shoulders. "Are you questioning my ability to do my job?"

"Never. I'm questioning whether or not you can survive if you continue like this." Alex leaned forward. "Right now, I don't think you're functioning well enough to make sound medical decisions." He frowned briefly and then continued. "Maggie and I had a hard trail to walk and we came out on the other side. I think you will too. Have you thought about going after Stacey? Telling her how you feel? Maybe offering her a ring instead of a job?"

"She's in Ethiopia," Cody said flatly.

Alex leaned toward him, pinning him with a look. "You fly, don't you? If you don't do something soon, I'm going to have to buy you out of the clinic because your sad face is starting to affect the morale around here. All I'm saying is think about it."

Cody did, for every hour of the day. Nothing Alex had said could Cody refute. He had been happy. Life had been good with Stacey in it. She had added to his life, not taken away, like Rachael had. The girls were crazy about her. He was too—heck, he was in love with her.

Was he really still letting Rachael control his life? He might have moved three thousand miles away from her yet what she had done governed every decision he made. Stacey had been right. It was time he let go. Trusted somebody. Admit that he could have that dream of a true partnership within a marriage, just with a different person. He hoped that person would be Stacey. It was finally time to move on with his life.

Just as shameful, he had looked down on Stacey for her lifestyle and had accused her of being a coward. He'd taken the high road of superiority in the knowledge that he had established a home. Living here on the island, he might not have been physically running, but what he'd been doing was certainly running emotionally. Never dating, never taking an interest in a woman, never opening up to someone. Until Stacey. He had let a destroyed dream and guilt rule his life for too long. His narrow world had become all about his girls and trying to protect them from life. What a horrible example to set for Jean and Lizzy.

Happiness was what he should be encouraging them to strive for. He'd had that with Stacey. Somehow he was going to get it back. The question now was how.

When Stacey had left Cody's house that Sunday, she'd gone back to her cottage and picked up her already packed bag. She'd made her way to the ferry in time to take an earlier one. There had been no one there to wave goodbye to. That had only added to her sadness.

She'd sat in the corner of the sparsely populated boat, not even looking out the window. Every fiber of her being had begged to stay but her mind had told her no. It wasn't to be. Nothing about her life was truly different than it had been before she'd come to Maple Island.

She had changed her plane reservation and ended up at her mother's door sooner than expected. The second the door to her mother's apartment had opened, Stacey had fallen into her arms. She had clung to her mother like she was the lifeline she was. Stacey's heart was broken and she'd run home. Regardless of the fact her mother's own life was so screwed up, she still remained the only constant in Stacey's. That evening she'd told her mother she was tired and had gone to bed early.

The next morning she'd woken in a small bedroom in her mother's apartment to the sounds of cars driving by, the trash truck banging and clanging, and people yelling through the open windows. She wasn't in paradise anymore.

This wasn't Maple Island, where the seagulls squawked as they fought over breakfast in the rolling waves and the sun shone warmly on her face. The one spot in all the world where Cody was, where his loving was so sweet it was almost painful. The place she'd chosen to leave behind.

She'd rolled over, burying her face in a pillow, and groaned. How had it come to this?

After their first kiss she'd never doubted it would be a difficult parting between her and Cody. Even knowing that, she'd never dreamed they wouldn't at least part friends. She couldn't believe she'd left with such ugliness between them. For all the wonderful memories she had stored away, those unpleasant few moments of their final fight tarnished them.

There was a knock on the bedroom door. Her mother asked, "Stacey, may I come in?"

"I guess so." There was no enthusiasm in her response. She sounded wretched even to her own ears.

Her mother came to sit on the bed like she used to do when Stacey had been a child. "You've been here a day and hardly gotten out of bed. I think it's time we talked."

Stacey knew that was true. She needed to understand things about her mother so she could reconcile her own beliefs. Cody had made her question them. Had she really been running all these years? Fearful of feeling anything for someone? Scared of being left? Stacey didn't want to live like that any longer. She wanted security and love. To feel special to someone. She wanted what she had lost with Cody.

"You get a shower and I'll fix us some pancakes and you can tell me what has you so out of sorts." This wasn't a request from her mother but a directive.

Left with no choice, Stacey crawled out of bed and headed for the tiny bath. She stood under the water until it turned cold.

There was a sharp rap on the door. "Pancakes in five."

Pancakes. She'd loved Cody's pancakes. Could see him standing at the stove, grinning, as he flipped one perfectly...

Stacey dressed, and with her hair still twisted in a towel she went to her mother's small galley kitchen. She took a seat at the two-person table next to a window overlooking a street with a few trees. Once again she longed for Maple Island.

They ate in silence. Mostly her mother ate. When her mother finished she placed her fork on her plate with a loud ping. Stacey jumped.

"Okay, spill."

Stacey fingered the bracelet Jean and Lizzy had given her. She rarely took it off. "I've been working for this doctor. He has two small girls."

"Aw, I suspected as much. This is about a man. He's gotten to you. I was wondering when you would finally let it happen."

Cody *had* gotten to her. Enough so that her entire world had tilted. She didn't know how to right it. "We got close, had an argument and then it was time for me to leave."

Her mother watched her closely. "There's more to it than that."

Her mom had always been able to read her expressions. Stacey hadn't realized that until this moment. She had believed her mother was oblivious to her and her feelings. Now she questioned whether or not she'd given her mother enough credit. "Do you mind if I ask you something?"

Her mother got up and poured them more tea then sat again. "What do you want to know?"

"Why couldn't you hold a marriage together?"

Her mother flinched then put her elbows on the table, holding the warm tea mug between her hands. "I don't know. Maybe because I was always searching for something from some man that he wasn't able to give me." She shrugged. "Or it might be that I can't open up enough to really let someone in. That I'm afraid they might see the real me and not like it. I know I've hurt you with my failed marriages. Your father, then your stepfather. I could see you missed him terribly. I hated myself for making you go through that."

"So your answer was to take me away from my friends as well by moving to Miami?" Some of Stacey's spirit had returned.

"That wasn't my best decision. I was running from the bill collectors."

Stacey had had no idea. She had to give her mom some sympathy there.

"I can't change what happened but what I can tell you is that if you ever find a man that you believe you can give your heart and soul to, and you know he can do the same to you, then grasp him and hold on for all your life. That's a precious thing that I've never had and wish desperately I could find. Don't let my abysmal track record spoil your happiness."

"It's still not too late for you." Stacey reached over and put her hand over her mother's. This type of heart-to-heart they had never had. Suddenly she felt sorry for her mother. Stacey had shared more with Cody in a few weeks than her mother had found in her lifetime with her various partners.

"Maybe not. The question is, have you found someone you could settle down with? Tell me about this doctor."

Stacey shared with her mother all about Cody and Jean and Lizzy, and Maple Island. The memories of their times together returned sweet and clear. Stacey finished with, "We had a huge fight. I had to leave and I won't see them again. I have a job in Ethiopia."

Her mother gave her a thoughtful look. "Do you love Cody?"

How like her mother to cut straight to the point. Stacey's eyes didn't waver as she answered, "With all my heart."

"Then do something about it."

"He offered me a job but said nothing about how he felt. I'm obligated to go to Ethiopia. After our fight I'm not sure he even wants to speak to me, let alone be willing to wait for me to come back."

"Then you need to decide if he's worth fighting for. Can you live without him? Probably. Will you be happy, though?" She shrugged.

Her mother still searched for what Stacey was confident she had already found with Cody. He and the girls had captured her heart. She would meet her obligation in Ethiopia until they could find a replacement for her. Then she would make arrangements to return to Maple Island. She intended to find out if Cody loved her as well.

Cody was coming out of surgery when Alex stopped him. "Do you have a sec?"

After their conversation two weeks earlier, Cody had taken hold of his emotions and stuffed them away in an effort to get his life back into line. He had called the agency that Stacey worked for and had been told that she was no longer employed by them. She had left no forwarding address. She had just disappeared. No, it was more like he had let her go.

Now he was only surviving because of the girls. Each day he hoped that Stacey might write and he would have a lead to what village she was working in in Ethiopia. It had been a month since she had left and every day he was disappointed when he looked through the mail. Somehow he had to find a way to contact her.

"Since you're not taking any interest in hiring a new clinical nurse and I'm worried about overworking the nurses we have, I've taken the liberty of having a staffing service set up a few interviews for you. The first one comes in today at three." With that, Alex walked away.

How like Alex to drop something like that in his lap when Cody least expected it. He had dawdled about replacing Stacey because it meant she was gone for good if he filled the position. He had been holding out for her return. He wanted her back in his professional life but more than that he wanted her in his private one as well.

That afternoon Cody was in his office. He picked up the phone. He had time to call one more nursing agency. He'd been working through a list of them, trying to find someone that knew something about Stacey. He'd already tried her cellphone and the number was no longer working. He'd even gone on social media and found nothing. "May I speak to someone who would know something about nurses assigned to Ethiopia?"

"I could probably help you with that information," came a voice he heard nightly in his dreams. *Stacey!*

Cody's head jerked toward the door. His heart clogged his throat. Was she actually here or was he just imagining it because he wanted it so desperately?

She smiled but there was still an unsure look in her eyes. "I'm here for a job interview."

He hung up the phone without saying another word and just stared at her. She was the most beautiful sight he'd ever seen. The simple pink dress she wore accentuated her coloring and her curves. It was demure while at the same time enticing. Her hair hung freely around her shoulders, bouncing with healthiness. His fingers tingled with the desire to run the silkiness through them. She wore the bracelet his daughters had given her on her wrist. Where had she come from? Had Alex put her up to this? He stood. "Hi, Stacey."

"Hello, Cody."

With great effort he stopped himself from circling the desk and scooping her up into his arms. What if that wasn't what she wanted? Maybe she just wanted the job but not him. That thought made him almost double over in pain. He'd said some nasty things to her the day she'd left. Yet here she was, interviewing for a job that would mean she would be working with him almost daily.

"How have you been?" With effort he kept his voice level, professional.

"Busy. I quit my job with the travel nursing agency but still made a short trip to Ethiopia to work until a replacement could be found. I've decided to try staying in one place for a while. I saw on the clinic website there was a job still open here, so I applied for it."

"Did Alex know it was you?" He'd never forgive the man for not putting him out of his misery as soon as he knew it was Stacey coming for the interview.

"Nope. At least, not until I saw him in the hall. He said something peculiar. Something about being damn tired of running a place for lonely hearts."

Cody chuckled. Alex was no doubt fed up with dealing with him and also having Salty unhappy about Mrs. Kerridge-Bates. Love hadn't run smoothly for them either, but at least they had finally sorted out their issues and had admitted to loving each other. They were even planning their wedding. Now, if he could just convince Stacey that they should go down the same path...

"So what makes you want to work at Maple Island Clinic?"

Her mouth quirked. "Do you conduct all your interviews standing up?"

"Uh...no, sorry. Come in and have a seat." She came in and closed the door, then took the chair in front of his desk.

Cody sat as well, clutching his hands in his lap. If he didn't touch her soon, he would die. Yet if he did, it might scare her off. She looked so cool and collected. As if she were unaffected by the weeks that had passed since they had seen one another.

"In answer to your question, you do."

"I do what?" He'd forgotten what he'd asked. She giggled. He loved that sound.

"You asked me why I wanted to work at the clinic and I said because of you."

Did he dare to hope? "Why is that?"

"Because you're the most amazing, giving and caring doctor and man that I know. You are a wonderful father, a good friend and most of all I want to be around you. Working with you would make me a better nurse and person."

Cody's heart swelled. Did she really believe that? He stood and circled the desk then sat on the corner of it within touching distance of her. "You do know that if you take this job, you would be a permanent staff member. Are you prepared to stay here for a lifetime?"

"I am." Her eyes didn't waver.

He gaze didn't leave hers. "I can be demanding, and misguided, and sometimes say things I regret. Can you deal with that?"

"I believe so. I often do the same thing." She continued to hold his gaze. Stacey had the most amazing green eyes.

"It sounds like we could get along well together." He knew exactly how well they could get along and wanted them to find that happiness again. "Do you have any questions for me?"

"I do have one." She looked down.

He waited. Was she afraid to ask him? Now, that was unlike the Stacey he knew.

Her eyes met his again. "Do you love me as much as I love you?"

His heart raced, his hands shook as he lifted her out of the chair and crushed her to him. He kissed her with all the passion that had built inside him while they'd been apart. It flowed freely over the dam he'd created to try to protect himself. She returned his kisses with the same abandon. He now had everything he wanted in life in his arms and he was going to do whatever it took to keep her there.

"I missed you so much. I've called everywhere, looking for you." He nibbled at her neck.

"Cody?"

"Yes?" He continued to kiss her eyes, her nose and her cheeks. He inhaled the peach smell he couldn't get enough of.

"You didn't answer my question." There was a hint of uncertainty in her voice.

He leaned away until he could meet her eyes. "I love you too. More than life."

* * *

Stacey lay in Cody's bed that evening, wrapped in his arms. Life took odd turns and sometimes gave a person something they never dreamed was possible. That had happened for her. She had what she had hoped for all her life—someone to love her, a place to call home and a man who would never leave her. Could her life get much better?

"Hey, what're you thinking about over there?"

"About how happy I am."

Cody rolled to her, placing a kiss on her bare shoulder. "You make me happy."

She cupped his cheek. "I'm sorry I said all those mean things to you."

"Don't be. I needed to hear them. You were right. That's why the girls are at my parents' and I'm here. I have to start letting go."

"I'm proud of you. What you said to me hit home as well. I talked to my mother, really talked. She's the one who convinced me to come and see you, to tell you how I felt. It turns out that in some ways she's been a good mother. I just didn't want to see it."

"It sounds like we have both made steps in the right direction." He gave her a tender kiss. Pulling away, he said, "It's about time for the girls to call. They'll be so excited to see you but they might ask questions we don't want to answer if we don't put some clothes on."

Not long after that Stacey could hear Cody already talking to the girls before she came out of the bathroom. They were video-chatting. She stepped up behind him and smiled into the screen at the two girls that she loved almost as much as she did their daddy.

"Hi, Jean. Hi, Lizzy."

"Stacey!" the girls squealed in unison.

"You came back. I knew you would," Jean said with a satisfied smile.

"I'm glad to be back. I missed you both so much. I look forward to hugging you when you get home."

"You're wearing the bracelet we gave you." Lizzy said, pointing.

"I am. I've thought about you both every day we have been apart." She squeezed Cody's shoulder. She'd thought of him every minute.

Cody pushed the chair back and spoke to Stacey. "Why don't you have a seat? I think the girls have something they want to ask you."

Stacey gave him a questioning look but took the spot he had vacated. She looked into the screen at the smiling faces. Cody came round beside her and went down on one knee, taking her hand.

"Okay, girls," Cody said.

"Will you marry us?" all three of them asked at the same time.

Stacey blinked back tears as she looked into Cody's eyes. "I can't think of anything I would love more."

She wrapped her arms around Cody's neck and they kissed to the sound of "Ooh!" coming from the girls.

EPILOGUE

STACEY FLOATED ON happiness like a hot-air balloon through a cloudless July sky. It was her wedding day. *Wedding day.*

Fleur fussed around her, tugging here and adjusting there, as Stacey prepared to walk down Cody's porch steps to the beach where he was waiting. "You look beautiful. I can hardly wait until Cody sees you. Your dress is perfect."

Stacey glanced down at the simple gauzy fabric with the pink ribbon at the waist. She carried a bouquet of pink roses that were a gift from Cody. "Thank you. Just think, you and Rick will be having your wedding day in only a couple of weeks."

Fleur stopped what she was doing. A serene look came over her face, along with a slight smile. She turned to Stacey. "There's nothing like marrying the man you love, is there?"

"No, there isn't." Seconds later the sound of Jean and Lizzy giggling drew her attention. They were coming up the path from the beach.

Jean called, "Stacey, you'd better come. Daddy's getting nervous, he said."

"I was just waiting for you two to escort me." Stacey

went down the steps to meet her future with a bright smile on her face.

"You're so pretty," Lizzy breathed in awe.

"You two look beautiful." The girls wore soft pink matching dresses that flowed in the slight breeze. Matching flowers circled their heads.

Fleur went down the steps carefully. At the bottom she spoke to Stacey. "Give me one minute to tell the guitar player to start playing and then you can come meet the groom." She disappeared between the rocks.

Stacey stepped down the stairs. "Are we ready, girls?"

Jean and Lizzy's faces turned serious as they started back toward the beach. Stacey followed close behind. Notes of the wedding march flowed on the ocean breeze as she stepped between the rocks to see Cody ahead, waiting for her at the end of the lines of chairs that formed an aisle. He had never looked more hand-some than he did then, dressed in a light gray suit with a crisp white shirt open at the neck. Alex, his best man, would stand beside him until she joined Cody in front of the pastor then Alex would take a seat next to Fleur.

The girls paused in front of Cody and he kissed the tops of their heads before they went to sit beside his mother and father on the right side front row. Across from them was her mother. She was smiling but her eyes held a glossy look.

When Cody's gaze found hers, Stacey's middle flut-tered. He took two steps forward and offered his hand. She grasped it and he brought her to him as they stared into each other's eyes.

The pastor cleared his throat and they guiltily turned to him.

The rest of the ceremony was a blur for Stacey. Before she knew it Cody was kissing her and they were going back down the aisle to applause and smiles. They continued until they got to the house. At the bottom of the steps Cody picked her up and swung her around then let her slide to her feet. "I love you, Mrs. Brennan."

She was now Mrs. Cody Brennan. Stacey Brennan. She liked the sound of all of it. "I love you, Dr. Brennan." She reached up and kissed him.

They climbed the stairs to the porch, where they would greet their guests before they went inside for the reception. The first to join them were the girls. They came running. Close behind them were Cody's parents.

"I'm hungry," Lizzy said as she reached them.

She and Cody laughed.

"I'm glad you're going to be our mother." Jean hugged her.

Stacey returned it tightly. "I am too."

"I'll see about them," his mother said. "This is your day." She hurried the girls on.

"Congratulations, son," his father said, with a handshake.

Just behind them was her mother. She hugged Stacey then Cody. "I wish you both the best." She looked at Stacey and smiled.

Soon Rick and Fleur were coming up the stairs, along with Alex and Maggie. They were all smiles.

After all the congratulations had been offered, Maggie said to no one in particular, "I'm sorry Rafael and Summer had to miss this but I know they're enjoying their honeymoon in Spain."

"When they get home, maybe we can all get together and share wedding pictures," Fleur suggested.

The men groaned.

Stacey's heart expanded. She'd not only gained Cody and the girls but this clinic "family" as well. For someone who had so little family of her own, she now had a lot.

Other members of the Maple Island community stopped to speak on their way inside. Soon she and Cody joined the crowd enjoying food and drinks. The first people they met near the wedding cake were Salty and Philomena.

"Congratulations, Doc." Salty offered his hand to Cody. "The steps were too much for us so we came round to the front door," Salty said in his gravelly voice. Philomena stood beside him, leaning on a decorative silver cane. "I told you a good woman is hard to find."

Philomena gave him a nudge. "Uh…and you found one, too."

Stacey leaned against Cody and squeezed his arm. She enjoyed the look of embarrassment that washed over Salty's face.

Philomena smiled at Stacey. "Beautiful bride and a beautiful wedding. I'm so happy for you both."

"Thank you." Stacey couldn't stop smiling. She looked around at the crowded room. She couldn't believe how much her life had changed in such a short time. For a person who'd had almost nobody in her life, she had now found a home and a community of what would become long-time friends.

Cody tugged her away so that it was only the two of them. He watched her closely. "What're you thinking?"

"Just that you have given me everything I've ever dreamed of and more. I love you so much."

He pulled her tight against him. "You have done exactly the same for me."

* * * * *

COMING SOON!

We really hope you enjoyed reading this book. If you're looking for more romance, be sure to head to the shops when new books are available on

Thursday 21st February

To see which titles are coming soon, please visit

millsandboon.co.uk/nextmonth

MILLS & BOON

Coming next month

A WIFE FOR THE SURGEON SHEIKH
Meredith Webber

Malik saw what little colour she'd had in her cheeks fade, and the tip of her tongue slide across her pale lips.

And found himself wanting nothing more than to take care of her—this small, fiercely protective woman. Not only to keep her safe but to lift the burden of fear from her slim shoulders.

To hold her, tell her it would all work out.

To hold her?

Get your mind back on the job.

But guilt at how he'd hurt her with his words made him reach out and touch one small, cold hand, where it lay in her lap.

'I'm sorry, I shouldn't have threatened you like that— you look exhausted, and all this has been a shock to you. No one should make decisions when they're tired, but there's a way out of this for all of us. Don't answer now, we will talk again in the morning. I shall phone your Mr Marshall and explain you won't be in to work.'

But she'd obviously stopped listening earlier in his conversation.

'A way out for all of us?' she asked, looking at him with a thousand questions in her lovely eyes.

'Of course,' he told her, and felt a small spurt of unexpected excitement even thinking about his solution.

'We shall get married,' he announced. 'That way Nim is both of ours and will be doubly protected.'

Her eyes had widened and although he hadn't thought she could get any paler, she was now sheet-white.

She stood up, and for a moment he thought she might physically attack him, but in the end she glared at him, and said, 'You must be mad!' before disappearing down the passage, presumably into her bedroom.

Malik realised there was no point in arguing, but the idea, which had come to him out of nowhere, was brilliant.

All he had to do was convince Lauren.

Her name rolled a little on his tongue and, inside his head, he tried it out a few times.

And his mind, for once, was not on Nimr, but on the woman he'd decided to marry...

Continue reading
A WIFE FOR THE SURGEON SHEIKH
Meredith Webber

Available next month
www.millsandboon.co.uk

LET'S TALK
Romance

For exclusive extracts, competitions
and special offers, find us online: